"In *Remembering the Osage Kid,* Mardi Oakley Medawar has told a complex tale, with an intricate plot and a host of interesting characters. For anyone new to Medawar's books, this will be a marvelous introduction. To readers familiar with her previous work, this is a welcome and pleasant surprise."

—Robert J. Conley, author of
Mountain Windsong: A Novel of the Trail of Tears

A BAD DAY TO DIE

Young Charlie panicked. . . .

He was running. Running for the horses, running away from his father's screams. He stumbled, crawled for several dozen inches, righted himself, and carried on running, his toes inside the summer moccasins being stabbed by the sharp rocks as he kicked back loose gravel and dust behind him, sprinting full tilt to where the horses were tied.

His father's screams were distant but they filled all of Charlie's hearing. And then there were shots. Five, six, seven shots. Charlie pulled up short, stood still, sweat running in rivulets down his heaving chest and back. His ears strained, but all that met him was silence.

A tiny cry escaped Charlie's throat. He hared off, running for all he was worth.

Books by Mardi Oakley Medawar

The Glory Days of Buffalo Egbert
a.k.a. People of the Whistling Waters

Remembering the Osage Kid

Rainwater on the White Road
a.k.a. Misty Hills of Home

Tay-Bodal *series*
Death at Rainy Mountain
Witch of the Palo Duro

For more information
visit: www.SpeakingVolumes.us

Remembering the Osage Kid

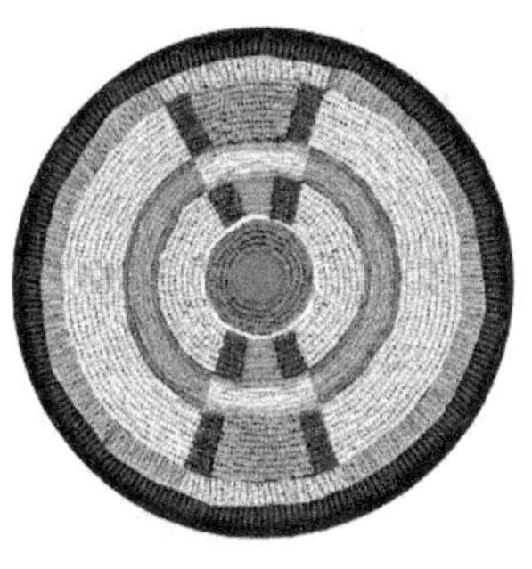

Mardi Oakley Medawar

SPEAKING VOLUMES, LLC
NAPLES, FLORIDA
2019

Remembering the Osage Kid

ISBN 978-1-61232-772-3

For my mother,
who is also my friend

CHAPTER ONE

On the morning of the last full day of C. R. Jones's life, he did something he hadn't done in years. He drove out to his son David's ranch, went directly to the stables, and asked a hired man to saddle a horse for him. The ranch hand was hesitant. The request had come from an eighty-five-year-old man. Even in advanced age C. R. Jones was very tall, his mind sharp and clear. And he was C. R. Jones. To refuse this legendary man anything was tantamount to cutting one's own throat. The horse was duly saddled and the ranch hand stood to the side, wondering if he should perhaps call Mister David as old C.R. climbed on, gave the horse its head, and rode away. The ranch hand dithered for an hour, then finally made the call from the stables to the main house, speaking first to Miz Irene, then to Mister David. Five minutes later, Mister David was in the stables, cussing up a storm as he mounted the waiting horse and took out after his father.

It was a beautiful June morning, the oppressive heat and humidity still a few tranquil hours away. C.R. rode with leisure the valleys and hillocks of this bluestem country known as the Osage Hills. He had been born on this land when it had existed in another time, an age so remote that now it was regarded as history. This never ceased to amaze C.R., that his yesterday had become ancient history. But something even more amazing, something C.R. never paused to consider, was that he had gone from that era into the technologically advanced twentieth century without a qualm. Now that vanished age called to him. He was Osage and Wah'Kon-Tah was calling to him in a voice that sounded like a skipping drum rhythm but was actually his own heartbeat. This was the last time his mortal eyes would see his country, his final opportunity to thank it for all it had provided. He stopped the horse on a hilltop in a stand of trees. This was his secret place, a place he hadn't visited in too many years. Standing quietly, he felt the presence like an assault. Bowing his head, C. R. Jones, one of the most powerful men in Oklahoma, wept.

By the time David picked up his father's trail, C.R. was doubling back. They missed each other by minutes and by about a half mile. When C.R. began his morning ride, the temperature had been a pleasant seventy-five degrees. Now it was over eighty-five. But it seemed nearer to ninety-five because of the humidity. At any rate, David was nearing heatstroke from the climate and infuriation. He was just nearing the hillock where C.R. had rested, when he saw the fresh hoof marks going in the opposite direction. Cursing, David turned the horse's head. He arrived back at the stables too late. His father had already been there and was gone again, driving for home. All of which meant that he, David, had spent the better part of the morning chasing smoke. He took his frustration out on the clump of ranch hands loitering in and around the stables, shouting at each and every one of them at the full volume of his voice. Then he headed for his office and there telephoned his mother and yelled at her for allowing Dad out for a morning wander.

David was forced to pause his tirade while his mother threw a little fit of her own. When her temper went on so long that she began repeating herself, David yelled over her voice. "Well, he's on his way home now, so he's all right, but if I were you, I'd lock him up until it's time for the party." Still livid, David slammed down the phone.

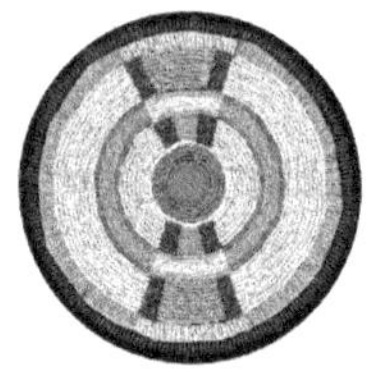

CHAPTER TWO

C.R.'s home had been, for the last fifty-odd years, an imposing estate set almost dead center among five hundred acres. Known locally as C.R.'s Place, it was "just down the road" from Frank's Place, meaning Frank Phillips's rustic retreat, a log cabin palace named Woolaroc.

C.R.'s place was not a rustic palace but a precise replica of a grand old home going to ruin somewhere in England. In this he felt he had one-upped Frank Phillips. C.R. and Frank had been friendly rivals in the oil business until the day the Osage Nation formally adopted Frank. The adoption enraged C.R. He was a "born to" Osage, a full-blood, and all but shunned by his own kind. The adoption of Frank Phillips, claiming him as an honored son, was viewed by C.R. as a united slap across his face. He was never friendly with Frank Phillips again. The first volley fired in this cold war came from C.R.'s building his English manor and then never inviting Frank in to see it.

The small town of Olla positioned haplessly between

the massive land holdings of the opposing oilmen rarely benefited from either. Olla was left to struggle to survive while the towns of Pawhuska (C.R.'s headquarters) and Bartlesville (Frank's) prospered. Following Frank's death, his retreat at Woolaroc became a museum, a state tourist attraction. Meanwhile, C.R.'s place remained what it had always been. A private home, a visible testament that in northeast Oklahoma oil money could do just about anything. As a further complement, the house was surrounded by twenty wonderfully landscaped acres, house and gardens enclosed behind high-bricked walls. Beyond the barrier walls lay God's reality—rolling hills, oceans of buffalo and bluestem grasses, pockets of blackjacks and scrub oaks.

And wind, the incessant prairie wind.

When C.R. arrived home, Emma, his wife for all of his adult life and the mother of his three sons, was waiting for him. And madder than a wet hen because he had gone out on a day when her hands were more than full with the final preparations for his birthday party. The second he walked through the doors, she ordered him off to his suite of rooms. His valet was directly behind him as C.R. trudged up the stairs. Still in a flap, Emma turned away, waving her arms as she vented her spleen at the florist.

Thirty years earlier, C.R. had fought the idea of a personal servant. The idea of another man dressing and undressing him was embarrassing. Gradually he became used to it, even grew to warm to the idea of being meticulously fussed over. He would never admit it, not even to himself, but the process of being prepared for the day, or for bed, was soothing. All he had to do was stand there while Edgar, his valet, saw to everything. And too, Edgar softly hummed while he tied a perfect Windsor knot, made the handkerchief in the pocket just so, brushed lint, or whatever, from the shoulders of the jacket Edgar had chosen for him to wear that day. C.R. zoned out while all of this humming and fussing was going on, any tension he may have felt draining from him in pleasant waves. Having Edgar to ease away stress was probably the reason C.R. had managed to live so long.

Edgar prepared him for his nap, taking away all the man- and horse-sweaty clothing as C.R. soaked in the bath. Then as Edgar dried and powdered him, C.R. enjoyed a cup of warm tea, setting the cup aside as Edgar slipped the nightshirt over his head. The curtains drawn, darkening his bedroom, Edgar tucked C.R. in for his nap, then discreetly took a chair on the far side of the room. C.R. lay in his bed, staring up at the ceiling. He wasn't the least bit sleepy, but he knew that a long night was ahead of him and a nap was probably one of Emma's better edicts.

"Edgar?"

"Sir?"

"Would you mind humming?"

"Anything in particular, sir?"

"No."

As Edgar hummed "Some Enchanted Evening," C. R. Jones began to drift off to sleep.

Five hours later, dressed in a tuxedo, his hands clasped behind his back, C.R. paced the foyer's black and white checkerboard marble back and forth, back and forth, just under the crystal chandelier. The final pace took him to the wall dominated by four large oil paintings, the largest a flattering portrait of himself done more than twenty years earlier. The three surrounding portraits were of his sons, Matt, David, and Harry.

Each son was handsome, blessedly gaining their features from their mother. C.R. was very grateful to Emma for his sons' good looks, for he had never been an overly attractive person. When he was fifteen, a nun told him that he was ruggedly ugly. She had been a kindly lady and had meant no offense, but her teasing statement was nonetheless true. In the prime of his manhood he had been sensuously ugly, broad-shouldered, standing six foot four. Time had lined his face, stooped his broad shoulders, changed his jet-black hair to white-gray, and leached the elasticity from his skin. He smiled as he remembered his granddaughter Hayley. At age three she had loved to sit on his lap and make tepees of the skin covering his knuckles. She would pull it up and then they would both watch during the interminable time it took for his skin to resettle. (A sliced apple turned brown more quickly.) Hayley thought his pinched skin standing straight up on its own was fascinating, something only her Pap-Paw could do. She even bragged about it.

"Me Pap-Paw gots pully skin. Want to see?"

Chuckling at the memory, C.R. looked at the portrait of his son Matt, mentally thanking him for Hayley. She was a grown woman now and he didn't see enough of her. Not since his retirement, when Matt, as the new president of Red Bird Oil, relocated the central office out of Pawhuska into Tulsa. Then Matt sent Hayley off to various schools, then the university. She was back home in Tulsa now, and he still didn't see enough of her.

When Matt moved the office, David, the first vice president, would not budge from the Rocking J. Because of the move, David had wanted to quit the company altogether, but Matt wouldn't allow that. He needed David, and the entire family knew why. Harry. So David drove into Tulsa twice a week or whenever Matt called him in on urgent matters.

Harry, the eldest son, had always lived in Tulsa. As president of the largest bank in Tulsa, he had little choice. Besides, Harry was a big-city person. Being stuck out in the Osage Hills had never suited him at all.

Since Matt's defection to Tulsa, the family flocked together only on holidays or special occasions. And because the city was a good two-hour drive, when the family gathered they stayed overnight. This was the real reason C.R. looked forward to the birthday party Emma had slaved to plan for months in advance. His children and smattering of their children would be under his roof again, their voices enlivening the house.

C.R. crossed the foyer to the family parlor, a comfortable room of overstuffed chairs and settees, a place he could sit quietly while he eagerly awaited the arrival of his family. Ordinarily this room was a place a man could put his feet up on the coffee table if he wanted to, even take a nap if one slipped up and caught him unawares, but today, thanks to that demented florist Emma had hired to decorate the house, the family parlor had the look and feel of a mortuary. He tried to ignore the high pollen count as he eased himself down onto a settee, propped the side of his head against his hand, his gaze drifting toward the fireplace. The open hearth was all but hidden behind a massive bird's-nest fern. His gaze traveled beyond the spiky fronds into the dark maw of the hearth. *To his astonishment, a fire began to glow. Then his mother's backside was toward him as she stirred the contents of a pan placed on a grill set close to the heart of the blaze. She was wearing a dull calico skirt and the ashy-gray blouse was tucked in at the waist. Her dark hair, tied in plaits, hung before her.*

When he blinked, she was gone, and behind the bulky fern once again there was only darkness. He sat very still, just his eyes moving as he surveyed the parlor. The brief vision unnerved him, and he could feel his heart stumbling along at an agitated pace. There followed a tingling sensation in his left arm, as if it had gone to sleep and was reluctant to wake up again. The sensation gradually subsided as he flexed his hand, squeezing and releasing a tightened fist while he concentrated on breathing, inhaling and exhaling in even streams. When the tingling abated, the tightness across his chest also eased. Bit by bit, he felt fine again. Except for his sinuses, they were beginning to feel the effect of the flowers. When the funny turn had completely passed, he forgot about it. What he could not forget, or ignore, was the overpowering flowery smell. It was becoming noxious. With a defeated feathery sigh he stood, left the room.

Directly across the foyer the double doors of the library stood open. The library was designated his special room. The truth of the matter was that from the very day he and Emma had moved into the completed house, the library frightened him. There were no windows in the library, and C.R. was mildly claustrophobic. It hardly mattered that the room was one thousand square feet in size, without windows, even with all the reading lamps turned on, the library was dark and felt confining. Like a jail cell. The memory of a specific cell came to him. Standing just outside the open doors, he peeked in just as a curious visitor might. What he saw were three walls of shelved books all neatly categorized. The wall facing him was dominated by a massive stone fireplace, its overmantel a polished mahogany. The only sounds in the room were his own breathing and the steady tick of the grandfather clock. Oriental carpets partially covered hardwood flooring, wing chairs, and tables with lamps the only furniture. To his immediate left a circular staircase wound upward, ending inside a galleried nook. His grandchildren used to play up there, and before them, his sons. The reading nook had never been anything more than a child's play fort even though Emma boasted about it, said the nook was the place true readers liked to hide.

C.R. turned away, giving serious thought to which room he might try next. He knew already that his most favorite haunt, the game room, was out of the question.

On any day but today the game room was a man's niche, a room of dark oak paneling and French windows that opened out onto a stone veranda. Cement urns containing dwarf conifers progressed down the wide stone steps that fed into a garden of bloodred roses and a tall yew maze. Dim sunlight and cool air from the veranda wafted through the open windows into the game room, and aided by paddle fans suspended from open beams, the air was always comfortable even during the hottest summer. In the winter, with the windows shut and the heavy curtains drawn, the somber oak absorbed the glow of the fire in the hearth, the lighting over the long bar and billiard table. The effect was a real English gentlemen's club replete with leather couches, a suit of armor, and a wall display of ancient rifles and pistols. But today this manly domain was stuffed to the rafters with flowers, and if a room had the ability to experience emotion, the game room felt humiliated. The main reception room was equally useless. Members of the staff were in there, all of them busy setting out whatever they were setting out, and he could hear the butler's irritated voice urging them to hurry. C.R. knew that there was no way he could wait for his family and guests in the middle of all that.

Standing near the staircase, he heard the slam of a door up on the second floor and then Emma's raised voice. He touched the elaborately carved newel post and smiled lightly as he listened to Emma yelling to her maid that the dressmaker had cut her evening dress in the wrong size. The maid must have disagreed, most likely, and said that Emma looked lovely, because he then heard Emma's distressed voice.

"Where's my husband¿" Emma yelled. "Tell him to come here. I want *his* opinion!"

The comedy was over. Not wishing to find himself embroiled in a weepy drama, he knew he had to find a quick hideout. He made a quick dash across the foyer to the front door. Seconds later he was outside, closing one of the big front doors quietly behind him. On the portico he drew an easy breath, looked out over the wide circular white-pea-gravel drive. Dead in the center of the drive was a fountain. Today water flowed. Normally it didn't. Summer was too hot, and he hated wasting valuable water on a needless display. Wintertime was far too cold, and the freezing water played bob with the plumbing. But as today was a special occasion, water arched and danced around the small statues, the sight embellishing the background of live oaks lining the drive and acres of velvety green lawns. The sound of purling water and the elegant view were calming. So calming that he didn't notice the blue bus parked far to his left in the drive until he heard a male voice. Turning his head to the sound, he saw musicians unloading cases from the vehicle's side cargo hold. A moment later the young men were being directed to walk around the far side of the house. As the musicians filed off, some of them smiled and waved, said, "Good evening, Mr. Jones." He dutifully smiled, waved. Within minutes they were gone and once again he was gazing beyond the spray of the fountain to the distant high walls surrounding the estate.

During the first year of its construction the house was treated as a local curiosity. Rattling Model T Fords loaded with picnickers came to gawk, spreading blankets around on the lawns, kids and dogs running amok while adults ate their lunches and marveled at the house. In those early days Emma was still struggling to learn how to be the person she felt he needed her to be. Then, too, she had been pregnant with Harry. There had been a lot of gossip back then. Gossip C.R. incurred. Emma loathed being the subject of local wagging tongues; she craved privacy. He hadn't realized just how badly she craved it until he came home late one summer evening. The brick masons had finished for the day and left behind them flats of stacked bricks, cement mixers, and other jumble of their trade. When he got out of his car to find out what the devil was going on, he found the marking trench, paced enough of it off to understand the need for so many bricks. Livid that Emma would order the construction without consulting him, he accused her of trying to trap him inside her personal prison. He had been so furious, he'd been tempted to hit her. If she hadn't been pregnant, he might have. But Emma stood her ground, went toe to toe with him against his rage and won.

The walls went up.

The citizens of Olla saw the walls as an insult and the people of Olla had long memories of first the renegade boy, then the surly natured young man known then as Charlie Jones. But when he hit oil, overnight he became known as Lucky Charlie. As his wealth increased, the townspeople slowly began to close their eyes to the fact that Charlie Jones remained a raging law unto himself. The brief time that he'd been tossed inside the jail and the town had been nearly jubilant was forgotten. But come those walls and suddenly everyone in Olla hated him all over again. He ceased to be known as Charlie. Suddenly he was C.R., one of the most powerful men in Oklahoma. A man to be mortally afraid of.

And he was absolutely and totally alone.

Entering the side garden, he proceeded to his favorite bench (even if it was made of solid concrete and numbed his rear end after a few minutes sitting on it), set in the shade of a towering tree. This was the garden he most frequented because it was the one garden devoid of flowers and flowering bushes. Emma had caused this "tree garden" to be created because here on the south side of the house the scorching prairie sun happily killed off any and all plants sprouting dainty petals. The space would have remained thoroughly barren if Emma had not heeded the advice of the gardeners and allowed various species of trees to be trucked in. The young trees responded to the light and space by filling out and stretching to the sky almost from the instant they were slammed into the prepared holes. Within five years the trees had grown so quickly and filled out so much that the tree garden was always dark with shade and filled with birdsong.

Seated on his special bench, he recalled the days when he used to sit here watching his sons playing baseball. Matt and David had played with the same rough-and-tumble enthusiasm they gave their adult lives. Matt and David were his Irish twins, born only nine and a half months apart, Matt the youngest. From infancy David and Matt had been a team against their older brother, Harry. To his credit, Harry met them head-on, but as he was odd man out and outnumbered, Harry hadn't much of a chance. He still didn't. And not just against Matt and David. C.R. worried quite a bit about Harry.

Five years ago, in 1960, the problems between the three brothers were exacerbated when C. R. Jones formally stepped down from power, handing over Red Bird Oil to Matt and David. Harry had been livid. He made no secret of his bitterness the night of C.R.'s farewell banquet.

C.R. had been thinking about his eldest son when he stepped to the rostrum to deliver his departing speech. Worrying about him, really. Yet seconds into the speech the problem of Harry dwindled, for in those eternal seconds as C.R. paused while reading the opening lines of his carefully prepared speech, the first of many long-buried memories hit him full bore and right between the eyes.

Badly shaken, he looked out over the sea of

expectant, smiling faces. Being an executive of an oil company is akin to belonging to an exclusive all-male club. C.R. owned his own oil company, therefore the lofty members of his company, as well as presidents and vice presidents of other companies, were in full attendance that night to honor the man, who, since the death of his one rival, Frank Phillips, had been the keeper of the keys to the clubhouse. In the murky gloom outside the spotlight trained on him, he could see their shadowy forms as they sat at tables smoking after-dinner cigars, sipping brandy, waiting for him to continue. He couldn't, for in those seconds he realized that the ghosts of his past had waited patiently for his undivided attention, and now that he was retiring, they would have it. He couldn't see the ghosts, but he could feel their determination. Gripping the sides of the rostrum, he envisioned the final portion of his life. In his mind's eye it spooled before him, an existence of long days and nights in which he would confront each and every specter and deal with each shade on his or her terms. For the first time in over sixty years, the great C. R. Jones was utterly terrified. Hearing the disconcerted murmuring beginning in his audience, and quickly moving to regain mastery of the awkward moment, he tapped a finger against the microphone. It responded loudly to the taps and then emitted a piercing whine.

"Something quit," he joked, speaking closely into the microphone. "At first I thought it was this thing, then I realized it was me."

Hardy laughter. The microphone didn't quit, C.R. did. *Gedit?*

While he waited for the forced laughter to subside so that he could get on with his speech, an idea formed. An idea of how to trap his worrisome ghosts. Feeling immeasurably better, C.R. sailed through his farewell address.

Following the banquet, he shunned the limousine,

preferring instead to be driven home by Matthew. He maintained a stony silence during the drive through the pitch-black miles of open prairie country. Finally entering the sleeping town of Olla, he began yelling for Matt to stop the car. The instant Matt slammed on the brakes, C.R. jumped out and ran to the only phone booth on the corner of the parade of buildings.

Matt immediately followed, waiting outside the phone booth, nervously rattling coins in his trouser pockets while his father made a call. A moment later, his father hung up and opened the booth's door and stepped out. Matt looked at him, his expression anxious.

"Daddy? Are you all right?"

"Almost."

Matt quickly scratched the side of his head. Then he exhaled a deep breath. Irritation seeping into his tone, he said, "Dad? Was that a business call? Because if it was, David and I—"

"Shut up, Matt."

Matt tossed his hands in the air. "Okay, if it isn't business, what is so urgent?"

"None of *your* business."

Matt knew when he was defeated, but after a few minutes of standing around with his father on the deserted street at nearly one o'clock in the morning, his impatience got the better of him.

"What are we doing now, Dad?"

"Waiting."

Fifteen minutes ticked by and then car lights were seen, the lights coming fast. The car pulled to a stop at the curb and the owner of the five and ten cents store leapt out, the man hitting the curb in a run, fumbling with keys and babbling apologies for having kept C. R. Jones waiting.

"Dad? What's—"

"Just get back in the car, Matthew,"

Matt was drumming his fingers against the steering

wheel when his father finally opened the car door and slid inside. He held a package close against his chest. Matthew eyed it.

C.R.'s tone almost childlike, he said, "I'd like to go home now, please. I'm very tired."

Sitting now on the butt-chilling concrete bench five years later, he remembered all of that and more. He remembered taking his package into his private suite, unwrapping it, and sitting down at his desk. He hadn't even bothered to remove his coat and tie before he took up the pen and began writing in one of the notepads. He was determined to trap all his ghosts in ink, but the biggest ghost was himself. He urgently needed to pass the history of his life and his greatest secret onto someone he considered trustworthy. The person to whom he wrote would appreciate this knowledge even though he might never appreciate the messenger. This person he was writing to had no time for the great C. R. Jones. As a matter of fact, he hated C. R. Jones. And the man was implacable, as hardheaded as solid granite, but there are times in a man's life when it is wiser to trust an enemy than it is to trust a friend. Especially when C.R.'s enemy also happened to be Cassie's son.

Cassie.

Charlie put a hand to his chest and leaned forward. The passage of years had not dulled the pain that grabbed his heart whenever he thought that name. And when he allowed himself to think it, she appeared in his mind's eye, perfect in every detail with her dimpled, bashful smile, long dark hair, waiflike body. He could see her now, so vividly that if he reached out his hand, he knew that he could touch her.

The pain in his chest increased, radiated down his arm. Blood trickled from his left nostril.

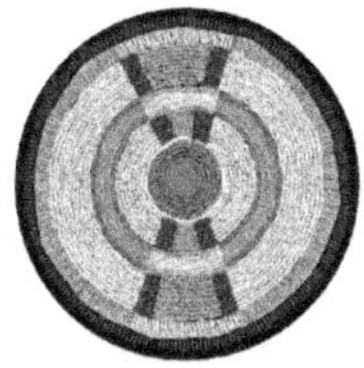

CHAPTER THREE

It had taken a long time for the pain to pass. He'd remained on the bench, suffering, as he listened to cars pulling into the drive, hearing the voices of his sons and their families as they made their way into the house. He used his silk handkerchief to wipe the blood from his face, then discarded it behind the cement bench. He still felt ill when he went around to the front of the house and entered the foyer. Acting as if nothing was wrong, he greeted his sons and their wives, yelled a hello to the sprinkling of grown-up grandchildren making their way up the stairs. Then the wives went off to the main room. Still standing in the foyer, C.R. had barely begun talking to his sons when Emma descended the stairs. Seeing her, her sons began to applaud, and she paused on the middle stair, acknowledging their appreciation. C.R. applauded too, for Emma indeed looked wonderful. Her hair was pinned up high and she was wearing a powdery-gray silk evening dress. Looking at his wife, it was hard to imagine her again as that skinny little thirteen-year-old girl wrapped up inside a blanket. She had been so frightened, her dark eyes shimmering with tears the day her father handed her over to be Charlie Jones's wife.

It had been cold in the church. The wedding was taking place in the late afternoon during the coldest month of winter, and the wood-burning stove wasn't putting out sufficient heat. The sky beyond the few windows in the church, even in the middle of the day, was dark and low, blending with the snowy ground. More snow was falling. It was the worst snowstorm in living memory. Charlie, dressed in the one good suit he owned, didn't feel the cold. He was already too numbed by dread. He was marrying Emma, a girl he didn't even know, while the woman he loved with all his soul was suffering at the hands of a man who did not deserve her. And there wasn't anything Charlie could do to help her or stop him.

Charlie's bride was standing next to him as the preaching man conducted the wedding service. As yet, he hadn't tried to get a look at her. She was small and bundled up from head to toe in a thick blanket. When it came time for him to make his vows and he turned, seeing the girl who was almost his wife, he first felt pleasantly surprised, then he was moved to pity. His bride was tiny. She was also exceptionally pretty. And so terrified, she was shaking. He brought his face close to the small face partially hidden inside the blanket folds. He said the vows in a strong, clear voice, and then he spoke just to her in a near whisper.

"Don't be afraid. I won't ever hurt you."

The promise was sealed with a warm kiss as they were pronounced man and wife, but his wedding vow proved itself to be a lie. All he had ever done was hurt her. He hadn't wanted to. It was just something he couldn't help. Emma had deserved a young man who would love her, make her happy. What she got instead was an indifferent husband, a lot of money, and three warring sons. But there was no time to roam that deep valley of guilt just then. Their guests were arriving and the butler was opening the doors.

"C.R," Emma whispered. "Please stop fidgeting." Then, all smiles, she turned away from him, extending a gloved hand to their first guests. Emma's biggest plus in the life of C. R. Jones was her knack for making complete strangers feel like close personal friends. She remembered names, faces, troubles, and victories of assorted folks, always sending timely cards and flowers as expressions of congratulations or profound sympathy. She was a genuinely caring lady, her smooth elegance ever in conflict with her husband's fierce business practices.

Still fidgeting, C.R. eased his weight from foot to foot as the multitude of guests streamed in through the open front doors, joined the reception's winding queue. C.R. and Emma were stationed like guards under the entrance portals of the main reception room, C.R. grinding his teeth into a smile. Inside the formal living room, waiters carrying silver trays offered the entering guests flutes of champagne. Glenn Miller–style music from the band situated out on the terrace helped swing everyone into the party mood. Even in the entrance of the main room, the music from the band was very loud. As C.R.'s hand was sincerely squeezed, personal messages had to be shouted next to his ear.

"You don't look eighty-five, C.R. I guarantee that."

"Happy birthday, C.R. And many, many, many more."

"C.R.! What a day, huh? We've had us some long years together, but we've still got a lot more years to run, don't we!"

Then there were the gushers. Those Emma invited strictly because they were so very good at gushing.

Squeeze, squeeze, squeeze. Gush, gush, gush.

"C.R. Can't tell ya how me and the wife appreciate being included on this special day."

"Mr. Jones, me an' the missus want to thank you for the invite."

"Was just telling your lady that the one complaint Oklahoma has with its favorite son is that he didn't produce more fine young men for the females of the territory. How come ya stopped at three, C.R.? My daughters got left out."

Who the hell was that?!

And then there was Kelly, beaming her impish smile, chuckling softly as she kissed her father-in-law's well-grooved cheek.

"Hi, Daddy!"

He found himself grinning widely as his onyx eyes crinkled and gazed into Kelly's bright blue eyes. "What are you doing, girl? And where's my worthless son?"

"Matt's hiding your present behind a bush. I wasn't supposed to say that, so you didn't hear it."

"Where are the children?"

"The last time I saw Chris he was in the kitchen talking on the phone. Best guess is he's conferring with a fellow Indian activist. You might want to prepare yourself for an evening of Chris skulking around as if he's on the lam from the FBI. Hayley's locked herself in her bedroom. Matt's invited another of his golden-boy engineers to be her dinner companion."

"Oh, Lord. I understand how she feels, but I'll be very upset if she misses my birthday party."

"Don't worry, Daddy. The children will be there when you blow out your candles. You know they never could resist a good bonfire."

"Kelly!" Emma barked, then sent her daughter-in-law a meaningful glare. "Dear, our guests are waiting."

Kelly placed a hand on her mouth and said sorry, sorry. Then, lifting the skirt of her evening dress, she playfully tiptoed away. Watching Kelly disappear into the mingling mob, C.R. realized that he was actually grinning, not simply forcing his lips wide. Thinking about Kelly, he went back to the arduous task of greeting well-wishers.

When Matt met Kelly, he was twenty, and Kelly barely nineteen. She was not a local girl. She was on summer holiday, visiting her aunt and uncle who lived in Olla. Meeting Matt, she had no idea of his identity. All she knew was that his name was Matthew Jones and that he was cute. For Kelly, that had been good enough. On the day they met, Matt was as grimy as any other oil-field roustabout. For her own reasons, Kelly's aunt had lived in fear of her niece learning who Matt actually was. Monitoring the courtship from day one, C.R. agreed with the worrying auntie, but for his own reasons. While Matt dated Kelly, C.R. had her investigated, and until he had the results of the investigation he initiated a code of silence. No one in Olla was prepared to tell Kelly just who it was she was actually dating.

C.R. had been more than pleased with the results of the investigation. The girl Matt had taken a shine to had proven to be squeaky clean. True, she was from a humble family, but C.R. didn't count that against her. Few families had escaped being humbled by the Depression. According to the report, Kelly was scheduled to begin beauty school in her home town of Monroe, Louisiana, beginning the ninth of September. If Matthew was in love with his new girlfriend, he had exactly three months to prevent her getting on the bus and riding out of his life. C.R. continued to monitor the developing romance. Through well-paid spies he knew exactly where Matt was taking Kelly and exactly what they were getting up to. It was coming on August when an ashen-faced Matt appeared in his office and confessed that he'd met a girl, that he loved her, and that he'd *accidentally* made said girl pregnant. Only willpower kept C.R. from laughing out loud.

Matt hated his father's office. Hated it not only because he had to worm past two secretaries to gain admittance but hated it because his father's office was so stark, impersonal. In this big room on the top of the Red Bird Oil building, the view from the windows was the refinery. The furniture was a desk, chairs, and telephones. There were no pictures on the walls, only graphs, flowcharts, and an enlarged map of Osage County. Added to this was his father's body language, which silently screamed, *What is it? Can't you see I'm busy!* Now Matt was bringing something highly personal inside this austere room, and his knees were knocking, his heart banging so loudly, he could barely hear his father's question.

"Matt? Can you please explain to me how you felt you could enjoy sex and prevent a pregnancy?"

"Well, I—I thought it was"—Matt lifted his shoulders in a dispirited shrug, cleared his tight throat—"you know, safe, in the truck."

C.R. ran a hand over his mouth, trying to wipe away the smile. "And why would you think that, Matthew?"

A scuffing of a booted foot, another lift of the shoulders, then Matt's mumbled response. "Because it always was before. With other girls."

C.R. bit his tongue so hard, he tasted blood. He waited while his son lost his timidity, straightened his spine, found the grit to look him in the eye.

"I know what you're thinking, Dad, but Kelly's not like the others. Kelly's great. She's the best thing that's ever happened to me. I'm marrying her, Dad. I really mean it. Even if you cut me out of the family, I'm still marrying Kelly. We'll go away and—"

"Shut up, Matthew."

Matt involuntarily jumped when his father's hand slapped the desktop. "Now, here's what you're going to do. You are going to take your young lady home to meet your mother. Then you will not move so much as a hair while you wait for me."

Matthew retreated a step as his father rose and straightened to his full six-foot-four-inch height. Matt gulped down the hardened lump in his throat and rasped, "W-what are you going to do¿"

C.R. casually arranged a stack of papers on his desk. "Me¿" He barked a laugh. "I'll be seeing to it that my frisky son is married before sundown." He seemed to forget Matthew's presence as he held a typed page and quietly read it. Then, raising a brow, he glanced up from the paper in his hand. In a perfectly even tone he asked, "Matthew¿ Why are you still here¿"

Matt turned, fled.

While the door was banging shut, C.R. chuckled and said under his breath, "Safe in the truck. My son the imbecile."

There were far too many guests to seat everyone in the dining room, so Emma had arranged for tables to be set out on the lawn and under a massive marquee should the early June weather attempt to thwart her with a seasonal shower. To save the lawn from being trampled, sheets of plywood had been laid out. The interior of the enormous tent looked like a five-star banquet hall, the months of planning by everyone involved on the project had been well rewarded. But C.R. mentally doffed his cap to Emma, the project's director.

To stave off the threat of encroaching dusk, thousands of white lights had been strung in the surrounding trees. Enough so that despite the leaves, the trees glowed like candles. Inside the marquee there were hundreds of real candles, on the tables and in standing candelabra. And, of course, there were flowers. Flowered centerpieces on every table, standing baskets in the corners, and streams of flowers cunningly arranged to hide the support poles of the marquee. As the guests entered and found their places at their assigned tables, the band retired. Four violinists and one cellist took over, filling the air with soft chamber music. But following the dinner, the swing band would be back to round off the evening with lively dancing.

Guests chatted with table partners, and formally attired waiters hopped about pouring wine, explaining the three choices of dinner starters: venison and cranberry pâté, crab mayonnaise, Parma ham with melon. Then they took orders from the selections of the main courses: roasted duck with cherry sauce, minted spring lamb, or prime rib. The dessert was a given—birthday cake. And everyone knew they were obliged to have a wedge.

Three tables of honor were set up on a raised stage, giving all the guests an unimpeded view of the governor and his lady, and the entire Jones family. C.R. hated dinner parties that had him on display. He always felt himself being watched as he cut into his food, and worse, while he chewed. A waiter took up C.R.'s napkin, snapped it open with a practiced flourish, and then draped it across C.R.'s lap. In those passing seconds C.R. heard his mother's voice.

"Charlie! Watch out for the pan."

His childhood home had only one room. His mother cooked in the fireplace, the cook pan shoved inside glowing embers. On cold mornings he liked to stand close to the hearth as he hurried to dress, and his mother was always certain that he would either step in the cook pan and ruin their breakfast or catch himself on fire. Inhaling deeply, C.R. could almost smell the beef and onions frying in the black cast-iron skillet.

"Mr. Jones¿"

Momentarily confused, C.R. looked up a the hovering waiter.

"Mr. Jones, which starter would you prefer, sir?"

Beef and onions.

Emma took over. "The ham and melon. It's his favorite."

No, it isn't.

"And then the duck with cherry sauce," Emma continued. "I'll be having the same."

The waiter turned to the governor, and while the governor and the waiter spoke and Emma bantered with the governor's wife, C.R. regressed once more.

"Charlie," his father said to him. The little boy looked at the empty jar his father held out to him. "Your mother needs more lucky crickets. But only get big crickets. Little crickets are bad luck."

It took hours to find just the right crickets, and he never knew what his mother actually did with them. All he knew was that twice a week in the summertime, the cricket jar would empty and his father would send him off to find more. It was only when he was a young man burning for the love a certain woman that he understood about the crickets.

Emma saw his smile and sat back in the chair, placing her hand on top of his as she whispered, "Have I done you proud?"

"Always," he muttered.

"But tonight," she pressed, "are you pleased with the party?"

"It's a wonderful party. I'm having a very nice time."

She looked away, beaming with pride as she surveyed her handiwork. She was always so afraid of events such as these, and her fear kept her going over each detail of a planned event until every last problem was solved to her perfectionist standard. As a result, Emma's parties were always lavish, always the talk of the state of Oklahoma, but she never felt her success until C.R. gave her his nod of approval.

Across the table, her son Harry caught her eye. He lifted a glass of wine, toasting her. Emma's smile faded. The one worry plaguing her was C.R.'s gift. That responsibility had been wrested from her, the boys insisting that this year they would choose it. She had no idea what it was, and none of them would tell her, not even David, who had been the family tattletale. The gift was a minor detail, but she didn't much care for the fact that even a minor detail attached to this special evening had been beyond her control. Any normal mother should feel able to trust her sons, but as not one of them had taken that much care when selecting their wives, how could she trust them to choose an appropriate gift for their father? And, dear God, if it was something awful, whatever would she say to the governor? *Pardon me, my sons are stupid?* Well, they were. All three of them. One only had to meet their wives to realize just how hopeless her boys were.

She tried to push her anxiety aside and enjoy the food, but her daughter-in-law Irene, David's wife, was making that a near impossibility. The woman was talking with her mouth full and gulping down the wine as if it were water. Across from Irene was Terri, Harry's wife. Emma watched as Terri daintily nibbled, then dabbed her mouth with the napkin. Emma might loathe the very air Terri breathed, but a least Terri had elegant manners and was impressive in public.

Kelly laughed loudly at something Matt said, her napkin coming quickly up to her mouth. Kelly had some manners, but that was all the credit Emma felt inclined to give her. At the other two tables her grandchildren were acting rowdy, but she didn't mind. It was a party and they were having a good time. Besides, she loved them and they loved her. She loved Chris most especially, even if he did tease her, call her Granny-Em.

After the meal the plates were cleared away and coffee was served. Then the big moment was at hand. Waiters and maids appeared from the left, flanking a dessert trolley, its caster wheels chugging under the weight of a five-tiered cake. The cake glowed in the light of burning candles ringing each layer. As the trolley entered the marquee, Harry stood, tapping a spoon lightly against the crystal water glass, ringing everyone's attention. Happy chattering gradually ceased as all heads turned in Harry's direction, a wide smile dominating every face.

Harry gloried in such moments. He was the president of Oklahoma National—the leading bank in Tulsa. Harry loved money. Consequently, Harry was a splendid bank president, and even more handsome than he had been in his youth. His hair was graying, but in a way that seemed contrived, and he wore a tuxedo with the ease of a second skin, looking relaxed and wonderful in it because he kept himself fit, athletically trim. A fullblood Osage, he was tall, dark, sophisticated, and with a set of teeth so dentally assisted white that when he smiled, the glare from those ivories was as blinding as a sudden religious conversion.

Teresa looked up at her husband adoringly, appearing to hang on his every word. But in private, Terri and Harry went after each other *with* words. Both were highly educated. Armed with impressive vocabularies, they knew exactly how to word-slash each other down to blood and bone. And they never raised their voices. No, they smiled and spoke almost lovingly as they took great chunks out of each other. It was the most chilling thing anyone could ever witness.

There was no small number in tonight's gathered assembly that didn't dread the day C. R. Jones popped his clogs and Harry made a hostile takeover bid against Red Bird Oil lock, stock, and refinery. Matthew was the president of Red Bird Oil and David the first vice president. So far they had held him off, but none of that would matter one whit to Steamroller Harry once the obstacle of his father was permanently removed.

"What," Harry asked solemnly, pompous-assedly, "does one give a man who has everything?" He paused for effect, briefly beaming that luminous smile. "A man who has done everything. Has provided his family, friends, and a multitude of employees with everything they could possibly need for happy, secure lives?"

Harry scanned the tables, playing Diogenes, albeit minus lamp, in search of an honest person. But he wasn't fooling this crowd with a heartfelt rhetorical. No one volunteered. Eyelashes didn't even quiver. One man at a far table, badly needing to cough, turned an alarming shade of blue in an effort to hold it in. Nodding sympathetically, seemingly united with them in their confounded state, Harry humbly admitted, "My brothers and I were also at a loss. It was Matt who finally provided the answer."

C.R. mentally chuckled. *Nice one, son. If I hate it, you've just made certain everyone knows who to blame.*

Harry nodded to Matt. On this cue, Matt folded his napkin, stood, and made his way around the tables, leaving the marquee. C.R. watched Matt cross the outside lawn, disappear behind a wall of rhododendrons. In Matt's brief absence, excited whisperings began to buzz. Harry waved the dessert trolley forward. The cake was on the move again, and the attending waiters sang, "Happy birthday to yooou." Guests stood to their feet, joining in. "Happy birthday to yooooou, happy birthday, C. Rrrrrr, Happy birthday toooo yoooooouu."

C.R. moved from pride of place toward the trolley, gearing himself to the task of blowing out the candles before a four-alarm fire ensued. Matt reappeared, and to C.R.'s utter amazement, Matt was steering a brand new bicycle.

Seeing the gift, Emma's brows shot up, wrinkling her

forehead, the creases threatening the pinned integrity of her chignon. Kelly began jumping up and down, clapping her hands as she laughed. C.R. was still so gobsmacked, he forgot the cake and its risk of fiery doom. He simply stood there, his lower jaw hanging, his eyes locked on the shiny red bicycle with plastic streamers swirling from the handlebar grips, and the big white bow tied to the seat.

Standing before him, Matt proclaimed in a loud voice, “Daddy, all of our lives you've told us that the only thing you'd ever wanted was a bicycle. How you worked from dawn to dusk trying to earn money to buy one. That by the time you finally had the money, you also had an oil company to run, a wife to support, and a house full of ungrateful children. Well, Dad, on behalf of your very grateful children and grandchildren, here's your bike. Happy birthday.”

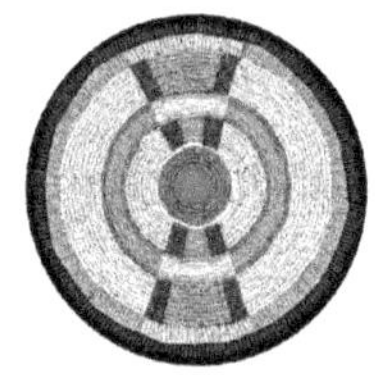

CHAPTER FOUR

The birthday party went on until past three in the morning. While guests were reluctant to call it a night, the grandchildren bolted upstairs to their waiting beds. Especially Hayley, who had embarrassed Matt the way she had been so rude to a young man whose only fault had been trying to be a pleasant dinner partner. When Hayley defected, the other grandchildren followed suit. Which only proved Matt's theory. The children of today were much too soft. Despite having over sixty years on his grandchildren, C.R. was managing to stay on his feet. Ever the host, he was there at the door to shake hands, thank each decamping guest for coming to his party. Matt, poised midway up the widely sweeping staircase, rested his weight against the thick banister as he looked down on the foreshortened view of his father. He was amazed that the old man had lasted the entire night. All things considered, it wasn't half bad for an eighty-five-year-old man accustomed to going off to bed at nine-thirty each and every night.

Matt twisted his lips to the side, bit at the inside of

his cheek. His father's forced laughter floated up to him as he endured the lengthy farewells.

He's stubborn, Matt thought. *Too stubborn to admit he's exhausted. That he's had enough.* Matt felt a prickle of irritation. *Why is Mama allowing this to go on?*

He caught sight of her moving off like a dowager empress, disappearing under the archway of the main reception room. Matt started back down the stairs ready and willing to bodily throw the lagging guests out on their ears, when the stragglers finally took the hint. Matt grinned at the speed his father used closing the door.

Still watching the scene below, he could hear his mother issuing orders. Exhausted as they were, the staff were now on double overtime wage. None of them were about to complain that they faced more long hours cleaning away every last ashtray, glass, and dish. The lady of the house could not tolerate untidiness, and she paid handsomely for services rendered. Besides, there was to be a family brunch the next day. It was mandatory all evidence of the party be eliminated.

Kelly came up the stairs. She held her shoes and the long skirt of her gown as her stocking feet plodded each step like a plow mule doggedly walking the acreage of featureless fields, pulling the plow, cleaving rock-hard dry soil. As Kelly tiredly stomped past her husband, she heard Emma's complaint even over the sounds of furniture being shoved around the vacuum cleaner's whine.

"You'd think at least one of my daughters would be here to help put things right!"

Matt heard Kelly's muttered response as she passed him. "She'd have a fit if one of us actually dared go in there."

Matt watched the roll and sway of his wife's hips as she ascended the stairs. Her sultry movements kindled an old familiar fire. The same fire he'd felt the first day he ever saw her walking away from him.

• • •

In 1937 Olla wasn't much of a town, and the name was far from thrilling. It was of French origin, meaning "pot." There had been a wealth of Frenchmen in the area during the dawn of the 1700s, possibly one of them dropped one. At any rate, the name stuck. Then and now, Olla was only twenty miles away from the bustling city of Pawhuska, and eleven miles out of Bartlesville. Because of the proximity of the Osage capital and Bartlesville, Olla didn't have a need for too many of its own stores, and the small shops that actually made up the town of Olla existed on pennies. Even in these days Olla looked like a wild west town. The few buildings lining both sides of the street were made of brick or clapboard, each with extended porch roofs to shade people walking the sidewalks. The sidewalks were made of wood and the main street was hardpan. And people parked their vehicles any way they wanted to.

In the thirties Olla's only amusement was one small café and a honky-tonk, the White Horse. Racially speaking, Olla has always been a mixed bag. Having once been an Osage village on the fringe of Osage County, Olla began its life as a town of a few dozen Osage citizens. But with the advent of oil, the whites moved in, building houses and the few stores. Then came the blacks, a few Mexicans, and one Chinese family.

On the day Matt met Kelly, he and his group of exhausted friends weren't in any mood to be in the White Horse. Hot and sweaty from the oppressive June heat, and wearing only patched and faded Levis and work boots, Matt and his fellow grain and feed store Romeos were also grimy. Working the oil patch was a dirty business. Because his father insisted his sons learn the oil trade from the bottom up, Matt on that day looked like any other shift-working roustabout. He blended in perfectly with his cronies as they all lolled in the shade of the feed store porch drinking cold sodas. Matt wasn't concerned about how he looked or smelled until he noticed the leggy thoroughbred colt walking tall inside the small herd of stubby mustang fillies. As the girls sauntered past, they stole glances at the young men blatantly ogling them. Kelly's head turned, and she briefly caught Matt's appraising gaze.

Smiling shyly, she tossed her mane of rich red-brown hair. She didn't giggle like the other girls. She broke the brief eye contact she shared with an open-mouthed Matt and carried on walking the dusty road, her curly chesnut hair swirling, and when she lowered her head, her hair hid her face. That's when he concentrated on her behind. The rim of the chilled RC Cola posed near his lips, he watched the smooth rhythm of her backside. The war beginning in Europe seemed to be having a wonderful side effect. Girls' dresses were becoming shorter. This girl's soft cotton dress stopped mid-knee, and he was treated to the full view of well-shaped legs ending at nicely turned ankles.

She was wearing a dusty pair of brown penny loafers and the obligatory dark line was absent on the backs of her calves. That meant she wasn't wearing stockings. He couldn't help but notice that the sun was doing a great job silhouetting her legs and upper thighs, which also meant she wasn't wearing a slip. Except for the thin material of the cotton dress, that beautiful girl was practically naked. As that thought rocketed through his brain, Matt's tongue firmly adhered itself to his upper palate.

Absently he handed the soft-drink bottle to his friend seated on a crate. He spoke to his friend but his line of sight remained fixed on the tall girl.

"Hang on to this a minute, Danny. An' don't try drinkin' it, 'cause I know exactly how much is left."

The instant Danny's hand closed around the chilled bottle, Matt sprinted off after that girl.

On their first date Matt took Kelly to the café, where they made a meal of hamburgers, fries, and Cokes. They sat in the corner booth until ten o'clock, talking until they were kicked out by the tired waitress who badly wanted to go home, put her feet up, and give her varicose veins a well-deserved rest.

Matt's only form of transport was an old jalopy truck. He had Kelly sit so close to him that she was practically in his lap, and even then he griped that she wasn't close enough. With her glued to his side, he drove to her aunt's house and they parked in the front yard, talking until after eleven. Impatiently, her aunt flicked the porch light on and off, signaling Kelly to say good night and come inside.

Kelly's hand was on the truck's door handle, but she didn't move it. Matt thought he heard a construction gang somewhere banging nails into solid wood. As he leaned in and lightly kissed her parted lips, he realized the sound was his own excited heartbeat.

Kissing her, he felt a jolt that almost knocked him senseless. For a full moment he couldn't move, could barely blink. He stared at her. She stared right back. The next thing he knew, he was grabbing her, pulling her against him, kissing her just as hard as he could. Her arms wrapped around his neck as she kissed him with a vigor that took his breath away. He heard low moans and couldn't decide if the moans were coming from him or from her. As the kiss intensified, he didn't care. Until she squirmed, tried to pull away.

"I have to go inside," she said in a whispery rush. "My aunt Alice is going crazy with the light switch."

"Just one more kiss," he begged. "Please, just one more."

Laughing, she shook her head as she tried to disengage herself from his hold. "Matt," she said, her voice firm, "I like kissing you too. I like it too much. And if we keep kissing, you'll think I'm cheap."

Matt emitted a short laugh. "Girl, I just blew a buck forty-five on your double hamburger, fries, and Coke. I don't know where you come from, but around here, that ain't cheap!"

She grabbed his face in one hand, forcing his lips into a fishy pucker. "My mama told me that just because a boy buys me a hamburger it doesn't mean he has the right to squeeze it out of me later. Now, walk me to the door like a gentleman."

Dutifully, hands sunk deep into his jeans pockets, Matt walked beside her on the brick path that led to the steps of the covered wooden porch. While they stood near the front door, Kelly's aunt Alice peered through a side window, holding the gauzy net curtain aside so they could clearly see her face and her disapproving scowl. His head lowered, Matt shoved his hands deeper inside his jeans pockets while Kelly, loud enough for her aunt to hear, thanked him for a lovely evening.

He raised his head, his expression hopeful. "Will you come out with me tomorrow night?"

She smiled happily. "I'd love to."

"And the night after and the night after?"

"Matt!"

"Hey," he said with a serious frown. "I'm kind of a jealous guy, okay? I don't want you ever kissing anyone but me."

Kelly put her finger to her mouth and made a shushing noise. "My aunt will hear you."

"Then you better find a way to shut me up or I'll start yelling it."

Hurriedly she tiptoed and kissed him into silence. Then she quickly escaped, the screen door and then the front door slamming shut behind her. Matt remained on the porch long after the porch light was turned off. He wanted Kelly to come out again, but he knew she wouldn't. He knew, too, that he should get in his truck and leave, but he couldn't. So he simply stood there as one by one the lights inside the house blinked out. In the darkness, crickets began to chirp and fireflies flitted. Finally he slunk away, climbed into his truck, drove for home. In his bed he lay wide awake, thinking of Kelly. Matt had never been on a roller coaster in his entire life but he'd heard about them. Heard about the thrill people felt while being hurtled down steep tracks at breathtaking speeds. Kissing Kelly felt just like that. And he liked it. He liked it so much, he felt too big for his skin. What he didn't like was having to wait the long hours before he could kiss her again.

"Is this what love is?" he asked the darkness. He felt a resounding yes. It was crazy, but so was risking one's life on a roller coaster. And once a guy signed on for either ride, there was nothing he could do but hang on.

The next evening Matt hurriedly drove to Kelly's house. The setting sun bathed the two-story dingy white clapboard house a flattering ochre. He arrived half an hour early, wearing a new pair of Levis that smelled only the way a brand-new pair straight from the dry goods shelf are able to smell. He also wore a stiffly starched short-sleeve cotton shirt and comfortable scuffed tan cowboy boots.

Because he was too early, he had to wait impatiently on the porch for Kelly. Finally she was there, standing within easy reach. Unfortunately, her aunt was on the other side of the screen door, talking a mile a minute as Kelly yes-ma'amed her, repeatedly reassuring the worrying woman that she would be home by ten. Her aunt was still talking as hand in hand Matt and Kelly raced down the porch steps and dashed for the truck.

Aunt Alice watched the rattletrap truck driving away. *I should tell her who he is. No. Maybe she'd do something silly if she knew. Girls can get foolish over men with money.*

The old truck clattered down the dusty main street of Olla, Kelly snuggling close to Matt. She raked one hand through her thick curls as she heaved a contented sigh. He glanced at her quickly. Kelly was the kind of girl who just got prettier every time a guy looked at her. She smelled clean from a recent bath, and because she sat so close, he could feel the warmth of her body. All these things made him excited. He couldn't wait to get her alone. Then she said something that had the effect of a bucket of cold water being dumped on his head.

"Aunt Alice is acting so strange. It started the minute my cousin Beth told her you had asked me out. All day she's pestered me with questions about what we did last night, what you told me about yourself. She didn't seem too happy with my answers." Kelly eased away from him, staring at his marvelous profile. "Is there something about you I should know?"

Matt's hands tightened on the steering wheel. He could tell her, this was the perfect opportunity. Evidently her aunt wanted the truth to come from him. Now was the opportune moment to tell Kelly the truth. Then again, if he told her that his father was one of the richest men in Oklahoma, that her uncle worked for his father, she might become nervous. He definitely did not want her nervous. Working his way through the hours that separated them, he'd made a lot of serious plans for tonight. Not one of those daydreams had included a long discussion about his father!

"Well, maybe she's concerned because I'm Osage. Osage people can be a little clanny and distant. But not this one. Not with you anyway."

Smiling, Kelly rested her head on his shoulder and tossed the discussion away entirely. "I missed you today. Isn't that odd?"

Relieved, Matt sat back, wrapped an arm around her shoulders, pulled her close against him, and kissed her forehead. "No, it's just what I wanted to hear."

"Are we going back to the booth at the café?"

"Nope. Got a special place in mind tonight."

"Is it far?"

"About five miles."

He kissed her forehead again. Five miles later, Matt parked the black Ford truck on the prairie, in the seclusion of a stand of cottonwood and blackjack trees. From behind the seat he produced a brown paper sack. Inside the sack were individually waxed-paper-wrapped peanut butter and honey sandwiches and two bottles of tepid RC Cola. He was grinning from ear to ear as he doled out the meal.

"I don't believe you did this!" she howled.

"I fixed it myself." Actually the cook had made the sandwiches, he'd merely wrapped them and put them in the bag.

A bite of sandwich in her mouth, Kelly was still laughing so much, she started choking. She laughed harder when Matt said, "Sweetheart, I don't want to rush you or anything, but we're losing valuable squeezing time."

She was wearing a dress that was practically the twin of the first dress he'd seen her in. The only difference between the two was the pastel coloring of the material. It was obvious both dresses had been cut from the same pattern—homemade the pair of them. And she still wasn't wearing stockings or a slip.

Matt's blood was racing like a fire through his veins. He pushed her down on the seat, kissing her deeply, his tongue exploring the warmth and softness of her mouth as he edged himself on top of her.

"Don't, Matt!" She pushed against his broad shoulders.

Those were the absolute last words he wanted to hear. But neither could he ignore them.

So he begged.

"Kelly, please. I want you so bad." He moved farther on top of her, the bulge inside his jeans pressing against her abdomen. One hand slid her skirt farther up her thighs. "I love you, Kelly."

"What?" She pushed him away, held him back the full length of her arms. As they stared at each other, his expression was utterly sincere, while hers was set in a frown. "How can you possibly say you love me when we've known each other for only two days?"

Bracing his weight on his arms, he looked down at her. "I don't know. It just kinda popped out."

Kelly began to worm around, trying to sit up. "Get off me, please."

"No." He shoved his face close to hers. "Listen to me, Kelly, I'm not lying. I really do love you. I don't know how it happened. Maybe I fell in love with you last night, or maybe it was when I first saw you walking in town. All I know is that last night I couldn't sleep for thinking about you, and all day I couldn't wait to be with you. Kel," he said, his tone earnest, "You're so pretty and so funny. I—I just can't seem to get enough of you." His hand brushed curls away from her face. "I'm sorry, I know I'm going too fast. I can't help it. I just want to love you. In every way that counts. In every way that's going to let me really believe you'll always be mine."

Tears shimmered on her lower lids, one sliding free, escaping into the hairline of her temple. Her blood was burning fiercely. Matt was glorious. His shirt was gone, wadded and discarded on the floorboard. His chest was smooth, well-muscled. She loved kissing his skin. It tasted rich, gingery. The truth was, she was crazy about him. Had been from the first moment he'd spoken to her. He'd walked backward as she marched steadily forward and he'd talked as briskly as he walked. Finally she stopped long enough to hear him chat her up.

She had been flattered beyond measure that he had singled her out from the group of girls. Being a tall girl, she was used to being the last at dances to be asked to dance. She was also used to the humiliation of sitting home on Saturday nights while her petite girlfriends were out and getting up to all kinds of mischief that they would share with her on Monday mornings before the bell rang summoning them to class. Kelly enviously listened, remembering that her Saturday night mischief had involved putting lemon in the rinse water after shampooing her hair. Then, her hair in curlers, she'd listened to radio comedy shows with her parents.

Because of her unusual height and less than voluptuous figure, Kelly was blind-date material. From puberty, she had been doomed to be the girl some poor, unsuspecting guy was stuck with for an evening of stiff conversation and worse, the almost painful moments of silence as her date mentally cursed his luck, and the couple they doubled-dated with tussled around in the backseat of the car, necking themselves into a happy oblivion.

And then, in front of her prettier cousin and all her cousin's attractive girlfriends, Too-Tall Kelly had been literally chased down the street by the most handsome young man in absolutely the whole wide world. And he was tall—wonderfully, wonderfully tall. And funny and intelligent and so very determined to make her like him.

Her cousin and friends had stood off at a respectable distance as Kelly and the stubborn young man spoke privately in the middle of the unpaved street. A light breeze played with the skirt of her dress. It also danced lightly through her hair. Then he said, sounding as if he meant it with all his heart, "Damn, you're gorgeous. Give a suffering guy a break. Please come out with me tonight."

At that moment, Kelly couldn't have cared less if he was a doctor, lawyer, Indian ditchdigger—the latter, judging by his appearance, more likely the case. What mattered was that he wanted her and she wanted him. On their first date, sitting in the booth, talking up a storm, he didn't mind that she had a brain, was witty. They bounced snappy patter with the rhythm of Bob Hope and Bing Crosby. Just talking to him was the most fun Kelly had since she had played with dolls.

Kissing him—there was no way to describe how she felt kissing him. And now he was telling her he loved her. Could it be true? Oh, God, please, let it be true!

"Really? You really, really love me?"

"Oh, baby." Matt heaved a deep, tortured sigh. "If you only knew how much."

Their son Chris was conceived on a starlit night out on the lone prairie, the only sounds those of night birds twittering in the blackjacks and the steady creaking of the rusting shocks underpinning an even rustier old Ford truck.

A month and a half later, on a Sunday afternoon, parked in "their" spot, Kelly sat tearful and frightened out of her mind. She wiped her eyes, then ran a hand under her nose as Matt sat watching her, one arm draping the steering wheel.

"It still hasn't started," she sobbed. "I knew this would happen. I just knew it!"

Matt was slightly terrified himself. He remembered his father's tiresome advice about being careful with his seed and all that, but he never believed he and Kelly would get in trouble in the truck. Didn't making babies involve big beds and pillows? Matt looked around the cramped quarters of the cab. Obviously not, because cramped conditions notwithstanding, they had managed to make Kelly pregnant.

Damn! We must be as fertile as a pair of turtles!

Were it any other girl, Matt would have strongly suspected this to be an elaborate act, that she was pretending to be pregnant in order to trap him into marriage. But he knew better. Aunt Alice and Cousin Beth hadn't spilled the beans about him and he knew why. Knew because Auntie Alice had taken him off to the kitchen one evening and gave him a sour-faced talking-to.

"I haven't told her who your daddy is. I don't want you tellin' her either. Since my husband works for your daddy, I can't stop you from seeing my niece, but I can stop you from gettin' her hopes up that you're serious about her. When she goes back to Louisiana in September, all she'll think is that she had herself a nice little summertime romance. If you care for my niece, please don't go impressin' her with that big house of yours. She came here a sweet, innocent girl, and I want her to go home just like that."

Matt was thoroughly discomfited, because without needing to impress Kelly with anything other than himself, she was no longer innocent. She hadn't been for weeks. Consumed with guilt, Matt lowered his head and muttered, "Yes, ma'am, Miss Alice."

Then there was his own knowledge of Kelly. She didn't have a pretentious bone in her body. She was so natural and so open that after a week of loving her, he had become terrified of her finding out who he was. The fear had grown into a living nightmare that she would find out and then promptly dump him, believing he had played her for a fool. Kelly did not suffer liars lightly, and to keep her in the dark for as long as possible, he had, by omission, been lying his head off.

He eased out from under the steering column and sat next to her, taking her in his arms. Her face was turned away from him as she stared numbly out the open passenger window, her elbow propped on the ledge, the fingers of her limp hand curled against her trembling mouth. Becoming heated by the feel of her in his arms, the gentle aroma of Midnight in Paris, Matt nuzzled her neck. It was a hell of a time to be horny, but he couldn't help it. His lust for her was so out of control that he didn't even have to be with her to be overwhelmed by it. All he had to do was say her name and his lower half rose to the occasion. Being near her merely made the condition ten times worse.

"Don't, Matt," she snapped. "Please, just—don't."

He blew a long stream of air out of his mouth and slumped back against the seat, staring up at the tattered material loosely covering the roof of the cab. It was a dingy brown that had seen its day. Scrawled permanently into its fraying weave was *Kelly*. Using his thumbnail, he had etched her name into the fabric. Having her name where he could see it made him feel happy, helped him feel that they were still together even during the long hours when they were apart. Now the sight of her name blinded him, accused him.

"Honey," he said softly. "Do you love me?"

"Yes," she snapped. Her tone carried the suggestion that the admission soured her mouth.

"Then will you please just trust me."

"I did trust you!" she cried. She turned her face farther away from him. "I trusted you when you said I wouldn't get pregnant. Well, I'm pregnant, Matthew!" Her voice rose another octave as she whirled and sent him a withering look. "I'm pregnant, and all you can think about is having me spread my legs one more time!"

"Hey!" Matt cried defensively. "That's not what I'm thinking at all."

"Oh, really?" she scoffed. "I'm having a nervous breakdown and all you want to do is nibble my ear! It certainly doesn't *feel* as if you're taking this seriously. It feels like—how do boys put it?—like you just want to tear off one more piece before you dump me. Well, thank you very much."

She was nearing hysteria as she wrenched open the cab door. Outside, she slammed the door hard enough to rock the truck.

"I can walk from here, Mr. Jones. And if you ever come near me again, I'll shoot you."

Matt's eyes half bugged out of his head as Kelly stormed off through the high, sun-scorched grass. Stunned, he watched her stomp away, watched as she angrily flung tears from her face with the back of her hand.

When she was a good distance, it finally occurred to him that she wasn't coming back to talk it out, most certainly not coming back to beg him to do the honorable thing. He quickly moved across the long seat and keyed the ignition.

Kelly ignored him as he drove slowly beside her, calling to her through the open window. "Baby, get in the truck."

"No!"

"Dammit, Kelly, I said get in the truck!"

"Go to hell, Matt Jones."

That's when Matt lost his temper. He stood on the brake and clutch and the truck came to an abrupt halt. The engine stalling noisily, Matt bolted out of the cab. Kelly's eyes grew wide as Matt barreled toward her. Panicked, she began to run.

"Kelly Jane Smith!" Matt bellowed as he chased her. "You better stop."

Kelly ran faster, her speed impeded by the tall grass, the irregularity of the ground.

Matt's booted feet ate up the distance between them. When he caught her, she lost the use of her legs. Her knees buckled and she began to crumple. Matt threw his arms around her, holding her against him, kissing the top of her sun-warmed head.

"Kelly," he crooned as she wept against him. "Kelly, I love you. You're not in trouble. We'll get married. I'm going to take care of you—and the baby."

"I'm so ashamed," she bawled, her body trembling as she sobbed.

"No, honey," he said, tears sounding in his voice. "Don't be ashamed of loving me. Please don't say that."

She turned up her tear-stained faced, and she looked

at him through red-rimmed eyes. "I'm not ashamed of loving you. I'm—I'm ashamed you feel you have to marry me."

Matt let go a chesty laugh. "Kelly! Do you honestly believe I was going to let you get on that bus in September? Honey, you weren't *ever* going anywhere."

His father amazed him. Matt's nerves were wire-thin as he stood in his father's office, confessing that he, at twenty, was about to become a father. C.R., seated behind his desk, stared hard at his third son, a tall young man with a head of thick black hair.

"Do you love this girl?" he asked in a surprisingly level tone.

"Dad, I love her so much I hurt. She's a real good girl. She was a virgin until me. And now, just because she loved me back, she's in trouble."

Matt's wary eyes met his father's. As if settling an argument between them, he said flatly, "I'm marrying her, Dad. And I'm marrying her before anyone knows she's in the family way. I'm not gonna have people around here laughing at her. Laughing at us. She's my girl and that's my baby. So you can throw me out of the family if you want to, but—"

"Shut up, Matt." C.R. was silent for a moment, enjoying the sight of his youngest son squirming like a worm on a hot rock. Then he ended Matt's torment. "I want you to take your little girl straight to the house. . . ."

Half an hour later, Matt's speeding truck raised a dust storm as he entered Aunt Alice's drive and slammed it to a halt on the sun-dried, stubby lawn. Kelly was seated on the porch, shelling peas with her aunt and cousin. All three women were surprised by Matt's highly dramatic appearance. Jumping to her feet, Kelly dropped the bowl from her lap, shelled peas and husks spilling on the plank flooring.

Matt laid on the horn. Between blasts he yelled, "Kelly! Get out here!"

Cold dread gripped Alice May Bingham. All this time Matt Jones had presented himself as a gentlemanly escort, but now he was acting crazy. Alice May was terrified of Indians, she hated it that her husband, needing work in a time when there was little work anywhere in the country, had brought her to a state filled with Indians. Her hands frantically grabbed for her niece. In a frightened voice she cried, "Don't do it, Kelly! Get in the house. We'll call the police!"

"It's all right, Aunt Alice," Kelly shouted over the blaring of the horn and Matt's shouts. She tore loose of her aunt's desperate grip and ran across the wide porch, skipped down the stairs, bolted for the truck. Matt popped the passenger door open and Kelly hopped in. As the truck spun its back tires, reversing out of the front lawn, Alice May stood on the lip of the porch, screaming Kelly's name. She got a lung full of gritty dust for her efforts.

Kelly was gone.

"Well, it's a humble little pile," Kelly declared cynically as the truck came to a stop in the drive of the great house. "Do your parents work here?"

Matt killed the engine. He couldn't make up his mind what he wanted to do first, laugh or kiss her. After a second's consideration, he did both. When he pulled away from her, Kelly's face still dreamy from the soulful kiss, he did what he should have done on their very first date.

He told the truth.

"But," she sputtered, "you work in the oil field! You wear jeans and—and you drive this truck!"

"Kelly," Matt sighed heavily, "my dad has a real hardon for the work ethic. He may have a lot of money, but none of his sons were ever spared from honest toil.

I've been working since I've known how to and now that I'm in college, I'm expected to work in the patch during the summers to pay back some of the money Dad forks out on my education."

Kelly sat there, her mouth hanging open. She didn't even seem to be breathing. How long could an unborn baby survive if the mother didn't breathe?

"Kelly!" he shouted.

He felt relieved when she immediately inhaled. Then she began to cry. He wasn't happy about the crying, but at least she was breathing.

"You should have told me, Matt!"

"Would you have gone out with me?"

"No!"

"Well, good reason not to tell you."

"My—my aunt should have told me."

Matt barked a laugh. "Hey, your aunt was afraid you might have sex with me if you knew. Believe it or not, she practically said that to my face. I didn't have the heart to tell her that you could be had for a peanut butter and honey sandwich."

Her arms folded under her small breasts, she sat ramrod straight and with a I'm-fuming-mad-at-you-Matthew-Jones expression on her face as she stared out the dust-coated windshield. "It wasn't just the sandwich."

Matt slid closer, placed his arm around her shoulders, and kissed the side of her face. "I know. It was my handsome face and manly charm."

"Oh, ha! It was the RC Cola. I was so thirsty, I thought I was going to die."

Laughing, Matt captured her face in his hands, kissed her mouth once, twice, three times. Then he rested his forehead against hers. "Kelly, no matter what my parents say, from now on it's just you and me. We stick together. Promise?"

Sniffing back a tear, she nodded.

• • •

Waiting for his father proved to be the longest twenty minutes of his life. Sitting on the veranda, Kelly and Matt sipped lemonade as Emma asked Kelly a stream of questions. Kelly answered, and given the circumstances, with amazing calm.

She had, during the previous fitful night's sleep, tried to envision meeting Matt's parents. Then there was the pressing problem of what to say to her own parents. In her mind she had rehearsed the telephone call she would make as soon as she and Matt had tied the knot. The rejected opener being: "Mama, Daddy—I'm in love and have married oil patch trash."

In view of the current bombshell, the call to Monroe, Louisiana, would undergo yet another revision. Her oil field Indian boy—and it still came as a shock to her—was loaded up to his copper-skinned gills in filthy lucre. So now, instead of being the white girl in love with their Osage son, as if that weren't enough of an obstacle, she faced the very real threat of his parents perceiving her as a scheming black-gold digger. She couldn't help but wonder which they would do first, try to buy her off, or boot her out with a few well-chosen, humiliating words. Kelly might appear unruffled as she sipped lemonade and answered each of his mother's endless questions, but inside she was a trembling wreck.

The sound of the front door slamming hard startled all three. Having been so involved with straining to keep polite small talk alive while each pondered separate worries, none of them had heard the car in the gravel drive. But the sound of the massive front door banging was a hard thing to miss. A heartbeat later Kelly heard, for the first time in her life, the sound of her future father-in-law's voice. It was strong, it was thunderous, and she would go to her grave remembering C. R. Jones exactly that way.

"MATTHEW!"

Matt's jaw instantly clenched. Emma's expression changed from surprised to alarmed. The blood in Kelly's face swiftly drained. Matt took her hand and muttered, "Here we go," and rose from his chair. Holding tightly to each other, ignoring Emma nipping at their heels with cries of "What's wrong, Matthew? Why does your father sound so angry?" they crossed the terrace and entered the house. His father, trailed by three men, two of whom Matt instantly recognized as his father's most trusted lieutenants, stormed through the main room, meeting the couple just as they passed through the curving portal of the formal dining room.

C.R. quickly appraised the young woman fearfully clinging to his son. Seeing the hard look in his father's eyes, Matt immediately assumed a defensive posture, pushing Kelly behind him, shielding her with his body. There was a lot to shield. The girl was remarkably tall, less than a few inches away from being as tall as his six-foot-three son. He had noticed quickly that she was all legs and that mother nature had given only the perfunctory nod by way of breasts.

But he knew exactly why Matt had fallen in love with her. It was those legs, those eyes, that shock of hair. Ignoring his combative son, C.R. sidestepped Matt and introduced himself to Kelly. Taking hold of her cold hand, he felt her tremble as her fair hand became lost inside his. But he saw courage shining from her sky-blue eyes, and at that instant he thoroughly approved of her.

The third man, a stranger to all of them, was the justice of the peace from Pawhuska. Emma, shocked out of her skull that her son was being married that very minute, ran out to pick fresh flowers for the bride. The petals of the flowers were still wet from the showering the gardener had given them. The flowers jittered and twitched in Kelly's clenched hand. The tiny storm her nerves created shook water from the held flowers, lightly soaking the front of her thin dress as the justice performed the ceremony.

The two men, one of whom was the head attorney for Red Bird Oil, the other an executive acting as witness, came by their lofty status primarily on the basis that they knew when and how to keep their mouths firmly shut. C.R. wrenched a ring off his wife's bejeweled hand and gave it over to Matt to use as a wedding ring until a proper one could be purchased. Oddly enough, Emma didn't squawk about losing the ring, and Kelly never asked for another one. But before an eight-pound-nine-ounce Christopher Charles bounced into the world, Matt bought Kelly a small gold band to wear with the opal ring purloined from his mother.

Kelly disappeared behind the door of the room they had lived in during the first weeks of their marriage before she and Matt went off to Norman, Oklahoma. While Matt attended the university, they lived in a tiny rental house. C.R. may have been miserly where living-expense money was concerned, but on the subject of his grandson's welfare, no price was too great. Christopher slept in the best crib, wore the best clothing. The young parents and their thoroughly pampered offspring were wildly happy.

Then Matt went off to war in Europe. Kelly, pregnant with their daughter Hayley, had lugged toddler Chris back to this palatial home to live in this house, to sleep in that room during the entire time Matt was away.

Matt, stirred by the memories he and Kelly had shared inside that room at the top of the stairs at the beginning of their marriage, when they were finally able to make love in a real bed, not cramped up in a truck, and the nights they'd known again when reunited after the war, skipped up the stairs, raced down the landing like an anxious bridegroom. He knocked softly before entering.

After so many years, Kelly was more than able to read her husband's mind. When Matt opened the door, she stood waiting for him. Her slinky silk evening gown lay on the floor like a wreath surrounding her ankles. She was absolutely naked, wearing only an inviting smile.

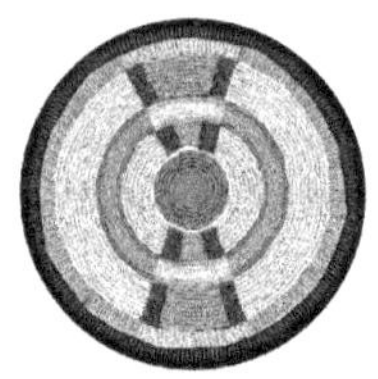

CHAPTER FIVE

It was almost noon. C.R. stood on the veranda enjoying the comfortable warmth of the new day. In the dining room Emma's fancy-pants butler—from Boston, not England, but close enough for Emma—was verbally abusing the two serving girls. The girls were doing their best at setting the brunch table properly, but there were just too many forks and spoons and knives.

C.R.'s heart went out to them. It had taken him years to get the hang of eating with an array of cutlery, always reminding himself, start with the ones on the end. Gradually, as course followed course, the cutlery dwindled. Closely following that golden rule of etiquette had, over time, lessened the trauma of using so many pieces of silverware. But laying it all out must be a living hell. Especially when one considered that the separate meals—breakfasts, brunches, dinners, and suppers—had separate requirements, thus separate modes of being laid out. C.R. did not envy those young girls suffering to learn their maid trade one little bit. He knew how to find oil, how to get it out of the ground, but setting dining tables for a living would have knocked him for six.

"Hi, Dad."

Standing there with his hands thrust deeply inside his trouser pockets, he was startled by the sound of Matt's voice.

"Oh, Matt," he breathed, his relief evident, "I thought you were Harry. Where is he anyway? He said last night he wanted to talk to me. That it was urgent. Then he went to bed. How urgent can something be if he can go to sleep?"

Matt chuckled lightly. "I wouldn't worry too much, Dad. With Harry, everything's urgent."

Both chuckled, then became quiet as they gave their attention to the glimmering garden, enjoying the display of sun-spangling light on the newly watered lawn and flowering hedges. This idyllic scene was, of course, thanks to Emma. She oversaw the continual care of the gardens with the same brutal efficiency she gave the running of the house. The sight of a dandelion coming to flower in the middle of a lawn, or the smallest mess in the house, never failed to send her scurrying into action. C.R. knew why she was this way. That her slavish devotion to the appearance of perfection stemmed from the lack of any perfection in their long marriage. For well over fifty years Emma had tried very hard to replace the person no one could ever replace. He didn't blame her for trying so hard, but her frenetic energy could be very wearing.

And, too, because of Emma, on a day that was heating up fast, begging for Bermuda shorts and loud Hawaiian shirts, here he was wearing what she called his morning suit. Thankfully it wasn't the British morning suit replete with gray swallowtail jacket, but the suit was gray and it had been made in England. Like the Boston butler, that was close enough.

Matt, on the other hand, looked dressed for tennis in

white cotton slacks and shirt. He wasn't wearing socks inside the slip-on white canvas shoes. C.R. stole a sidelong glance at his son. Matt looked a decade younger than his actual age. He was fit, trim, and handsome. Add to this that he was also the president of a successful oil company, Matt's sex appeal soared off the charts. Women blatantly threw themselves at him, and nine times out of ten, they flirted with him right in front of Kelly.

C.R., as ruggedly ugly as he knew himself to be, had in his younger days been treated to the same flattering pursuit. Women were strongly attracted to power and money. C.R. had both. So much, in fact, that even though he had a face that could crack porcelain, women wanted him. But because he was forever in love with a woman he could never have, and because he deeply respected Emma, Charlie never availed himself of the charms so freely offered. From what he knew of Matt, his son had never yielded to this temptation either. Matt's refusals must have boggled the enamored minds of the women chasing him. In this age of youth worship, Kelly must seem to them to be so far over the hill, she couldn't possibly remember the hump.

What these insipid women failed to grasp was that Matt was so besotted with Kelly that when he looked at her, he didn't see the crow's-feet crinkling the corners of her eyes or the gray beginning to streak her chestnut hair. And it did the other women no good whatsoever to flaunt their well-endowed boobies. Matt wasn't a booby man. He never had been. He was strictly a leg man, and Kelly had four miles more leg than any woman in the state. Plus, she was the best friend Matt had ever known. Kelly never had to worry about Matt and other women. Like a pair of swans, Matt and Kelly had mated for life. C.R. thought about that for a moment. Then in his mind's eye he saw his own swan.

Cassie.

The family assembled in the dining room. Harry and Teresa, David and Irene, Matt and Kelly. Their son, Christopher, was the only grandchild present. The others had skipped out. Hayley, Matt and Kelly's daughter, had been the only fleeing grandchild to pause long enough to have a private chat with C.R. before making her dash for Tulsa. Charlie loved Hayley almost to the point of violence. He had loved her in this way since the day of her birth. He hated hospitals and Emma had practically dragged him by the hair to visit Kelly on the maternity wing.

"Matt's not here and that baby needs a male to hold it and welcome it to the family."

C.R. grudgingly complied, but the moment Kelly lay the tiny bundled newborn in his arms and Hayley opened her eyes slightly, smiling a tiny smile, C.R. was instantly his little granddaughter's doting slave.

"Look! She's smiling at me."

Emma peered at the baby. Having mothered three babies, she knew when a baby was screwing itself up for a bowel moment. But considering the effort it had taken to get him inside a hospital, she didn't correct him.

"This baby really knows me," he said proudly.

"Yes, she does."

Carefully holding the baby, C.R. walked over to the bed and sat down close to Kelly.

"She's perfect. Can I have her?"

Kelly laughed softly. "Of course you can."

And that was that. From day one, Hayley belonged to C.R. Throughout Hayley's life C.R. made it his business to spoil her. If Hayley had asked for the moon, her Pap-Paw would have found a way to get it for her. But three weeks earlier Hayley asked for something more down to earth. Something that he would have to first fight Matt and then his most implacable enemy before he would be able to grant her wish. During their conference that morning, when he'd tried to reassure her, her tears and pleadings almost destroyed him. Now, toying with the food on his plate, C.R. wished his little Hayley had asked him for the moon.

Matt glanced toward the head of the table. "Hey, Dad? Are you going to give your present a try today?"

"He is not!" Emma snapped. "What kind of present was that? I would have said something last night, but I didn't want to cause a scene. How could you boys give your father a bicycle! Have you all gone crazy? Your father doesn't know how to ride a bicycle, and he's too old to learn."

C.R. cleared his throat. It was something he did when he wanted everyone's full attention. As always, it worked.

"I like my present," he said with a tone of finality. "It's the best present anyone has ever given to me. And yes, I'm going to ride it. In fact, as soon as we've eaten, I'm saddling up."

The Jones boys surrounded C.R. as he sat on his brand-new bicycle. Because the bicycle couldn't gain sufficient purchase on the gravel drive, it had been wheeled outside the gates. Now they were on pavement, all of the sons talking at once, trying to outshout one another as they gave their father instructions on how to properly ride the thing.

The women, Emma in the forefront, stood in the archway of the open gates, all of them squinting against the bright glare of the sun, and with hands against their foreheads shielding their eyes. When her daughters-in-law began to bicker among themselves, Emma's patience began to unravel. She had three seemingly intelligent sons, and not one of them had married a woman she could stand. They were three completely different women, and each one of them got on her nerves in three completely different ways. The first daughter-in-law had been Teresa. She was the first to teach Emma that if a beautiful thing was yellow and it glittered, then it was probably fool's gold.

Teresa had been staying for the Christmas season with relatives. Family, who, as it happened, were well-placed acquaintances of C.R.'s. Teresa's kin were comfortably situated in Tulsa. Teresa, unfortunately, was their visiting poor relation. Even though Emma was made aware of the girl's meager circumstance, she couldn't help but admire the way Teresa wore borrowed party dresses with grace and poise.

And the girl had such an excellent pedigree. She was from an old southern aristocratic family. The girl so impressed her that Emma hadn't minded at all that Teresa's immediate family had fallen on hard times. Caught up with Teresa's airs and graces, Emma was also a little more than enthralled that Teresa's family could be traced back to wealthy Virginia plantation owners and from there to the very courts of the kings of England.

Emma was told by the breathy hostess of the Christmas fête, who was but a mere third cousin to her indigent houseguest, that Teresa was the direct descendant of the second son of an English earl who'd set up his son as a gentleman colonial tobacco farmer. The family had weathered all the winds of change, the Revolution—being on the right side with General Washington—the Civil War—they had not put all their money in Confederate capital, they had run blockades instead, making even more money bootlegging guns to the South for the cause—but unfortunately the family had met its financial Waterloo at the onset of the Great Depression.

Emma did not hold her father's massive stock losses against Teresa. Teresa was the most gently spoken, ladylike girl she had ever met. She even admired Terri's father. He wasn't a whiner.

"Had a bit of bad luck on the old exchange" was all he said concerning his recent ruin.

After their marriage, Terri seemed genuinely smitten with Harry, looking up to him, always saying, "Yes, Harry," whether she was agreeing with something he'd said or answering his summons to refill his drink glass. And Harry had loved her solid devotion. The marriage had been quite good for the first five years. Years spent in England, while Harry studied at University College, Oxford.

Terri had wanted to live permanently in England, where her family connections had meant everything and Harry had been reduced to the status of the rich Red Indian person she'd happened to marry. Returning to Oklahoma meant having to submit to Harry's will again, being thought of as second best. Terri was secretly tired of being grateful to Harry for marrying her. She had grown to like his dependence on her for a change. But after five years of Teresa being the grand lady, Harry was tired of their role reversal and he was determined that their small children would be spared the depravation and the dangers of war. And in England, Harry wasn't considered too old to be in the war. Harry wasn't interested in saving that arrogant little rock called Great Britain from the dreaded Jerries. In his opinion, the Germans would only improve the place, taking a mired government in hand and making it work more efficiently, something the waffling Brits seemed incapable of doing. Besides, the entire Royal Family were Germans. Why England was so terrified of being invaded by more Germans was beyond him.

So Harry and Terri came home to the safety of America. Shortly after their return, cracks in the marital foundation began to appear.

Yes, Harry was gradually replaced by a sardonic *Oh, how silly.* Then came the squabbles, the no-holds-barred insults, neither caring that the rest of their astonished family was present. They remained together for the sake of the children, never mind that the three children didn't especially care for being the glue holding their parents' marriage together. When each child came of age, they escaped. Son Eric was now a doctor living in Florida. Daughters Natalie and Amy were married, one living in New York, the other California, in La Jolla. Now Terri and Harry's marriage was, for all intents and purposes, as dead as a three-for-a-penny doornail. The only thing preventing its well-deserved burial was Terri's stubborn refusal to let go of the corpse. Emma knew she wasn't supposed to know the full truth, that Harry no longer even lived with Terri, but she did know. *Everyone* knew.

Oh, God, and then there was Irene. David and Irene had a strong marriage, but Emma needed an even stronger drink as a bracer against the fact of Irene.

Irene was half Jewish. That was not the problem. The problem began and ended with Irene bending so far backward to be completely non-Jewish that she was so Oklahoma, a person would swear she'd been born wearing cowboy boots. It grated on Emma's nerves that Irene could also be so maddeningly self-deprecating. Irene could at the worst possible moment come out with idiocies such as "My daddy used to work for C.R," giving the misleading impression that the man had merely slopped through the mire of drilling mud. The fact was, Irene's father had been a brilliant contract lawyer who saved C.R.'s company more times than anyone would care to count. He also owned a cattle ranch, the Rocking J, which after he died, Irene, as his only child, inherited, lock, stock, and branding irons.

Even before they were married, Irene had thoroughly corrupted David. During the first months of their courtship, David dropped out of Princeton and went to live on the ranch like a beer-swilling cowboy. He never left. The only reason he was still involved with the family company was that Matt needed him. Otherwise he would have spent every minute of his life punching cows. David and Irene had two daughters, Sharon and Ruth. Emma couldn't stand them either. They were too much like their mother. In other words, real *country*. Yee-haw. Which meant that when they went off to college, both were so hicky, they gave Okies a bad name. And just like their mother, they stayed that way. Sharon, built like her father and possessing her mother's skewed values, became a veterinarian. Emma had no worry about Sharon ever marrying and breeding after her own kind. It wasn't likely that any man would ever warm up to a big woman who made a living wrestling bull calves to the ground, changing them from bulls to steers.

But Irene was very proud of Sharon. Even over a good dinner Irene could be counted on to start off table chatter with "Guess how many mountain oysters Sharon whacked today?"

Ruth married a trucker. Again, Irene's low-rent way of describing anything. Ruth's husband single-handedly ran Red Bird Oil trucking. He wore a suit and worked in an office. Emma strongly suspected the man didn't even know how to drive an oil truck.

Like their mother, the two daughters habitually sat at the ranch house kitchen table, drinking Cokes from the bottle, smoking forty packs of cigarettes between them while picking their back teeth with the stems of wooden matches. *Yeeeeee-hawww.*

Next, there was Kelly.

Emma held a solid grudge against Kelly. That girl had virtually appeared out of nowhere, marrying Matt on the same day Emma met her. Following the shock of their marriage, Emma quietly had Kelly investigated, learning that her new daughter-in-law came from a severely modest background. She had been born and raised in Monroe, Louisiana, to hardworking but lower-middle-income parents. Kelly had been merely visiting Oklahoma for the summer when Matt met her. She had been due to leave in September, but instead she'd slunk her way into the family by putting her feet in the air and writhing on her back. Chris had been a honeymoon baby the way F.D.R. had been a Republican! Despite the truth, Kelly still managed to make every male in the family, especially C.R., treat her as if she were an all-wise, all-knowing Madonna.

That just infuriated the fire out of Emma.

She was relieved of her bitter thoughts by the sight of her laughing husband almost falling off the bicycle. "Oh, I can't stand this," she snarled. "This is the most ridiculous thing he's ever done."

"Don't blame Harry," Terri said smugly. "He tried to talk Matt out of buying the bicycle, but Matt just wouldn't listen."

"Thank you, Terri," Kelly said acidly.

Terri's eyes narrowed, sending Kelly a warning look.

Irene moved closer to Kelly, muttering in her nasal, twangy voice, "I swear, if she says one more syrupy thing about Harry, I'll throw up all over her pointy-toed Italian shoes."

Instantly furious, Terri whirled on Irene. "Oh, why don't you just go back in the house and chain-smoke and gnaw a whole lumberyard of matches!"

Irene laughed. "Honey, I hope you didn't waste your whole night thinking up such a great comeback. If you did, then you sure wasted some good lovin' time." Irene placed a hand against her mouth and laughed again. "Oops! I guess I forgot who I was talking to—"

"Irene!" Kelly shouted.

Startled, Irene was confused by Kelly's livid expression. Instantly on the defensive, she mewled, "Well, Kel, I'm only saying what everybody knows."

Terri was far from appreciative of Kelly's intervention. In a waspish tone she said, "Thank you, but I don't need you to defend me from trash."

Irene sucked in a ragged breath, then went on the attack. "Who you callin' trash, you jumped-up apple-seller's daughter¿ My daddy was making good money working for C.R. while your daddy was standing on street corners begging nickels."

Kelly moved beside Emma, removing herself from the conflict.

Rapidly stabbing her chest with her index finger, Terri raged, "My father was a gentleman. And for your information, despite his circumstance, he made certain that I went to college, which is more than your father ever did for you."

"Yeah, but if I had *wanted* to go to college, *I* wouldn't have had to wait tables to do it."

Terry turned away, pointing her perfectly formed nose skyward. "I refuse to trade further remarks with someone so utterly beneath me."

"Beneath you¿!" Irene bawled. "Honey, you'd have to climb a forty-foot ladder just to kiss my ass."

"You're despicable."

"You're frigid."

"Please stop fighting," Kelly pleaded.

"Shut up, Kelly!" Terri and Irene shouted in unison.

Glaring over her shoulder at the group of women she heartily despised, Emma quickly ended the bickering when she said through gritted teeth, "C.R. is about to break his neck. I'd appreciate a moment of respectful silence."

• • •

"Pedal, Dad!" Matt laughed as he and his son Chris ran alongside the wobbly bicycle.

C.R. was sweating from every pore of his body as the bicycle he struggled hard to manage jiggled and swayed as if it suffered Saint Vitus' dance. His heart was thudding rapidly. He could feel each and every beat and hear the whoosh of blood in his ears. The sound drowned out everything, even the voices of Matt and Chris as they trotted beside him, shouting encouragement. He pedaled harder, building up a respectable speed and all the while becoming more and more aware of the searing pain in his chest preventing his drawing anything beyond a shallow breath. Then there was the fiery tingle in his left arm. It was numbing his hand. He could no longer feel that hand gripping the handlebar.

And then came the flashes—half-second images—blasting through his mind like the channels on a television set being quickly changed.

A girl, young, mixed blood—her face so clear that in that second everything else was blotted out. Then, just as suddenly, she was gone, replaced by the image of his father, hanging crucifix fashion between two trees. He heard his father screaming as the fire beneath his bare feet licked his flesh. Then one by one there were the faces of cowboys, laughing as they watched his father's suffering.

The channel switched again. He saw a young boy, hiding, then running away from the grisly scene. C.R. felt himself leave his body, become one with the boy. He felt the child's rampant heartbeat, tasted his fear, felt each slash of the spiky branches as the boy crashed through bramble. He felt the jagged edges of rocks stabbing the soles of his feet through the thin moccasins, and in the distance he heard much too clearly the sound of his father's dying voice.

C.R. slammed back into his eighty-five-year-old body, realized with a shock that he was on an unstable bicycle, that he was too weak to control it. When he glanced at his son and grandson running along beside, he wanted to call out to them for help, but he was stopped by the fact that he had no idea who they were. They were complete strangers. How could he ask complete strangers for help? Then a new pain, as violent as a shotgun blast hit his chest. Oddly, his thoughts became completely clear. He knew his son, his grandson, as well as something else.

I'm having a heart attack.

Blood erupted from his nose. A waterfall of blood. Distantly he heard voices shouting as the bicycle slid out from under him. There was no feeling other than the pain ripping his chest as he hit the ground and lay there, concerned faces surrounding him, everything going white.

In the middle of the blinding white, a girl with waist-length hair as dark as midnight and eyes shining with love beckoned.

Cassie!

Charlie hurriedly scrambled to his feet and she came to him, leaping into his opened arms.

Cassie. Charlie held her tightly, swung her off her feet, and laughed like a happy fool.

"Daddy!" Matt screamed into his dead father's strangely peaceful face. *"Daddy!"*

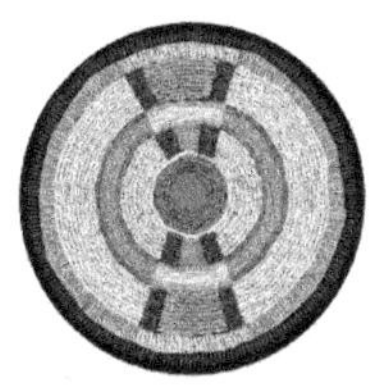

CHAPTER SIX

Tornadoes, prairie fires, oil company lawyers, and gossip are the fastest-moving natural calamities known to Oklahoma. In a small town like Olla, tornadoes and gossip ran neck and neck. Owning a combination hardware, plumbing, and building supply store, the only majorly successful store in Olla, Everett Jakomin helped the town in the advent of one while he listened attentively to the other. And why not? Gossip was now his primary entertainment.

Being French-Osage, he was not as tall as many Osage men grow to be. Everett was only six feet two. He had a very nice-looking face which was barely lined, and almond-shaped eyes with orbs so dark that the corneas blended with the irises. A pair of glasses perched on the end of a Romanesque nose, and a full, sensuous mouth was pursed beneath as he thoughtfully listened to a customer at the counter. The more he listened, the more irritated he became, and he raked his fingers through salt-and-pepper hair that was cut closely around almost feminine ears.

While his wife had been alive, stuffing him with good home cooking, he had sported a bit of a gut. But he had been on his own for the past three years, either eating at the café, Katie's Steak 'N' Spuds, or cooking for himself.

The gut was gone.

Everett hated to cook. Grilling a steak or frying an egg was about the best he could do. Therefore, he ate a lot of Wheaties. The food at the café was quite good, but he went there primarily to socialize. Especially with the café's owner. In the past two years the owner of Katie's Steak 'N' Spuds was the only woman he cared to spend time with. But he was convinced that she merely considered him to be a good friend. And because she was such a young woman, nearly twenty years his junior, quietly admiring Katie Little Hill was about as far as Everett dared to take their relationship.

For an intelligent man, Everett Jakomin was as blind as cheese mold to the fact that quite a few women in Olla, Katie Little Hill included, admired the breath out of him. With good reason. He was a successful businessman, middle-aged—if he planned to live to be one hundred and six—and despite his bashful manner he could be quite a charmer. The biggest plus was that he was also a sexy hunk of masculinity, with a striking resemblance to James Garner. Oh, yes, women, especially the good widowed sisters of Grace Baptist Church, admired Everett Jakomin quite a bit. And they certainly had the opportunity, because Everett attended church every Sunday morning and evening without fail. But not because he was a hard-line Southern Baptist. He went because his late wife, Anna, had devoted so much of her life to Grace Baptist, and when he was in the church, he felt her presence.

Everett shifted his weight from foot to foot as he looked impatiently over the glasses perched on the end of his nose. Glasses he needed only for reading, not for seeing. At this moment in his life, he wished he weren't seeing Dickie Lovett.

A small, wiry man, Dickie was a plumber who always looked and smelled as if he personally crawled through a drainpipe in order to clear it. His odor was offending Everett's nose as he leaned across the counter, and his conversation was quickly becoming as offensive as his smell. Yet Dickie persisted, disregarding Everett's hindering scowl as he continued to voice his particular slant on the recent death of C. R. Jones.

"I'm bettin' it was Harry what killed him. Bought that bicycle just so's the ol' man would flop over dead tryin' to ride it. Purty tricky when ya think about it, Ev. Now you just watch an' see him pick off his brothers one by one."

Dickie stretched his oblong head forward, revealing more of his thin, grimy neck beneath the collar of his work shirt. His beady eyes narrowed as he blatantly studied Everett.

"Ya know, Ev—you an' Harry look a lot alike. I always did think that. 'Course, you look like a man an' he looks like a sissy, but in the face there's a 'semblance."

Everett chuckled deeply as he checked Dickie's order list. "All us Osage look alike to you, Dickie."

Dickie slapped the countertop and brayed with laughter. "That you do, Ev. Tall an' butt-ugly, ever' last one of ya."

Everett smiled as he shook his head. One of the double-glassed doors opened, and into the expansive store stepped Matt Jones. The silence that came over the establishment and its sprinkling of customers was immediate and eerie. Matt Jones stood there, wearing gray slacks, an expensive-looking short-sleeve sport shirt, and gray Hush Puppy loafers. Despite his neat appearance, he looked haggard, as if he had aged ten years overnight. No one spoke or moved as he crossed the wide terra-cotta-tiled shop floor and approached the counter. He was careful to stand a few feet away from the odious Dickie. Up close, Matt's complexion was even more sallow. Everett removed his glasses, setting them down on the counter, wondering if he should offer Matt his condolences. Then, on second thought, no. He was not sorry that C. R. Jones was dead and any allusion that he might be would not be well received by C.R.'s son. Not knowing what to do, Everett simply stared back at Matt.

"Good morning," Matt managed in a painfully tight voice.

Everett opened his mouth, but he was too late. Dickie jumped right in as if the address had been intended for him. Grinning like a bat from ear to encrusted ear, Dickie chimed his customary response to this particular salutation.

"Hey, good morning this morning! If tomorrow morning is like this morning, it'll be another fine morning in the morning."

Everett and Matt looked at the little ferret of a human with silent and united disapproval.

In a somber voice Everett said, "May I help you, Mr. Jones?"

"Yes, Mr. Jakomin. I wonder if I might speak with you privately for a moment?"

"Certainly."

Everett nodded to his counter assistant, a young man named Tommy Knife. Tommy wore his dark hair long and habitually tossed his head, flipping his hair away from his eyes. Because Matthew Jones was in the store, Tommy's eyes were especially wide as he flipped his hair and looked at Everett with the expression of a flustered rabbit.

"Tommy, would you finish Dickie's order, please? I'll be in my office." Then to Matt, as Everett raised the counter partition to allow Matt to walk through, he said solemnly, "Please come this way, Mr. Jones."

Watching the departing men, Tommy absently picked up Everett's glasses, putting them in his shirt pocket. Later, when Everett began yelling that his glasses were lost, Tommy would just as absently hand them over. Keeping Everett's glasses safe was not part of his job description, it was simply a habit he'd developed to prevent his boss from tearing up the stockroom whenever his glasses were missing. Tommy wasn't thinking about Everett or the glasses he'd put away safely in his shirt pocket. He was watching Dickie. Watching Dickie slither toward the partition, the upper half of his body hanging across the width of the counter, his crusty clothing leaving a dirty trail on the Formica. Dickie was almost there when Tommy's voice mildly warned, "Don't even think about it, Dickie. You step one toe behind this counter and you'll find yourself having to drive to Pawhuska every time you need a ballcock."

Unflappable, Dickie simply grinned his bat grin. Lying halfway over the counter, Dickie said, "Wonder what one of the Jones boys wants with Ev?"

"It'll be about the funeral," Tommy grunted, trying to sound nonchalant, as if a Jones appearing in the store were an everyday occurrence. He walked away from the counter, beginning to busy himself with Dickie's order. His back turned to the plumber, he studied the many pigeonholed shelves of boxed parts on the back wall. "Ya gotta remember, Dickie, Ev's on the council," Tommy said as he pulled out boxes, looked inside, shoved them back again. "Maybe the Jones family wants old C.R. buried with honors the way old Chief Bacon Rind was buried. My grandfather says that that was some funeral. The president and senators and all kinds of important people came. He said there were so many cars filled with folks that the cars stretched back for miles and miles. They buried Bacon Rind up on a hill and in the old timey Osage way. Hasn't been another funeral like it since. I'll bet hard money Mr. Jones is in there right now putting the pressure on Ev for C.R. to get buried just like that."

"Think it'll happen?" Dickie breathed excitedly.

His back still turned to the counter, Tommy examined the contents of another box of parts. "No. Not while Ev's on the council."

"Ev could really stop it?"

"Yep."

Dickie scratched his chin. "Boy-hidy, ain't that just somethin'? When he was alive, old man Jones told most ever'body how to live. But the second he croaks, it's up to Ev to say how he can be dead. Now, that's just *reeeally* somethin'."

"Dickie!" Tommy barked. "Is it three or five shunt valves you need. I can't read Ev's writing."

"It's two five-inchers."

"Well, hell, Dickie!" Tommy laughed. He turned at the waist, looking back at the plumber. "Looks like you gotta go to Pawhuska after all. We're out of the five-inchers."

Dickie straightened, slapped the Formica, and said musically, "Whelp. There goes the morning!"

Everett closed the office door and motioned for Matt to have a seat on one of the two battered chairs positioned in front of a cluttered desk. The office was small, windowless. It was lit by overhead fluorescent tubes. The unnatural light made everything seem white-blue. Filing cabinets lined one wall. Shelves containing thick order books crowded another wall. An old, well-used electric percolator and a variety of coffee mugs stood on a wobbly-looking hostess trolley. The desk was the central piece of the office, taking up most of the floor space.

Everett, a born diplomat, did not move to sit behind his desk. Matt sat down, and even though there was barely a foot of space separating them, and Everett wasn't comfortable being this close to a Jones, he took the second nearby chair. Waiting for Matt to speak first, Everett sat forward, bent at the waist, his arms on his thighs, hands together, fingers entwined and hanging between parted knees.

Matt worried his lower lip and remained quiet for a stretch of minutes. Everett was patient. He knew the younger man was battling both his grief and his pride. It was a terrible thing to lose a loved one. And equally terrible to be forced to come to a long-standing adversary in need of a personal favor. Everett was prepared to give Matt all the time he needed. Matt managed to gather himself, and although he had to clear his throat twice, he finally spoke.

"Exactly how well did you know my father?"

"I've known him all my life," Everett returned softly. "And as you well know, we've never been friends."

Matt nodded, seemingly digesting this statement as he stared at the far wall. His face slowly turning bright with anger, Matt looked again at Everett Jakomin.

"Then would you please explain this to me?" He pulled a folded envelope out of his shirt pocket and handed it over.

Everett unfolded the long envelope and read the inscription. Without his glasses the words were a bit blurry, but he read them well enough: "To be opened on my death. C. R. Jones."

As the envelope was already opened, Everett withdrew the single page. He held the paper back a bit and the writing sharpened. There were only a few lines.

"It is my request that Everett Jakomin see to all funeral arrangements. He is also to be the executor of my last will and testament. My will is not to be read until he either agrees to be my agent, or six months have passed."

And then the familiar scrawl—C. R. Jones.

Everett pulled his chin tight against his neck. He read the note again, a puzzled expression, like a visible question mark, apparent on his face.

"Do you know why he would simply give you so much power?" Matt asked, his tone bitter.

Everett shook his head as if to clear it and handed the letter and envelope back to Matt, who snatched them, shoving the two separate pieces roughly inside his shirt pocket.

"I don't have any idea," Everett replied. "This is not something I would ever agree to. No offense, but dead or alive, I've never wanted anything to do with your father."

"Why did you hate him so much?"

"That's personal. It was supposed to be kept just between him and me. Somehow along the way Harry got into it, and then you. I always felt that was a little sad. And needless. My dispute with C.R. had nothing to do with either of you. I've always counted it a blessing that David had the good sense to keep out of it."

"David was more involved that you realize. He's the first vice president of Red Bird, if you recall. And my fight with you was because of Red Bird, not my dad." Matt pointed an accusing finger. "You brought the war to me, not the other way around."

"That isn't true."

"Yes, it is."

"I have never meant to offend you. As a member of the council, I've only ever acted for the good of the Nation."

"Bullshit. *Everything* you've done as a council member you've done for the sheer pleasure of pushing around anyone named Jones."

As Everett opened his mouth to protest, Matt waved an impatient arm. "I'm tired, Mr. Jakomin, and I didn't come here to fight with you about our past differences. I came here for an entirely different purpose. I came to ask about you and my father."

Everett looked at Matt levelly. In a quietly firm voice he answered, "As I said, what passed between C.R. and me was personal."

Steam seemed to pour out of Matt's nose and ears as he fought back his temper. "He's dead now, Mr. Jakomin. He's at Johnston's Mortuary, lying . . . " His voice broke. He put a shaking hand to his brow, hitched another sob. "Helpless. And he's . . . alone."

Matt raised his head, his eyes brimming with tears. In a husky voice he spoke through clenched teeth, his fist pounding his leg, punctuating each word. "Not one of us can help him. Not one of us can do a thing, not even Harry, who threatened to burn Johnston's down to the ground. We're helpless because Dad left the matter of his burial to you. And not only in this note," Matt half shouted, slapping the accursed message in his chest pocket. "That he left for us to find. Believe me, if it had been the only copy, we would have torn it up and tossed it to the wind. But he outfoxed us. With the Johnston brothers he left a witnessed, notarized letter of instruction. With his attorneys, the same damn thing. So now he's going to be on that slab until you decide what's to be done about him. Everything has been left for you. Bury him, execute his will, provide for his widow, his grandchildren. He wants you to do everything, and I want to know why! I want to know why his own sons weren't good enough. It's my right to know, and you'd better tell me."

"Perhaps," Everett sighed, leaning heavily back in the chair, "it was his way of blackmailing me into allowing an honored warrior's funeral."

"I'm not buying that," Matt said contemptuously, shaking his head, running a hand over his mouth and chin. "Majority still rules on the council. You're only one vote. One against fifteen. My father *needed* you the way Napoleon needed piles. No, Mr. Jakomin. What my father said was he *wanted* you. Big difference, wouldn't you say, between needing and wanting?"

Matt's voice grew stronger as anger overpowered grief. "This should have been left for Harry. By tradition, burying our father is his right. It's no secret there isn't any love lost between us, but Harry's my brother, so you'll forgive me for having a real hard time understanding why my father chose you. I thought I knew him, understood him. Now I'm completely lost."

Everett ran his thumb and second finger along the curve of his nose, pinching the bridge. Then he sighed heavily and sat back in the chair. "I wish I could give you the answers you need, but I'm afraid I'm a little bit lost too."

"So," Matt challenged, "what do we do now, Mr. Jakomin?"

Everett raked his thick hair away from his face with his fingers as he billowed his cheeks and blew a long stream of air out of his mouth. "Well, the only thing I can think of is we go over to Johnston's and see about getting C.R. buried."

Everett hated funerals. Hated them because of Anna.

A year before she died, Anna had broken her leg. She had been shopping with two of her women friends in Bartlesville. They were running to cross the street, all three women eager to get to the dress shop, where a sale was in progress. Right after Anna stepped off the curb, she stumbled and broke her leg. She was taken to the Jane Phillips Medical Center-Hospital in Bartlesville. Everett was called and immediately he rushed to be with her.

Stress break.

That was what the doctors initially said. Everett had teased Anna, saying he hadn't realized hotfooting it across a street to get to a store offering fifty percent off summer dresses could be so stressful. But a day later, when the results of the blood tests and additional X rays they had been told were strictly routine came back and they learned the real reason for the snap in her left tibia, all joking ceased.

Bone cancer.

A year of hell began on that morning, in that hospital room, in the company of a strained-faced young doctor who stammered badly as he told them that Anna's chances ranged between zero and none, that she was too advanced, that had she been diagnosed even a month before she stepped off the curb, it still would have been too late. Without knowing it, she had been dying for over a year. The unexplainable weight loss she had been so happy about, all of the aches and pains she'd ignored, putting the discomforts down to symptoms of advancing age, were signals that her body was steadily devouring itself.

Then came the radiation and chemotherapy treatments in a desperate attempt to at least slow down the disease. Anna lost more weight and so rapidly that practically overnight she became a brittle skeleton. Next she lost her hair. Finally, and because the cancer was in her liver, she died. When the hospital orderlies came for her, Everett wouldn't allow them to take her on the gurney to the hospital morgue. Instead, he lifted her from her bed and carried her like a limp bride. It was a hard walk but an easy burden. When his lovely Anna died, she weighed little more than seventy pounds.

Next came Johnston's.

He hadn't really known what to expect when he entered the mortuary. In truth, he had been too grief-stricken to spare it much thought. Even so, Johnston's had been something of a shock.

The first thing that hit him was the noticeable absence of music. He'd been disappointed that there wasn't a looped, piped-in recording of the Mormon

Tabernacle Choir. Except for the rattle of a typewriter from one of the cubbyhole offices, the mortuary was stone quiet. Not knowing what to do, he meekly stood inside the entrance of the one-story building. Quite a bit of time passed, and then one of the Johnston grandsons, a kid barely passed twenty, skinny and pasty-faced, came strolling out of one of the back offices. The kid, who turned out to be a fully qualified mortician, looked more like a trainee used car salesman. He was wearing jeans, an old shirt, and eating a ham sandwich. Seeing Everett standing in the Foyer of Peace, the kid looked a little surprised as he hurriedly swallowed the great lump of food in his mouth and said, "Uh—can I hep ya?"

And the place had smelled so bad. Like Pine Sol and something else Everett couldn't name and didn't think he'd ever want to. How could a guy eat in a place like that? Were his nostrils completely burned out? Hastily discarding his sandwich, the kid ushered him into the coffin room. Again, as Everett examined the shiny coffins on display and the kid described the features of each, he had the dreamy feeling that he was considering a reliable secondhand car, not a repository for Anna's earthly remains. After only a few minutes he chose a nice blue coffin. Anna loved blue. She used to say it was God's favorite color and that's why it was hers. Then back in a small office he and the kid filled out forms and made arrangements for Anna to be transported from the Jane Phillips Hospital. He remembered the kid laughing as he carefully filled out the forms.

"Hey! You're a lefty. Mind telling me how you can write with your hand all curled around like that?"

Everett looked up, and when their eyes met, the kid's smile did a slow fade. He could tell that the kid was instantly sorry he'd spoken out of turn, and Everett was instantly sorry that someone so young had to deal with death day in and day out. To ease them both past the awkward silence, Everett offered a feeble smile. "Some other time, maybe."

The kid remained quiet while Everett finished with the forms. As Everett handed them over, the kid stammered, "Uh, Mr. Jakomin? I promise, we'll take real good care of your wife. I'll see to her myself."

His inconsolable sorrow and his pitiful gratitude to a kid he didn't even know almost brought Everett to his knees. The back of his throat locked; he could only manage a wheezing thank-you before he left Johnston's with all the speed he could muster.

For the two days and nights Anna was in Johnston's, Everett knew she was well watched over. The kid inadvertently let him know this when Everett had brought in the last dress Anna would ever wear.

"This is a little too big for her," the kid said. "But don't worry. I'll have it altered."

"I'll pay for the—"

"Don't worry about a thing, Mr. Jakomin. Please. I'm taking care of her. I know how special Miz Anna is. I promise, she's gonna look really pretty."

She did. The kid had even gone out and bought a nice wig to cover her tiny bald head. The kid did a good job with the makeup to mask her unnatural yellow complexion, and he even put lipstick on her lips. When Everett saw her again, she was in her pretty blue coffin. She looked so sweet, but not at all like his Anna. She reminded him more of a plastic doll lying on its back, its hinged eyes closed. He didn't want to hurt the kid's feelings, but the pretty little plastic doll in the blue box was not his Anna. His Anna was gone, beyond his reach.

On the day of the funeral, in a hearse so shiny it gleamed like a black diamond, the doll-like Anna was taken to the cemetery for the private graveside service. It was presided over by Pastor Bob and attended by their three children, Martha, Robert, and Nathaniel, and

Everett and Anna's five little grandchildren. Grace Baptist Church had gone all-out for the church service; hundreds of people turned out and there had been standing room only.

For over a dozen years Anna had taught Sunday school, the eighth-graders, an age group no one else would touch with a cattle prod the length of at least twenty of Noah's cubits. Yet Anna had taken the kids on and year after year each eighth-grade class adored her. With her as their teacher, the eighth-grade class became the cornerstone of the Wednesday night youth fellowship, the Baptist Youth for Christ. Younger kids couldn't wait to grow up and be in Miz Anna's class. And as her former pupils became old enough to go off to wherever life took them, a great number remembered to send her birthday and Christmas cards. Everett's clerk, Tommy Knife, had been one of Anna's kids. As a young man of twenty, Tommy Knife was hardworking, went to night school to build up credits to go on to a university. Tommy Knife was strictly teetotal. That's the way the majority of Anna's Grace Baptist kids turned out. They and her own children were her living memorials.

Added to all of this, she still found time to sing a hearty alto in the church choir. Everybody at Grace Baptist had loved his Anna. And that's why they turned out for the church service in record numbers. But Everett loved her more and his grief was private. Stubbornly, he kept the graveside service that way. Just as every Saturday, no matter the weather, he tended Anna's grave.

He hadn't set foot in Johnston's since, and now he was going there again, walking the paved sidewalk beside a surly, indignant Jones boy. The muggy heat of the too-hot day was clammy on his skin, thick inside his lungs, and he was suffering this heat and the offensive company of Matthew Jones for reasons only God and C. R. Jones knew. Nearing the end of the street there stood Bennie Stone Calf. Bennie was misshapen, with a big head and stunted body. Although he was in his early twenties, Bennie's mental age was somewhere around six. He also had a pronounced speech impediment.

Despite the heat, Bennie was wearing baggy jeans, a lone-sleeved shirt, heavy socks with black hightop sneakers, and a blue Dodgers baseball cap. Ever since Bennie had fallen in love with the television private eye Peter Gunn, he had taken to standing out on the street corners, staring at people, especially people in passing cars, because he believed that this was what private eyes did. They stared. Matt Jones tried to walk around Bennie, avoid him as much as possible. Then he looked close to apoplexy when Everett paused and spoke to Bennie.

"You watching it all, Bennie?"

Bennie nodded as he narrowed his eyes, indicating that his private eyes were on the case.

"Don't you stand out here too long," Everett admonished. "It's too hot."

Bennie's voice was thick, his words mangled. "I dum't feef it. Dum't hurt mem."

Everett fished a quarter out of his trouser pocket and handed it over. "You go get yourself a cold drink, Bennie. I mean it. Your eyes will start hurting if the rest of you gets thirsty."

Bennie stared at the coin in the palm of his hand. Then he looked up at Everett, to Matt Jones, then to Everett again, tilting his head in Matt's direction. "Him daddy dead."

"Yes, Bennie," Everett said patiently. "His father died."

"Mem mama said him daddy had bimcycle."

"That's true."

"Wherem bimcycle? Mem can hab it?"

Matt fidgeted as Everett's eyes glided in his direction. Matt turned his head away, his jawline twitching. Bennie tugged Everett's arm.

"Mem hab bimcycle nowm¿"

Matt nodded. Everett placed his hand on Bennie's rounded shoulder. "Yes, Bennie, Mr. Jones said you can have the bicycle. Now go get yourself that cold drink."

Bennie scooted off, his private eyeing replaced by the joy of the promised bicycle. Matt and Everett continued their walk to the mortuary.

"Giving that boy C.R.'s bicycle is really nice of you," Everett said. "Bennie's had a hard life. His mother was an alcoholic, which is why I believe he's the way he is. His grandmother takes care of him. It's her he calls mama. Bennie's had a lot of love but not much else. He'll take good care of your father's bicy—"

"Please shut up," Matt shouted. His conflicting emotions, grief, and seething anger erupted further. "I'll make sure the bike is delivered, but I don't care one thing about it or that moron."

Everett and Matt continued on without another word passing between them.

When at last they arrived, Matt opened the glass door of the mortuary. The blast of frigid air-conditioning washed over them as Matt held the door for Everett to enter. Once inside the Foyer of Peace, Johnston's surprised Everett yet again.

Both Johnston brothers were there to greet them. They looked old and ancient enough to be measuring themselves for one of their own boxes. They were wearing suits and looking tremendously worried. The younger Johnston continually moved his hands, appearing to be giving them a good soaping. His eyes danced, flitting from corner to corner as if he half expected a bogeyman to leap out at him from behind a partially open office door. The cold air was still pungent with Pine Sol. And the kid was standing in the background. He was three years older now, suitably dressed for the somber occasion and without sandwich in hand. Everett caught his eye and the kid nodded a silent hello.

Then Harry came barreling out of one of the offices and all hell broke loose. "Soapy" Johnston, Everett's mental name for the slightly younger mortician, leapt out of Harry's path. Good move. If Soapy hadn't jumped, Harry would have plowed right through him. Harry was coming straight for Everett, his balled fist poised as he shouted, "You sonofabitch!"

Matt caught him just before Harry could deliver the blow intended for Everett's face. Harry was still yelling, using every term he could think of to debase Everett's parentage as he and Matt twisted around in a macabre dance.

"Hey!" Everett shouted. "I'm only here because I was asked. I don't know anything more than anyone else."

Huffing and puffing, Harry began to settle as he glared at Everett, but just in case, Matt continued to hold on to him. Everett was good at glaring, too, and he glared holes through Harry.

"If you try to hit me again, Harold Jones, I'm gone and you and your daddy can rot in hell or right here in Johnston's. I promise. It won't make one hair's bit of difference to me."

Matt gave his enraged brother a hard shake. "Dammit, Harry, calm down."

"Uh, Mr. Jakomin?" the eldest Johnston said apologetically. "Would you follow me, please?" The man turned, and Everett made a move to follow him.

"I'm going too," Harry yelled.

Standing well away from him, unsure of how tightly his brother held on to him, the mortician, even more apologetically, said to Harry, "No, sir. I'm afraid you can't. The departed Mr. Jones's instructions were that this conversation remain private."

• • •

Everett took a seat as the mortician settled himself behind the imitation wood desk. Everett tried to erase it from his mind that it looked like a car dealer's desk. The man opened a side drawer, and with considerable effort lifted out a cardboard box. Too heavy for the frail-looking man to hand over, he placed it down on the desktop and slid it toward Everett.

Looking down at the box, Everett raised a quizzical brow.

"That's for you. Quite apart from the actual estate. Mr. Jones requested two things. First, you, uh, are to view him."

"What?!"

"View him. You know, go back into the, uh, Sleep Room and view him."

"Are you talking about the refrigerator room?"

"Yes, well." Johnston indignantly cleared his throat. "We prefer to call it the Sleep Room."

"Get a grip!" Everett barked. "We're talking about a room full of freezers."

"Nevertheless." Johnston raised a shaking hand. "Mr. Jones requested you view his remains in this, uh, transitional state. He insisted on it."

Everett tilted his head to the side and bird-eyed the older man. "What's the second thing?"

"You're to read the contents of the box. It contains his memoirs. They are extremely confidential and must not to be shown to anyone else. Especially the members of his family. If you refuse, I have been instructed to destroy the box."

"Oh, yeah? Well, what if I say I've read it but I haven't?"

"I'm afraid, Mr. Jakomin," the man sighed wearily. He swiveled in his chair, turning slightly to present a bone-weary profile. Evidently the death and burial of C. R. Jones was causing him an understandable amount of anxiety. "I would know. And in that case, I have the authority to instruct his attorneys to hold up the reading of the will for a period of six months."

The man noisily cleared his dry throat again and swiveled back to face Everett, resting his arms on the desktop.

"So what you're saying is that you already know just how he wants to be buried."

"Oh, yes." The man rapidly blinked watery blue eyes. "Mr. Jones was quite specific. But without your cooperation my hands are tied."

"He's blackmailing me," Everett said flatly.

He was silent for a moment as he considered the trap C. R. Jones had clearly and quite cunningly laid for him. Be a good boy, read the memoirs, and find the answer to how C. R. Jones wishes to be buried. Not only would Everett have that on his conscience for the rest of his life, but the family would probably find ways to sue him for everything he owned. He was so stuck, he could have sworn he heard C.R. laughing.

But why me? Why didn't you stick this with another enemy? Lord knows you had a whole country to choose from, and every last one of them is far more deserving.

Livid that even in C.R.'s final moments he had chosen to play a game he knew would drive him, Everett, stark staring crazy, the shopowner leaned forward in the chair and asked tightly, "Can't Harry fight this?"

Johnston steepled his fingers. "No. Legal proceedings would take at least a year. As he made his own lawyers party to his terms, I'm afraid there is nothing Harry can legally do."

Everett sighed and sat back heavily. "Well, I guess I can't blame Harry for wanting to hit me. If my dad had pulled this, I'd want to take a swing at somebody too. I guess it was lucky for me he died a broke drunk. It sure saved me from the nonsense a rich old fool can think up."

Slapping the arms of the chair, Everett stood. The mortician shakily rose a second behind him. Everett glanced at the man and said mournfully, "Let's go on to the Sleep Room. The quicker we can get this over with, the better."

Everett stood before what looked like a giant filing cabinet and watched as a drawer was guided out by two white-coated attendants. The heavy sheet covering C.R. was slowly pulled back, and Everett looked down on the man credited with the ruination of his father's life. Looking at C.R., Everett heard his father's life-long lament.

"You wanna know why I drink, son? You just ask that bastard Jones an' quit goin' on at me. He can tell ya. Oh, yeah. C. R. Jones knows everythin'."

Everett experienced the most profound shock of the day when he viewed the great C. R. Jones's earthly remains. He had more than expected to see C.R. twisted and contorted in his last efforts to fight off death. Instead, C.R. looked strangely peaceful, as if his final moment had been the happiest of his life. Everett looked up wonderingly at the old mortician standing on the other side of the body.

Johnston nodded his head slightly and said, "I'll just leave you now. When you wish to speak to me again, I'll be in my office."

He left Everett gazing at C. R. Jones and in the safe-keeping of two attendants, who moved away and stood quietly on the other side of the room. Forcing himself to breathe, Everett stared at the body for a very long time, vividly recalling the first time he had ever seen C. R. Jones. He had been a very little boy and C. R. Jones had seemed a giant. A giant who went down on one knee to look him in the eye. Next he remembered every fight, every harsh word they had traded through the years. Mostly he remembered the odd expression that had once flitted across C.R.'s face during the occasion of their most heated debate before the council. A debate Everett won. He hadn't known then, just as he didn't know now, what that look actually meant, but he had the impression that it was admiration, that C.R. believed him to be worthy. Of what? This burial fiasco?

Everett leaned in close and whispered, "What game are you playing now, old man?"

Hesitantly, he put out a hand and almost lovingly stroked the dead man's hair. Everett was as surprised as the two waiting attendants when he looked back over his shoulder and asked, "May I have a lock of his hair, please?"

Within seconds he began to realize his full authority in all things concerning C. R. Jones. The attendants were only too eager to grant his request. And if he hadn't stopped them, instructing that they simply snip a small amount and from the back of the head, they might have scalped C.R. Everett had no idea why he wanted a lock of C.R.'s hair, maybe it was a latent coup-counting thing, who knew. All he did know was that he wanted it, that he needed it, and that he would always keep it safe. Now, with that lock of hair sealed in a small envelope and nestled in his shirt pocket, Everett was shown into the coffin room, where Harry and Matt were said to be waiting for him.

After he entered and the double doors were closed, giving the three men privacy, Harry shot him a look that boldly announced that he was still more than eager to tear Everett's heart out. Matt simply looked sad. Everett was severely tempted to go to Matt and give him a comforting hug. But a hug from Everett Jakomin would hardly be welcome. His feud with the Jones clan had begun long before the three men in the coffin room were born. It had been a feud between their fathers that had been passed on to the sons. None of them, not even

Everett, knew the details of the feud. It had simply been enough for the sons to hate the man their respective fathers singled out for hatred. When as young men they learned to hate each other for their own separate reasons, the unknown original reason between the fathers was deemed too unimportant to question. Obeying wiser instincts, Everett made no move toward Matt. He remained standing in front of the closed doors until he was noticed.

"We," Matt struggled, "we were just . . . looking at the coffins. Trying to decide . . ." His voice trailed off.

"Choose any one you want," Everett said quietly.

"Oh, thank you so very much," Harry sniped, pushing himself away from the coffin he leaned against. With a menacing stride he approached Everett, stopping just two feet away from him. "You can't know how much we appreciate your being so obliging."

The muscle in Everett's jaw ticked as he and Harry glowered for a long, edgy moment, their eyes locked, neither of them blinking. Finally, Harry broke contact, and even in this, a small victory for Everett, Harry raged.

"Just who the hell do you think you are?!"

"I'm beginning to wonder that myself. As I have been given to understand it, I now control everything, the funeral, and for the next six months, your lives."

Harry visibly paled.

Matt merely nodded thoughtfully and then asked, "What are you going to do?"

Everett looked away, ran a hand through his hair. "Exactly what C.R. wanted me to do. I'll make sure he's buried and then I'll execute his will to the best of my ability."

Matt turned his pained face away. Harry continued to glare suspiciously. Matt gentled the heavy silence permeating the room with a lifeless "Thank you."

Harry rounded on his brother. "What in the blue hell are you thanking him for?!"

"Oh, shut up, Harry," Matt cried. As if trying to squeeze away the sound of his brother's voice, he pressed his hands against his ears. "Just please, for once in your life, shut the hell up."

Everett sat on a padded folding chair, watching and listening to the brothers examining and arguing the merits of each display coffin. Finally, they chose one. A heavy oak coffin with pale blue satin interior.

"Solid oak with lead lining," Harry said. "It'll last forever. Dad will be safe and dry inside this. Nothing will be able to get at him."

This was an important feature for Harry. He had never gotten over the ghastly childhood tune, "The worms crawl in, the worms crawl out, the worms play pinochle on your snout . . ."

No, safe inside a lead lined casket, worms would not get at Harry's daddy. And that meant Harry would be able to sleep at night not having to worry about it. Or dream about it. He wouldn't wake up screaming in his mistress's arms because of the nightmares his father's death was already causing.

Like last night.

He had wanted to stay in his father's house to be there for his mother. As the eldest son and primary heir, it was his duty to stay, and he'd planned to do exactly that. Then, as he and his brothers went through their father's effects, they found the note. Unable to understand it, the note was shown to Emma. Until she read that scrap of paper, she had been holding up amazingly well. But that note turned her to stone.

"I thought it was over," she whispered. "After all these years I—" She looked up at her perplexed sons. "I was wrong."

She wouldn't say any more. She took to her room and Matt called the family doctor, who administered a sedative. The brothers retired to the study, where they immediately had a knock-down drag-out fight between themselves and their father's attorney. So hurt that his father had, prior to his death, conspired behind his back, and unwilling to believe that neither David nor Matt knew anything about it, Harry stormed out of the house. He wasn't really worried about his mother as he drove back to Tulsa. She was out for the count and had the rest of the family, even Terri, staying with her. If Mama woke up, she would have more comfort and concern than she could deal with, whereas Harry had nothing.

He needed Alisa and he needed her desperately. Alisa would help him through his pain. She always did. And tonight he brought in pain by the bucketload. Only Alisa understood him, knew that the biggest fear in his life was his fear of death. As long as his father had been alive, Harry had managed to lock the fear away. Now his father was dead and Harry's horrifying fear, coupled with the fact that his father had effectively disowned him, was loose and playing havoc with his mind.

"Oh, Jesus, help me!" Harry cried. He sat in bed, every inch of his well-toned body bathed in a cold sweat. The small clock on the nightstand read four, and for the third time during the long, near-sleepless night, Alisa dutifully popped up beside him.

"I'm having a heart attack!" Harry panicked.

Alisa prised his hands away from his chest. Then she took hold of his chin and forced Harry to look at her. "Harry," she said firmly. "You're not having a heart attack."

"But it hurts, Liss," he whined.

"It's grief, Harry. Your daddy died this morning. That's why your heart hurts."

Harry leaned against her, sobbing. Alisa, his mistress of ten years, stroked the back of his head while he cried like a frightened child. Alisa's ample breasts were warm and comforting. Gradually, he felt safe again. The way he always felt safe with her.

Alisa Boone, a full-blood Cherokee, did not look like a kept mistress. She didn't act like on either. She wasn't showy, wasn't demanding. Harry's wife *was* showy and demanding. Harry definitely did not need another Terri.

It was trite but true—life often is—that Harry met Alisa at the bank. She had been a teller. She was also short, running to pudgy, four years junior to Harry—quite old for mistress material—and in a word, dowdy. Alisa wouldn't have known haute couture if it gave her a good slap across the face.

But from the first day he met her, Harry felt relaxed with her. So relaxed that within months he promoted her from teller to his personal assistant. Working in close contact day after day, Harry began to lust after Alisa. His lust trebled when she firmly refused his advances. During the year Alisa held him off, he fell desperately in love with her. So in love that to have her he had literally gone down on both knees to Terri begging her for a divorce.

Terri laughed in his face.

Her laughter ringing in his ears, and feeling hopelessly trapped with no one to turn to, he appeared at Alisa's door at midnight that same night. It was a rainy night, and when she unlocked the door, Harry was soaked to the skin.

And he was crying.

Alisa let him in, finally accepting him completely, his fears, his weaknesses, even his trapped state. And she loved him. Ten years later they were still together but in a nice residential house in a quiet, upper-middle-class neighborhood. A neighborhood filled with people who knew full well who Harry was, and wise to the nature of his relationship with Alisa. After a couple of years a few of their less self-righteous neighbors got over their disapproval of the couple living in sin in their midst and accepted Harry and Alisa as just another couple. During the summers they and the friendly neighbors discussed the crabgrass infesting their lawns and invited each other for backyard barbecues. It was a dull, ordinary life Harry never expected to live but enjoyed anyway.

Harry's address became 112 Birch Street, abandoning Terri to rattle around in the big house situated in Tulsa's prestigious Utica Square. Matt and Kelly's house was only three streets away, but even when Harry still lived with Terri, the brothers never visited. The secluded homes did not have house numbers. Each house was named. Matt and Kelly's house was named Seven Oaks. Terri's house was named Red Bird's Nest. Which was sad, considering all three of her chicks had flown the nest and Harry was only ever there during the dinner parties given to entertain business associates. Keeping his two lives separate, Harry's secretary notified him whenever there was a function at the house in the square requiring his attendance. Then he would change his clothes at 112 Birch and drive to the Nest. After the guests were gone, like a guest himself he thanked Terri for the nice evening and went home to Alisa.

"I say we take this," Harry said with finality.

Matt sent a furtive glance in Everett's direction while Harry busily inspected the depth and lushness of the casket interior. When Everett nodded, Matt spoke to his brother.

"If you want it, Harry, you can have it."

Those words sounded a wrong note. Disturbed, Everett's brows furrowed as he leaned back, stuck his long legs out, crossing them at the ankles, and studied Matt. His fingers toying with his chin, Everett realized that ongoing animosities aside, he didn't actually know Matt or Harry all that well. Matt's statement to his older brother hadn't sounded like he was giving in. No, what it inferred was Matt's allowance of Harry's choice. Everett thought about that as the two brothers conferred. When he looked up, he was just in time to see Matt put his hand on Harry's shoulder. Harry nodded as Matt spoke softly. Then Harry said, "Thank you."

Another wrong note sounded. In fact, it had been as loud as a gong. There was a complexity between the Jones brothers he couldn't quite figure out. This small puzzle gave rise to a thousand and one other questions. Questions like familiar luggage he'd carried around with him all his life. And the answers were most probably in the box. Suddenly, he couldn't wait to collect the box and begin reading C.R.'s memoirs. He tried to be patient, but almost another hour passed before the Jones boys finished the arrangements about the coffin. Then Everett had to wait it out until he was certain they were gone. Only then did he collect the box, carrying it against his hip during the long walk back to the store. Once the box was set on the passenger seat of his flashy red sports car, Everett drove home with considerable speed.

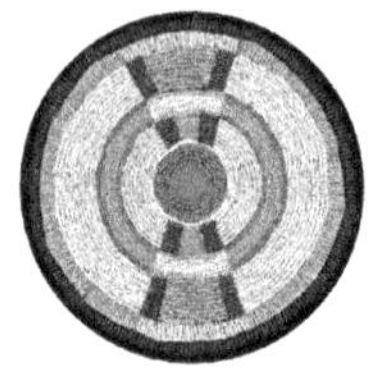

CHAPTER SEVEN

Within minutes of arriving home, Everett found a pair of reading glasses in the kitchen drawer and put them on. He owned a total of eight pair. Although his prescription hadn't changed since his mid-forties, he bought a new pair every year. Not because collecting glasses was a thing he loved, quite the contrary, he hated having to wear glasses. Which was precisely why he needed so many. He was either irritated or in a hurry whenever he removed a pair with a tossing motion. Later on, when the glasses were needed, he would have no idea where they were.

It had been Anna who suggested he have a second pair. Little did she realize her well-meaning suggestion would spark a craze. Six pair were kept in the house, while two remained at the hardware store. At home he'd developed the habit of putting the glasses in a drawer in the kitchen. But at the store Everett was too pushed for time to form this useful routine. Were it not for Tommy Knife's prudence, a good portion of Everett's workday would have been spent tearing apart his desk in a maddened search.

The glasses on his face, Everett went to the kitchen table, where he spent a bit of time struggling to open the sealed box the mortician had given to him. Once the seals were broken and the box open, inside he found six very ordinary-looking writing tablets. He took out the first tablet and, sitting down on a chair, placed it on the table, laying back the top cover.

Hello, Everett.

The salutation caused him to recoil slightly. Blinking rapidly, he looked at it again. Then he sat back with a vocal, "Huh!" and had himself a bit of a think.

He didn't know why he was so surprised. After all, C.R. had left the memoirs to him. But beginning the thing so casually, as if he didn't doubt for a second that Everett would agree to his list of demands, was a trifle unnerving. Especially as in life C.R. had never referred to him as anything other than Mr. Jakomin or Everett-Jakomin, expelling both Christian and surname in one breath. "Hello, Everett" was completely out of character, and now Everett was wondering just when these memoirs had been written.

He searched the box, opening and closing each tablet rapidly in his search for an opening date, which any decent diarist would be certain to begin with.

But not C.R.

Everett closed the cover on the final tablet and sat very still, staring at all six tablets spread out over the tabletop. The covers had once been red, but because of age, the color had mellowed to a dusty pink. Even the old familiar pen-and-ink drawing of an Indian chief in full feather bonnet profile, encircled by a heavy border, had dulled. Everett opened the cover of the first tablet again, ignoring the writing as he studied the faded black ink scrawled across cheap pulp paper imprinted with milky-blue lines. These were a schoolkid's writing tablets. It needn't be said that C.R. could have afforded goldleafed pages had his goal been to loftily immortalize himself.

Everett ran a hand over his mouth and thought. Ol' Soapy Johnston had said that the contents of the box were to be destroyed, and Everett could tell that Soapy hadn't been comfortable with Everett taking the box out of the mortuary. By the time Everett retrieved the box he had been too eager to leave to hear much more of Soapy's instructions. Now, looking at the writing tablets, he knew that they hadn't been written by a man planning one last scam. These tablets had been written years earlier, and especially for him. And as Soapy sensed, they were strictly private. Too private to be allowed to exist once Everett finished reading them. Which meant that C.R. had written the whole unvarnished truth in these disposable tablets and that truth would very probably hurt and/or destroy a whole lot of people.

Everett's stomach clenched painfully. A finger of chilly fear traced the length of his spine. A deafening silence filled Anna's sunny kitchen as he experienced a small taste of what it must have actually been like to be as all-powerful as C. R. Jones.

He didn't like it. In fact, having that kind of power scared the living snot out of him. Shaking, Everett stood. The plastic pads on the chair's flattened chrome feet had long-ago worn away. Bare metal scraped the linoleum flooring as he pushed the chair back with his legs. He went to the stove and turned on the gas burner under the coffeepot. He needed coffee and he needed it right then. Waiting for the coffee to heat, he fished the pack of Pall Malls from his shirt pocket. He had been a hardcore smoker when he and Anna were first married, but gave it up cold turkey when Anna became pregnant with their daughter Martha. The rank smell of cigarette smoke made Anna so ill that he had been afraid she would puke herself into a miscarriage if he didn't stop smoking in a hurry.

Six months after Anna's funeral he took up smoking again. Primarily because he was bored, because Anna wasn't around to complain about the smell in the house, and because his favorite TV western star, starring on his favorite TV western show, highly recommended it.

"Pall Malls," the star declared, "My cigarette. I can light it at both ends."

So Everett bought a carton of Pall Malls and every Wednesday night smoked along with his hero. When after a month he was thoroughly hooked and puffing away morning, noon, and night, he couldn't help but wonder about the boast. Okay, supposing the guy did light his cigarette at both ends. What did he do then? Smoke it in the middle? Applying Zippo flame to just one end, Everett inhaled deeply, held the smoke for a brief second, then blew it out in a blue plume. Through the gauzy smoke, dancing like a breeze-tumbled lace curtain, he leaned against the counter and stared at the first page of the first tablet lying open on the table.

The coffee was boiling.

Hello, Everett.

I've waited a long time to talk to you. All of your life really. I know what I have to say can never take place man to man, face-to-face. Neither your pride nor, for that matter, mine would allow that to happen. So now I'm dead and you're feeling boxed in. I can only imagine how much you hate that, and if there was any other way, believe me I would have chosen it. But there isn't, so you'll just have to sit still for a bit and allow me to explain just how and why the animosity between us began. I'm not asking your forgiveness. All I'm asking is a fair hearing.

Any Osage child knows that we Osage once lived on the Missouri, that our name is Wah-Sha-She, Children of the Middle Waters. But to personalize this history, I want you to know that my father's father came from a place on the Missouri known to us as the Place of Many Swans, that my grandfather was the third son of a great chief. That old warrior's name had been Bear Chief. It's a traditional name in our family, always passed on to the grandson, skipping a generation. When I was born in the spring of 1876, that name was given to me. When I was enrolled in school, I was given three white names to surround my real name. Charles Richard Bear Chief Jones.

That's me.

Keeping the name Bear Chief was to honor that ancient warrior who fought against George Washington on the side of the French. He was supposed to have been very brave and very important to our people. Anyway, my grandfather, the second Bear Chief in our family, and his wife, had just been newly married and living in a village on the Missouri, when the Osage, in 1847, were forced to move to Kansas. Less than a decade later, the Osage were forced to move to Oklahoma because the Kansas reservation was sold out from under them. This part of Oklahoma had always been the hind end of our dwindled domain. It was good for hunting buffalo, but as we were forest and river people, we never lived here. The first wave of Cherokees were relocated to Oklahoma in 1836. The second wave hit about 1840. These two factions fought with each other and those Cherokees wishing to escape the internal strife took over this upper section of our hunting country that became known as the Cherokee Strip. Then the government came along and decided that there was room enough for the Osage in this strip too. The Cherokees didn't care for that very much, so the money that had been given to our nation for our Kansas lands had to be paid to the Cherokees for the return of our own hunting ground.

The Cherokees have always been a farming people, living in houses, wearing fancy clothing, the men even wearing turbans. That's why we called them the People with Things on Their Heads. The most remarkable thing about them was that every last one of them could read and write. Having wild Osage for neighbors did not sit well with them and we Osage were a bit irked that we had to pay for something that was ours. This new Washington deal made for bad blood, and a lot of killing went on between the Osage and the Cherokees. When they weren't shooting at us or each other, they were writing angry letters to Washington. Which were ignored. When the American Civil War came along, the Confederates promised them a better deal (the extermination of us) and so the Cherokees became Confederates.

And lost again.

Meanwhile, we Osage were paying close attention to the old prophet Paw Hunka. He had predicted this move and told the people not to be sad about having to sell our lands in Kansas to white settlers because we were going to a better place. To a land holding a great secret. He said the white men believed this land was worth nothing, but that they were wrong. And when they realized their error the white men would come again, waving money. No truer words were ever spoken. We successfully held on to our land until Oklahoma became a state and the Osage Reservation became Osage County. Then our lands came up for sale again to ranchers, homesteaders, but what they could not get, what they could never own, was the secret Paw Hunka said the land held.

Oil.

I was born during a time when Jake Bartles was building himself a village located on the Caney River. You've always known it as Bartlesville. Jake had married into the Cherokees and was trading up a storm with them. Us poor old Osage didn't interest him at all. We didn't have a thing except for lands rich in bluestem grass and pesky blackjacks. Plus the Major, our Quaker agent who was thrifty with our dollars and didn't like Jake Bartles even one little bit, wouldn't let him on our reserve. He was a good man, the Major, and even though he changed too much of our way of life and listened more to the more progressive French/Osage, he genuinely cared about us as a whole Nation.

When the cowboys started driving their herds through our lands, taking their steers to market from Texas, it was the Major who saw to it that the trail bosses paid for the grass their herds ate and the damage the great herds left in their wake. When the railroads started sniffing around, the Major got huge settlements on the land they needed to lay their tracks. The Osage became fairly prosperous. The Major banked our money and as a tribe we were almost as well off as we had been in the days when the Osage ruled the entire Missouri and the French had to worry about keeping us friendly.

The Osage reservation in the Major's day was divided up into clans, and these clans lived apart just as they had in the old days on the Missouri. Following the American Civil War, Indian Territory as it was known prior to statehood, was a wild place. We had all the outlaws running loose inside it, the really famous ones. The Territory *was* the Wild West. Everything outside the Territory was tamed and whipped. Belle Starr used to pinch my cheeks and call me "Love-cake" and her outlaw Cherokee husband, Sam Starr, taught me how to shoot. But I'm getting ahead of myself. All that happened after my father was killed and I was left alone to jump up by myself.

When I was six, the reservation had two schools. One Quaker, one Catholic. The Major insisted that all children attend school. When he noticed on his records that I had come of age, the Major drove out to our house (some folks still lived in lodges but my father built us a one-room stone house) located out on the edge of the reserve. The Major used to call on folks all the time, so we weren't really surprised when he drove up to our place in his two-mule surrey. What was surprising was his telling my father that I had to go to one of the schools. That my father had no say in the discussion. The only choice my father had was which school I would attend.

To this day I do not know why my father told the Major that we were of the Black Robes, meaning Catholic. His saying that effected my life forever. I cannot count how many times since that day I have wondered how I might have turned out had he simply allowed me to go off to the non-Catholic school. Nor can I shake the very vivid memory of my standing beside my father's long legs being very careful to keep the surprise from my expression while he told the Major that we were a Catholic family.

That was the first time I had ever heard anything about it. I had never been to a Catholic Mass in the whole of my young life. Not only that, but my father used to stand outside our house and pray in a loud voice to Wah'Kon-Tah each and every dawn. Faith in the old Osage god was the only religion I knew, but for some reason the Major accepted my father's word that we were practicing Catholics. Less than an hour later, and with me sitting in the surrey with a bundle containing all my personal possessions between my bare feet, the Major drove me to the Catholic school and enrolled me that very day.

The headmaster of the school was an old Jesuit named Père Blanc. He looked like a piece of year-old jerked meat wrapped up in black cloth and he was just as tough. The nuns were frightened to death of him. So were all the kids having to live at the school and address him as Father. I suffered more than one beating my first weak in school because I refused to call him Father. To me that was sacrilege. That old priest wasn't anything like my father. My father was a gentle-speaking man. Père Blanc was a yeller. He had a deep bass voice and only one volume.

Loud.

There were wide welts from the belt all over my back, but the beatings didn't break me. What finally did was the nuns cutting my hair off, putting a bowl on my head and cutting around it. Mind you, it took five of them to do it.

"Hold him!" Sister Catherine yelled.

"We're trying, Sister," a younger nun shouted. "He's stronger than he looks."

Charlie squirmed, twisted and screamed as he heard and felt the scissors. He kicked out at the old nun and the scissors flew from her hand, somersaulted in the air and falling, grazed her hand. Blood quickly appeared and now in a rage, she slapped Charlie across the mouth, spinning his head. The bowl fell away, clattered to the floor. One nun scurried to retrieve it, and as a form of further punishment clamped it down hard on Charlie's twisting head.

Sister Catherine, holding a hand over her wound, growled into his tear-stained face. "You filthy little heathen. Kick me again and I'll shave you baldheaded." Straightening, she glared at the younger nuns. "One of you come around here and hold his legs."

Once it was done, my long hair lying on the floor and all around the stool they held me down on, my spirit crumbled. I was so ashamed, I couldn't even look at my own shadow. After that I shuffled through the regimented days, going to class, taking my place in the dinner line, going to bed. The days were long and awful but the nights were worse. In the night, that's when my situation would hit me pretty hard and I would just cry and cry. But softly so no one heard me.

The school was more like an army training camp than a school. We all wore uniforms and we marched everywhere, to classes, to meals, and to church. We had one play period during the day and that was considered a privilege. If you were bad, but not so bad as to warrant the strap, then you lost play privilege. The supreme rule was not to speak unless spoken to. That was a rule that I kept without any difficulty. There wasn't anyone I cared to speak to and at that juncture in my life I couldn't have spoken even if I had wanted to. The only languages that were allowed were English and French. I didn't know a word of French and my English was sparse. If I muttered one word of Osage, I got the strap. I appeared to be a model pupil, but in reality I didn't understand one thing that was going on in class. I was like a parrot, I repeated what I was supposed to say but the words coming out of my mouth had no meaning. Then one morning I woke up understanding everybody. I'm telling you the truth. It seemed to happen just like that. I went to bed still feeling as dumb as a post and woke up the next morning fully cognizant. I'll bet hard money that was exactly the way Paul felt when he experienced blinding conversion. And like Paul, I was excited. I wanted to talk and talk, show people that I really could answer and know what I was actually saying. Wouldn't you know it, that was the one day I wasn't called on once to answer a question. So I had to keep my mouth shut. Keep the secret to myself. That was a frustrating thing for a kid to have to do, but the discipline taught me a great lesson. It taught me how to keep myself to myself.

Sister Catherine, the nun who had cut off my hair,

was the first person to realize my new ability. Some days later, she pulled me out of the marching line and spoke to me. She was a tall, angular woman, her features severe because she ate so little. Her philosophy held that people should always leave the table hungry, that remaining hungry caused people to be grateful for the food God provided and their prayers more fervent. When mealtimes ended, as a joke some of the boys would lightly tap the tabletop and whisper, "Are you hungry, table?"

The habit she wore made her look older than her real age and the heavy lines around her mouth had been caused not by smiling but from perpetually grinding her teeth. Looking up at her was not a pleasant thing to do, and being singled out by her always meant trouble. My knees were knocking pretty hard when she pulled me out of the line, and I had to stand there, looking up at her, wondering what infraction I could be guilty of. It never occurred to me that she was about to lavish praise. But she did, in her severe way, of course.

"Charles," she said in a heavily somber tone, "I know you understand what I'm saying, so spare me any pretense that you don't. You have a quick mind, young Charles. However, what has impressed me is your mastery of your tongue. Do not digress. A wise man always keeps his own counsel, never forgetting that an unruly tongue is the cause of a man's damnation."

Then she shoved me back into the line and walked away. I called her Mother after that and I never kicked her again whenever she cut my hair. Finally satisfied that the wild Indian in their custody had been partially tamed, Père Blanc quickly forgot my existence. I only ever saw him when I accidentally crossed the path he trounced, his robes flying behind him, and he yelled for me to get the hell out of his way. I didn't believe for a moment that he recognized me as I leapt clear of him. I had become just one more kid in his life, and Père Blanc didn't like kids. And he despised the Territory. But to give him his due, that old man made certain of three things.

One, that we were all baptised Roman Catholic. Two, that we received Communion daily. And three, that we were educated. More terrified of Père Blanc than we were of death, we learned to read our McGuffey's Readers backwards and forwards, add large columns of numbers, and spout the multiplication tables more easily than we could say our own names. As for history, we only learned about the times of Christ and the never-ending list of saints and popes. As I said, the only second language allowed to be spoken in school was French. The Osage language was completely forbidden, and those caught speaking a word of it got the blood beaten out of them.

That should tell you even more about the school. That it was racially biased. All of the children (it was a mixed boarding school, girls dormitory on one side, boys on the other) were French/Osage. The mixed bloods were a supremely arrogant group. I was the only full-blood. To understand that level of hell you have to realize that in those days the French/Osage used to maintain themselves as a separate group. They were a sequestered tribe within the Nation. They had their own section of the reserve, their own laws, and French was their dominant language. The only times I can remember their mixing with the rest of the Nation was on Annuity Day, but even then they were renowned for keeping themselves to themselves.

Before I go on, I have to tell you about Annuity Day. For a kid, it was like Christmas but even better because it came twice a year. On Annuity Day the Major handed out the dividends on the interest our tribal money had accrued in the banks. Everyone came in from all over the reserve, not just for the money but because all of the clans would be together. Camps were set up all around the council house, which was down the hill from the Major's big two-story house. Traders came in and set up selling stalls. Annuity Day was actually a three-day carnival. During the days, the women haggled over bolts of cloth, sewing threads, and tiny glass beads for making jewelry. The men gambled, wrestled, and raced horses. We kids ran, played, and ate candy until we were ill. At night there were songs around bonfires and old men told exciting stories. The French/Osage had their own camp activities. During daylight hours they were polite, but at night they stayed in their own camps.

So maybe you can appreciate how I was treated in their school. After the priest stopped beating me, the boys started. I, who hadn't ever raised a hand against anyone in the whole of my young life, had to learn fast how to fight, because those boys would have beaten me to death if I hadn't.

When I went home for two weeks during that first summer of school, my own parents didn't know me. I had changed so much in manner: grim, arrogant, as well as aggressively defensive. I might have mastered my unruly tongue at school, but the minute I was home, I let it rip. As far as I was concerned, everything bad in my life was my father's fault, and I hated him. I even hated my mother for letting him send me away, cast me into a living hell. As you can imagine, for the first few days following my being landed on their doorstep, my mother and father treated me like an unwelcome stranger. At the end of those short weeks, they had just barely gotten me back to normal, when the Major's surrey arrived and he took me back to that hellhole and the nightmare started all over again.

There is one other thing you should know about that school. Something you should bear in mind as you continue to read this. The girls didn't last long. They got checked in when they were about five, but come the time of their first sign of womanhood, their fathers showed up with a man either his age or a little bit (not much) younger than himself, demanding the girl.

Now, at this time we still had two traditions that the old Major couldn't abide. One, the practice of polygamy, which had been our custom since the dawn of time; two, child brides. The Major repeatedly bucked heads with the tribal council on these issues. Girls at the Quaker school were solidly under the Major's protection until they were eighteen, but at the Catholic school, Père Blanc was fully in charge.

Père Blanc did not object to girl brides. Hell, he even performed the marriage Mass. When I was there, I saw little twelve-year-old girls, scared and crying, dragged into the church and married off to men old enough to be their fathers. Not to put too fine a point on it, forced marriages were done solely for the sake of mixed-racial purity, because in those days a French/Osage girl had to marry a French/Osage man. It was their law, and if the girl in question did not feel called to be a nun, then Père Blanc married her off according to French/Osage law. And until the girls were married, they were watched over like they were walking nuggets of precious gold.

The boys, on the other hand, were different. Once they turned sixteen and were out of school, French/Osage boys could do just about anything they wanted to, which is how they got the reputation of being heartbreakers. Until they became of manly age (thirty and over) and were expected to marry and settle down, the French/Osage males ran riot through the outlying female communities. Which caused the Major a lot of problems when angry daddies showed up at the agency threatening to shoot the Major's pacifist ass off.

From now on, when you hear Olla townies bragging that they're part French-Osage, go ahead and grin. They got that blood from their great-grandmothers crawling out of bedroom windows to meet their

French/Osage lovers in the barn. And you can bet every nickel you'll ever own in this life that any child produced as a result of those late-night liaisons was born on the wrong side of the blanket. It couldn't have happened any other way, because back then French/Osage boys weren't allowed to marry outside of their own kind either.

I'm not telling you this as an interesting historical footnote, Everett. I'm telling you in the hope that you will pound these little-known facts into your head and hold them there while I tell you about the year I turned ten. The year when two things happened that changed the path my life would take and in a roundabout way guaranteed that you would even have a life. One, my father was killed. Two, I saw for the first time the little French/Osage girl I would love forever.

Cassie DuPree. Your mother.

The telephone rang brutally, startling him and causing him to jump in the chair. Then he looked over his shoulder at the wall-mounted phone above the kitchen counter. He didn't want to answer it, didn't want to be interrupted, especially then, but the telephone was insistent. After six rings Everett marked his place in the tablet, dog-earring the bottom corner of the page, crossed the room, and lifted the receiver. Before he had the chance to say hello, he heard Matt's croaky voice.

"I hate to ask, but could you come to the house? Right now? My mother would like to speak to you. She's in a bad way, Mr. Jakomin. If you could just spare her a minute, I'd be very grateful."

He wanted to say no. Consoling widows was never

his long suit, and besides, he wanted to read, but Matt Jones sounded pathetic.

With a dispirited sigh Everett said, "I can be there in half an hour."

"Thank you."

Both hung up.

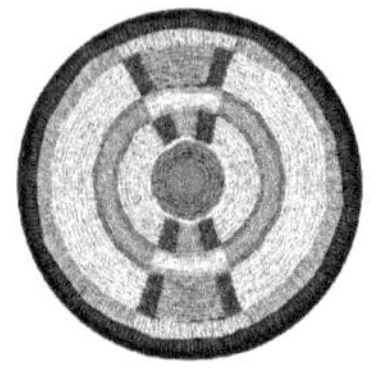

CHAPTER EIGHT

Everett recognized Matt's daughter the instant she opened one of the front doors even though Miss Hayley Jones was hardly one to trod the streets of Olla. She had been raised in Tulsa, then had been packed off to schools in the East. Now she was out of school and her picture was always in the Tulsa newspapers. At twenty-two, wealthy, single, and stunningly attractive, everything Hayley Jones said or did was considered hot news. Meeting her in person, Everett couldn't help but notice that she was very tall. The black and white newspaper photos didn't do her justice. What looked merely like dark hair in print was in life auburn. She also had amazing olive-green-colored eyes.

"Mr. Jakomin," she said in a breathy whisper, "may I speak with you a moment?"

As she was physically blocking the door, he didn't see he had much of an option. "Of course, Miss Jones."

She began wringing her hands as her eyes darted like frightened minnows. He tried to catch them with his, but they were too quick.

"Well, of course you know that I've been seeing Nath—"

Everett's eyes flew wide and Hayley's eyes finally locked with his.

"Oh," she said softly. "I—I see that he . . ." Her words trailed off. Embarrassment etched her face as Hayley wrung her hands more. Everett wasn't trying to catch her eyes again, he was fuming as he thought about Nath.

Everett's youngest son was an artist. A sculptor. He was extremely talented, but if it weren't for Everett's pitching in with the rent money for the studio apartment Nath kept in Tulsa, Nath would be homeless as well as broke. Up until that second, Everett had no idea that the paths of his son, the flat-broke artist, and Miss Hayley Jones, the oil heiress, had ever crossed. Nath had certainly kept that one close to his chest. And with good reason. Neither Matt nor Everett would have approved. The disapproval wouldn't have been so much because of the feud, at least not on Everett's part, it would have stemmed from the fact that the couple in question traveled in such vastly different circles. A poor young man going around with a rich young woman is never a good idea. Financially Nath would never be able to keep up with Miss Jones and her crowd of friends, and it would be absurd for him to try. That apparently Nath was being absurd made Everett angry.

"Miss Jones," he said tightly, "I don't believe you and I should continue this discussion. Not only is now the wrong time, but this is a conversation I should be having with my son."

"Yes," she said meekly. "But it's just that Nath and I— Well, you see, Mr. Jakomin, we—" She bit back whatever else she was about to confess. He studied her as she composed herself, then stood aside, permitting Everett to enter the house. Walking quickly, her high heels clicking against the checkerboard marble flooring, she led him to a closed door on the left.

Everett had never even been near the Jones mansion let alone inside it. The place had the feel of a palace, but he wasn't given much of an opportunity to see beyond the foyer because Hayley had opened the door and entered the room. This parlor where C.R. had once felt comfortable enough to put his feet up on the furniture immediately overwhelmed Everett. The plush chairs and settees certainly made his brand-new Naugahyde La-Z-Boy seem crappy, and he suddenly wished he had worn a suit, not just a good pair of khaki slacks and sport shirt. He felt immediately relieved that the three Jones boys scowling at him from across the room weren't wearing suits either.

The sons and wives were standing beside an older woman reclined on a couch. Hayley politely but needlessly announced Everett and then she scuddled out, closing the door behind her. The second Hayley was gone, Everett felt abandoned to an unfriendly crowd. And then Irene Jones marched right up to him, extending her work-rough hand. Irene was the one Jones wife Everett saw quite a bit around Olla. She drove an old station wagon with ROCKING J emblazoned on the sides, and when she visited various stores her white-blond hair was in a simple ponytail and she invariably wore jeans, men's shirts, and boots. Today her hair lay around her shoulders and she was wearing a neat dress, a single strand of pearls around her long neck, and low-heeled shoes. She looked self-conscious and awkward. Taking her hand, Everett found her grip firm and she spoke to him with a chain smoker's gravelly voice.

"Hi. I'm Irene. David's wife."

David first met Irene at the party his mother gave to welcome her sons home from their eastern colleges.

The party had been stocked with young girls claiming direct kinship to the most important men in Oklahoma. At C.R's insistence, an invitation had been extended the daughter of his company attorney.

Irene came, looking like a herring caught up in the swirl of angelfish. A thoroughgoing tomboy, Irene did not blend well in a refined crowd. And as soon as she was ushered into the main room she knew that her dress and her hair were completely wrong for the occasion. Seeing her, the young men in tuxedos, their short hair slicked hard against their skulls, grinned, turned their heads away, and whispered among themselves. The young women, their svelte figures revealed in curve-hugging silk gowns, their bobbed hair possessing more waves than the Atlantic, rolled mascared eyes and furrowed thin pencil-drawn eyebrows. Irene was wearing a hooped gown, and her white-blond hair was done in ringlets. Had the party been a cotillion, she would have been a belle.

It was not a cotillion.

Noticing the new arrival, David stepped away from a group of young men and studied her. Harry and the others looked as well and promptly snickered.

His tone repentant, Harry hastily explained Irene's presence to his snobbish eastern school pals. "We let the rubes in when my father owes them a favor."

David moved close to his brother and whispered next to Harry's ear, "Now tell them how you tried to date her two years ago and the little rube wouldn't even talk to you."

Harry winced. As David walked away, Harry's narrowed eyes flung daggers at David's back.

Irene was so nervous, she felt on the verge of throwing up. Against her will her father had hauled her, kicking and screaming, to the party, and now he was holed up somewhere in the house with C.R. to make certain she didn't sneak out before the party was over.

To make matters worse, he had timed her arrival so that she would make a noticeable entrance. Which meant everyone would be given the opportunity to stare at her and make her feel as asinine as she knew she looked. Now they were ignoring her, and she was just standing on her own, not knowing what to do. Her stomach pitched furiously and made a noise which a few nearest her heard quite clearly. Giggles ensued as an abashed Irene placed both hands on top of her flat but gurgling stomach.

In those seconds she almost hated her father for having forced her into this situation. She was an Oklahoma cowgirl, nothing more, nothing less. And now she was all done up like a dog's dinner standing on her own, balanced precariously on high heels, at a party she didn't want to attend and certainly didn't feel welcome at. To add insult to injury, her feet hurt, and because she wasn't use to standing on her toes she could feel her wobbly ankles beginning to swell. She placed a hand to her temple as her father's voice shouted inside her brain.

"Irene! You stop that pouting. These are nice kids and you're going to have a good time. Besides, you can't spend your life chasing around with ranch hands."

"But I like ranch hands!"

"Life is not one long rodeo, Irene. You have to grow up an' start being a young lady."

"Hello."

With a gasp, she looked up into David Jones's smiling face. She hadn't seen him in years, and in that time he had changed, becoming more handsome, certainly more polished. She remembered coming to this house as a child and attending birthday parties given in turn for each of the boys. Back then David had been her favorite because he could always be counted on for a game of marbles when the organized party fun turned tedious. The invitations to further parties stopped when the boys reached an age they no longer appreciated the inclusion of little girls. When the Jones boys began to like girls again, tomboy Irene didn't make the party lists. But because the Rocking J was within spitting distance of the Jones house, she always knew when there was a party. Knew too that she hadn't been included.

She felt she got even whenever she saw any of the boys driving their cars along the road that was shared by the house and the ranch. As their cars approached, she pretended she didn't see the customary wave, nor did she wave in response. It was a small retaliation, but it let them know she didn't give a fig about any one of them. Then two years earlier Harry came to the ranch with his father. When Harry saw her, he couldn't stop remarking about how grown-up she had gotten to be and that she'd turned out to be so pretty. He'd meant it all to be complimentary, but it had the reverse effect. He called her a couple of times after that, but by then she'd learned that Harry was rumored to be involved with a girl named Terri who was currently back east. Not anyone's second fiddle, Irene promptly let Harry know by her standoffish response that she just wasn't interested. Now, here she was at one of the famous Jones boys parties and David, her very first crush, was standing too close. She had gotten over the burning crush she'd had on David at the age of nine. She was in no mood at present to risk being rejected by him again, the way she had been when David first turned on her, called her just a stupid girl. Even now the memory hurt.

"Go away," she said sullenly.

David's head snapped back. "Excuse me?"

Irene gritted her teeth. "Go away."

David gave her another once-over. Beneath that ill-fitting, old-fashioned dress—where had she gotten it?—there was a hint of a terrific figure. Her long white-blond hair had been forced into an unbecoming wreath of curls. Yet her pretty little face attracted him like a bee to a flower. He couldn't help but smile as he studied her turned-up nose and rosebud mouth that badly needed kissing. A lot of kissing. The thing he liked best was her coloring. Irene was deeply tanned even though that night she had tried to hide the tan under pale face-powder.

"Irene? Don't you remember me? I'm David."

"Of course I remember you. Please leave me alone."

He bent at the knees and tried to catch her eye. She turned her face, deliberately showing him a disapproving profile.

"This is a social," he said. "Didn't you come here to be social?"

"For your information, my father forced me to come. And your father probably told you to be nice to me."

"No, he didn't. I'm talking to you because I want to."

She rolled her eyes upward. When he smiled widely, even though she fought it, she couldn't prevent her response of a trace of a smile. That's when he noticed the dimple at the corner of her mouth. David loved dimples. They were his weakness. A girl with a dimple could make him act like a fool. He still wanted to kiss her pouting mouth, but he badly wanted to kiss that dimple.

"Hey," he cried. "I have an idea. If you really want to hide until the party's over, you could come with me out to the garden. I was going there anyway to sneak a smoke."

She rolled her eyes again. "I'm supposed to believe that?"

"Yeah. Look, my mom has a fit if anyone smokes in the house. She says that's what the verandas are for."

Irene seemed to consider what he said, then asked timidly, "Could, could I have a smoke too?"

"Hey, you bet!" Gallantly, David offered his arm.

As she placed her hand in the bend of his elbow, her fair brows furrowed. "But just don't get any funny ideas while we're out there in the dark."

Laughing, he placed his hand over hers. "I wouldn't dream of it."

Sitting down on a bench proved a problem, as the hoop wasn't cooperative. With David's help Irene finally conquered the thing and then they sat side by side, sharing a cigarette as soft music drifted out to them. They talked about all sorts of things and once she was relaxed, Irene's earthy wit had David rolling with laughter. Positive now that he did not want to share her attention with anyone, he left her briefly, going back inside only long enough to steal two glasses and a bottle of wine. The hours they spent together on the veranda felt more like minutes, and before they knew it, the party was over.

"Great," she said with a relieved sigh, "I can go home now."

He was glad it was dark. Had there been anything brighter than starlight, she would have seen the twinge of hurt cross his face. He took her hand, stood before her, and bowed at the waist.

"Please allow me to see you out."

As he walked her through the house, he knew that he couldn't leave it like this. He had to see her again. And in a more befitting costume. They found her father, Peter Waterman, in the foyer standing next to C.R. Still holding her hand, David blatantly lied.

"Irene's invited me to the ranch tomorrow, Mr. Waterman. We thought it would be nice to go on a picnic."

Irene's face drained.

Peter Waterman positively crowed his delight. "Well

isn't that nice. You just come on out, David. We'll be happy to have you."

"I can be there about eleven."

"That's fine," Peter Waterman said enthusiastically. "That's just fine. We'll see you then, son." To his somnambulistic daughter he said, "Irene, say thank-you to C.R. for inviting you to the party."

Irene almost curtsied as she said woodenly, "Thank you, Mr. Jones, for inviting me to the party. It was very nice."

"I'm glad you could come, Irene," C.R. said softly. "From now on, don't be such a stranger."

"Thank you, sir."

"Boy," Irene said with a disapproving shake of her head, "he's sure got you buffaloed."

David was sitting on a giant horse Irene had introduced as Red. In the corral, as David clambered awkwardly into the saddle, Red had tried to bite his leg. The attempt did not bode well. David gritted his teeth as they then set out at a canter toward the picnic site. David could be very stubborn, and even though he was terrified of the horse, he was determined to stay in the saddle. As Irene rode ahead, he thought back over the previous hour.

Driving his snappy white roadster through the gates and up the dusty drive, he was amazed that he hadn't remembered just how impressive the Rocking J was. Never mind that the Rocking J was a close neighbor, he hadn't visited the ranch in nearly a decade. As his car sped by, the painted black wood fencing surrounding the pastures seemed to disappear until all he could see were acres of bluestem. Then there was the house. It was a one-story structure with two separate wings. Behind the house the ranch spread out for miles, dotted with corrals, outbuildings, a small house for the foreman and his family, a bunkhouse for the common hands, three barns, and a stable. Irene had been waiting in the front drive as he drove in, parked the roadster, and climbed out. She was wearing a pair of tight jeans, a sleeveless shirt, and boots. Her hair, freed from the forced curls, lay smoothly behind her shoulders. She was gorgeous. And furious, refusing to speak to him as they walked to the corrals. In the barn a hand was just finishing the task of saddling two horses. Irene pointed to one and said, "You get Red." She was in the saddle and riding off at a canter while Red was trying to nip David's leg.

Two miles away from the corrals, Red lost interest in following after the lead horse. As David hadn't ridden since he was ten years old, Big Red sensed fear and made the most of it. While David halfheartedly kicked, Big Red blithely crunched grass. Fuming, Irene returned and maneuvered her horse beside Red, yelling at David.

"You can't let him buffalo you like this. You can't just let him graze when he wants to."

"He's hungry."

"Hungry, my aunt Maud. Red knows better than this and so should you. What kinda Osage lets a horse just do anything it wants to?"

"A rich one with a roadster."

"You are a sad piece of work, David Jones."

She used her reins to whack Big Red's flank. Red took off, David careening drunkenly.

"Let him know you're in the saddle, David!" she screamed as David bounced recklessly.

"Red!" he shouted. "I'm in the saddle! I'm in the saddle, boy!"

"Oh, what a goober," Irene muttered. When Red and David disappeared over the rise, she whipped her own mount into a gallop. She didn't really want to save him, but she knew her father would be upset if she did nothing while David Jones broke his idiot neck.

• • •

Their picnic consisted of sitting in the shade of a gnarled tree, drinking bottles of warm soda and eating egg salad sandwiches. Irene still wasn't happy. Like the party the night before, she clearly wanted this picnic over with as quickly as possible. As for David, there wasn't a bone or muscle in his body that wasn't screaming in agony, but the thing that hurt him the most was Irene's attitude.

"Why don't you like me?"

Draining the last of the soda pop, the unexpected question caused her to choke. She sputtered, then began to cough uncontrollably. David pounded her back until she cried "enough." Breathing deeply through her nose, she frowned at him.

"Look, David, we haven't seen each other since we were kids, and we live right next door. You can't expect me to fall over happy just because you've decided to come see me after all this time. It was nice of you to be friendly last night, but that was last night. The party's over. Now you should stick with playing tennis with your college pals and leave me alone."

David took a long slug of soda and wiped his mouth with the back of his hand. He pulled his upper lip over his teeth and held on to it with the bottom set as he stared off over the vast terrain that was the Rocking J ranch.

"Irene, I wasn't just being nice to you. And even though you've tried to kill me today, I still like you."

A flutter of excitement played hob with the egg salad sandwich in her stomach. Ignoring it, she cried, "When did I try to kill you?"

"When you put me on the killer horse from hell!" he shouted.

Irene fell to the side, laughing. "My mother rides Red! I knew I should have put you on Elmer."

"I wish you had."

Irene stopped laughing, sat up, and leaned in until

she was almost nose to nose with him. "For your information, Elmer's put five ranch hands in the hospital. If I had put you on Elmer, he would have bounced your butt clear to the moon."

David scoffed, "If he's so dangerous, why haven't you had him shot?"

"You lunatic! Elmer's got the best bloodlines in the whole state! He could kill or cripple a hundred men and he'd still be worth more than all of them stuck together. The stud fees alone—"

"Can I kiss you?"

Jolted by the question, she stared openmouthed. Several seconds passed before she found her voice. "If I let you kiss me, will you go home?"

"No."

Without missing a beat, she said, "Okay, then, you can kiss me. But nothing sloppy."

David sounded a laugh. "But I just said I wouldn't go away."

"I know. That's why I said yes."

It was a chaste kiss, just a brief brushing of lips. When he tried to grab her, make a better kiss, she pulled away, jumping to her feet.

Standing over him, her hands on her hips, she said firmly, "That's all you get, bub, till you learn to sit a horse like a man. Or even better, like an Osage."

C.R. watched his second son cripple in each and every day at sundown for two solid weeks. He didn't bother to ask how the riding lessons were going. It was more than obvious that they were painful. After the third week, David bounced into his father's study as happy as a lively puppy.

"Dad! Irene let me out of the corral! We even raced and I almost won! Her father said I was doing so well that if it was all right with you, I could spend the summer working as a full-time hand. That means I'd be sleeping in the bunkhouse and everything!"

"Would you like that, David?"

"Yeah! I love the ranch." He sat down and leaned over his father's desk. "You'll never guess what happened today. If I hadn't seen it, I probably wouldn't have believed it, but a cow got stuck inside a stand of blackjacks and was just running around bawling her head off. I drove out in the truck with the foreman and a hand to rescue it. Bert, he's the foreman, said that if we couldn't get it out, the cow would die. And do you know why, Dad? It's because of the way the trees grow." He used his gloved hands to demonstrate. "See, the top branches grow straight up, but the bottom branches of a blackjack grow down, and those bottom branches are as sharp as swords. They can cut a cow to pieces. And because the trees grow so close together, once a cow gets in, she can't get out. We had to use machetes and even then we made only a dent in it, and the flies, man, the flies almost ate me alive.

"That cow was almost crazy, but Samuel managed to get a rope on her and it took all three of us to drag her out. But the reason she went into that blackjack stand was because she was trying to drop a calf and she wanted shade. But the minute she knew she was in trouble, she forgot about trying to pass that calf. We could see tiny hooves just poking out under the tail and Bert started yelling that her contractions must have stopped. Then Samuel yelled at me, and we wrestled her to the ground while Bert ran to get another rope out of the truck. When he had it, he tied it around the little hooves and he goes back to the truck again. By then I had no idea what was going on, but I stayed on her neck just like Bert told me to and then Samuel yells, "Haul away, Bert." Bert put the truck in reverse, and even though he took it slow, that calf came flying out of there." David slapped his work-gloved hand against dusty chaps. "It was the damnedest thing I've ever seen, and that was just on a boring day, Dad."

"How's Irene?"

"Hey, she's just great." David beamed. "She said to say hi. Dad, do you know she can make a buttermilk biscuit so light, it practically floats in the air? She can ride a horse better than a man and make biscuits too. She's some girl."

"I think you should grab her, David."

Grinning, David wriggled his eyebrows. "Already have, Dad."

Before David left for his eastern school that September, he and Irene were formally engaged. After three months the separation proved to be too painful for them, and David quit college and came home. They were married by Christmas and David went to the Rocking J to live in a house Peter Waterman and C.R. had built a mile from the main house. Ten years later, following Peter Waterman's death, David and Irene and their two little girls moved into the main house.

The Rocking J had been so named because the land the ranch occupied was secretly leased from C.R., the lease valid only for Peter Waterman's lifetime. In the days when the deal had been made, no one was willing to sell a New York Jew one square foot of land, and because of a promise C.R. had made to his father, he couldn't sell his land either. But he could rent it. Which is what he did. As both men grew older, they both worried about Irene. C.R. assured Peter that should the worst happen, he was prepared to pay her what the ranch was worth, but the Rocking J was Irene's greatest love. Both men became worried when she refused to go to college, refused to date any young man who might take her away from her singular passion.

Working to spare her from the truth, C.R. and Peter Waterman conspired to match Irene with C.R.'s oldest son. When she turned her nose up at Harry, both fathers despaired, Peter because he didn't believe the scheme would work, C.R. because he had hoped Harry's involvement with Irene would put paid to the nonsense Emma was brewing matching Harry with that southern blueblood. C.R. knew in his heart of hearts Terri was not the woman for Harry. His oldest son needed a practical woman, not a woman content to live in a bygone dreamworld. Inviting Irene to the party had been intended as another stab at matching her with Harry. It was blind luck that instead, Irene and David had paired off.

At the time, he hadn't considered his second son a possibility because he'd believed David was still too young for a serious romance. Evidently he wasn't, because David fell hard for Irene. So hard that after only a few months back in college, David had practically run all the way home from Princeton in his desperation to marry her. In hindsight, C.R. saw the match as being right. David loved the ranch almost as much as he loved Irene. And married to David, the Rocking J would always be Irene's home, but more important, the land would be in the hands of a Jones. All of this meant that Peter Waterman could eventually go peacefully to his grave and that C.R. would not demean his own father's death.

"Mrs. Jones," Everett said, pumping Irene's hand, "I've always wanted to personally thank you for Rocking J's business. Will you be needing the standard order for fence posts come autumn?"

"Yeah, I was about to have the foreman call with the numbers, but—"

"Irene!" David snapped. As Irene and Everett looked

blankly at him, David's tone softened. "Honey, the man has come to talk to Mama."

"Oh. I'm sorry, Dee." Irene turned back to Everett. "Mr. Jakomin? Would you like a glass of tea?"

"Yes, ma'am, I sure would."

"I'll get it for ya." Before she left his side she said in a whisper, "Don't let 'em smell fear."

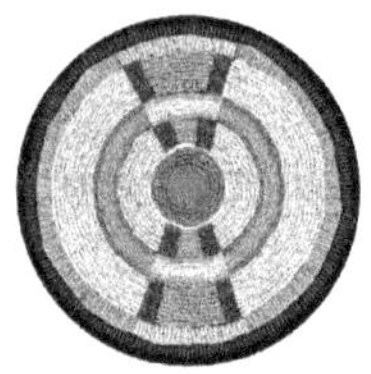

CHAPTER NINE

Meeting Emma Jones proved to be highly uncomfortable. Fortunately, the interview lasted only a few moments. Just long enough to drink the tall glass of iced tea and give his assurances that C.R. would be buried in a timely fashion. Mrs. Jones was understandably distraught, and Everett felt angry that he, a virtual stranger, had been thrown at her in a time when she was so vulnerable. He was even angrier that her sons, most especially Harry, had done nothing to ease the situation. If anything, Harry's rage had only added to his mother's emotional torment.

Taking Everett's hand, she looked at him for a long time. Her eyes were dull, moving sluggishly. Her facial features were a little too loose to be normal. Everett guessed correctly that she was on a powerful sedative.

"What has my husband told you about all this?" she asked slurrily.

Everett stopped himself just before he mentioned the writing tablets. The answers everyone wanted were in the tablets, but C.R.'s family weren't meant to know about the memoirs, and Everett was bound by his promise not to tell. The most he could do was sit there and feel like a jackass. Everett placed his hand on top of hers. Her mouth trembled and tears were forming in her eyes. Even in advanced age she was a handsome woman. If they'd met under different circumstances, when she was in control, immaculately groomed, he knew she would be magnificent. Even strongly drugged and in the depths of despair she was still almost magnificent. Knowing only too well what it felt like to lose a loved one, he responded to her need. Without bothering to think through exactly whom he was comforting, he wrapped his arm around her shoulders and held her close.

"I will not hurt you," he whispered. "I promise."

She closed her eyes as tears streamed her face. Everett's words reminded her of another time, another man making that very same promise. He promised he wouldn't, but . . . Running away from the memory brought her back to the moment, reminded her just who was speaking to her now. Inadvertently, and without ever knowing it, the man holding her had already hurt her very much and simply by his existence. C.R. had always strove to keep her from knowing just how involved he remained with Everett Jakomin's life and welfare, but she knew.

Her head felt heavy and she rested her forehead against his, speaking softly, just to Everett.

"I knew you before you were born, you know. Knew you after too. You were a pretty little boy. Your hair used to be so light. Almost . . . blond." Her head slumped, coming to rest on his shoulder as she lost the battle against the sedatives. He had to strain to hear her last muffled words. "Blond hair. Too French to be . . ."

He did not care for the direction this slurry conversation was headed. And then a coldness filled him as he remembered C.R.'s scrawled words.

"I met your mother. Cassie DuPree."

Dear God.

His mind locked on that one horrific possibility, he felt almost dead from the neck up by the time Matt and David relieved him of their mother. But before they helped her walk away, he heard her mumble, "Not . . . Charlie's."

Feeling immensely relieved and foolish that he had even for a second seriously considered a distraught woman's ramblings concerning his paternity, Everett stood, eager now to leave, be away from this house, away from these people. Kelly and Irene saw Everett out, walking beside him toward the front double doors. Irene was highly talkative. She carried on a one-sided conversation with him while Kelly, Matt's wife, glanced at him now and again out of the corner of her eye.

These furtive glances revived Everett's attention. Kelly Jones's glancing looks and silence made him acutely aware of her. At the door Irene continued her low-voiced concerns for the delicate state of her mother-in-law's mental health. Kelly abandoned covert peeking. Facing Everett, she studied him openly, the way one might study a new strain of virus under a microscope. As Irene finished her lengthy list of concerns, and before Everett could speak the trite yet comforting utterances so expected during times such as these, Kelly cut him off.

"Nath must come to the funeral."

Everett's head snapped in her direction. "Excuse me?"

"Your son, Nath," Kelly said calmly. "Of course you're aware he and Hayley have become good friends. She needs him now, and I insist he be included in whatever arrangements you intend to make. I could speak to him personally. It would be one less thing for you to do."

"Uh," Everett faltered, "I believe I'd like to do that myself."

"Then please tell him his presence is required."

He felt his temper rise as she continued to regard him, expected him to say—what? Yes, here's my son, you rich folks just play with him as much as you want to? Oh, fat chance. As soon as he got his hands on Nathaniel Jakomin, there wouldn't be much of him left for anyone to play with. And now Everett knew he'd better say his good-byes and leave before he let slip something unforgivably rude.

Kelly Jones proved to be a hard person to walk away from. Her hand on his arm stopping him, she said curtly, "If you need any help with the arrangements, please call. Matt and I, as well as Harry and Terri, have temporarily moved in with Mother. But my bedroom has a private line. Perhaps I should give you the number."

"Well, ma'am, I—"

"Oh, never mind," she said. "I just remembered. Nath has it."

A heartbeat later Everett found himself standing outside, the door swinging closed behind him. He turned his head until his chin lined with his shoulder and he scowled darkly at the doors.

Nath has it, he mockingly seethed. Then he mentally raged. What the devil is my son doing with the private telephone number to Mrs. Matthew Jones's bedroom?

So angry now he was smoldering, he marched the width of the portico, descended the steps. The gravel crunched loudly as he made his way to his car, opened the door, and climbed inside. In the house the two women heard the car engine start, then leaving the drive.

There was fire in Irene's eyes. "I thought you said Nath was going to talk to him."

Kelly scraped her bottom lip with her teeth. "Last night he said he would. I can only assume that Nath has tried but for some reason keeps missing his father."

"Well, he'd better get him and get him fast," Irene scoffed. Then her tone softened. "How's Hayley holding up?"

As if hearing her name, Hayley appeared in the archway of the main room. From across the foyer, Kelly looked at her daughter, shook her head. Hayley dissolved into tears and ran back into the distant room.

Irene threw up her hands. "Well, I guess that answers my question. I can't believe how bad C.R.'s screwed everything up. It just wasn't like him to handle things like this. He sure picked a real wrong time to die."

"I'm sure C.R. didn't do it on purpose, Irene."

Irene took Kelly's arm as they walked through the foyer. "How much does Nath favor his daddy?"

Kelly smiled wanly. "There's a strong resemblance, but Nath is the much better-looking of the two."

Irene stopped. There were two things in life she appreciated to her very core. One was a good horse. The second was a good-looking man. Everett Jakomin was a very good-looking man. "Oh, then I can't wait to meet his kid."

Both women quickly shut up as Matt rounded the corner. His body language, his steely expression, left them no doubt that he was as mad as a hornet.

"Is he gone?"

"He just left," Kelly answered. Irene and Kelly remained stock-still as Matt stormed up the stairway.

Irene sent Kelly a worried glance. Kelly was staring up the stairway, watching her husband. In the business world, Matt was an aggressive warrior, a persona he shed each night before entering the front door of their home. Throughout the decades of being his wife, Kelly knew only the loving side of Matt, the gentle man who didn't mind taking out the garbage. But she knew the other side existed and she feared that part of him that was unforgiving and showed no quarter.

Irene patted her hand. "It's gonna be all right, Kel. It really is, hon. I just know it in my bones."

Kelly watched until Matt disappeared, heard him slam their bedroom door. Her nerves were ragged. Never before had she kept anything secret from him, but Matt was forcing her to keep this one. If only C.R. hadn't died. But he had died and now she would have to face Matt all alone. It would not be pleasant. With anything to do with Chris, Matt simply expected his son to get on with it, prove his manhood.

"There's the cold, cruel world son, hit it."

But not Hayley. Oh, no. Hayley had to be protected. She had to have the very best because nothing else would do. And Matt's image of the best had shifted from the material to the matrimonial. With the same zeal he had chosen almost everything Hayley had ever owned, he was now *interviewing* likely candidates to be his future son-in-law.

Kelly had tried not to argue or worry because she felt that C.R. was a major ace up her sleeve. Then C.R. died. There went the ace. As if that wasn't awful enough, before C.R. was even cold, Everett Jakomin had been thrust into their lives, and his unexpected intrusion was by written decree of C.R. Matt was so furious and so hurt that he couldn't see beyond his fury or his pain. Today he was close to hating his father. Hating him for dying, hating him for passing over his own sons in favor of a man who continually opposed C.R., a man who, over the years he had been on the council, blocked oil lease sites until he had squeezed as much money out of Red Bird Oil as he could get.

"That's sacred ground. You can't test on sacred ground." This, invariably, was the excuse Everett Jakomin gave to stop the Red Bird geologists in their tracks. Months and obscene amounts of money were wasted until it was decided just how sacred the proposed drill site was. Then, even before oil was discovered, Everett drove a hard bargain to make certain the lease went for the highest price possible. When the oil came in, there he was again, always demanding audits in order to guarantee that the bulk of the profits went into Osage Nation coffers. Matt and David, as president and first vice president of Red Bird Oil, had millions of dollars worth of reason to despise Everett Jakomin. And, in turn, Everett Jakomin's son.

The knot inside Kelly's stomach tightened. Vaguely, she felt Irene wrap an arm around her shoulders, pull her away from the staircase, tell her again that everything would be all right. Irene had known her secret for weeks. As of last night, so did David. As Irene led her out of the foyer, Kelly too vividly recalled the encounter and again heard David's wrath.

Kelly had gone to Rocking J hours after the family had found C.R.'s damnable little missive, which had turned a bad situation from sincerely awful to rabidly bug-nutty. The coroner had barely taken C.R.'s remains away for death verification when the screaming and tearing of hair began. Kelly had retreated into a daze for the remainder of the day, but by early evening her little secret was too weighty to bear. She drove to the ranch, meaning only to talk it all through once again with Irene. But then Irene sucker-punched her.

"Honey, this is gettin' bigger than both of us. You're gonna have to talk to Dee." Not taking Kelly's cries of *Oh, God no!* for an answer, Irene propelled her into David's study.

David was at his desk, on the telephone. When he heard the door open and then close, the phone still at his ear, David turned in his chair. All Kelly could think as he smiled briefly and motioned her in was how much David looked like Matt. Nervously, she sat down in the chair near his desk. He talked a few minutes more on the phone, then hung up, wiping a hand across his face.

"What can I do for you, Kel?"

In a faltering voice she told him, and as David listened, his face visibly hardened. When she was finished, he jumped out of his chair and began to rage.

"For the love of God, Kelly! How could you do it? Don't you even know what you've done?" Sorely tempted to hit her, David raked his hand through his hair. He paced the floor of his study. He stopped, and his face twisted with loathing, he glared at her.

"Who else knows?"

"Only Irene."

"Then we keep it that way," David fumed. "You just keep your mouth shut until this mess about Dad has been cleared up. Have you got that?!"

David's fury being just a foretaste of what she could expect from Matt, Kelly wept.

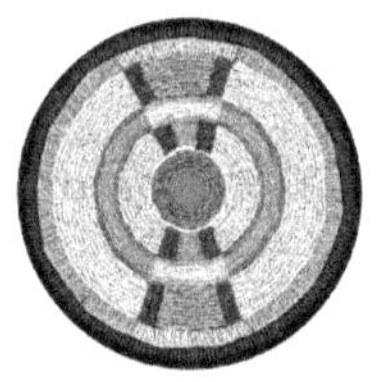

CHAPTER TEN

Everett drove his red Corvette out the gates and met tarmac. Last year, when Chevrolet introduced the two-seater sports car, he'd bought the first one set out on the showroom floor. The car clashed with his staid personality, and his children had teased him unmercifully about it, but he'd bought the Corvette because he'd needed a radical change. Besides, he could no longer stand driving the Ford coupe. Every time he started the Ford he expected to see Anna on the passenger side and then he would have to remind himself why she wasn't there. Then there would be that awful pain. Changing cars was easier than dealing daily with that pain. He'd been tempted to sell the house for the same reason, but in the end he just couldn't. He settled for repainting the exterior and interior in different shades and then completely redecorating. Except for the kitchen.

Anna's kitchen was sacrosanct.

Now that he was used to driving the Corvette, used to its power and speed, he was hard in love with it. The day he bought it he paid cash and then drove through town, waving to folks on the street strictly for the pleasure of having them stop and gawk as he cruised by. Now that the novelty was gone, few could remember him driving anything else. As soon as the red car came into view, folks waved without batting an eye. Even his daughter Martha was used to his car, and that spoke volumes. Martha was a prissy soul, and when he first bought the car she had been horrified. But his sons, especially Nath, had fallen over laughing.

"What's next, Dad? Will you be hanging out at the A & W, flirting with the carhops?"

"Maybe."

"Then you should sit really low in the seat so they can't see how old you are."

"Thank you, Nathaniel. Get out of my car."

" 'Vette, Dad. It's called a 'Vette. If you're gonna drive it, the least you can do is get the name right, okay?"

The pavement of the private road was narrow, barely wide enough room for two cars to pass each other. As Everett was the only one using it, he didn't have to worry about anything except the black road ahead while he fumbled in his shirt pocket for a cigarette. Everett adjusted his rump in the leather bucket seat. On hot days like today, Everett's bucket felt too big for the seat, but that was a different worry. He punched the lighter and stuck a cigarette in his mouth as he waited for the lighter to pop. When it did, he applied the red glow and puffed energetically. Relaxing a bit, he propped his left elbow out the open window, resting his arm on the frame. Memories flickered through his mind, memories of his childhood, his father.

Delbert Jakomin had been a hard-boiled drunk. He had been a drinker before Everett was born and progressively grew worse. And when he was at his drunkest, he cursed C. R. Jones. By the time Everett was twenty-five, Delbert's liver had given up trying to process the booze from his blood. His had not been a peaceful death, nor was it sudden. He was in the hospital for months. In his final weeks he was bloated, discolored, every breath a torment. Still, Delbert Jakomin clung to life. Everett suspected that his father was more terrified of dying than letting go of his suffering. And so during those months he wasted away, becoming even more bloated and turning the color of a ripe pumpkin. The most terrible memory Everett owned were the last moments of his father's life. Delbert spent them screaming to God for five more minutes, just five more minutes. Everett couldn't understand why, when his father had wasted the whole of his life, five more minutes would seem so important. And try as he might, he had never gotten over the guilt of being glad that God hadn't been listening. Ready or not, Delbert Jakomin died four minutes short and in mid-scream.

Everett made the sharp left that led out on the two-lane highway. The traffic on the state road was spotty. Even so, Everett adjusted himself in the seat and willed himself to be more alert. Until he thought about Nath and all concerns for driving safely evaporated. In his frustration with his son, he yelled at C. R. Jones.

"I'm not happy that my son is seeing your granddaughter. I'm not happy at all." He stabbed out the cigarette in the full-to-the-rim ashtray.

"I want you to know something right now. If it weren't for your wife, I wouldn't care if the Johnstons cremated you. And it would give me great pleasure to tie up your will for the next six months. But I can't do that because you made me responsible for your wife. In the old days one man would have to trust another pretty damned hard to do something like that. These aren't the old days, C.R., and I never wanted your trust. You forced it on me. I really don't care about the sad story of your life, and I especially don't care about your sons.

From now on, whatever I have to do, I'll do for the sake of your wife. No woman should be left with the foolishness you've put on her, and I think you're a real sonofabitch for doing it. So I'll read your damn memoirs, but I have to be honest, I can't see how anything you've written will ever justify the damage you've caused." Everett fumed a bit more, then started in again.

"A man is supposed to live on through his sons. If that's true, then, brother, you're in trouble. You produced three soul suckers who should be approached only by a legion of priests, a basketload of fresh garlic, a gallon of holy water, and several very large crucifixes. And I'll never be able to thank you enough for putting me right in the middle of them alone and unarmed."

With relief he finally pulled into his own driveway. His concrete drive was oil-spotted and it wasn't a million miles long like C.R.'s. Widthwise, there was just enough for two cars to be parked side by side. He switched off the ignition and sat listening to the heated engine tick as he fully appreciated the peace of his tree-lined neighborhood.

Everett's house was a modest brick-faced single-story structure dubbed ranch-style. His house was the only single-story house in the neighborhood, and it was also the newest. The oldest house was a grand two-story white house complete with columns on the front porch, a second-story veranda, and a breezeway over the side entrance drive. Built sometime during the 1890s, the old house had recently been inherited by Miss Milly's daughter, Miss Darlin'. Miss Darlin' wasn't her real name, Everett wasn't certain if he'd ever really heard her real name. Miss Milly called her daughter Darlin' and so did everyone else. At any rate, Miss Darlin' was seventy-two. She lived her whole life in the house down the street. When Everett and Anna moved into the neighborhood, Miss Darlin' was in charge of her aging mother saying that her mother didn't have much longer. Miss Milly outlived Anna.

Miss Milly and Miss Darlin' were lovely, gently bred ladies always the first to appear on the doorstep of neighbors experiencing difficulties. As frail as she had been, when Miss Milly learned that Anna was in the hospital, she had been standing right by the side of Miss Darlin' the day Everett forced himself to answer the doorbell. The ladies not only brought words of comfort, they brought a baking dish containing their famous peaches and cream cake, a dish they prepared only for those suffering a most dire situation. Being the recipient of one of their cakes closed the chapter on Everett's denial. Holding the baking dish in his hands began his hard acceptance that his Anna was terminal. That she was never coming home. When he went to the hospital later that day, he ended Anna's treatments. He'd expected a fight, but even the doctors had been relieved that he had come to that decision.

"We can keep her comfortable," one of them said.

And Everett knew this was all he had left to hope for. That his Anna would be . . . comfortable.

He stayed with her all through the next days and nights that Anna peacefully slipped away. The last day of her life, Anna had refused the morphine injections. She was clear of mind and without pain. She even laughed and joked with the kids, and as they left, she told each one how much she loved them as they kissed her good-bye.

Everett had thought she was asleep as she lay with her eyes closed. He sat by her bed, reading a book, when he heard her weak voice say, "Do you see them, Ev?"

He quickly put the book aside, hovered over her, his large arms framing her small head. "See who, sweetheart?"

"Angels." With great effort she licked her dry lips. Then in a voice filled with wonder she cried, "Oh!"

And she was gone.

Miss Milly was the only person he knew during those first bleak weeks following Anna's death that didn't say "It was God's will." What Miss Milly said instead was "Everett, don't you let me catch you crawlin' into that grave after Anna. Your children an' your grandchildren need you too much for that kinda nonsense. Now, you pull yourself up and start livin' the way God and Anna herself expects you to."

He greatly mourned Miss Milly's recent passing, and because he worried about Miss Darlin', especially now that she had a live-in housekeeper and there was something about that woman that he just didn't like, Everett checked on Miss Darlin' three, sometimes, four times a week.

His quiet yearnings for the days when Anna had been alive and the elderly ladies down the street had been spry ended as one memory replaced another and he felt a laugh bubbling deep inside him. The favorite story of the neighborhood began on the day when Nath had been six. Having proudly attended his very first Vacation Bible School class, Nath had learned that the original people on Earth were called Adam and Eve. The minute he came home from church he marched his little self down to Miss Milly's. The ladies were sitting on their front porch, doing their embroidery work. Standing at the bottom of their steps, Nath demanded to know why Miss Milly and Miss Darlin' would change their names from the names God Himself had given to them. Needless to say, the ladies were a trifle undone. Especially Miss Darlin'. It isn't every day a spinster lady is credited for having founded the human race. Before Nath marched himself off again, he strongly warned them not to give away any more apples from their overgrown apple tree. Most especially not to his daddy, because his mama wouldn't like his daddy wearing fig leaves because she already didn't like it when his daddy wore boxer shorts to the breakfast table. Now, there was a nugget the two ladies—as well as Everett—could have lived happily without their knowing. Being ladies of the old school, the incident would have ended with them. It had been only by chance that their closest neighbor, Bill Parker, had heard the whole thing while pruning in his yard. Bill Parker did not hesitate. He spread that story faster than the prairie winds can blow, and even now on a dull day in the neighborhood, it was repeated.

All of the homes were widely spaced on acre-and-a-half lots. Being such an old neighborhood, all the homes had their own water wells and septic systems. The fronting road had been tarmacked over seven years before, which was a blessing, cutting down the dust generated by passing cars, but there was still no sign of the sidewalks the candidates for Olla town council had faithfully promised. Everett was secretly glad that five elections had come and gone and still the sidewalks had yet to materialize. He hadn't wanted them in the first place. He loved the way the trees lined the road, their canopy arching and meeting, spangling the shadowed blacktop with bursts of sunlight streaming through the thick growth of elm and maple leaves. If the town council made good its promise about the sidewalks, the first thing the work crew would have to do is take out nearly every one of the trees. And then the neighborhood would lose its most cherished possession. Its tangible aura of permanence. Still sitting in his car, looking down the road, Everett vowed then and there that sidewalks would go in over his very dead body. Then he noticed that the lawns belonging to his neighbors were vivid green, while his was nearing a lemon yellow. He couldn't help but notice that his bedding plants were leaning, en masse, toward the watering hose coiled under the spigot.

"It's too hot to water right now," he said, speaking in a reasonable tone to the plants the way Anna used to. "But I'll give ya'll a real good soaking sometime after sundown."

It was a vague promise, and the shriveling plants knew it, but his conscience a bit clearer, Everett climbed out of his car and walked along the side of the house. As he entered the back door, the sun was gliding toward the west, darkening the east-facing kitchen. Absently, he flipped on the wall switch, cueing the overhead neon. The artificial lights flickered, annoying his vision as he closed the door. On the kitchen table the box of memoirs patiently waited. He was expected to call Johnston's in the morning about the funeral preparations. Which meant he would have to spend the whole of the evening reading if he had any hope of being prepared. C.R.'s final request had all the feel of a game show with Everett as the contestant nervously awaiting the sixty-four-thousand-dollar question.

"A nice plot with a twelve-foot-high statue of the archangel Michael standing guard?"

BEEEEEP.

"Wrong answer, Mr. Jakomin. But you take away a nice portable television set and two hundred dollars in cash."

Everett prepared a fresh pot of coffee. He was setting it on the stove, when the telephone rang. He gave the instrument a baleful glare.

"That better not be another Jones."

It was Nath. Just the boy he wanted to talk to. But first he allowed Nath to squirm.

"Hi, Dad. I've, uh, been calling you all day."

Coldly Everett answered, "I'm sorry I missed your calls, son. As you undoubtedly know, I've been a bit busy."

"Uh, yeah. I know all about it. Do you know why C.R. wants you to handle his funeral?"

"No."

"That's kind of hard to believe, Dad."

"Well, Nath, I'm having a hard time believing some of the things I've been hearing about you lately. You care to tell me how long you have been seeing Miss Hayley Jones?"

When Nath answered, he sounded wounded. "I was going to tell you about that."

"When?"

"Well, today, as a matter of fact. That's why I'm calling you."

Everett raised his voice to a shout. "Nathaniel, just how mixed up are you with Hayley Jones?"

Dead silence.

Everett held on to the receiver, listening to his son breathe. Then Nath began to speak haltingly. "Well, you know, Dad. She's a pretty girl and I'm a healthy guy, so we just sort of—"

"Nathaniel! I have never in your whole life told you who you could be friends with, but you know how I feel about that family. I don't care how pretty she is or how healthy you are, I don't approve of you going out with her. Am I getting through to you, my son?"

"Yes. Man, you must have had a rough day."

"I have and it's not over. The next time you talk to her, you just tell little Miss Hayley Jones three things. One, that everything to do with her grandfather is under control. Two, that you are breaking it off with her, and three, that no, you will not be at the funeral to hold her hand. Am I getting through to you, Nathaniel?"

"Now, hang on a minute, Dad—"

"No, I won't. I meant every word I said. Now, good night."

Everett slammed the receiver down. Breathing hard,

he stared at the wall phone. He couldn't help remembering what C.R. had written about long-ago French/Osage males. History seemed determined to repeat itself. Little Hayley Jones was crawling out her bedroom window, meeting a certain French/Osage young man named Nathaniel Jakomin, and Matthew Jones would be out for a certain young man's blood if he ever got wind of it.

Taking a calming breath, he remembered something else. That Hayley's mother already knew. Not only that, she even seemed bent on the liaison. Why else would she demand Nath attend the funeral? Everett shook his head. Mrs. Kelly Jones could demand until she turned blue in the face. Nath was his son, his concern, and thanks to C.R., he had full authority on the funeral's guest list. Therefore Nath would *not* attend the funeral. That was his last word on the subject. And he didn't want any more interrupting telephone calls either. He took the receiver off the hook and slammed it down on the counter with a loud bang.

His jaws locked tighter than the back cheeks of a bull walking uphill, Everett grabbed his glasses and the waiting writing pad and headed for the living room and the solace of his recliner. Within seconds of being kicked back in the chair, despite his recent and highly vocal assurances that he was no longer interested in the minute details of C.R.'s life, he became deeply engrossed.

I was kind of a gangly ten-year-old, tall and skinny as a stick. As I had been in school for four years and was considered to be one of the brightest boys in class, I was also mouthy. I had an opinion about everything, and when I was home I drove my father crazy with them. As I told you, French/Osage people were progressive. I was progressing right along with them while my father remained uncompromisingly conservative.

My father's name was Eagle's Feather and he was a big man. He wore a breechcloth and leggings and he wore his hair in the traditional fashion, shaved on both sides and with a scalp lock and roach. His ears were pierced from the lobe to the center, and silvery chains hung from each puncture. He also had tattoos around his wrists, biceps, and along his collarbone. The tattoos were sharp geometric designs and ashy-black in color. Before I was taken off to school, I wanted my ears pierced, but I wanted the tattoos the most. I couldn't wait to get them, as I recall, but tattooing was done on boys only when they reached warrior age. At ten, still six years away from that age, I thought earrings on a man looked stupid and I no longer wanted to be tattooed. What I wanted was my father to take out his earrings and hide his tattoos under a shirt because the sight of his earrings and tattoos embarrassed me. But then, during the time when I was a ten-year-old know-it-all, everything about my father embarrassed me. Especially the way he spoke.

In school, the Osage language had been all but knocked out of my head. It had been replaced with English and a working knowledge of French. When I was home, I demanded my parents speak only English to me. What a little prig. My mother couldn't even speak English, so in order to communicate with me she had to point at something and then look at me questioningly. My father spoke English the same way he spoke Osage, sentences back to front. I knew better than to try to correct him, but I did roll my eyes and sigh heavily while he did his best to comply with my asinine edict. He should have slapped me naked and hid my clothes, but he was a gentle man; raising his hand against a child was not his way. Because of my surly nature, my mother became shy around me. When I came home for that last summer of my childhood, my father tried to spare her my irritating company as much as possible. That was the reason I went with him on that steaming hot day to round up stray cattle.

That morning I was given the task of saddling the two horses. It was not even seven in the morning and already the day was heating up. There wasn't one cloud in the sky, and the sun was all over me like a suffocating blanket. A stubborn little cuss, I was wearing jeans and my legs were frying inside them. If I'd had a working brain in my head, I would have dressed for the weather, but I was too proud to give my father the small satisfaction of heeding his advice. Besides, I felt I was obliging him enough going without a shirt and wearing moccasins instead of my school boots.

Finally, naked as a flea except for the breechcloth and moccasins, he came out of the house carrying a cloth bundle containing our lunch and our day's ration of water in a battered canteen. Without a word to me he threw his long leg over the horse and then there he was, sitting in the saddle, tying the lunch bundle to the horn, then draping the canteen strap over the bundle. His being able to mount a horse without using stirrups was quite a sight, but then, my father was almost six feet seven. He didn't use stirrups when he rode either. They weren't long enough, so in a time before my living memory, he'd cut the stirrups off. As I was growing like a weed, I remember sitting there, staring at him, feeling confident that by next summer I would be cutting my stirrups off too, and that when I did, I would be superior to my father in every way. No bones about it, when I was ten I had to be just about the biggest little gonad ever to draw a breath.

Regret is a hard thing to live with, Everett. It's worse than guilt, worse than hate, twelve times worse than unrequited love. I have three regrets. Two of those are the thoughts I harbored for my father and for the way I treated him on the very last day of his life. Oh, sure, I've got a bucketload of guilt where Emma and each of my sons are concerned, but I know in my heart that if I had to do it all over again, I wouldn't change a thing. But just the thought of my father fills me with such deep regret that I drown in it. If I could have that man back for just one minute, one measly minute, I would throw my arms around him and beg him to forgive me. But I can't because there isn't enough money in the world to buy even a minute from God. He owns time, He calls all the shots. And that's fair. Once He gave me for free all the time I needed to tell my father that I loved him, that I was proud of him. It's hardly God's fault that I frittered those precious moments away.

My father took off at a gallop, leaving me to follow behind. That mare I rode had a butt-busting and brain-jarring trot. For a good part of the morning I was all alone, following the tracks my father left for me. It was getting up to noon when I finally spotted him. Well, actually, I found his horse first. It was tied to a scrub bush and munching grass. Dismounting, I tied my horse next to it and climbed the hill. My father was already on top, lying on his stomach, watching something on the other side of the hill. Hearing my approach, he hand-signaled for me to get down, so I did, low-crawling the remaining distance until I was beside him. Then my eyes almost bugged out of my head. My father had been watching his stray head of cattle being rustled by three rough-looking cowboys.

Charlie felt a tremor of fear as his father began to rise.

"No!"

Eagle's Feather looked to his side, gratified by the worry plainly apparent on his son's face. "Be well in heart, Bear Chief. Me come back."

"No! We ought to tell the Major."

Eagle's Feather sent his son a wan smile. "Eagle's Feather land, this. Bear Chief land, this." Pointing to the cowboys, he said. "Him give me cow, go away land."

In my heart I know there was nothing I could do but lie on the flat of my stomach, grip and tear at blades of grass, and watch as my unarmed father descended the knoll, waving his long arms over his head to attract the drovers' attention. Lucklessly, he gained it. More than gut instinct told me that those three trespassers were dangerous. I could read, and thanks to the newspapers Père Blanc subscribed to and then passed on to us boys when he was finished with them, I knew all about the steady rise of outlaws in the Territory. My father, stuck off on his own for ninety percent of his time, wasn't fully aware of this new encroachment.

Outlawry in Indian Territory was reaching its zenith. Murders, rapes, town shootups, bank robberies, bush-wackings, were everyday occurrences. The Jameses, the Starrs, and the Youngers were the principal desperadoes, and for the most part they stayed in the southern area of Cherokee country. What my father failed to realize was that hundreds of lesser outlaws, all vying for their share of notoriety, were meaner, more deadly, and they were moving north. As the law chased them, Hanging Judge Parker's officers in particular, these outlaws were journeying more and more "up the Osage," as the newspapers phrased it, finding safe haven in the outposts of Tulsey Town, as Tulsa was then called, and Catoosa.

Tulsey Town was a wide-open cattle town, but Catoosa was simply an open door into hell with no other ambitions. If a man had so much as a decent toe bone, he didn't last a day in Catoosa. And according to the fiery editorials I'd read, neither town was overly fussy about bills of ownership for the cattle loaded onto the trains destined for St. Louis. The cowboys my father hailed were heading in the direction of Tulsey

Town and Catoosa. Realizing this, every blood cell in my body froze. Just as I opened my mouth to shout, call my father back, the cowboys drew out their pistols and "got the drop," as newspapers phrased it, on him.

A lump the size of Kansas formed in my throat. I couldn't even whisper, let alone shout around it. All I could do was watch as my father raised his hands and tried to reason with that trio of scum.

Charlie heard one of the outlaws say, "Let's get him in the brush!" The cattle-rustling temporarily forgotten, Eagle's Feather was shoved toward a stand of elders and cottonwoods.

Low-crawling backward until he was certain he would not be seen, Charlie ran to the base of the hillock, sliding the last few yards on his side until he was in a dry-wash gulley. Running the gully in a crouch, he made for the tree-sheltered area where the men had taken his father. He ducked low behind scrub trees as the men were tying his father between two strong trees. Next they began hauling Eagle's Feather off his feet, leaving him to dangle about a foot off the ground. One of the outlaws, his back turned toward Charlie, squatted directly under Eagle's Feather. Charlie couldn't see exactly what the squatting outlaw was doing, but he heard his father yelling. He knew his father's words were for him, not his captors.

"Land belong me. Never sell! Never."

"We don't want your damn land, ya idiot," a standing outlaw jeered.

"Hey!" the kneeling outlaw yelled. "He almost kicked me in the head."

The leader of the outlaws took a riding quirt and lashed Eagle's Feather across the back. Making no sound, not even a grunt, Eagle's Feather flinched with each strike.

"Never sell land!" Eagle's Feather shouted. "Promise!"

"I promise," Charlie whispered as he sobbed.

"Go away. Go fast!"

"What in the hell's he squawlin' about?"

The outlaw came around and then used the quirt across

Eagle's Feather's face. "We'll go when we're good an' damn ready." Then, turning to the crouching outlaw, he barked. "Get that fire lit so's we can get the hell out of here."

Knowing his father was about to die, Charlie panicked.

He couldn't remember how he had gotten out of his hiding place without being seen or heard. None of that mattered anymore. He had, and now he was running. Running for the horses, running away from his father's screams. He stumbled, crawled for several dozen inches, righted himself, and carried on running, his toes inside the summer moccasins being stabbed by the sharp rocks as he kicked back loose gravel and dust behind him in his sprint to where the horses were tied.

His father's screams were distant, but they filled all of Charlie's hearing. And then there were shots. Five, six, seven shots. Charlie pulled up short, stood still, sweat running in rivulets down his heaving chest and back. His ears strained, but all that met him was silence.

A tiny cry escaped Charlie's throat. He hared off, running for all he was worth, his heart thudding dangerously in his chest as he ran and ran. He saw the waiting horses, but unable to stop, he passed them by. He ran for another mile, not caring where, as tears flooded his eyes, flew away from him as he vainly tried to outrun the horror of his father's murder, tried to outdistance a memory which would be, for the remainder of his life, inescapable.

Everett took a deep breath. Took another. He closed the cover of the tablet.

"Well . . . damn."

Handling it as if the writing pad were fine china, he set it on the sidetable, leaned forward in the recliner, pulling himself into an upright position. He remained still for few minutes, then rose and walked to the kitchen.

The disengaged receiver beeped its fury. Everett

cleared the line, and drawing a card from his shirt pocket, dialed the printed number. After six rings a voice answered.

"Mr. Johnston?" He had no idea which Johnston he was speaking to, but at that point either would do. "Yeah, this is Everett Jakomin." Everett cleared his throat noisily. "I know I said I'd get back to you tomorrow morning, but I'd appreciate it if I could have just a little more time."

Johnston launched himself into a lengthy harangue about the wake being scheduled for the evening of day after tomorrow, going on to say that Mrs. Jones's house staff were seeing to the details, coordinating same with the Johnston brothers. The upshot of the conversation was that the mortician said he could comfortably wait until the evening of the wake for Everett's final instructions regarding the funeral itself.

Ending the call, Everett went back to his recliner and sat staring at nothing for a very long time.

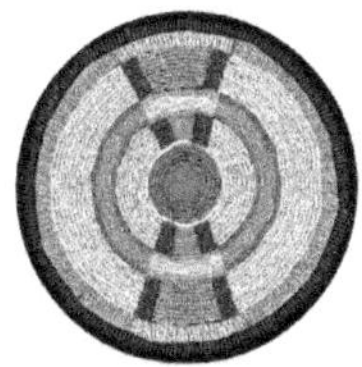

CHAPTER ELEVEN

Everett couldn't bring himself to read the second journal. Journal number one had been more than enough. But neither could he sleep. Instead, he sat out on the back screened-in porch, rocking in a ladder-back rocking chair, listening to the sounds of the night, watching the blinks of courting fireflies. It was midnight when he remembered the parched bedding plants. It was one in the morning when he finally got off his duff and left the porch to fulfill his promise.

And that was how his son Nath found him.

Everett was so preoccupied with his thoughts and his given task of watering the plants and the lawn that he didn't notice the twin beams of headlights briefly catching him in the glare. Nor did he hear the car pull into the drive, or the car door as it opened and shut with a thunk. But gradually he became aware of the tall masculine form beside him and recognized that shadowy figure as his son. The two stood quietly together as Everett continued to spray the shrubs and flowers.

"Your mama planted all of this."

"I know, Dad."

Everett, sidestepping closer to his son, continued spraying the beds. "I swear, that woman could make rocks grow. Anything she planted took off like a rocket. I've always had a real job clipping it all back to stop the bushes from taking over the house. It was right after she planted the ivy on the south wall that we saw that movie, *Invasion of the Body Snatchers*. Well, sir, that ivy took off so fast, sealing off the side of the house and climbing up to the roof, that I became convinced that ivy was from outer space. I told her so an' she'd just laughed, sayin' that the ivy had come from Hill Top Nursery, an' then I said, 'Yeah, but the owners of the nursery are out-of-towners. How do we know they really moved here from Oklahoma City? What if they're from Venus? What if they brought a few Venus ivy clippings to Earth with them?' Then one morning," Everett said as he turned off the nozzle, "I woke up and found that damn ivy all over me."

Nath, his hands shoved deep in his jeans pockets, rocked back on his heels in surprise. "You're kidding!"

Everett threw down the hose, and father and son walked toward the back gate of the yard.

"Nope. You know your mama was a practical joker. She went out that particular morning at the crack of dawn, whacked off an armload of ivy, and carefully spread it all over me while I lay in bed sleeping. When I woke up and found myself covered with green and white leaves, I did some serious screaming. And I never watched another scary movie with her again." Closing and locking the gate behind them, he said with a chuckle, "That made two things I wouldn't do with her."

As they approached the back porch, climbed the stairs, and entered through the slightly ajar screened door, Nath asked, "What was the other thing?"

Everett answered in a flat tone. "Fly."

He left Nath to make himself comfortable in one of the rockers while he went into the kitchen and retrieved two bottles of Coke. After popping the caps, he returned to the porch, casually handing his son one of the bottles before seating himself in the other rocker. Both men sat in silence, sipping and rocking. Finally, Nath couldn't stand it anymore.

"When did you and Mama ever fly? I only remember us driving places. Mama would be fanning herself with roadmaps while you were getting us so lost, we needed the state police to find us, and in the meantime your three kids, the only fruits of your loins, were trying to kill each other in the backseat."

Everett dryly said, "And your mama would say"—his voice became falsetto—" 'You children, don't be ugly now. Your daddy's trying to drive.' "

Nath laughed. "Oh, yeah and I remember you yelling, 'Honey! Damm it! Hit 'em! Just hit 'em!' "

Everett tilted the Coke bottle, toasting his son. "To the good times."

Nath clinked his Coke against his father's. Then they were comfortably silent, just sipping and rocking. Sharing memories felt so very good. Especially on a sleepless night.

"Yep," Everett said, breaking the silence. "Those were the days, all right."

"So, when did you and Mama ever fly?"

Everett sat back in the rocker, gazing sightlessly through the haze of the screens and into the pitch beyond.

"It was the year before you were born. Your mama wanted to go to Hollywood and see the movie stars. Especially Roy Rogers. Your mama was secretly in love with old Roy. She used to buy every movie magazine that had him in it. But what really impressed her was the knowledge that he was a good Christian and that he made Dale hang out the family wash just like they were regular people.

"So, to make her fondest wish of meeting Roy Rogers come true, I bought the airplane tickets and we left your brother and sister with your nana." Everett began to rock his chair steadily. "Your mama and I had never flown before. All we knew was that we were supposed to get all dressed up so we could be crammed inside a plane for a few hours. And before we did that, why, your mama had to telephone every member of the family, every friend we had in the world, and even a few minor acquaintances, just to rub it in that we were flying somewhere."

Everett took another drink from the Coke bottle. "Your mama was real good with the bragging part. Worked that telephone day and night, making everybody she could think of jealous. And come the day we went into Tulsa to catch the flight, she looked beautiful. And let me tell you, she pranced around in that airport in what she called her flying outfit, which was an emerald-green suit-dress and matching hat, like a proud queen. But once we were in the plane and the thing jumped into the sky, the thrill of flying left your mother completely."

"We were only in the air five whole minutes when a big fat woman decided she had to go to the toilet. The second your mama caught sight of her waddling up the aisle, your mama started yelling, 'For God's sake, sit down! You're rocking the airplane!' "

Nath's laughter exploded. Everett ignored his son's gales as he continued. "Of course, it was only turbulence, but your mama was convinced that the plane's dippin' and buckin' was all the fat lady's fault. But the thing that really caused her to flip was the old woman dying."

"What?"

"Died, son. A woman died."

"The fat woman? What happened? Did her bladder pop because Mom wouldn't let her go to the toilet?"

Everett laughed out loud. "No, Nath. Try to keep up. The fat lady was fine. She was mad at your mama for embarrassing her, but otherwise she was fine. It was a little old woman who died. Bless her heart, she was in her seventies and was on her way to California, to see her great-grandchildren. Anyway"—Everett finished off his Coke and set the bottle down next to the rocker—"she was slightly deaf and she was sitting on the opposite side of the aisle from us and beside a young man who was half crazy because he was going to California to get married. He looked as if he had been drinking for about a week and hadn't slept during any of it. He didn't like sitting next to a little old deaf lady who was yelling at him about what a lucky young man he was. That marriage was a blessing from God. He didn't impress me as someone all that eager to get blessed. When he couldn't take her yelling conversation anymore, the stewardess allowed him to move up to a seat closer to the front. The stewardess didn't want to do that at first, but she gave in because the guy was begging to get some sleep an' he wasn't going to get any sitting next to a woman intent on making conversation at the top of her lungs.

"He wasn't gone for more than a half an hour, your mama was recovering nicely from the fact that the fat woman wasn't moving and the ride was getting smoother, when lo and behold, the stewardess discovers that the little old lady wasn't sleeping, but stone dead.

"It was all I could do to keep your mama calm while the cabin crew dragged the old lady out of her seat and up the aisle to the galley. The old lady was hidden, except for her feet, which, unfortunately, sort of stuck out from behind the galley wall. I tried to keep your mama distracted from the poor old soul's feet by praying with her through every mile we traveled.

"But after a while, it started to get time for the stewardesses to serve lunch. Well, they couldn't really do that with a body lying on the galley floor, so they hauled her away, and wouldn't you know, they set her next to the nervous bridegroom, who was by then sound asleep.

"We got our lunch, but halfway through it there came the most god-awful yelling. The bridegroom had woken up and found himself sitting next to a stiffening corpse. He responded bravely to this by tearing through the plane screaming his guts up.

"As you might imagine, that ended lunch. The plane made an emergency landing in Phoenix to remove the old lady, but your mama insisted that we get off too. Right behind us was the fat lady and the scared groom. I don't know whatever happened to them, but we took the train back to Tulsa. Your mama never got to meet Roy Rogers or exchange laundry tips with Dale like she told everybody she was going to do, but it didn't seem to bother her, because she never mentioned going to California again."

Everett shook his head sorrowfully. "This family always did have sour luck when it came to vacations. Want to hear about the time your mama accidentally blew out every lightbulb in a motel in Texas? I know you don't remember that because that was the vacation when we all went to see the Alamo and you were only three years old."

"Daddy!" Nath yelled, the knees of his long legs touching his chest as he sat doubled up with laughter. "Please quit. I can't take any more!"

Disinclined to show Nath any mercy, Everett droned on. "We had to slip out during the dead of night before the manager realized we'd been illegally cooking in our room and your mama's electric skillet had overloaded his circuits. When we snuck out, there was just one lone pitiful bulb burning over the vacancy sign. I never did get my egg she'd been cooking. In a panic she flushed it down the commode to get rid of the evidence. Oh, yeah, and your brother Bobby almost started a race riot because when we finally got to the Alamo it seemed like every Mexican in Texas was in line with us and then Bobby yelled, 'Hey, Dad! Looks like Davy Crockett's still gonna havta put up a pretty good fight.' "

Nath had pitched forward, out of the rocker, and now lay belly-down on the porch, making strangled noises. When he finally went quiet, Everett said, "Let's go in the house, son. I'll make some fresh coffee and we can talk about what's keeping us both so wide awake at almost three o'clock in the morning."

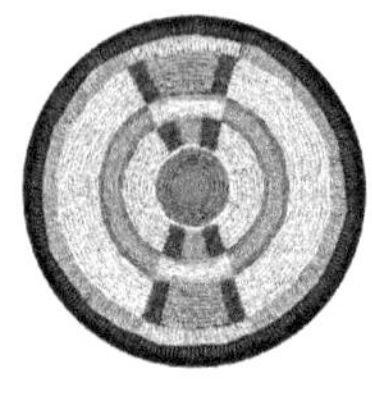

CHAPTER TWELVE

Nath took a seat at the kitchen table while his father stood at the work counter filling the old-fashioned coffeepot. Even though his father sold electric percolators in his hardware store, personally, he had little use for them. He claimed percolators made weak, tinny-tasting coffee. Nath watched his father and felt both amusement and pride. His father was a good father. The best. Nath loved him.

And he loved this house. He loved it for its peace and security. Mostly he loved it because of all the memories contained within these walls. In this house he had learned to walk and talk. In the driveway and then the fronting street he had learned to ride a bicycle. In due time his father had taught him how to drive a car. In this very kitchen his mother always waited for him to come home from school. And when he did, he'd sit at the table and enjoy the snack she had ready and waiting.

In this house he had fought with his brother Robert, teased his sister Martha—calling her MarthaMartyMae, his young idea of a beautiful name, saying it all in one breath over and over until Martha burst into tears, pleading for him to stop. When he wouldn't, because younger brothers are like sharks on the trail of blood when it comes to sibling torment, Martha ran to Mama begging, "Mama make him stop! Make him stop!"

She did. With one look. That look was known in the family as Mama Means Business. She didn't use her special look often, but when she did, the A-bomb had nothing on Mama. But unlike the A-bomb, which made a lot of noise, Mama was quietly deadly. And extremely polite.

"Please, Nath, go to your bedroom and pull your toy box into the hall. Then I would appreciate it very much if you would go back in your room and read that lovely book, *Treasure Island*. I'll call you when it's all right for you to go outside and play."

Nath gulped noisily. "Will I be in my room for a long, long time, Mama?"

Anna knelt before her youngest son. She adored Nath. He was a smaller version of her Everett. The corner of Nath's cherubic mouth twitched, and she could see the twin reflections of herself in his ebony eyes. Never wanting the image of his mother to be a fearful one, Anna tossed back her shoulder-length beauty-shop-permed dark hair and pushed her smiling face closer to his.

"You won't really be in your room, Nath."

He canted his head to the side. "I won't?"

Anna lovingly touched his round cheek. "No. Not if you're *properly* reading. Whenever someone is *properly* reading, then they can go wherever their imagination takes them. Imagination is a wonderful gift from God, Nath. But it's also like a muscle in your arm. If you don't use it, it won't be strong. Now, teasing your sister and making her cry proved to me that your imagination muscle is very weak. Someone with a strong imagination would be able to think of better ways to amuse himself. So, for your punishment, you will exercise your mind."

"But for how long, Mama?" Nath cried.

Anna smiled again. "I'll leave it to you to tell me."

Going to his room, he had no idea what she meant by that. All he did know was that there was a good possibility he would miss the afternoon baseball game. Then his friends would be mad at him because he played shortstop and he just happened to be the best shortstop in the whole world, and his team was never able to win a game without him. His team losing today would be all his dumb sister's fault.

There was just one thing wrong with Mama's idea for exercising his imagination muscle. Nath hated to read. Reading always made him go to sleep. Perhaps, he decided as he dragged his toy box into the hall, he could play at something quietly and if he was really, really quiet then his mother would *think* he was reading. He eased open the lid of his toy box and had a look inside at his stuff. Every bit of it was noisy, even his yo-yos. They were whistlers. Then he spotted the cardboard box of clay his aunt Libby had given him for Christmas. Nath had never even opened the box. Opening it now, he saw sticks of colored clay individually wrapped in cellophane. Playing with clay would not be noisy. Nath took the box of clay and went into his bedroom, closing the door.

When two hours passed, Anna decided to steal a peek at her son. What she saw amazed her, and in her amazement, she entered, standing behind him as Nath worked at his desk. Feeling her presence, Nath's nimble fingers froze. He remained completely still as Anna knelt down beside his chair, more closely examining the colorful sculpture of a standing warrior.

"This is wonderful, Nathie," she breathed. "Where did you get this idea?"

Feeling there might be hope for his being forgiven for yet another act of disobedience, Nath quickly showed his mother the picture book. "From here, Mama. See?"

Anna examined the printed painting on the page, then looked again at the clay figure. Nath's model was perfect, almost as if the painted warrior had stepped out of the page in the book.

"Oh, Nathie, that imagination muscle of yours has really grown today."

Nath's expression was a question mark. "It has?"

"Yes. This is wonderful."

"But, Mama, I—I was just . . . playing."

Laughing, she kissed the side of her son's head. "That's what imagination is all about, Nathie. It's about flying high and free, playing inside your own mind." Anna stood. "You can go outside now."

Nath lowered his head. "I—I kinda want to finish my warrior."

She rested her hand on top of his head. "Take all the time you need. I'm just going to run into town for a few minutes. I won't be long."

At the five-and-ten, Anna bought Nath three more boxes of clay.

His bedroom was still exactly as he had left it. His old teddy bear was still on his bed and the walls were still decorated with high school pennants. On the shelves and under glass domes to protect them were dozens of his clay sculptures, ones his mother couldn't bear to see him dismantle. Thinking about his mother, he missed her with every fiber of his being. He missed her peaceful, strong nature. He missed the way she just naturally understood things. He could tell her anything and she would listen and nod, understanding the way he felt, sometimes, especially during the confused puberty years, even explaining to him how he felt.

He needed her now. God, how he needed her. His life was a mess, rapidly getting messier. There was no one to turn to now except his father, and his father could be a hard guy to work with during a crisis. Dad had always been the reactionary, while Mom had been the thinker. Knowing this, Nath couldn't help but remember the day his dad had caught him smoking in the garage. Dad had pulled out his belt and was about to apply it to Nath's backside, when his mother came to the rescue.

"Everett," she'd said evenly. "Let Nath go."

The hand holding the belt poised over his head and Nath's squirming body tucked hard against his side, Everett shouted, "I'm gonna wear him out, Anna, and this time you can't stop me."

"I won't," she said. "Not if you promise that after you whip him you'll turn the belt on yourself."

Everett's eyes flew wide. "What are you talking about?"

"I'm talking about you sneaking cigarettes at the store. If you're going to smoke, your son is going to smoke. That's just the way it works, Ev. Sons learn from their fathers, and Nath has learned from you."

"I have never smoked in front of my children!" Everett shouted.

"True, but you have smoked from time to time. We've all smelled it, Ev. The Juicy Fruit chewing gum hasn't fooled anyone, dear."

Wishing again that his mother were there when he needed her a heck of a lot more than he had that day in the garage, Nath sighed deeply. For the past five months, most especially during the last two months, he'd been lying to his father. The reason he was there now in his mother's kitchen was to put an end to the lies. He trembled slightly as he imagined how his father, the reactionary, would take the truth about Hayley.

• • •

Nath met Hayley on the night they each attended a gallery show in Tulsa. It had been a one-man show, and that one man was not Nath. A novice in the art world, Nath used the excuse of the show to put himself out there, let his face be seen, hand out a few business cards to the right people, and to avail himself of the free food from the buffet.

The moment they were introduced by a mutual friend, Nath couldn't take his eyes off Hayley even though she was very rude to him and escaped, taking refuge within a group of young people who interspersed every particle of their conversations with, "Oh, yah." This expression immediately let the inferior masses know that their group was very rich, very eastern-school. But mostly that their group was a closed clique, membership obtained soley by birth.

Even at a glance it was abundantly clear Nathaniel Jakomin did not belong even to the fringe element of Hayley Jones's crowd. It wasn't just their expensive clothing that set them apart, it was their superior manner. And being supremely superior, they looked askance at the very tall, lean young man in the cheap suit and—gad, can you believe it? Long hair tied back!—as Nath continually passed them by. He stopped passing when he heard a young woman standing close to Hayley hoot, "Who does he think he is? Geronimo?"

Despite the damning comment from her friend, Hayley began to eye the young man slinking away. His face was almost too pretty to belong to a man, and the ponytail was, in a word, exciting. She felt her heart flutter when, as he spoke to a couple of other artists, he smiled broadly, then laughed a rich, mellow laugh.

He's beautiful.

At that second she imagined herself in bed with him, lying in his arms, mesmerized as his beautifully formed mouth neared hers. And then all that hair, set free of the band holding it in a queue, falling forward as he looked down at her.

Hot flash!

Feeling as if she were suddenly burning up, Hayley pulled rapidly at the silky bodice of her evening dress. Concerned for the pinkish color and the tiny beads of sweat forming across Hayley's upper lip, her best friend Claudia nudged her.

"I say, Old Crap, are you all right? You look like death on a stick."

Her throat tight, Hayley shook her head. "I think the salmon was off."

Claudia pulled a face. "You're not going to heave or anything, are you? I mean, that's really so offputting when done in public. Especially for the people nibbling like rats at the mushroom pâté."

Hayley fanned her face with the program. "Shut up, Claudia."

Sometime close to midnight, all of Nath's business cards had been handed out to the right people and the buffet of free food had been cleared away. Having no other reason to remain, Nath made for the exit. He was on the sidewalk when he realized that Hayley Jones had followed him out. She made some noise about the salmon and needing air, but the electricity between them was so great that Nath wasn't listening. She didn't retreat as he advanced on her. She didn't flinch or offer a word of protest when he captured her face inside his hands. They stared at each other for a moment, and then he brought his face closer and kissed her. Before either of them knew it, they were necking hard and heavy right there on the street corner.

During the next weeks the romance flourished, changing from unabashed lust into love. Two months ago, love led them into marriage. Although the marriage thing had been completely unplanned. It just happened. Just like everything just happened where Nath and Hayley were concerned.

The day they married, he'd sold a bronze piece to a private buyer and received two thousand dollars. *Two thousand!* He felt rich and invincible as he walked to the car. Inside, Hayley was listening to the radio while she waited. Insanely he proposed within seconds of opening the car door and sliding behind the steering wheel. Just as insanely, Hayley said yes. After that, mutual insanity ruled. Almost as if they were daring each other to be the first to back out, they looked up a justice of the peace in the telephone book, drove to the man's house. Through the standard justice of the peace parlor-wedding ceremony, they were still daring each other. And then suddenly the question of who would back out first was made moot.

They were married.

They had been married for two days when Hayley summoned the nerve to tell her parents she was moving out of her father's home and taking a luxury apartment. When her father blew his top, Hayley tearfully confessed to her mother just why she was moving out. Kelly then became a co-conspirator, soothing Matt's temper. The day Nath moved into the apartment with Hayley, keeping his efficiency apartment as a studio, Kelly was on the telephone to C.R., blubbering for his help.

"Hayley's got herself a fine young man," C.R. said, surprising the whey out of Kelly. "You just stop crying and leave Matt to me."

Two weeks into the new arrangement, Nath and Hayley realized that they liked being married. They liked it a lot. But they knew, too, that they couldn't keep their marriage a secret forever. When the truth hit the fan, the fallout would be nasty.

In a panic, Hayley did what she always did when she was afraid. She ran to her grandfather. She was stunned that he already seemed to know her secret, that her marriage to Nath Jakomin hadn't surprised him one little bit. What he did say was that a combined effort would be needed to bring Matt around. At his bidding, Kelly was again pulled into the loop, and putting their three heads together, they decided it would be best that Hayley's marriage remain a secret until after the excitement of C.R.'s big birthday party. The morning after the party, Hayley again confronted her grandfather. He wasn't looking well, and that worried her even though he reassured her that he was fine, that he had the situation under control. As impatient as she was to have the matter out in the open, completely settled, she had to wait, trust her grandfather a day or two longer. And two hours later she received the call that her much-loved grandfather was dead. Hayley became hysterical with grief and Nath became terrified. With C.R. gone, nothing stood between them and Matt Jones's vengeful wrath.

Just when he thought nothing could possibly get any worse, it did. The Jones family went into a tailspin over the fact that C. R. Jones had made Everett Jakomin the executor of his will. Then the Jones boys began beating the war drum against any human being named Jakomin. Nath could no longer trust Hayley as he had, because when she wasn't walking around like a zombie or curled up in bed weeping her heart out, she was screaming at him. Suddenly being in the apartment with her was like being locked up in a small room with a foaming-at-the-mouth Tasmanian devil. He always knew she had a temper, but man, he'd never suspected just how bad her temper could be!

Next, their lone ally, Kelly Jones, became shaky. Without C.R., it was clear to Nath that Kelly Jones was almost mortally afraid of her husband learning about their daughter's marriage. And after turning to her brother-in-law David, testing the waters so to speak,

Kelly completely lost her cool. From what Nath could gather from the tidbits Hayley slung at him, things were getting even uglier in the mansion. Since C.R.'s death, the entire family had moved in with Mama Jones, and while she lay in her room sedated out of her skull, the rest of the family were going after one another with knives. The only thing keeping them even remotely united was their shared hatred of Everett Jakomin.

What really chapped Nath's lips was that Hayley was siding with her family. Nath knew this for a fact because he'd listened in on the bedroom extension to Hayley's conversation with her brother Chris. She was still on the phone with her brother when Nath came out of the bedroom, marriage certificate in hand. Her voice caught midsentence when he stabbed his finger against the line that read Hayley Jones *Jakomin*. Hayley quickly hung up the phone and then she came after him like a Fury. Nath stood his ground, and the result was the grandmother of all fights. And Hayley packed her bags. He knew she had gone to hole up in the enemy camp, and even though he was still so mad at her, he couldn't see straight, he wanted her back so badly.

He came back to the moment when Everett placed a cup of coffee in front of him and then sat down, the rectangular tabletop the only space between them. Looking at his troubled son, Everett gingerly asked, "Is she pregnant?"

His expression aghast, Nath jumped in the chair. "Hell no!" Then his eyes slew to the corners. *At least I don't think so.*

Calmly, Everett blew on the coffee before venturing a taste.

"I'm glad to hear it. I've been worrying that's what you came to tell me."

Nath fidgeted. *When the hell was her last period?*

Trying desperately to remember, his hands nervously

turned the cup of hot coffee on the table. Staring at the black contents of the cup, Nath cleared his throat. "Daddy . . ."

Everett braced himself. At this age Nath called him Daddy only when things were bad. Very bad.

"Just how much do you hate the Joneses?"

Feeling inexpressibly sad, Everett set his cup down, resting his arms on the table. He studied his son's troubled features for a long time. Then a memory banged through. The memory of Anna coming into the house with baby Nath on her hip.

"You'll never guess what, Ev!" Anna beamed. "Our Nathie has been chosen as a final candidate for the Spring Pow-Wow's Beautiful Baby Contest."

Everett threw a fit. He didn't approve of beauty contests, especially a beauty contest involving his son as a contestant. But Anna wouldn't listen and Nath remained a candidate. And won. The prize had been a professional photograph of Nath and said photograph had been proudly framed and was still hanging over the mantel. Everett was glad he had that photograph. It was all he had left of the baby who had grown up much too fast.

Nath was still waiting for an answer. Haltingly, Everett tried to give him one. "I don't really hate the Joneses. My dad tried to teach me to hate from the time I was a little boy. He was very specific about who to hate. C. R. Jones. For half my life I had no idea why I was supposed to hate him, but living with a man like my father, it was smarter not to ask questions.

"It wasn't long after I came home from boarding school that I met your mother. I thank God every day that she was such a loving and patient person. It's because of her that I don't hate the Joneses, but even she couldn't stop me not liking them. After my father died, it became easier for me to lay any remaining bitterness to rest with him. It would have been left at that if C.R. hadn't started pushing me, forcing me to push back. Then his sons got into it and I felt surrounded. Sometimes I've had to fight them dirty, but I figured, so what. When it's four against one, the one does what he has to do. But what I have never done is defend myself on a personal level. A wise man leaves mud-slinging alone because mud always sticks to the last person to throw it. So anytime one of the Jones boys cut up rough with me, I went after their soft target. Their wallets.

"Using this defense, I've hurt them real bad over the years, and anyone named Jones is slow to forgive anyone who's cost them money. This is why I don't want you running with Matt's daughter. Because of me, Matt Jones will go after you with everything he's got. So as of now, I'm not asking and I'm not begging, I'm telling. Whatever you have to do to get out of this love affair with Hayley Jones, you do it. You do it right now, before it costs you everything you have and everything you ever hope to be. You're not just playing with fire here, Nath. You're playing with molten lava. Believe me, all it'll do is get all over you and burn you to a crisp."

His father's eyes nailed him from across the table. Nath quickly looked away.

"Dad? Can you at least tell me what it is you're doing for C.R.? Everybody knows it's something, and the Jones people are going nuts trying to figure out what it is."

"It's none of their business," Everett said flatly. "It's between me and C.R. And like it or not, this is one time his sons can't jump in the middle."

"Is he giving you all of his money?"

Everett leaned back and laughed. "Well, if he has, I guarantee you one thing. The Jones boys and I will quickly find ourselves fighting the war of the century. Which is another reason I want you in the clear."

Nath lowered his head. He knew when he was

defeated. Everything seemed so hopeless. If C.R. had disinherited his sons, and they fought back the way Nath knew they would, Hayley would never come back to him. Most likely she'd curse the day they'd met and file for a divorce. Everyone seemed to have their own need for revenge lately, so what chance did some poor shmo in love have against all the back-biting and hate? Especially now that Hayley had chosen sides. So why was he there? Why was he even considering telling his father that he was married, when for all intents and purposes the marriage was over!

Suddenly he felt weary beyond his years, a desiccated old man. A pair of lungs as deeply cracked and brittle as a dried mudhole painfully inhaled, exhaled. Feeling his bones turning to powder, Nath stood, said good night to his father. As he left the house, he made plans to move out of the apartment and back into the efficiency studio. It would be better if he simply left on his own, save Hayley the embarrassment of having him forcibly evicted. But just thinking of packing his belongings and voluntarily walking out of Hayley's life hurt so much. And there was no one to hold him, no one to help ease him through this awful emptiness.

Mama? Why did you have to die?

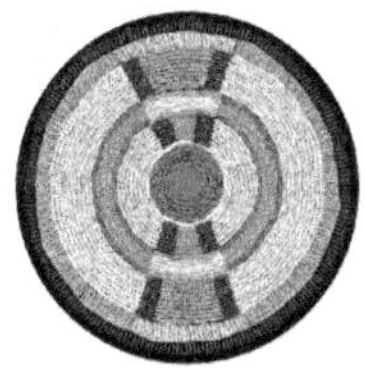

CHAPTER THIRTEEN

In the murky predawn light, Everett stood on the lawn, watching his son reverse out of the drive. Nath, pausing between the necessary change of gears, waved good-bye to his father. Everett raised a hand and held it in place the entire time his son drove away. He was worried about Nath. On a good day, as a kid, Nath'd had trouble locating his own behind even when using both hands and a roadmap. Now he was a grown man, and tonight Nath still seemed lost in a fog. Perhaps it was because he was artistic that common sense eluded him. Or, as in this case, because his thought processes were being victimized by another part of his anatomy. Whatever, it was long past the time for Nath to accept responsibility for himself. The only way Everett could think to help him was to cut off Nath's dependency on fatherly aid. Which would mean Everett learning to say no to Nath.

If you want to be an artist and still pay your rent, then you'll have to do what the other struggling artists are doing. You're going to have to break down and get a part-time job.

Saying no to his youngest son, especially on the issue of money, was hard especially, as even thinking it he could almost hear Anna sucking a long, worry-riddled breath through clenched teeth. But his wife's heavenly worries aside, he felt he'd already made a good start on the no business.

No, you can't go out to play with Hayley Jones anymore. Or words to that effect.

Admittedly, he had spoken to Nath like a child, which was probably the reason Nath clammed up, but in a situation like this, Nath had to be spoken down to. He needed to be taken in hand, told directly that this kind of romantic codswallop hadn't worked for Romeo and Juliet and it most certainly wouldn't work for him.

Everett turned, walked to the front porch. Climbing the steps, he felt a little more at peace with his new plan of cutting Nath financially loose. If anything, Nath's being flat broke would hasten the doom of his liaison with Hayley. By his silence it was abundantly clear that Nath was reluctant to follow the direct order he'd been issued. To be blunt, Everett wasn't inclined to trust his son to obey. But once Nath's living-expense money dried up, Miss Hayley Jones would be in for a shock. Her playmate's free time would be gobbled up by his needing to wash dishes or pump gas. Everett could trust Nath to work at mindless menial jobs in order to survive, saving his best mental and physical efforts for his art. Anyone really knowing Nath would expect nothing less. All of his young adult life *everything* had taken second place to Nath's art. Once the bloom was off the romantic rose, Hayley would find herself waiting for Nath more than she actually saw Nath. As socially active as Miss Hayley Jones was, sitting around waiting for a forgetful lover to call would not be endured for very long. Everett prayed Hayley would quickly realize that she would always come in second to Nath's true love and hopefully before Matt learned of his daughter's escapade with the enemy's son.

Thinking about Matt going after Nath, purposely ruining his son's life and career simply because he'd dare to love Princess Hayley, a circle of burning rage formed at the top of Everett's brain and rapidly descended, covering his face like a suffocating mask. A cry escaping his lips, Everett fiercely yanked open the screen door and in a popping bang it hit the outer wall. It banged again when it closed behind him.

"Touch my kid," Everett warned, "and I swear . . ." His words trailed off. Standing in the silent living room, a snarl twisted his face as he clenched and unclenched his fists. "Don't even think about hurting Nath. I mean it, Matt. I *really* mean it." What made the moment satisfying was that by his own hand C.R. had given him all the power he would ever need to stomp Matt Jones deep into the ground.

Thank you, C.R.

Nath drove home to an empty apartment. Fully clothed, he fell across the bed. His head swallowed by the downy pillow, he almost didn't hear the bedside telephone ringing. He answered on the third ring.

"Where have you been?" Hayley's whispery voice demanded.

"I went to talk to my dad. Why? What did you think? That I was out rambling with other women?"

"I didn't know what to think," she said acidly. "But I wouldn't put it past you to be with some chippy at a time like this."

"Hey! I love you too. Even if you have spit on my name and left my bed."

"I didn't do anything of the kind."

"Yes, you did, Mrs. Jakomin. And if you're calling at four in the morning just to tell me you want a divorce, *I* wouldn't be surprised."

Hayley began to sob softly. Clutching the phone hard against his ear, Nath sat up.

"Pumpkin? Are you crying?"

"No!"

Nath grinned. "Yes, you are. You're crying because you miss me."

"You are unbelievably conceited, Nath Jakomin."

"Yeah, and I'm something else."

"Oh, really? And just what would that be?"

"Yours. Forever, Hayley."

Silence stretched for several seconds and then Hayley sniffed, "I—I want to come home."

"Pumpkin, come home just as fast as you can."

Everett tried sleeping. He tried very hard. His body was exhausted but his mind wouldn't settle down. Which was understandable, as this had been a highly unusual day, and he, through the whole of it, had overloaded his system with caffeine and nicotine. To make things worse, the night was almost as warm as the day had been. His house did not have air-conditioning. It had only ever had standing floor fans, and normally those were good enough. But not tonight. He couldn't stop sweating, and the salty sweat made every inch of his skin feel itchy.

Frustrated, he beat his pillows into submission, tried a new sleeping position. Then he lay there almost feeling the sun rising as he listened to the end of the crickets' night song. Next would come the birds beginning their morning song. Usually he liked nothing better than sitting on the porch, listening to the end of one and the beginning of the other while enjoying his first cup of coffee. At present he could only imagine the joyful noise of birds pissing him off. But before the crickets quit and the birds began, he raised his head, listening to an extremely loud cricket. One of the insectile singers sounded too close, too loud. And in the closet.

Throwing the light covers away from his body, Everett left the bed.

The closet was dark and cluttered, an environmental condition crickets loved best. This one loved the closet atmosphere so much that it was rubbing its back legs in a happy delirium. The noise stopped immediately when Everett pulled the string switch of the overhead lightbulb. Startled by the light, the cricket tried to hop to a safer haven behind a pair of shoes. That's when Everett spotted it. Sounding a war cry, the great cricket hunt was on, Everett moving around inside the closet in a crouch, the cricket hopping for safety behind shoes and shoeboxes. Finally with a "Gotcha!" Jiminy was trapped beneath Everett's cupped hands. Carefully he maneuvered the cricket until he was able to pick it up, carry it out of the bedroom. On the back porch steps he released the cricket, watched it hop into the cover of bushes without so much as a farewell wave of its antenna.

"That was a big sucker," Everett grunted in a laugh. No longer interested in trying to sleep, Everett went back into the house and retrieved the box containing C.R.'s handwritten memoirs. In the soft morning sunshine streaming in through the kitchen windows, Everett sat at the table, reading.

I just kept running, Everett. I couldn't stop. Natural instincts told me to go home, but the growing guilt and shame of abandoning my father wouldn't let me. I didn't know how I'd ever face my mother, tell her about my father and my cowardice, so I ran in the opposite direction. I hoped my mother would think I had been killed too. It wouldn't have been a small deception. I felt dead, separate from my body, my spirit hovering just above the corporeal part of me that was running. In this state I didn't feel heat, sweat, straining muscles, or fatigue. I felt nothing but my immortal disgrace.

I don't know how long I ran. I was a pretty strong kid and time had lost its meaning. I may have run for a few hours or the entire day. All I do know is that my body ran until it dropped, and then my spirit slammed back inside its mortal cage, and it felt so heavy and confining that I couldn't get up or get out again. Then I was asleep. No, not asleep. Unconscious. There were no dreams, nothing more than a bottomless blackness.

It was dusk, the sky turning deep purple, the clouds on the horizon a darker gray-mauve. Shadows on the ground were deceptive, bushes, rocks appearing to be great holes. The group of four riders riding two abreast slowed their mounts. The only woman in the group spoke, and she was giving the horseman beside her a tongue-lashing.

"Sam, sometimes I cannot believe the way you think. Your brains seem as bent as a dog's hind leg. How can you sit there right next to me an' tell me that you're gonna put our whole nine hundred dollars in a bank?"

"Dammit, Belle, what's wrong with that?"

Belle Starr reined up her horse. Her husband Sam reined up beside her. Sam's two brothers continued riding on ahead. Whenever Sam and Belle fell into fussing, other family members wisely stayed out of their business.

Belle waved a hand as she cried, "For the love of Our Good Christ Almighty, you know how unsafe banks can be."

"Well, the bank I put our money in will be safe, Sugar-Bee," Sam replied with a slight whine. "I'll make certain-sure."

"You big lunkskull. There's a lot of thieves runnin' around lately. They're startin' to ruin the Territory for everybody. Things is gettin' so bad, a helpless woman don't even feel safe enough to sleep in her own bed no more. I'm tellin' you, Sam, you put our hard-earned money in a bank an' you can just

wave it good-bye. Why you'd even want to put it in a bank in the first place is a mystery to me."

" 'Cause Ellis says that bankers are startin' to pay folks for puttin' money in their safes. He says they call it interest. Well, getting more money for my money makes me real interested."

Still stewing, Belle sat back in the saddle. There were times when she felt more like a mother to her near-decade-and-a-half-younger husband than she did his wife. Her tone taking on more patience, she said, "Sam, banks is payin' people money to bank with them because they're losing business. An' the reason they're losing business is because of fellas just like you. Bank robbers. Besides, when you put money in a bank, you gotta be able to tell the bankin' man where you got the money. What you gonna tell him, Love-Cake? That you got nine hundred dollars for selling a herd of horses that weren't even yours to begin with? You gonna admit that, darlin', an' get yourself hung?"

Sam frowned deeply, his lips a pronounced pucker under his nose as he thought over what Belle had said. "Whoa, I didn't know about that part, Belle. I could get myself in a whole lot of trouble."

"Yes, you could, sweet-pie. Besides which, even if you did get away with it, I know sooner or later you'd forget which bank was which and you'd rob your own by mistake. So I'm telling you, the best thing to do is what we've always done. What you need to do is—"

"Hey!!"

Startled by Ellis's shout, Belle and Sam turned their heads in unison.

"Belle!" William's tone was urgent. "We found something. I think you better get over here and give it a look."

Sam and Belle kneed their horses.

All four knelt around the boy's body, Belle's hand at the child's throat feeling the weak pulse.

"This child is tryin' to die," she said sadly.

One of Sam's two brothers asked softly, "Belle? He got a wound or somethin' som'wheres?"

She sat back on her legs, her full skirts acting as a comfortable padding between her bottom and her calves. "Now, how am I supposed to know that? I can't see anything. We're gonna have to build up a fire so's I can look him over proper."

Sam's thumb struck a match. It blazed for a few seconds, enough time for him to see the profile of the child. Then he blew the match out. "No need for none of that, Sugar-Love. This here child just oughtta go ahead an' die."

"Sam Starr," Belle hollered. "Don't make me slap ya now. How can you squat there an' say a boy child should just go on an' die?"

"Belle, this here is a wild Osage's child. It ain't good for nothin'."

"Sometimes you take the rag off the bush, Sam Starr. You just really do. I am not gonna leave this baby out here to die on his own. If he's gonna die, he's gonna do it the way God intended all men oughta die. In a woman's arms. Now, you help me lift him up, an', Ellis! You an' your worthless brother get to makin' up a fire so's I can see a little bit of what I'm doin'."

The next thing I recall was that it was dark and hands were lifting me. I heard voices that sounded a long way off. I do remember realizing that these voices were speaking English. The murdering cowboys had me. I hadn't outrun them. As terrifying as that thought was, I couldn't help myself. I blacked out.

When I woke up again, you can imagine my surprise to find a woman looking down at me. It was still dark, but there was a campfire. And my shivering body was wrapped inside warming blankets. At first the woman peering at me looked orange and old. But not real old. She was what you would call mature. And her looks leaned toward handsome. Not pretty or beautiful: handsome. That's the only word that ever really fit Belle Starr.

Of course I'd heard of her. Everybody in the Territory and half the world had heard of her. She'd already been in more newspapers than any other woman alive, and that includes Annie Oakley, but the newspapers always described Belle Starr as the beautiful, daring outlaw queen. When I read every word, I imagined her as a very young woman with long, flowing hair, wearing beautiful clothes, looking grand and flashy as she sat sidesaddle on a half-wild black stallion.

The real Belle, on first acquaintance, was something of a disappointment. She wore plain dresses that fit her well, kept her thin, graying brown hair pulled back in a tidy bun. Her nose was a bit too turned up and pointy. Her upper lip was thin. Her eyes were widely spaced and a trifle sunken, the surrounding lashes were light-colored and sparse. Her rounded chin had a deep cleft almost as if it had been neatly cut. Put all of this together in your mind and you'll have to agree that there wasn't anything gaudy about Belle Starr. But what I came to learn to love about her was her deep voice and very folksy, no nonsense manner of speaking.

When my eyes were able to focus and I realized that the woman caring for me wasn't a dream, she called back over her shoulder, "Sam. The little chigger's awake." Then to me she said, "You just rest easy, honey-cake. Mama-Belle won't let nobody hurt'cha."

Sam. Belle.

The two names instantly clicked inside my skull, and suddenly I was bright and alert. And what I felt was sheer terror. Those two names carried a long and bloody history in the Territory. But the surname Starr, most especially.

To understand Sam and Belle Starr, you have to know their full background, beginning with old James Starr. Father of Tom Starr. And Tom Starr, Sam's father, was a man legend for death and cruelty.

The Starrs were Cherokee. They came to the Territory around 1836. Came on their own trot, following after Major Ridge. Ridge had signed a treaty with the government agreeing to relocate and give up their home country in the East. Because Ridge complied with the removal policy as set down by Andrew Jackson, his followers weren't treated too badly. That is, if you can believe for a second that having all of their lands, their homes, and their property confiscated and given over to their white neighbors was kindly meant. But as a reward for giving up everything and going peacefully, Ridge's group was taken out in wagons and they were fed while en route to the Territory which was to be their permanent home.

Granted, Ridge saved his people untold physical suffering in the long run, but his signing away Cherokee land without the full vote of the governing council directly defied Cherokee law. Signing a treaty the entire Nation hadn't agreed to carried the death penalty. But Ridge knew that his life scarcely mattered in the balance of things. By signing his name to the document that gave away all of North and South Carolina and a hefty portion of Georgia, he saved his followers from suffering what the holdouts endured on the Trail of Tears, a fate that befell supporters of Chief John Ross. Now there was a group of even bigger holdouts who, during the time Ridge was signing and Ross was accusing Ridge of being a traitor, advocated taking to the mountains. Neither Ridge nor Ross was inclined to listen to them, but that group of Cherokees did take to the hills, and even though bounties were placed on their heads and bounty hunters made a good living for a while, their children and their children's children remained in North Carolina. Eventually they were granted amnesty and have become since known as the Eastern Band. If Ridge and or Ross had listened to this smaller group, perhaps none of the bloody mess that happened within the Cherokee Nation would have happened. But they didn't and it did and this is the way it went.

Ross's half of the Nation was forcibly relocated, finally showing up in the Territory in 1838. Their numbers had been greatly reduced by the forced march and inhuman deprivation. By this time, Ridge's group was well entrenched, having built homes, started farms. When the survivors of Ross's group arrived, Ross shifted the blame of his people's suffering away from himself and onto Ridge. As you might imagine, Ross's people, seeing how well Ridge's people were getting on, quickly agreed with their leader. As Ross's party slowly recovered, tensions were building within the Nation. It got worse when Ross declared that he was the only rightful chief.

Ridge, who had gotten used to being head chief in the Territory, and disinclined to share this power with the come-lately Ross, disagreed. Their power struggle went beyond the walls of the council building, dividing the Nation straight down the middle. Those siding with Ridge were called the Treaty party. Those siding with Ross were called—what else?—the Ross party.

The political posturing turned nasty when Ross declared Ridge an enemy of the Nation for having illegally signed a treaty that as a direct result caused the forceable eviction of the entire Nation from their natural homelands. This charge carried the death penalty, and Ross demanded that Ridge be executed forthwith. To back his play, members of his group promptly assassinated Major Ridge and Ridge's son, John.

Being one of the first followers of Ridge, and the most vocal against Ross, James Starr was duly marked for death too. But old James was foxy. During the subsequent years of killing and revenge-killing that began with Ridge's murder, Ross's posse finally caught up with James Starr in 1847. They finally tracked him to his hideout and shot him down in a hail of bullets as he stood on his own front porch.

By this time, James's son Tom was living a good ten miles from his father's holdings and was the father of a large family of mean-to-the-bone sons. Tom was a huge man. Nearly six foot eight. People used to mistake him for being an Osage because he was so big. And Old Tom was as crazy as a bedbug and as evil-natured as a copperhead snake. As Tom buried his well-shot-up daddy, he vowed there and then to kill ten Rossers for every bullet hole in his father. Which meant a fair amount of killing, because James had thirty-six holes in him.

Even before his father, James Starr, was gunned down, Tom Starr had a black reputation. But after Tom put James in the ground, Tom's reputation turned even blacker. There is a story, a true one, that as Tom burned down a house with a family of Rossers inside it, a little boy belonging to the family escaped the flames. Tom picked that child up and calmly tossed his little body back into the inferno. To his startled henchmen Tom said, "A Rosser is a Rosser no matter the age. And allowed to grow, that boy woulda come lookin' for me."

Now you've got the picture of Tom Starr. Sam's daddy. Belle's father-in-law.

All of this was common knowledge back in my day, but history has a way of becoming glossed over, so I will not be surprised if this is all news to you. For you see, the state of Oklahoma had done everything it can do to bury its wild Territory days. But as this past is a very viable part of my own, responsible for creating the kind of man I would one day become, I do not feel one twinge of remorse of dredging it all up again.

I will, because otherwise my hand will fall off if I try to write it all out for you, skip over the remaining years of the Cherokee Civil War, and then the American Civil War. Hell, I wasn't even born then anyway, so I will now bring you back to Belle: my unlikely deliverer. The lady who saved me from dying at a truly tender age. If only for this act of kindness the woman deserves someone who will write the truth about her. The books and now the movies that have been produced are so obtuse and more often so downright silly that they've caused me to weep.

Belle was born in 1848, in Missouri, as Myra Shirley. She married her first no-good, James C. Reed, in Texas, in the year 1866. By James she had two children. A daughter, Pearl. A son, Eddie. James Reed was what was politely termed a gentleman of the road. Bluntly put, he robbed stagecoaches. And he ran with the Youngers, who in turn hid out quite a bit at Tom Starr's compound. The Youngers were in and out of Tom's place so much, in fact, the goosenecked creek the outlaws had to cross in order to get in to Tom's hideout, Tom named Younger's Bend.

Now, here's where we set the record straight about the men in Belle's life. For a good number of years she was Mrs. Myra Reed. Please do not think for a moment she had no idea what James was up to when he robbed stagecoaches. She did. And she spent money as fast as James could rob it, dressing herself and her children up in fine clothing, living in a nice house, and scaring the living whey out of her neighbors when they muttered disgruntled words about maybe talking to the law. It was through her husband, James, that she eventually met the Youngers and the Starrs. Bear in mind that when she met Tom Starr she was a married woman with two children. When things got hot in Texas, Belle would take her two children and put up on Tom's hospitality. And Tom loved her. As villainous as that old bugger was, he had a real love for the ladies and he had a great sense of humor. Belle's running to him played on his gentlemanly nature, and the antics Belle could get up to kept him laughing.

Sam Starr, Tom's son, was during all of this a mere child of twelve. This fact effectively shooting all to hell and gone the absurd tales concerning Belle's long and torrid romance with Sam, the pair of them supposedly making James a cuckold. Blue Duck, yet another Cherokee outlaw Belle was supposed to have run wild and made free with, was during this time a boy barely in his teens and living with his parents, going by his true name, Bluford Duck. During these post–Civil War days, Bluford was not an outlaw, nor was there, during this period, any woman known as Belle Starr.

Blue Duck's so-called unholy reign of terror didn't even begin until his early twenties, when he made the mistake of stealing a horse. His outlaw career ended just as abruptly. When he finally met Myra, she was by then married to her third husband, Sam Starr, and was widely known as Belle Starr. Belle knew Bluford for about five hot minutes when she consented to pose for a photograph with him. But before the photograph had time to develop, the vigilantes had already taken Blue Duck outside and hanged him for horse-thieving. Every ounce of his infamous notoriety has been based solely on this lone photograph with Belle.

I have never found western movies overly thrilling. Men my age and older lived the Wild West days and every man jack will tell you that the Wild West was not a place anyone would choose to live if given a better choice. The simple, barefaced truth, a thing you will not find in novels or movies, is that more Indians were killed by starvation and cholera than were killed by soldiers. Hunger and disease were the two ingredients responsible for defeating the Nations. As for the Cavalry, a greater number of soldiers died as a result of dysentery than on the glorious field of battle. But no one wants to read about Indians starving to death, and I can't think of anyone who'd pay good money to watch a movie about a troop of soldiers fighting life-threatening cases of the runs, so history, as it actually happened, has, for entertainment's sake, been understandably set aside. But this in no way excuses the muddying of historic lives lived to the full, most especially Belle's.

Anyway, after James Reed's life was cut short by a deputy's bullet, our Belle, still known as Myra, quickly married Bruce Younger. Bruce was Cole Younger's cousin. Legend has Belle and Cole inseparably linked, but this is completely wrong. She only ever fancied Bruce. She told me out of her own mouth that they were married, although no official record of their marriage was ever found.

Belle was the type of woman who never felt the need to lie about anything except her age, which is, after all, a woman's prerogative, not a lie. The Belle I knew was of a forthright temperament; however, I will admit that she was completely incapable of feeling the slightest amount of shame. She told the truth simply because it never occurred to her to lie, and should her truths cause anyone to feel uncomfortable, for the life of her she could not understand their sensitivities. Had she merely shacked up with Bruce Younger for a while, I know the woman would have said so and then laughed her head off when anyone blushed. This is why I have always believed Belle and what she told me in the form of bedtime stories during the nights of the many weeks I lived in her home and in her company. She had been very friendly with Cole, but not as it is commonly recounted, in the biblical sense. Cole was her adviser, her confidant, nothing more. Our Belle was, throughout the whole of her life, strictly a one-man woman. True, she had three husbands, but she was faithful to every one of them. It was not her fault that each died on her, thus sending her on to the next.

According to Belle, one day Bruce Younger simply disappeared. She waited two years for his return. Reports came to her all during her wait that he had been killed, but she waited anyway, hoping the reports would be proved wrong. Then something happened in

Texas. Belle was never clear on just what, but whatever it was, it made her afraid. So afraid that she sent her two children away, separating them, sending Pearl to one sister, Eddie to another relative. That just about killed her. She loved her children and wrote to them every week. Then the trouble in Texas had her on the move and in fear for her very life. A creature of habit, she ran to Tom Starr.

As I said, Tom Starr was very fond of Belle. So fond of her that he wanted her in his family. The only likely candidate was his youngest son, Sam. When Belle finally married Sam, he was twenty-three and she admitted to being thirty-two but was most likely nearer forty. Her marriage certificate said twenty-eight. Her marriage to Sam automatically made her a Cherokee Nation citizen, and so she settled in the Territory for good. Sam was a good-looking son-of-a-buck, not nearly as tall as his father, Tom, but still a good-sized young man. He also had an agreeable baby face that sparked much interest among the local female population. Once he was married to Myra, now known as Belle, she reined him in hard. In those days it was still all right for Cherokee men to have more than one wife, but Belle was not inclined to share.

My guess is Belle was the primary reason Sam didn't turn out to be as mean as his daddy, Tom. Admittedly, like his father, Sam was a thoroughgoing outlaw, but Belle's mothering love softened him enough so that he wasn't quite as nasty as his father and his brothers tended to be. Although Sam did have a hard streak. On the afternoon they found me near death, Sam thought they should leave me and allow nature to take its fatal course. If it hadn't been for Belle, there is no doubt in my mind that Sam would have left me to die. Animosity existed between the Osage and the Cherokee Nations, and it was not unusual for one to kill the other. Osage regarded Cherokees as trespassers and Cherokees regarded Osage as subhuman. To Sam's way of thinking, by allowing me to die he would be doing me a favor.

It was a few days into our acquaintance when I was told that the Starrs, Belle, Sam, and Sam's two brothers, Ellis and William, had found my unconscious little body while making their way home from Catoosa. There, they had just sold a herd of rustled horses. And it was because of those very same horses that a few months later, Sam, and then finally Belle, would be shot dead. Ambushed, their murderers never identified. The mystery of their deaths would spark theories and wild fables, the worst in my mind that Belle was shot down by one or both of her own children. The most laughable theory has Sam shooting Belle for trifling with Cole, and then turning the gun on himself. None of that is true. Sam and Belle died because of a herd of horses. That's the beginning and the end of it.

Everett, as nonsensical as it may seem, the men and women of the Oklahoma Territory could make a whole lot of mischief, rob banks, hold up stages, even murder folks. They could do all of that and still walk around as free as a breeze, but if they took to stealing horses, they had to watch their backs. Horse-stealing was the Territory's one unforgivable crime. A person had to be real certain he or she could defend themselves against all comers before laying hands on someone else's horse. When I met Sam and Belle, the Starrs had been playing loose with the law for a long time. And they had been getting away with it for so long that they felt invulnerable. Which is natural enough when you consider everyone was scared to death of them. I don't believe it ever impressed either one of them that violating the one unforgivable crime would make someone angry enough to stop being afraid. Which is what happened and why Sam and Belle died.

But I don't want to dwell on that. It makes me sad. I

want to tell you now about Sam. Why he became, and remained, my hero, even though because of him I shot and killed two men.

Charlie woke to bright sunshine, his eyes gummy and every fiber of his being shrieking in agony. He sat up slowly and carefully. Two men, rolled up in sleeping blankets, lay a distance away. A third man knelt by the fire, holding a coffeepot, pouring steaming black liquid into a tin cup. Charlie felt something bump his side. Looking fearfully left, he spied Belle Starr. She lay next to him, a blanket pulled up close to her face. She sounded a slight grunt as she stirred in her sleep. The man by the fire looked back in Charlie's direction. He set the coffeepot and the cup down. He made hand signs to Charlie to be quiet and to come to him. Although his abused body protested the activity, Charlie obeyed.

The boy's moccasins were in tatters. His feet looked like expanded sausages on the brink of exploding their encasing skins. He hobbled, pain etching his face with each step as he edged closer to Sam. Sam shook his head sadly. The boy looked to be a manly little fellow, braving his pain without complaint.

Poor li'l ol' chigger, Sam thought. He's a savage Osage. He's better off dead. Belle shoulda just let us leave him.

But to the boy, as Charlie stood as near to Sam Starr as he dared, Sam said, "Sit, kid. Before you drop."

Charlie eased himself to the ground, sitting cross-legged, waiting quietly.

"You want some coffee or some water?"

"Water, please. Sir."

Sam raised an eyebrow. Sir. Unless they were staring down the barrel of his pistol, folks weren't inclined to address Sam Starr as sir. Never mind that the boy was a full-blood Osage, Sam found himself warming to him. He handed the boy a full canteen.

"Don't drink too much too fast," Sam warned. "You'll twist your guts."

"Thank you, sir," Charlie said. Watching Sam Starr warily, he tipped back his head and drank from the canteen.

Charlie was startled by Sam's blurted out question. "Kid, where'd the hell you get such a stupid haircut?"

"S-s-school, sir."

Sam squinted, canting his head. "You runnin' from the school, are ya?"

"No, sir. I'm running from desperadoes."

Sam was perfectly still for a moment, then he threw back his head, braying laughter.

Sam was still talking to Charlie and frying thick slabs of bacon when Belle and his older brothers woke. Belle was a bit astonished that her husband and the Osage boy were sitting side by side, speaking in low, serious tones, but she didn't disturb them as she prepared a pan of corn bread to go with the bacon. Then Sam called to his two brothers.

"William, Ellis, come over here an' listen to this."

Belle kept a mother's eye on the situation as she mixed the corn bread batter. All three Starrs were listening intently to the Osage child. Belle could tell that the boy was feeling safer in their company, but whatever he was saying was hard for him to tell. When he lowered his head, began to cry, Belle joined the group, sitting herself down behind the boy, wrapping her arms around him. Her hand against the side of his face, she held his head against her breasts.

"It's all right, little sugar-muffin. Everything's all right."

Fortified by Belle's comfort, Charlie struggled to continue the horrible tale. When he finished, the Starrs silently stared at each other. After an interminable amount of time, Belle turned Charlie, holding his upper arms firmly in her hands.

"Little soul, I want you to think very hard and describe each one of those cowboys."

Charlie remained mute. Not because he couldn't describe them. He could. Too easily. Their hated images were all too clear. He was afraid to describe them and the Starrs understood why. A common dread in all Native American cultures is that to speak evil is to summon it. Charlie did not want those three bad persons to come and harm his new friends. By maintaining his silence, he was protecting the Starrs.

But Belle was the only non-Indian in the group. She did not understand, nor did she have any patience with Charlie's silence. Shaking him, she yelled in his face, "Love-cake, open your mouth an' tell us what those hombres look like."

Charlie sent Sam a pleading look. It was then that Sam Starr made the first move in capturing Charlie's reverence. He placed a firm hand on the boy's shoulder and said, "It's safe. We will be safe. No harm will ever come to any of us because of you. I promise. You just tell me everything you can remember. Don't leave one thing out."

Belle's hands released him as Charlie turned away from her and spoke somberly to Sam. He described each man in detail—height, weight, color of hair, even the patterns made by sweat and dirt staining their clothing. When he was finished, Sam had all three men as locked in his mind as they were in the boy's.

Then that appeared to be the end of it. All four Starrs seemed to dismiss the discussion completely as they settled down to eat their morning meal. Following breakfast, Charlie feeling as full as a tick, tried not to cry or flinch while Belle tended his swollen, abraded feet. While she was busily engaged, Sam and his brothers saddled their horses.

Charlie glanced fearfully at the Outlaw Queen. "Where they going?"

"They got a little errand to run," she answered crisply. "Don't you be worrin' about them. You jest try not to wiggle so much. I can't hep ya proper if you're gonna worm around like a flibbertigibbet."

The three Starrs rode away, Sam turning in the saddle, smiling and waving to Charlie. "Hold the camp, Chigger. Don't let no bad boys mess with my woman."

That was a long, hot day, Everett, but that's not the reason it stays so vividly in my mind. It stays because of Belle, because she fascinated me so much. And the more I got to know her, the more I realized that the exciting tales the tabloids made up about her paled a thousand times over in the presence of the genuine Belle Starr. The male Starrs were gone the whole day. I was not stupid. I did not pester Belle further as to their whereabouts. Besides, I was still struggling with my father's death. One minute I believed it. The next, I didn't.

Late in the afternoon, Belle and I gathered wood for the camp. She had my feet all bound up and I was able to walk a little more comfortably. She'd pinned a dainty hat onto her head, making her look more like a Sunday-school teacher than an outlaw queen. As we gathered wood, I talked to her in a way I had not talked to anyone before, nor, for that matter, since. Writing this journal for you to read is the closest I have ever come to confiding my fears and sorrows to another person since that day.

When I started crying, begging her to take me back to my father because I was certain by then that he might still be alive, I'll never forget how she looked. She stood there in that well-tailored long, dark dress with that prim hat on her head, holding twisted sticks of wood in her arms. As she looked at me, her expression softened and her eyes misted.

"Honey-cake," she said in a low, teary voice. "Your pap is dead."

She dropped the load of kindling and I hobbled to her. She held me, stroking the back of my head while I clung to her, blubbering all over her skirts.

In 1941 I went into Tulsa, all by myself, to see a movie, just because of its title: *Belle Starr* - The Bandit Queen. It was in full color and starred Randolph Scott as Cole Younger and Gene Tierney as Belle. Gene Tierney was a pretty woman. And she looked even better in Technicolor. But she wasn't a patch on the real Belle standing in the full white-yellow blaze of the prairie sun, her arms opened to a hurting, frightened little boy.

Charlie had finally learned all the words to the song "Shall We Gather at the River," and sang along with Belle as they sat on a blanket facing each other. The hot day was at last cooling slightly, and the sky a panorama of sunset's brilliant colors. Their combined voices began to fade as the thudding hooves of horses were heard.

In small stages Belle turned at the waist and faced the distant riders. The words of the song were beginning to fade from her voice as she calmly picked up the six-shooter lying by her side. Shielding her eyes with one hand, cocking back the hammer of the pistol with the other, Belle was still half muttering the song as she waited. Charlie's heart did not beat again until he heard her emit a sigh and then ease the hammer down. The riders coming up in at an easy lope were the Starrs, and Belle stood and broadly waved her husband and brothers-in-law into the camp.

Behind the Starrs were two men on foot. They were roped around the waist and they staggered from exhaustion. From the look of them, they had been struggling to keep pace with the three horsemen for a lot of miles. Instantly recognizing the two men, Charlie jumped to his injured feet. As the three riders and their two struggling prisoners neared, Charlie could feel himself turning to stone. Meanwhile, yelling her head off, Belle advanced on the returning Starrs.

"Dammit, Sam! The child said there were three of 'em."

Dismounting, Sam replied with a half laugh. "There were, woman. But I had to plug one to convince these here two that comin' with us was a fine idea."

Still in a huff, Belle left her husband, walking to the two men who lay collapsed in a pile, one on top of the other. She kicked at one, then the next. There was no response from either.

"These're lookin' kinda dead too." Whirling, her skirts fanning slightly and brushing up dust, Belle cried disgust-

edly, "Dammit all to hell, Sam! I told you I wanted 'em for the boy!"

Sam approached her, chucking her lightly under the chin. Inclining his head, he kissed her frowning lips. "They'll be fit enough come mornin'. But right now, woman, me an' the brothers could use some food an' coffee. Quit yellin' at me an' make yourself useful."

As sunlight faded and the campfire quickly became the only light source, the Starrs ignored their prisoners. The only one even vaguely aware of their presence was Charlie. He couldn't stop staring at them. As darkness swallowed their forms, he continued to stare, acutely aware of the nearness of his father's murderers. He didn't hear the conversation around the campfire, he heard only the two killers, their breathing, their occasional stirring. Although the Starrs had rolled up in their blankets and were soundly asleep, Charlie sat throughout the night. Staring. On guard. The heavy pistol Sam had given him clutched tightly in his hands.

Come the murky gray light of predawn, Charlie was numb to all emotions except consuming hate. Sam woke, left his bedroll, and walking past Charlie, tapped the boy lightly on the head.

"Come on, (pronounced own) Chigger."

Wordlessly, Charlie rose, tagging after the long-legged Cherokee outlaw.

Charlie carefully set the gun down as he and Sam Starr stood, watering the same blades of buffalo grass. Hearing Sam chortle, Charlie twisted his head, looked up. Sam looked down at him, chuckling louder.

"That's a hell of a third leg you're growin' yourself, little hoss."

Charlie's cheeks darkened with embarrassment. He wished he could stop peeing and hide himself, but his bladder was emptying itself in a forceful stream. With Sam adding to the noise, the combined sound was impressive, like the steady drum of a urinating bull buffalo. Charlie had no choice but to endure Sam's good-natured teasing.

"Best not let Belle see that. Otherwise, she'll have you when you grow up the way she latched on to me." Sam laughed again. "You're lookin' kinda scared. That does you credit. Belle's got a fearsome appetite for lovin'. It put the two men before me in the ground. I suspect she left 'em too weak to duck when the law shot at 'em."

He laughed harder as he adjusted himself inside his jeans. Waiting while Charlie struggled to button his trousers, Sam said, "Belle's the kinda woman that when she loves a man she loves him mightily. You might want to remember that before you just haul out an' let fly in front of her." He winked and clicked his tongue. "You could be next, Chigger."

Hastily picking up the six-shooter, Charlie scrambled after Sam Starr as the outlaw ambled off. Sam Starr was a man quickly becoming, and the man who would remain, Charlie's lifetime hero. Primarily because Sam had come into his young life when he was most susceptible. He'd just newly lost his father, but in reality, Charlie had felt fatherless for quite a while, blaming Eagle's Feather for the beatings, the rough treatment, and the loneliness he'd endured at the school. The blaming began on the occasion of Charlie's first home visit. Certain his father would save him, he told Eagle's Feather of his misery. All Eagle's Feather had done was shake his head sadly and say, "That's the way of it."

The Cherokees have almost the same fatalist expression. During their time together, Charlie heard Sam Starr say it as a matter of course, but because Sam said it in Cherokee— S-gi-dv nu-s-di *"That's the way it is"—for nearly half his life, Charlie had no idea what it was he was hearing, or because he idolized Sam and tossed the expression around in the same manner, what he was repeating.*

But now there was Sam. Sam, who was strong and dangerous. Sam, who was not afraid of anything or anyone. Sam, who had gone after three murdering men without a flicker of concern. This was the bravest thing Charlie felt he had ever witnessed, and he could not think of anything better than growing up to be exactly like Sam Starr.

Panting as he half ran to keep up, Charlie asked, "How come you call me Chigger?"

Sam stopped, looking down at the boy. He didn't miss the hero-worship radiating from the boy's dark eyes.

"First, kid, you tell me what a chigger is."

With a slight lift of his shoulders, Charlie replied, "It's just a little red bug."

Sam smiled broadly. "That's right. An' so are you. You're just a wild little Osage. A chigger. Me, I'm from a civilized nation. Now you know your place, kid."

Charlie lowered his head. Looking back up at Sam, he asked worriedly, "Does being a chigger make me a bad person?"

"Depends."

"On what?"

"On how bad you wanna be. As long as you got that"—Sam Starr pointed to the pistol Charlie held against his chest—"it's down to you to decide when bein' called chigger is all right an' when it ain't. You ever use a gun?"

"No, sir."

"Then we best fix that."

Belle and the others woke to the sounds of shots being fired and Sam cussing.

"Dammit, Charlie! Keep your eyes open. You just wasted another round."

"Did I hit something?"

"Hell no. An' you ain't supposed to hafta ask. When you fire a gun you're supposed to know if you hit or miss. Now, you shoot 'er again. An' if you close your eyes one more time, you're gonna feel my boot connectin' with your chiggery little butt-hole."

Belle and her in-laws ignored the noise as they stirred the camp to life, building up the fire, working to make coffee and cook breakfast. The firing continued, and gradually, Sam's swearing lessened, being replaced by the sounds of whooping laughter. The popping gunshots still sounded as Sam sloped *into the camp and squatted down by his wife, accepting the cup of coffee she poured for him.*

"He's doing well?" Belle asked.

Sam sipped and nodded. Winking to his brothers, he said, "Little Chigger takes to the gun the way a six-legged red bug takes to blood."

Sam and his brothers laughed.

Belle worried her lower lip. "Think he's ready in his heart to—"

"He's ready. Readiest boy-child I ever met." Sam handed her the emptied cup and stood. "You might want to give them fellas some coffee, Belle. It's the last they're ever gonna get."

Charlie could hardly see. Droplets of sweat seeped into his eyes, the salt stinging and blurring his vision. He blinked rapidly to clear them as Sam Starr crouched behind him, droning softly in his ear. Charlie held the gun in both hands, his arms straight, elbows locked. His feet were wide apart in the shootist's stance Sam had taught him. Still, the barrel of the gun trembled as Charlie aimed at one of the two cowboy outlaws standing on his knees. The man's bare head was bent to his chest. He wept loudly. Charlie maintained his aim on the target.

"Is he the one, Charlie?" Sam said against his ear. "Is he the one that started the fire under your daddy's feet?"

Charlie flinched at the memory. Slowly, he nodded. He was terrified knowing exactly what Sam Starr expected him to do. Because of his mounting terror, his entire body was soggy with sweat. The palms of his hands were so damp that the heavy gun was slippery. Keeping it steady in his hands required considerable effort.

"I know you're feelin' scared, Charlie, but look at him. Look at him an' remember your daddy screaming. Look at him an' remember the way he laughed at your daddy. He ain't laughin' now though, is he?"

Charlie's answer was a throaty growl. "No."

"Why ain't he laughin', Charlie?"

" 'Cause I got a gun."

"That's right," Sam snickered. "Ooooh, scary, scary. Little Chigger's got a gun, so now Mr. Bad Man's boo-hooin'. But you can make him laugh again, Charlie. All you gotta do is put the gun down an' walk off like a baby, an' that piece of trash is gonna laugh. He's gonna laugh at you an' he's gonna keep on laughin' about what he did to your daddy. You want that, Charlie? You always want to hear your daddy screamin' while the man who made him scream is livin' good an' laughin'?"

Charlie felt his hatred treble. A cooling breeze came from nowhere, magically drying the sweat on his face, his body. In a hardened voice Charlie answered, "No."

The breeze turned into a wind. The wind whipped at Charlie's hair, his clothing. Peripherally, Charlie saw Belle standing in front of her two brothers-in-law. The wind caught Belle's skirts, billowing them back behind her, flattening the front against her legs. Belle steadied the prim hat on her head, holding it by the brim with one hand. She said not one word. She watched Charlie.

And waited.

But Sam's voice became stronger.

"Your daddy's blood is calling to you, Charlie. You can either prove yourself to be a man, revenge your daddy, or you can spend the rest of your life as Charlie the Chigger. 'Cause that's all you'll ever be if you don't do it, Charlie. You'll just be a little no-account red bug for folks to step on."

"I ain't no damn chigger!" Charlie yelled at the top of his voice.

"Who you yellin' at, Charlie?"

"Him! I'm yellin' at him!"

Sam's voice dropped to a hissing whisper, "Why?"

In an uncontrollable rage, Charlie yelled more loudly, "You killed my daddy! You killed my daddy, you rotten go-to-hell bastard!"

Sam nudged Charlie's spine. "Get him, kid."

His eyes wide open, Charlie fired. The bullet struck in the center of his target's abdomen and the cowboy fell to the side, screaming as his body bucked in spasms. His screams were as terrible as the screams trapped inside Charlie's mind. The killer's identical screams fueled further rage. To stop the screaming, Charlie fired again and again as he ran toward the downed man.

The second cowboy, knowing he was next, began to scream. His terror merely served to draw Charlie's attention and he fired, the bullet striking the man's left shoulder. Now both cowboys were writhing on the ground, yelling and bleeding. Charlie wanted them to shut up. Wanted them to stop twitching. Standing between them, he fired back and forth between them until the gun clicked. It clicked five more times before Belle reached him. Instead of pulling the boy away, she handed him a fresh gun. His features just as twisted as his emotional state, Charlie snatched the gun from her hand and fired until it, too, merely clicked. Only then did Belle take the boy to her, hold him against her even though his balled fists beat at her hips as he continued to rage, his cries muffled in the thickness of her skirts.

Brother William stooped, retrieving the spent pistols lying on the ground. Brother Ellis's booted foot toed one of the downed cowboys. Looking back over his shoulder at his younger brother, Sam, Ellis said, "I do believe these here boys have gone to their reward."

Sam lifted his hat, adjusting it on his head, the brim shading his eyes from the beating sun. "Best make certain-sure, Ellis. The kid was firin' kinda wild."

Needing precious little prompting, Ellis unholstered his revolver and shot each thoroughly holed and bloody man neatly between the eyes. Resting the smoking barrel of the gun against his shoulder, again Ellis looked at Sam. "She's done."

Everett removed his glasses, rubbed his grainy eyes with his thumb and forefinger. He was mentally and physically spent. Playing the forced role of C.R.'s confessor was a grueling business. Almost as a fleeting thought he remembered what he'd said as he drove away from C.R.'s palace.

I don't care about the sad story of your life. . . .

Everett wasn't so certain anymore. What he was certain of was that he needed a shower and some food. The shower was taken care of in a matter of minutes. He felt somewhat refreshed as he dressed, but not enough to handle cooking. Then, too, he didn't want to be alone.

Without a second's hesitation he drove to his home away from home, Katie's Steak 'N' Spuds. The food there was always good, but the company was better. The company being the café's petite owner. Katie O'Malley Little Hill was half Osage, half Irish, a divorcée who from the time she was twenty-five ran her own business and raised two daughters all by herself. Everett thought the world of Katie. His feelings for her had slowly developed beyond friendship, but he was determined Katie would never know. He didn't want to embarrass her.

The café was air-conditioned as well as being equipped with six slowly turning paddle fans, evenly spaced along the ceiling. The cooled air felt good. Especially as outside the temperature was over ninety degrees and the humidity factor somewhere around eighty percent. On days such as this, those unable to afford anything more that oscillating fans tended to linger inside businesses that were air-conditioned. Everett's air-conditioned supply store always did its best business during the dog days of summer, so it hardly surprised him to find Katie's air-conditioned café packed to the rafters. Standing near the counter, he scanned the restaurant. Three waitresses bustled around, serving, taking orders. Katie usually stood at the register, either taking money or greeting her customers. Today she was absent from her post.

As one harried waitress darted by, Everett lifted his chin and called out to her. There are some people who go through their entire lives with a single expression. Some wear a perpetual frown, others a silly grin. Maybelle's expression announced that life was wearing her down to a frazzle, and she always looked in a hurry even when she was standing still.

"Hey, Maybelle? Did Katie stay home today?"

The young woman brushed long tendrils of dampened hair away from her face. Maybelle was a young mother struggling to support herself and her babies because her husband had decided to take a hike. Women in that predicament always found work with Katie.

"She's in the kitchen, Ev. On the phone, screamin' at one of her girls."

Feeling relieved, a smile curved his lips. "Which one?"

"The one with the no-good boyfriend." Maybelle took another impatient swipe at the dark brown hair hanging across her right eye. "Ev, I hope you're not in a big rush to eat. We've run out of tables and folks are taking their own sweet time over their food."

Everett laughed. "Don't upset yourself, May. I'll go in the kitchen and beg a piece of cheese or something."

A grin thinned Maybelle's lips. She wondered if Everett realized how transparent he was. Probably not. Before scurrying off, Maybelle said, "Well, I'm sure you remember where the kitchen is."

"Yes, I do."

Everett shouldered his way through a group of diners standing at the counter, waiting to pay their bills. Maybelle dashed for the register, and her nimble fingers were flying over the keys as he entered the kitchen through the swinging door.

Katie stood on the other side of the large kitchen,

talking on the wall phone, one finger plugging her ear to block the noise of the shouting and pot-banging the cooks made. He stood there for a brief moment, looking at Katie's backside.

She wore her usual faded jeans, white T-shirt, and cowboy boots. Her long black hair, still without a trace of gray, was tied behind her in a single braid. In jeans, Katie had the nicest little backside in town. Half the attraction of her café was the treat of watching Katie walk away from a table. Forcing his gaze from her rump, he went to the coffee urn, grabbed a still-warm-from-the-washer cup.

Filled cup in hand, he meandered over to Katie, leaned against the wall. He felt a rustle of excitement when he gained a fleeting dark-eyed glance from Katie and she smiled faintly. Then she was yelling again into the phone.

"*No!* That's unacceptable, Gem. I don't care if you are nineteen, you still live in your mama's house. I lay in bed just as wide eyed as an owl until two in the morning. I was still wide awake when you managed to wander in at two-thirty."

She listened, then fired back, "Yeah, I knew you were at Ed's party, but knowing that didn't mean I could just close my eyes and go to sleep."

She listened again for about a second. "I'll tell you why not. What if you left the party early, what if, while you're driving home you got a flat or something? You know yourself Ed wouldn't think to call me to let me know you're on your way home even if God spoke to him out of a burning bush and told him to do it. So Ed would be thinking that you're home safe while I'm thinkin' you're with him. But the whole time we're both thinking two different things, you're stuck in a broken-down car and a rapist is trying to crowbar you out!"

She stopped yelling long enough to listen. Everett fought the urge to laugh. The bizarre twists of Katie

Little Hill's mind never failed to entertain him. He wasn't alone.

"Stop laughing, Gemma!" Katie shouted. "An' listen to this." She was completely silent for a split second. "That was the sound of your mama *not* laughing. Now, you hear me good, little girl. One more stunt like last night an' you'll find yourself looking for somewhere else to live, and don't give me any more garbage about how Ed's promised he'll take care of you. If I've told you once, I've told you a thousand times, Ed's got all he can do taking care of Ed. I will never understand how you think you can count on a man whose one brag is that he filled out an unemployment form correctly!

"As of this morning, *your* life has come down to two choices. You're either going to college in September, or you're slingin' steaks for your mama. I mean it, Gemma. I've had all I'm gonna take off you. It just burns my liver that nineteen years ago I paid good money to a doctor to deliver me a baby daughter who would respect and obey her mama. I'm half a mind to march myself right back to that man and demand a refund. Or even better, maybe I'll just sue him for malpractice. Now, that's all I got to say to you, Gemma Little Hill. Except for this. Do the laundry!"

Katie slammed the phone down, and from the corner of her glittering eyes, she threatened Everett. "You so much as grin and I'll hurt you."

Everett pressed his lips together as he raised a hand in surrender. Making a disgusted sound in her throat, Katie steamrolled past him. Quickly setting the cup on the drainer of the stainless steel sinks, he bolted after her, following her out to the open concrete back porch. He reached her just as she was sitting down on the edge of the porch. Directly behind her were open vegetable crates and standing burlap bags filled with potatoes. As Everett sat down beside her, Katie ignored him. Waiting for her temper to settle, they sat in silence, their legs hanging over the edge, Everett swinging his feet in small circles.

"Give me a cigarette, Ev," she finally said. Everett lit two cigarettes and passed one to her. Katie took it, her high temper still evident as she smoked.

"Kara has never given me one tap of trouble," she said more to herself than to Everett. "That kid makes straight A's and wouldn't have a boyfriend if one fell out of the sky and landed on her. With my luck, she'll probably grow up to be a nun, go off to some god-forsaken country an' die of a peculiar disease nobody ever heard of until they named the thing, karaitus.

"But I'll still have my Gemma. She'll be alive and well an' poppin' out baby after baby from that good-for-nothing Ed Redland and then she'll wag every last one of them home to me."

Everett could no longer contain it. He was rocking with laughter when Katie punched his arm and yelled over his racket. "I'm glad you think this is so funny. I haven't had any sleep, I've been working since six this morning, and that flea-brained daughter of mine has been laid up in bed nearly the whole livelong day!"

Everett apologized and did his best to sympathize. It was not difficult. Because of Nath, he was also minus a night's sleep. Had he known Katie was awake, he might have called her.

Might have.

"I was wide awake because of one of my kids too."

Katie looked at him, her finely formed features softening. Katie was raised Osage. Except for her legendary Irish temper, she knew nothing about being Irish. And being an Osage, she waited for Everett, not pressing him, allowing him to speak in his own good time.

Five minutes of companionable silence passed, and then Everett said, "I found out yesterday that Nath has been running around with Hayley Jones."

Katie gasped sharply. "Oh, my God, Ev. As if you weren't having enough trouble with the Joneses."

He glanced at her. "You know about that too, do ya¿"

Katie waved a limp hand. "Everett, think about it. This is Olla. I knew just about everything there was to know five minutes after you and Matt Jones left together for the funeral home. And I've got to tell you, I wasn't lying awake worrying about just Gemma last night. A lot of my worrying was for you. But in the cold light of day it's handier to blame Gemma. Does that make me an unfit mother¿"

Everett grinned from ear to ear.

Katie lightly slapped his arm. "Now tell me some stuff I don't know. Tell me how you found out about Nath running around with Matt Jones's girl."

Everett's grin withered, his expression and his tone turning sour. "She practically told me herself when I went to the house."

"Whose house¿"

"C.R.'s."

Katie jumped with excitement. "You've been inside C. R. Jones's house!"

"Yeah. Yesterday afternoon. I went there to talk to Mrs. Jones. I met the whole fam-damnily. An' let me tell you, that's some group. Count yourself lucky that you've missed them as customers."

Katie pushed her face close to his. "I'll have you know, Everett Jakomin, that Mrs. David Jones just happens to love my chicken salad sandwiches. She gets chicken salad on a roll to go every time she comes in this town."

"Well, good for her. But none of the others have ever trotted their butts in here, have they¿"

Katie glared at him. "Are you trying to rub that in my face¿"

"No. I'm just trying to make you see how completely tasteless and arrogant those people are!"

"Oh."

"Can we talk about something else now?"

"No." Then, seeing his forlorn expression, Katie laughed, shaking her head, the single braid moving across her spine like a windshield wiper blade. "Oh, all right, Mr. Everett. Don't pout. We'll talk about something else if you really want to."

Everett brightened.

Until she verbally knee-capped him. "I guess you know that for two years I've been waiting for you to ask me out."

Everett soundlessly gasped, then could do little else beyond gape.

Even when Anna had been alive, Katie had a crush on Everett. After Anna's death, Katie waited through his year of grieving, then waited two more years. She wouldn't be saying anything now if she weren't exhausted. When Katie was *really* tired, the repress button in her brain became stuck. It was undeniably stuck now. So stuck that she thought it was wildly funny that Everett was sitting there looking all set to fly off as fast as a scalded turkey buzzard. She put her hand on his arm to keep him grounded.

"Ev, you don't have to look so scared. I'm just talking about us having supper. It's not like we've never eaten together before. I'd just like for us to eat someplace else for a change. And I'd like to do that tonight."

"But you're tired!" he panicked.

"Oh, please. I'm just tired of my kids."

Everett swallowed with great difficulty. "Well—I—uh—have something I have to do for C.R. an'—uh—I kind of have to—"

"Do what?"

"Uh—read."

"*Read!* What does he want you to read?"

"That part's a secret."

Katie moved closer. "I won't tell anybody."

He felt himself drowning in her eyes. His head spinning, he gripped the concrete edge to prevent himself from falling off the porch. "I really can't tell you, Katie. I shouldn't have even said that much."

She moved closer, sitting so close that every time he breathed, he inhaled her. Katie Little Hill's womanly musk was emphasized by the combination of cooking odors and a splash of a delicately flowered cologne. In Everett's opinion, there wasn't anything sexier than a beautiful woman who could cook. And this beautiful woman was pinning him with her eyes the way a collector pins a rare butterfly.

"Tell me," she said in a low tone.

"No. I can't. I swore I wouldn't."

Katie screwed her face up. "Everett Jakomin, you just—"

"Fry your liver."

"Yes, you do. And like it or not, I'm coming to your house around seven *with* our supper. Have you got that?"

His eyes wide with wonder, Everett nodded.

"Good."

She jumped to her booted feet and marched away, entering the kitchen. In a mild stupor, Everett listened as Katie yelled at the cooks. Then suddenly she was standing behind the screen door, yelling at him.

"Did you want a steak sandwich or not?"

"Yes."

"To go?"

"Yes, please."

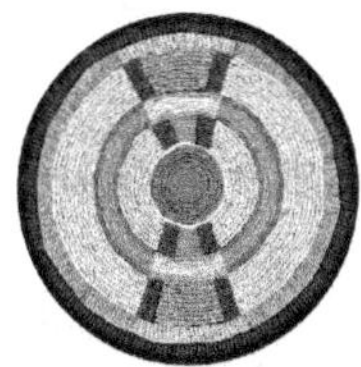

CHAPTER FOURTEEN

Eating the steak sandwich without tasting a single bite of it, Everett drove for home and in the process broke all speed laws. Buddy Williams, the local speed buster, sat in his cruiser, his face behind a magazine. His head bobbed up as Everett's car whipped by. Recognizing the red Corvette and knowing Everett Jakomin to be a motorist who received more warnings about driving too slow, especially through town, where Everett was prone to stop the car in the middle of the street and have a chat with folks on the sidewalk, Buddy did not key the ignition or press the siren button. Instead, he watched the red sports car become a distant spot as he chewed the inside of his cheek.

"Gotta be haulin' butt because of the Jones business. Can't think of one thing else that'd make Everett Jakomin move so damn fast."

Shaking his head, Buddy went back to the *Playboy* magazine, thumbing to his second favorite section, the Unabashed Dictionary page. He liked the jokes but mostly he liked the pen and ink drawings of the little semi-nude Femline, wishing there really were such things and that he could have one.

Everett Jakomin's major breach of Oklahoma law was completely forgotten as Buddy thumbed the magazine and lost himself dreaming of having his very own little Femline.

Everett hit the kitchen in a dead run. He didn't stop running until he reached the utility closet, pulling out the vacuum cleaner and assorted cleaning supplies. His house wasn't really a mess, but then neither was it *woman clean*. Having been a married man for nearly half his life, Everett knew the difference between comfortably tidy and woman clean. In a woman-clean house a man's nostrils were continually assaulted. Bathrooms and kitchen smelled of bleach while the living room and bedrooms ponged of lemon furniture wax. And everything existing under the roof was shiny. Even the children. Everett had a lot of work ahead of him if he hoped to wipe away three years of bachelor living before Katie turned up.

Around four the physical activity and lack of sleep had worn him down. He collapsed, sprawling on the couch. Before he could defend himself from it, a nap grabbed him. He dreamed about Katie. Kissing Katie. He was thoroughly enjoying the kiss, when Anna was suddenly there. Feeling like an adulterer caught in the act, he released his hold on Katie and with a sad expression, Katie disappeared.

Turning to face his wife, he felt awash with guilt. Anna smiled as she came to stand beside him, her hand reaching up to lightly stroke his worried forehead. She looked so pretty. So Anna. The way she looked before the sickness, before her death. He was thrilled to pieces that she wasn't wearing the dress she'd been buried in. She was wearing, instead, a simple cotton dress. A dress that would look all right should she have to answer the doorbell. Dresses too good to wear every day she called her Sunday clothes, and Sunday clothes required garter belts, stockings, and slips. Day dresses had no such needs, and her shoes were typically a pair of scuffed loafers. Looking down, he felt himself grin. She was wearing the loafers too. Anna slipped her hand in his and he held on to it very tightly as he gazed down at her precious face.

Anna always considered herself plain primarily because she never wore makeup and quietly envied women who did. But she could never get the hang of makeup, not even lipstick, and the one time she'd tried plucking her brows it had been so painful that it put her off ever trying again. Her hair was her one and only vanity. Anna liked to go the hairdresser to have her hair cut and permed. Her dream was that her dark hair would be made to look like Elizabeth Taylor's.

"*It's time, Ev,*" she said softly.

"Time for what?"

"*For you to be happy again.*"

"I am happy."

Anna shook her head, sighed, withdrawing her hand despite Everett's best effort to hold onto her.

I have to go.

NO!

Yes, Everett. I have to leave and you must let me go. Completely.

"Anna!"

Everett woke with a start. Shaken, he sat up, wiping his tear-streaked face with his hands. A gentle breeze came through the open windows, ruffling the gauzy sheers hanging between the heavier curtains. Otherwise, the house was still.

He remained on the couch for a very long time, remembering Anna the way she really was, practical and yet a die-hard romantic. How many times had he known her to play matchmaker? Too many times to count. It used to drive him crazy, but she ignored him on the issue because she just could not stand the thought of anyone being alone, unloved. That thought led to the next, a thought he hadn't ever considered, the thought of how his being alone for three years must have made Anna feel. Now, like a frightened sparrow chick being forced out of the nest by its mother, he felt Anna pushing him. Pushing him toward . . .

Katie.

Anna would approve of Katie because when she was alive she had more than approved of Katie. She even admired her. Admired her for her business skills, admired her for the way she single-handedly raised two daughters. But Anna admired her even more because she knew Katie to be a very good person.

"There isn't a man in this town who wouldn't fall down happy if Katie Little Hill looked at him twice, but she won't do it. And do you know why, Ev?"

"Nope."

"Because she has her heart set on someone special."

Everett felt himself grow cold inside. That conversation had taken place in the hospital days after they had been given Anna's prognosis. Of course, everyone in Olla knew the results almost immediately, and not knowing what else to do, Katie had sent a big box of freshly made Cowboy Cookies to the hospital via messenger. Anna loved Cowboy Cookies beyond an obsession. And because the cookies were so time-consuming to make, Anna showed her appreciation by eating each cookie in tiny bites. She had been doing exactly that when she talked to him about Katie Little Hill. Still in emotional shambles caused by Anna's prognosis, all the small talk she was attempting to make flew right over his head.

Until now.

Katie's image flashed inside his brain. His heart began to pound rapidly. Katie was coming at seven.

Quickly he glanced at the carriage clock on the mantel. Quarter to six. Everett leapt from the couch.

He took his second shower of the day, this time shampooing his hair until it squeaked. He dressed in his best tan trousers and a pale turquoise short-sleeve shirt. He hastily shoved sockless feet into brown loafers. He still had five minutes. Five precious minutes to calm down and look cool and relaxed before Katie turned up. Then the doorbell sounded. Everett forgot calm and cool in a breakneck run for the door. A happy grin was on his face as he opened it.

And Nath stood there.

Everett's grin died.

"I brought pizza," Nath said, showing the flat, grease-soaked container. Nath was ecstatic now that Hayley was home, that she had chosen him over her family. Now it was his turn to make the same commitment. Nath was there to tell his father the truth and let the chips fall where they may. But doing the dreaded deed over a pizza might give him a needed edge. How loud could his father yell with his mouth full?

Everett tried to block his son's entrance, tell him that now was not a good time, but Nath was a young man on a mission. He barely noticed his father's bulk as he barged on through. Just inside the house, Nath paused, his chin level with his shoulder as he studied his father. Everett's expression was a worried frown as he closed the front door.

"Dad! Are you wearing some of Mom's perfume?"

Everett gasped sharply, then yelled, "No, I am not! If you must know, I'm wearing a new aftershave that I got as a sample in the mail. I think it smells so great, I might even buy myself a bottle of it."

Nath barked a laugh. "Dad, how great can an after-shave be if they're sending samples to Indians?" Before his father could answer, Nath looked away and said, "The old homestead's looking pretty good." Nath's eyes narrowed. "Wait a minute. You're smelling like a flower and now I see that the house is all clean. Dad? You wanna tell me what's going on?"

Everett began to squirm. The doorbell rang.

Nath and Everett stood as if bolted to the wall-to-wall carpeting.

The bell sounded again.

Nath said, as if issuing a dare, "Why don't I get it?"

"No!"

Nath and Everett both moved for the door, Everett muscling his son out only because Nath was hampered by the hot pizza box in his hands. But he could hover just behind, which is what Nath did, his eyes widening in shocked surprise.

Even for Katie Little Hill, she looked gorgeous. Instead of her customary jeans, she was wearing a sleeveless blue sundress. The boots were gone, replaced by white flats. And she was wearing makeup. Not a lot. Just enough to be serious. Only her hair looked the same, brushed away from her face, tied into a single braid that extended to her small waist.

"For a minute there," Katie said as she breezed in, shoving two grocery bags into Everett's limp arms, "I thought you had changed your mind about having me over for supper. I even imagined you crawling around on the floor pretending you weren't home." She smiled broadly at Nath. "Hi, Nath! Gosh, I haven't seen you in ages."

Nath closed his hanging mouth. "I—I've been kind of busy." Then he looked meaningfully at his father. "Dad, could I see you in the kitchen. Please."

Shifting the two paper bags in his arms, Everett sighed. "Take a seat, Katie. I'll be right with you."

Setting the bags of groceries on the counter, Everett's frowning eyes lanced Nath. Tossing the pizza box on the counter beside the bags, Nath frowned right back.

"Talk," Nath demanded. "Tell me just what you think you're doing bringing another woman inside my mama's house."

Everett felt anger rip right through him. "That's not another woman. That's my friend. One of the best friends I've ever had."

Nath lifted a corner of his mouth in a mocking snarl. "Oh, yeah, right. Katie Little Hill, the town fox, is here only because she's friends with my dad."

"That's right."

"That's bull!" Nath shouted.

Steaming, Everett said, "Nathaniel, I have a right to have a woman friend if I want one."

Nath began to wave his arms as he shouted louder. "Fine! Make friends with all the women you want, just don't bring them into my mama's house. And here's another thing. Don't date a woman who's not that much older than your own daughter. It's sick, Dad, and it makes me sick!"

"Now you know how I felt when I heard about you and Hayley Jones."

"Leave Hayley out of this!"

"I will not. It wouldn't surprise me one bit that after you promised me you wouldn't see her anymore, you crawled back into her bed."

"At least I wasn't crawling around with her in my mama's bed!"

It took Everett every ounce of his strength to stop himself from balling his fist and hitting his son in the mouth. Breathing hard, he said, "I would advise you not to say one more word. You're about a hair's-breadth away from getting a whipping. I am still your father, Nathaniel Jakomin, and it's not your place to tell me who I can have as my friend."

Nath's handsome features contorted as he advanced on his father and growled in his face. "And you don't have the right to tell me I can't have Hayley. You've just lost your rights in that department, *Dad*."

"No, I haven't."

"Yes, you have."

"Nathaniel! For your own good, I forbid you to see Hayley Jones."

"You can't forbid squat! Hayley and I are married."

All the blood left Everett's face. "You're what?"

"Married. We've been married for the past two months. And you know something else, Dad? We're staying married. I don't care what you say, and she doesn't care what her father says, we're staying together and there's nothing either one of you can do to stop us."

Everett placed his hands against his face. "Oh, my God."

"Praying isn't going to help," Nath snorted. "If you don't want Hayley, then you can't have me. But don't try blaming Hayley for that either. From the way things seem to be changing around here, you would have lost me anyway. If you're gonna run around with young women, bring them inside my mama's house without worrying how your kids might feel about it, then I don't want you for my father."

Everett straightened and grabbed Nath's arm as Nath turned to go. "Before your righteous anger has you storming out of here, you're going to hear what I've got to say. If you and Hayley are married, then God help you both, because I'm not lifting a finger. And don't you ever, ever, as long as you live, talk to me the way you just did, or I'll mop the floor with you. Anna was my wife long before you were ever born. If you think for five minutes that I'd ever do anything to disgrace her, then, young man, you've got another think comin'. Now, I am telling you for the last time, Katie is my friend. She was also your mama's friend. If you don't like her being in *my* house, then don't let the door hit you in the butt, and don't forget your pizza."

Having heard every word, Katie sat like a piece of

solid stone while Nath slammed out of the house. She glanced at Everett standing in the archway of the dinning room. He looked angry as well as thoroughly embarrassed. Katie softly cleared her throat.

"Since you had a steak sandwich for lunch, I thought for supper we'd have fried chicken."

Helping Katie prepare the meal calmed Everett. Within minutes he was learning the fine art of double-dipping chicken pieces. Beaten eggs and milk in one bowl, seasoned flour in another, Katie walked him through the procedure, first dipping a piece of chicken into the liquid mixture, then placing it into the flour mixture, repeating steps one and two. Easy. But not for Everett. His pieces of chicken came through the process looking so gummy and sad that Katie politely put them aside, saying she would fry those last.

"I think it'll be easier if I just come over every time you crave fried chicken," she teased.

Everett became very still. Then his double-dipped hand purposely touched hers. "You—you'd come?"

Katie looked up at him, her eyes soft and warm. "Yes."

Both looked quickly away. Everett went to the sink, washed the sticky paste from his hands. Speaking over the running water, he said, "I'm sorry about what you heard. I didn't expect Nath to—" Breath left him in a rush when her arms encircled his waist and she rested the side of her face against his back. The water was still running, Everett's hands remained under the flow. He tried to breathe. He felt as clumsy with breathing as he had felt handling the chicken pieces.

"It's all right, Ev," she said. "I got an earful from my kids too."

Both her girls, Gemma and Kara, hero-worshiped their father. A man who did not deserve one speck of their love. He remembered to call at Christmas, but that was about it. Remembering to call on the girls' birthdays was beyond him. When he called at Christmas, he was vague about where he was, even more vague about what he was doing. Being vague was Mikey's cagy way of avoiding paying Katie money for child support.

Mikey and Katie married in their teens. By their early twenties, their marriage was over. Mikey Little Hill did not like being a husband. He liked even less being the father of two baby girls. What Mikey liked was riding a motorcycle, drinking beer, and staying out all night with his friends. The all-nighters became a series of days and nights. The first few times this happened, Katie made frantic telephone calls trying to find out if her husband was dead or alive. His being away for days on end became routine. Katie's primary concern was that there would be enough food in the house for the children. A few times Mikey went out on a binge, there hadn't been.

During Mikey's final episode, Katie walked the long miles, both babies on her hips, to her father's house. He gave her five dollars and told her that was as much as he was going to help her with, while she stayed living with that no-good. Katie then walked all the way back to the rented trailer she and Mikey called home. With the five dollars she bought milk, bread, and a giant box of cereal. Just enough food to feed her children for the next three days, five, if she didn't eat too. Katie felt isolated, hurt. The next day Mikey came home so hungover, he looked like death warmed up. The first words out of his mouth was that he'd been fired. Then he said he wanted something hot to eat. Katie said she would be happy to fry him up a divorce.

Mikey just looked at her out of bleary eyes for a long while, then he snickered. "Hey, that's great, Suggie. I'll take mine sunny-side up." With that he just went to bed, sleeping for two straight days. While he slept, Katie worried he hadn't understood her about the divorce.

Then she worried that he had understood and didn't give a damn. In both cases, she worried about what she would do. She did not have a high school diploma or marketable skills. Nearing nineteen, her single talent seemed to be her ability to conceive at the drop of a man's britches. This would not help her feed the babies she already had. As difficult as life was with Mikey, she was terrified by the prospect of life without him.

Bone-weary and weepy, she tried to feed her hungry babies the remaining milk and cereal. As near to starvation as they were, they fought the spoon. Until that moment it never occurred to her that even the hungry craved a change in diet. Then she had an ugly vision. A vision of herself worn out and dried up by the age of thirty, surrounded by even more crying children she couldn't feed. That's when she knew that however hard or frightening it seemed, she had to break it off with Mikey. She had to get out while she had only the two children to consider.

She finally heard him moving around in the back of the trailer. Bracing herself for a fight, she went to their cramped bedroom. She didn't know if she was relieved or hurt as she stood in the narrow doorway watching him stuff clothing in the old knapsack he used whenever he went on his biking escapades.

"I'll be out of your hair in a few minutes, Sug," he said casually. "I'll give you a call when I get to where I'm going."

So that was it. Mikey had heard and he'd understood that she wanted a divorce. And he was happy to give her one. That settled, the adrenaline pumping in her system also settled. Calmly, she spoke to Mikey.

"Do you have any money you can give me?"

He stopped packing, looked back over his shoulder, and laughed.

That was the last time she saw Mikey Little Hill. Her children had been raised on the photographs he occasionally sent and the telephone calls he made once a year. The only time she'd ever had a permanent address for him was during the year he lived in Denver. He lived with a woman and he didn't bother to explain their relationship. Not that Katie actually cared. All she needed from Mikey was an address, a place of record to send the reams of paperwork generated by the process of getting a divorce. She had a hunch that it had been his reading the court directive ordering him to pay sixty dollars a month for child support that prompted Mikey to move on.

Katie waited until he was three months delinquent in said child support before calling the Denver number. The woman answering said that Mikey had disappeared, that he owed her money too. Five hundred and forty dollars and sixty-five cents to be exact. Katie wished her luck getting it. The woman wished Katie luck trying to collect child support. Katie thanked her, as she needed luck. She needed it in the worst way. The situation at her parents' house was becoming unbearable. Her mother had taken over her children and her father's vocabulary had dwindled to "I told you so's." She needed a place of her own to raise her children herself, but she had only one skill. She could cook.

The banks didn't view her dexterity with a fry pan as solid collateral. C.R.'s eldest son, Mr. Harry-the-bank-manager Jones, all but threw her bodily out of his bank. But two days later she received a letter from C. R. Jones. The brief letter stated the day and time for a private appointment. Dressed in her nicest clothing, Katie used her father's car and drove to Pawhuska. As soon as she gave her name to the receptionist, she was shown straight in to C. R. Jones's office. The moment his secretary opened the door to his office, C. R. Jones never took his eyes off her. His quiet stare was the most unnerving thing imaginable. Somehow, without tripping and falling down on her face, Katie managed to enter the room and stand before this legendary person. He didn't say a word, merely indicated with his hand the chair beside her quivering form. Happy to relieve her trembling legs of the weight of her body, she took a chair and sat rigidly on it as she faced his desk.

And waited.

Until that moment she had never seen C. R. Jones in the flesh. But like everyone else, she knew that he had once been an outlaw, that he had managed to escape being hung for murder, that he had become a prosperous oil tycoon by nefarious means. He was still considered an outlaw by the Osage Nation. Knowing all about his fierce reputation, Katie expected to meet a man nine feet tall and able to breathe fire and brimstone. The real C. R. Jones came as something of a pleasant shock.

He was a huge man with a gentle voice and he breathed ordinary air. From what she could see of his clothing, as he sat behind his desk, he was impeccably dressed. His features were less than handsome, his face very broad, his cheekbones so high that his eyes were dark crescent-shaped slits. His nose jutted out long and thick. A newly fledged hawk could have landed on C. R. Jones's nose and rested comfortably. His square jawline flared out to meet large ears, further elongated by advancing age. She knew this unnatural bend of the jawline was caused by the erosion of solid bone yielding to the incessant pull of muscle; the signature of a man victimized by the habit of grinding his back teeth.

C. R. Jones was swarthy, his deep coloring at odds with silvery hair cut in an idiosyncratic style. The top of his hair was long enough to brush straight back, but on the sides, from his big ears to the top of his temples, the hair was clipped so closely to the skull that on first glance appeared to be growing out from a recent shave. When he turned his head briefly, Katie's eyes bulged.

Seeing him in profile, seeing the way the crown was neatly swept back all the way to the collar of his shirt, Katie realized what she was seeing was a modern version of the old-fashioned roach cut.

Hearing her slight gasp, C.R. swiveled in his chair, propped his elbows on the desktop, entwined the fingers of his hands together. His grim mouth partially hidden behind his hands, his glittering dark eyes gazed at her. Finally, he untangled his fingers, leaned back in the chair.

"I've heard about your troubles," he began, his tone still gentle. "I've also been made aware of your idea concerning a new café in Olla. Although my son Harry thinks the idea amusing, as far as I'm concerned, Olla could use a good café. It hasn't had one since the war. Every town needs a café, and while I applaud your insight into Olla's need, I can't help but question your ability to manage a new business.

"What I propose is this, I will finance your idea for the standard term of seven years. During that time I will be your very silent partner, handling the business end until I am confident you can take over every aspect of the concern. I will leave the cooking and building of patronage strictly to you, but one leak of our arrangement outside the confines of this office will automatically terminate any agreement and you will then owe me the full sum of the loan, plus nine percent interest. Are we clear?"

Katie could only swallow and nod.

As he filled out a check he said, "I know you're probably aching to ask why I'm doing this." He tore the check out of the large company checkbook, blew the ink dry. Handing the check over, he said the last word he would ever speak to her directly. "Don't."

Katie took C. R. Jones's check and with most of the money bought the dilapidated White Horse Bar. Then she spent what was left gutting the old building, redecorating, and buying the equipment she would need to feed future customers. As agreed, she told no one the truth about how she, a woman without one tap of collateral, had managed to secure such a huge loan. Her father laughed off inquiries, saying his Katie was half Irish and Irish people just didn't understand the word no.

Only Katie knew how far from the truth her father was, because no banker under heaven would have surprised a client the way C.R. surprised her the day before the café opened. She had been busy with the million last-minute details, when a big truck pulled into the red dirt parking lot. She yelled through the locked glass doors at the three men on the other side.

"We're closed. We don't open until tomorrow."

"Yes, ma'am," one man said. "I understand that. We're just deliverin' the sign. We were told we had ta get it installed in your big winda here by this afternoon."

She nervously signed the paper on the clipboard and then just stood back while the three men took over the café. When they left, cursive glowing red neon proclaimed KATIE'S STEAKS 'N' SPUDS. Well into the night Katie stood outside her restaurant, staring at the sign glowing in the center of the plate glass window. Naming the café was something she'd tried to do during all the work and worry of bringing it near completion. She hadn't been able to think of a single name she liked, and wasn't about to spend a nickel on any type of sign until a name hit her as being perfect.

This name *was* perfect. Just as C.R.'s costly and thoughtful gift was perfect. With all of her heart she wanted to call or send a note to her silent partner, but that was impossible. C.R. had set up a special account with the Osage Federal Bank. She could begin repaying the loan as soon as she was financially able, but she could not, under any circumstances or on any level, communicate with C. R. Jones. Filled with a deepening sadness that she would never to be able to properly thank the person who had helped her so much, the glowing sign began to blur as tears welled, then spilled.

To repay C. R. Jones, Katie worked like a dog through the seven years of their secret partnership. During those years she lived in a little one-bedroom rental house. It was only after she had repaid C.R. and their partnership duly ended that she looked into buying her own home. As luck would have it, a three-bedroom house came on the market. The house was a 1930s vintage and the plumbing iffy. Katie bought it for almost a song. Once the expense of replumbing and restoring the house was paid in full, she bought a brand-new car to celebrate the tenth anniversary of her divorce. For the first time in all those ten years, Katie felt happy. Or at least she'd convinced herself mightily that she was happy, convinced herself, too, that she would never again need another man in her life.

And then Anna Jakomin died.

After that, Katie could no longer deny the strong physical attraction she felt for one of her best customers, Everett Jakomin. Patiently she waited through his first year of mourning. Then she waited another two years, hoping he would notice that their friendship could very easily develop into something more. Finally, today it seemed he was becoming blearily aware, and for the remainder of the day Katie had been waltzing on air, only to trip over a horrible bump in a dark cloud.

Mikey's continued hold on her.

Though he wouldn't recognize the children if he passed them on the street, Mikey indirectly put the boot on her first date with Everett. Mikey didn't know it, of course, and would have laughed if told, but the damage he caused could be traced straight back to his Christmas calls to the girls. Calls he'd made in the first years of their separation out of a vague sense of guilt and continued only because the Christmas calls had devolved into a weird tradition. Year after year Mikey talked to his daughters about the day he would return and they would be a family again. Until tonight, as she dressed to be with Everett, it never dawned on her just how much her daughters believed Mikey's Christmas swill. But as she hadn't ever gone out on a date with anyone, their belief that one day they would be a whole family again had never been put to the test. Even in her hindsight their opposition to the fact that she was getting all dressed up to be with a man seemed surreal.

Gemma screamed and cried. Kara ran off to her room in a flood of tears. Evidently she had given them far too much credit for having the good sense to realize that Daddy hadn't done one thing for them since his contribution to their conception. Katie made it her business to knock some of Mikey's crap out of their heads.

"This is the first date I've had since your deadbeat father walked out on us. He's never coming back, and I wouldn't let him in the house even if he did. Every rag on your body, every morsel of food you've ever shoveled into your mouth, you've had because I worked myself into the ground to make sure you had it. And I'll tell you something else, Gemma Little Hill, I'm going on this date with Everett Jakomin because I deserve to have a good time. Now, get your little sorry self out of my way."

Gemma looked as if she'd been kicked in the gut, and from the back bedroom Kara's wailing reached new heights. Resolute in her plan to be with the man she had been yearning after for years, Katie walked out on her girls and straight into Nath. Sitting in Everett's living room, she heard every word of Nath's highly vocal opposition to her presence in his mama's house.

Kids. Ya gotta love 'em. The question is *why*? The only two things kids are good at is worrying the breath out of their parents and popping off their ugly little mouths.

Everett was enjoying the moments of physical contact until he felt her shaking. Suddenly concerned, he turned and her arms fell away. Her head was lowered and she was making small whimpering sounds. His wet hands on her bare arms, he bent at the knees as he tried to look her in the face. Katie raised her head.

"Katie? Please don't cry."

She ran a hand under her nose. "I can't help it. If this lull in the evening is the only part of our first date we'll remember as the fun part, then I think we're in trouble."

For a split second he was stymied, then he laughed, throwing his arms around her, hugging her hard as they laughed together.

Over supper they avoided any mention of their children, concentrating the table talk instead on Olla's score of more colorful characters. Sharing stories, Katie and Everett laughed a lot, the easy companionship they'd shared over the years kicking in. When the meal was finished, Everett placed a floor fan on the back porch. The whir of the fan would stir the muggy air while they enjoyed coffee and strawberry shortcake. While Katie prepared the tray in the kitchen, Everett busily placed the rocking chairs closer together. Then he dashed into the kitchen to carry the heavy tray for her.

"Man, this is good," Everett said, eating the dessert. "I don't know how you always seem to make something so simple taste so special."

"I add a drop of vanilla and a sprinkle of sugar in the cream before I whip it up."

"That's it?"

"That's it. But don't tell anybody. I'll lose business if women start copying me."

"Recipes kind of a cutthroat thing, are they?"

"Yep. Especially when it comes to cobblers. Every

man in this town, including you, Mr. Everett, come into my place even when they're not hungry for a cup of coffee and a bowl of cobbler. You wouldn't believe how many calls I get from wives asking for my recipe. Oh, please, like I'm going to tell them I add a dash of nutmeg to the batter. If they knew that, I'd go broke overnight."

Everett took the empty plate from her, placed it with his on the TV tray table. They sat back in their chairs, rocking, watching the night sky through the porch's screening and listening to the crickets singing over the gentle whirring of the floor fan. In the distance there was a flash in the sky that backlit the edges of swollen clouds.

"That storm will be here in no time at all," Everett said softly. "My lawn's sure going to appreciate the watering."

Katie chuckled. "I noticed it sounded a little crunchy when I walked across it."

His hand slipped away from the armrest of his chair, snaked to the side, covered and then rested on hers.

Katie's heart nervously fluttered. She hoped Everett was working up the nerve to kiss her.

"Katie¿" he said hesitantly. "I need to talk to someone. Someone I can trust not to repeat anything I say in confidence."

You mean the way you used to trust Anna, Katie thought. As lightly as she could, she said, "I trusted you with my recipes, Ev. That's something I wouldn't trust to my own mother."

Everett chuckled deeply in his chest. "I guess you got me there." He was silent for a moment. During the passing of seconds they heard the rumble of thunder and watched lightning brighten the sky in a series of flashes as they held hands and rocked in the chairs. "Something has been bugging the britches off me," he said grimly. "Something to do with C.R. You know I told you he left me some stuff to read?" She nodded. "Well, he left me his memoirs. And here's the spooky part. He wrote them just for me."

"How do you know?"

"Because he talks straight to me, Katie. He throws my name around like he was sitting in the room with me. When I first started reading it, I didn't care about him or his life, but—"

"Now you do."

Everett slumped in the chair. "Yeah."

Katie turned in the chair. "Now I want to tell you a secret, Everett. I met C. R. Jones. He was not the ogre I'd always heard he was. The man I met was a gentle man, a caring man. He helped me when no one else would. His only condition was that I not tell how I got the money to start the café."

"He what!"

"It's true," she said. "And I'll tell you something else. I'd be willing to bet that there are hundreds more around here that he helped. It would be just like him to make each and every one of them swear to the same kind of secrecy he made me swear to."

"Why would he do that?"

"I don't know. But his terms were very clear. If I told anyone, even my parents, the agreement would end and I would be worse off than before."

Everett could think of nothing to say. He could only look at her, his expression thoroughly baffled.

Katie sat forward. "Listen to me, Ev. The C.R. I knew for years was an extremely private person. He wouldn't just trust anyone coming down the pike. If he left me his memoirs, I'd feel privileged. It's all right if you're beginning to have second thoughts about him, even admire him. C. R. Jones was a worthy man. What I will never understand is why he went to extreme lengths to hide that part of himself from the world. And while you're thinking about that, try this. I'll bet his granddaughter is a good person too. She'd have to be for Nath to love her."

Everett scowled. "I don't want to talk about that, Katie. I'm still too mad at Nath."

"Why? Because he married the girl he loved and felt he had to keep it a secret from you? Or because he lost his head because another woman was in his mother's house?"

Everett fidgeted. "Both things."

Katie sat back and rocked her chair. "My goodness, that's a lot to be mad about."

"Yes, it is. I should have decked him."

"Well, I'm glad you didn't. I admire a man who's in control of himself."

Feeling proud, Everett grinned. Then Katie ambushed him.

"What are you going to do to protect Nath and Hayley when Matt goes on a rampage?"

"Not one thing!" he shouted.

Katie laughed softly. "No, really, what are you going to do?"

Humbled, Everett muttered, "Use Matt's own money against him if I have to."

"Good plan, Ev. I like it."

Still defensive, he barked, "Well, even if I can't stand him, Nath is still my kid."

"Yes, he is."

Everett peered at her. "Are you mad at Nath for what he said?"

"Nope. But I really liked the part where you said I would be in your house as much as you wanted me to be."

"Really?"

"Uh-huh. I hope that's a lot, Everett. I don't know how to tell you this except straight out, but I have a crush on you."

"You do?"

"Uh-huh."

They rocked in silence for a few moments, their eyes meeting and holding through the first boom of thunder. Rain began to pour down in a solid sheet, the rapid tattoo of large droplets on the porch roof sounding like hail. Leaning toward each other, they kissed.

His hand tightened on hers. "Katie? Would you like . . . to stay the night?"

"Yes."

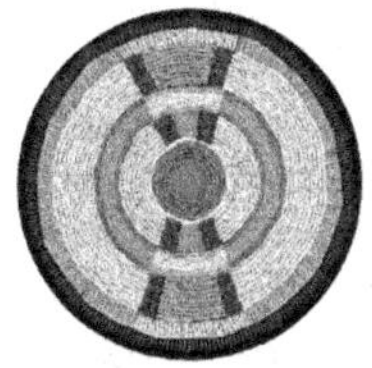

CHAPTER FIFTEEN

The storm dwindled to a steady rain. Everett lay on his side, watching Katie sleep, marveling at her. Making love to her had been the most natural experience, as if they had done so hundreds of times before, each knowing exactly where to touch, how to kiss. And for the first time in four years, he felt whole again, as if a vital piece of his soul had been restored. In the back of his mind he heard Nath's snarling tone, warning him not to take Katie into his mama's bed.

He hadn't.

The big four-poster he'd shared with Anna had been given away to Goodwill before she died. He'd had to give it away. He knew she would never be in that bed again, and being in it without her filled him with an inexpressible grief. So months before she died, he called Goodwill to come and take it. After that, when he wasn't sleeping at the hospital, he slept on the couch. The new bedroom suite, the new bed he now shared with Katie, he'd purchased sometime during his first year of widowerhood. Everett felt completely free of the guilt Nath had tried to ram down his throat. He also knew he would happily and guiltlessly make love to Katie again if she would only wake up. Hope springing eternal, he placed his hand on her bare shoulder. Katie muffled in her sleep and turned on her side, her curled spine facing him as she snuggled her face deeply into the pillow. Everett heaved a saddened sigh. Wide awake, he eased himself out of bed.

In the kitchen he stood in front of the stove, beginning to light the burner under the coffeepot, when Katie's voice yelled inside his head. *"Ev! You drink too much coffee. What's wrong with a little orange juice now and then?"* Everett turned off the gas, went to the refrigerator instead. Then he smiled at the sight of real live honest-to-God leftovers sitting on the shelves of his refrigerator. Now, there was a sight he'd missed without ever realizing it. A woman filled up every part of a man's life. Even his refrigerator. Grinning, Everett grabbed the juice pitcher and poured himself a tall glass. He was tempted to drink the juice, go back to bed, snuggle against Katie, and listen to the rain dancing on the roof, but he could almost feel C.R. patiently waiting for him. Knowing Katie would understand, he went to the living room and his recliner, switched on the table lamp. Picking up the memoirs, Everett found his reading glasses and made himself comfortable.

After shooting down the two men who had been the focus of my entire capacity to fear and hate, I was so drained of life, I entered a catatonic state. Like an animated doll, I stood when told to stand, sat when told to sit, and ate the food given to me with the same vigor. Belle held me a lot, stroked my hair, called me Honey-Muffin, and hummed a variety of gospel songs. I have no idea how long this went on. Retreating into blankness robs a person of time perception. At any rate, I wasn't in a fit state to be alone, and the Starrs had to leave. Feeling responsible for me, they decided to take me with them. Well, actually it was Sam who cast the deciding vote when he picked me up, held my limp form against his waist, and carried me to his horse.

The notorious Starr compound was situated far to the southwestern part of the Territory. It was a long ride and my first time off the Osage reserve. I don't remember the trip, Everett. Unless you're crazy, you don't just gun down two unarmed men and ride off on a three-day tour of the countryside, enjoying the sights. By the second day of travel, my spirit began to rally. The coming back to myself felt like the gradual waking from a dream I couldn't remember. I gave up trying to remember when I realized that I was on a fast-moving horse and tucked safely inside Sam Starr's arms. I wasn't afraid, I felt too safe to be afraid. Sam had powerful arms, and while I was deep inside them I just knew nothing would ever get me. But the minute he realized that I was beginning to rally, he tried to shift me behind him. I kicked up a yelling fuss that tickled the fire out of Belle but embarrassed the stuffing out of Sam. He really got mad, saying that if I wasn't careful I'd grow up to be a nancy. I had no idea what that meant, but it sounded serious. Enough anyway to make me quit squalling while he placed me behind him.

The last day of travel was not an easy ride. The outlaws were on their constant guard and nervous. Their tension made me pretty nervous too, and the heat and humidity of their home country was so high, I could barely breathe and my brains felt like cotton wool. Then we entered a canyon so narrow that the horses had to proceed single file. My fuzzy brain brightened a bit when I saw the posted lookouts from above. They waved down to us, then stood on the ledges with their rifles resting on their shoulders, watching us the whole time it took us to ride through the canyon. That spooked me, Everett. It was solid proof that these outlaws were in hard control of their domain and anyone entering there lived purely by their grace and favor. Now that I was all the way in, I had no idea if they would ever let me out again. As Sam had relaxed somewhat, I put to him the question of my eventual departure. The asking took every bit of guts I had, but I asked.

Sam laughed and said, "Kid, you can leave the day I know you'll be all right by your ownself. Till then, Belle'll appreciate the extra help around the place."

So there it was. As far as Sam was concerned, I could be with them for weeks, months, possibly years. Don't get the idea that the Starrs were interested in nursemaiding a ten-year-old orphan. They weren't. But they did have a skewed sense of responsibility for my continued welfare. Until the day Sam believed I was capable of taking myself home, I could count on a life of being their houseboy servant.

Their house was a complete surprise. The newspapers I'd read had made it seem that the Starrs lived in a huge mansion, that they could afford the best of everything because of their constant thieving. But after meeting the outlaw queen for myself and then seeing her outlaw palace, I learned right then and there how stupid it is to believe solidly in the printed word. Their house was not a mansion. It was a shack. An old, small one-story, mean-looking shack with a sagging covered front porch. Off the back side they'd slapped on a lean-to which was the kitchen. There were two barns and three outbuildings where "guests" could take their ease when visiting.

For three months I lived in the Starrs' house. I slept in the lean-to kitchen, on the floor next to the wood stove. Belle had tried to make the inside of the house as nice as she could. In the parlor, bright calico cloth was pasted onto the walls, concealing gray clapboard, and lacy curtains covered the small framed windows. The wood floors squeaked with every footstep, the sound only faintly muted by braided rugs. The only nice rug was in the parlor. It was what Belle called an Ayrab rug. She said her first husband got it for her.

"Out of the best house in Abilene."

Silly me, until I was nineteen I thought she meant a rich person's house.

The main parlor wall had framed photographs hung in order of the subject's importance. As if each photograph was a breathing person, Belle introduced me to the folks on her wall of fame, beginning with her first husband, James Reed. Everyone was there, her children, Eddie and Pearl, and the Youngers. The largest photograph and given pride of place was an oval, time-smoky image of old Tom Starr. My first days in the house were spent being told the exploits of each and every person in the photographs, and whenever Belle became stuck for detail, she hollered for Sam. That's when I realized Sam was a natural storyteller. Especially when he was on the subject of his daddy. Sam would come into the parlor, making himself comfortable in a chair while I sat at his feet. He took up Belle's dangling thread in the tale and went on from there, literally for hours and with barely a pause for breath. Listening to Sam Starr was a thoroughly mesmerising experience. For a kid, listening to Sam telling true-life stories was a great way to spend the day. His stories sure beat the boogers out of anything the kids of today get out of television sets.

I will, however, have to admit that the evenings in the Starr household leaned dramatically toward the strange. Belle had an old upright piano in the parlor and in her mind a gracious lady passed the evenings with music. So while Sam and the boys were in the kitchen playing poker, betting hard and heavy every ill-gotten dime to their names, Belle had me sitting beside her on the bench while she banged the piano and taught me to sing every song she knew. I wasn't much of a singer, but then, neither was Belle. Our croaky duets would promptly end when our singing grated every last nerve in Sam's body so badly that he started losing at poker. Then in frustration he'd take off one of his boots and fling it at us, typically missing Belle but always managing to hit me squarely in my back. Then Belle would yell at him, "Sam! Why'd you hit this baby?" And he would yell, "Woman, he ain't no baby. An' he ain't no singer either. Why don'tcha send him on in here an' let's see if he can at least play a decent hand of poker."

Believe me, I wanted to go. Belle's gracious musical evenings gave me a headache and I wanted to be with Sam. But Belle would not allow me to learn to play poker. She told me very firmly that poker would corrupt my young soul. Having no idea that her first husband, James Reed, had been a diehard gambler, I was left in amazement that she would view a card game as being more evil than teaching a child to shoot down two men, then allowing this same child to live with notorious outlaws. But that was Belle. Undaunted by Sam's begging her to close the piano lid for the night, she opened up yet another sheet of music and said, "Charlie-Babe, you're gonna like this one." And we would sing. Often under a hail of boots flying in my direction.

The Starrs lived their lives according to Indian time. Meaning they never went to bed until they were sleepy. This could be anywhere around two or three in the morning. Then they'd wake up the next day just whenever they happened to. I was used to living my life according to the school clock, going to bed at eight every night, waking up at five. It took my poor little body a full month to acclimate, and during the acclimation I existed on two or three hours' sleep within a twenty-four-hour time period. I was also used to eating at regular intervals, another thing the Starrs were even more haphazard about than sleeping. This was primarily because the men had to wait for food until Belle felt in the mood to cook, which wasn't often. Finally, out of desperation, I offered my negligible cookery skills. Belle jumped on that idea like a chicken on a June bug, and before I knew it, I was the cook, dishwasher, and laundry boy. In between times, I chopped wood. Let me tell you something, hanging out with outlaws may be every boy's dream, but the reality of it is that it's a lot of grubby work. I quickly learned that it's not only armies that march on their bellies. Outlaws do too. I must have fried five mountains of potatoes and onions and stirred more pots of cooking beans than I ever want to remember. Belle's contribution to the effort was her infamous corn bread, which invariably burned because she wouldn't trust me to touch it, not even to take it out of the oven, and then she'd forget about it until it smoked up the kitchen. In a choking panic I'd yell for her and she'd come running. And she cussed with every step.

"Why didn't you holler sooner?" she'd cry. "I should know better than to let some little toe-rag chile run my kitchen."

I of course was thoroughly contrite and repentant, but Sam and his Merry Men remained unfazed. According to Sam, it was some of the best corn bread Belle had ever made. In between shoveling down beans and potatoes, they simply cracked off the corn bread's blackest bits and buttered up whatever was left. By the time I was finally allowed to crawl onto my pallet, I'd lay there for a spell, wishing like crazy I was back in school, sleeping in my comfortable bed and living my days within the confines of a regimented schedule. It's funny how the little things in life are missed so much almost from the instant they're taken away. When I had been in school my greatest wish had been for unbridled freedom. That wish had been granted. And at age ten I learned my first wise truth.

Unbridled freedom is scary.

But the discomforts of working all day, staying awake half the night and then sleeping on a hard floor, finally gave me the gumption I needed. I turned to Sam. No, actually what I did was I escaped out of the back of the house and I ran to Sam. Just as fast as my little legs would carry me. He'd saved me once from certain death, and I was counting hard on his saving me from Belle's tender mercies—before her brand of mothering killed me.

In the twinkling of Sam's malevolent eye, I was promoted. I turned in my apron, paring knife, and washboard, only to find myself being hoisted aboard a horse Sam described as green-broke, but in truth that plug hadn't been broken green or any other color. What it was was nasty. I was so terrified, my hands were like paralysed claws on the reins. I couldn't have let go for love nor money. I hung on while that animal bucked every brain cell in my head just as loose as a drunken goose. There wasn't a slender hope in hell that I would be rescued, because Sam and the boys sat themselves along the fence railing, laughing and yelling, "Ride 'im, kid! Bust that nag!"

I'm telling you, Everett, after they finally pulled me off that horse, if I had been able to draw my legs together, I would have walked myself all the way home. But my little legs were so bowed out that my feet were turned in and I was standing on my ankles. I was so tired that night, I curled up under the kitchen table and passed out, oblivious to the card game being played over my head, the booted feet nudging my body, and the singing and piano-banging racket Belle was making in the parlor. In spite of all the noise, I went immediately to sleep and stayed asleep until the next morning, when Sam dragged me out by my ankles from underneath the table.

"Got a few more horses, kid," he laughed.

Sick with fear, my clawed hands scraped the floorboards and I kicked and screamed. That's when Sam's hand whacked my tender behind. That smack hurt so bad, tears sprang to my eyes. Sam didn't appear to notice I was crying as he stood me to my feet.

"Listen to me, kid," he said, his voice flat and intimidating. "In this outfit a man rides till he falls, then he gets up an' rides again. *S-gi-dv nu-s-di.* (That's the way it is)."

I was too weak to hang on to the reins as I had the day before. My body was just too numb to be scared. Then, too, on the second day of my bronco-busting career, I no longer feared death. I was actually praying for it. The new horse Sam put me on did its best to oblige bouncing me off the ground more than it bounced me in the saddle. Sam got mad. He was so determined I was going to ride that plug to a walk so it knew who was boss, he tied me in the saddle. Which meant that horse had to work even harder to get rid of me.

It did.

Sam said that horse had a lot of heart. I will leave it to your imagination my opinion on the matter. Anyway, I finally rode it until the horse was winded and lathered, didn't have one more bounce left to its name. When Sam pulled me off that sour nag, every bone in my body felt disconnected. I couldn't stand for trying, and I'd slobbered myself with the blood from loosened teeth and the hole I'd bitten in my tongue.

Belle was so upset by the sight of me that after Sam carried me inside the house and lay me down on the parlor's settee, she screamed and chased him around the room, smacking him on the head. I remember lying on the lumpy settee, watching the fracas, listening as Sam yelled defensively about just doin' what he had to do to make a man out of me. If I could have moved my swollen tongue, I know I would have yelled "Hit him again, Belle!"

My recovery took nearly a week. During that time I was given the privilege of sleeping in a cot set up inside Belle and Sam's room. During the day the door to the bedroom was closed. I thought it was so that I would not be disturbed while I slept. I should have known better. The Starrs weren't ones to lavish this type of consideration. The door was kept closed to keep me out of earshot. During those few blissful days, I was aware of the many comings and goings in the house. I heard horses and voices, but the Starr household was, to be kind, such a lively place that strangers coming and going during all hours of the day and night were far from unusual.

During the daylight hours Sam sent Belle off to a neighbor lady's house, the neighbor lady being the wife of a member of the Starr gang. As soon as she was gone, the house filled up with men. I could hear them talking, but safe and snug in bed and behind the closed bedroom door I couldn't make out what was being said in the outer rooms. Nor was I concerned enough to leave the bed and eavesdrop. I was enjoying too much the luxury of being left completely alone, being allowed simply to sleep while my body healed.

The nights were different. I quickly learned to dread Belle and Sam coming to bed, because as soon as they did I was treated to sounds I'd never heard before. Sounds that made me feel . . . peculiar. I ignored their noise as best I could, but Belle Starr enjoyed sex more than any woman I've ever known. Even with a pillow over my head and my fingers jammed in my ears it was impossible to fully block out the noises of her passion. No one was more glad than I when Belle finally said I was fit enough to go back to my sleeping pallet in the kitchen. But her pronouncement hadn't come soon enough. After sharing the bedroom with her, I couldn't look at Belle in the motherly the way I had before, nor could I meet her eye without turning fifty shades of red. True to form, Belle was oblivious to my prepubescent embarrassment.

Once I was able to walk outside and breathe fresh air, the first thing I noticed was that the mood in the Starr compound had changed. The men I knew to be practical jokers by nature had turned moody, and they barely spoke. The man who made me the most nervous was Sam. He was going around with a face as dark as thunder, and when he looked at me, he made me feel invisible. You have to remember, Everett, that during this portion of my life I viewed Sam Starr as my idol. He had come along within hours of my father's murder, and in my grief and confusion I attached all of my boyhood needs to him. I would have done anything to please Sam Starr, and it crushed me beyond despair to be slighted by him. Eager to please, I quickly volunteered to help break more horses. When he said "It's been done, kid" and kept on walking as if even being near me irked him, I hit a new wall of grief.

In a funk, I went back to my former duties. The next few days were spent sitting on the back steps of the lean-to kitchen, peeling potatoes or plucking the dead chickens Belle planned to fry for supper. When I wasn't doing that, I chopped wood or plunged my little arms deep in hot lye-soapy washtubs, scrubbing laundry against the washboard. I was scrubbing away the day Sam suddenly appeared. The instant his shadow drifted over me, I froze. He stared at me for a full minute, his face unreadable. All he said as he turned to walk away were the very words he'd said once before, out on the prairie.

"Come on, kid."

That was enough. I dried my hands and arms and ran after him. I followed him all the way to the barn and then straight through it, out of the small back door. I kept on following until he stopped about a hundred yards behind the barn. When I caught up with him, he was spinning the cylinder of a six-shooter.

Sam looked up as Charlie approached, came to a stop. "Kid," he said in a flat tone. "It's time we get serious about this man business." He handed over the loaded gun. "Back here you're far enough away so's you won't kill nothin' I think's important, so this'll be your practice spot. From now on you bring yourself out here ever' day an' you shoot until you're good enough."

Squinting, his head canted to the side, Charlie clutched the gun and looked at Sam Starr. "How will I know when I'm good enough?"

Sam smiled faintly. "I'll tell ya."

Nodding, Charlie muttered, "Oh."

Going down on one knee, Sam looked the boy in the face. "Listen to me, kid, you got to be ready. There's lots of things goin' on, stuff I won't even talk over with Belle."

"How come?"

" 'Cause she's got a temper an' she'll make ever'thing twice as worse." He shook a warning finger in Charlie's face. "You best not tell her I said that, you hear me?"

"Yes, Sam."

Sam placed his hands on the boy's shoulders. "I got to be easy in my mind that my Belle's set. An' I got to be easy about you too. Charlie, it's time for you to start walkin' the Man Road."

Charlie had no idea what Sam was talking about, but he nodded as if he fully understood.

Sam emitted a deep sigh and said thoughtfully, "I started walkin' the Man Road when I was younger than you. Times were hard an' my daddy needed me." He looked back at the boy. "I ain't pushin' you ahead of your time. You're old enough, but even if you wasn't old enough in age, you're old enough where it counts." Sam's index finger pushed against Charlie's chest. "You're old enough in here.

"This world's a real ugly place, Charlie. A man's got to match ugly for ugly if he's gonna protect and provide for those he cares about. An' here's somethin' else I want you to always remember. Never go after an enemy when you're full up with hate. Always wait until your heart goes cold and your mind gets clear. Then you get him out on your ground. An' you let him see the bullet comin', Charlie. It's the fear in his eyes that'll take away your hate. Ain't nothin' else ever gonna work."

Sam was quiet for a moment, allowing the boy to remember the cowboys, remember the fear they had shown in the final moments of their lives. Charlie's mouth twitched as he looked again at Sam Starr.

Sam smiled. "You don't hate 'em no more."

"No," Charlie said softly.

Sam stood, lightly patted Charlie's back. "Cold vengeance works ever'time. You remember that an' you'll be all right. You'll be even better if you grow up smart enough to keep out of the path of a strong-headed woman."

"But what do I do if a strong-headed woman gets me?"

Sam Starr chortled softly. "Be damned if I know, kid."

Feeling that I had somehow managed to crawl back into Sam Starr's good graces, and determined to stay there, I practiced from first sun to last light each and every day. Sometimes Sam's brothers and their pals would come out and watch me, but mostly I was alone. Then one day Sam came to my practice spot and told me I was good enough. As a reward, he fitted me with my own gun holster, buckling it around my narrow hips, telling me all about the importance of slinging a holster low and tying it down on the leg so I could always get my gun fast. Then he asked me how would I like to ride out with him and the boys. I couldn't say yes fast enough. During the many weeks since my arrival into the Starr compound, I hadn't stepped one toe out of it. I wanted to be free of the compound's restraining quality, but most of all, I wanted to be with Sam. I wanted to ride by his side, bask in his reflected glory.

How was I supposed to know that our little day trip would include robbing a bank?

But it did, and we sure robbed her.

The name of the town was Wichita Falls. No, not Kansas—Texas. A little town just a spit and a throw from the Red River. Near the turn of the century, Wichita Falls, Texas, was no more than a mud hole with a few buildings around it. Ordinarily Sam wouldn't have bothered a bank in such a little-bitty town, but he was pressed. Things I knew nothing about were closing in on him. He needed quick cash. But what he told me was that our taking on a little bank was more suited to breaking me into the robbing trade, that in the future the banks we'd rob would get bigger as I learned the stick-up craft. Small bank aside, the minute he filled me in on the plans for the robbery, I was awash with conflicting emotions. On the one hand, I was scared pea-green. On the other, I wanted to prove myself to Sam. The second hand proved mightier than the first. I focused my resolve and did my best to look just as tough as I could while I walked around, patting the trusty six-shooter hanging off my hip. Ellis Starr hooted, "Look at him strut. I'm tellin' ya, fellas, we got a genu-wine bad boy ridin' with us."

We didn't do the bank robbery like they're done in the movies. We didn't ride straight into town, riding our horses in a walk down the main street of the town while meaningfully eyeing the citizenry. Nope, we quietly rode around the town, staying to the back roads. Then we crept into an alleyway that ran between the bank and another building. Because of the southern positioning of the sun, it was fairly dark in that alley. My instructions were achingly simple. All I had to do was wait in the alley and hold on to the horses while Sam and the gang did the actual sticking-up. It was when they left me to do this that things became a little screwy.

I had never seen bubble gum in my whole life, so when a boy about my age walked along the sunny boardwalk with this big bubble coming out of his face, I forgot everything Sam told me. Now, hanging out with outlaws for a long period of time markedly alters a person's sense of social graces. Any normal kid would have called out, "Hey! What's that big bubble on your face?" Then the second kid would have walked into the alleyway (of course not thinking it strange for one minute that the other kid was holding on to eight saddled horses) and would have explained the joys of bubble gum, perhaps even offering a piece.

Not me. I drew my gun and shot right through that bubble. I have to say that it had to be the best shot I have ever made. That bullet barely skimmed the kid's nose when it hit the bubble dead center. The boy, however, did not appreciate my skill. The gun blast ringing in his ears, and bubble gum smeared all over his face, the kid started screaming his lungs loose. He was so scared that he didn't even have the sense to run away. He just stood there, screaming. As it was considered to be just another uneventful day in a small town, a gunshot and a screaming child instantly attracted a lot of attention. When concerned adults came rushing to the boy's aid, I realized I'd made a fatal faux pas in the old bank-robbing business. Not only that, but in the same moment I was aiming my gun at the bubble, Sam and the boys had been drawing theirs, training them on the people inside the bank. The second my gun fired, one of Sam's women hostages started shrieking that they were all going to die. She was so vocal that Sam had to outyell her when he shouted, "Who the hell fired that gun!"

Ellis said that it sounded maybe like it came from outside, and the Starr gang, thinking they were surrounded by the law, were rightfully concerned. They grabbed as much money as they could and started out of the bank. During their hasty exit, Sam yelled to his brother William, "Tell that Osage kid to get them damn horses around here!"

Now, he could have just said "Tell Charlie . . ." But he didn't. While his brother William ran for me, Sam and his pals were guarding the boardwalk, six-guns at the ready, the barrels following the scattering targets otherwise known as the people of Wichita Falls. One of the targets was Bubble-Gum Boy, who was still screaming but was now being carried to safety in the arms of a running man. Ellis remained in the bank to guard his brother's back from the shotgun the bank manager was certain to haul out just as soon as he thought it was safe enough to be brave.

While Sam waited for me and Ellis covered the folks in the bank, Ellis clearly heard the men with their hands in the air muttering among themselves.

"The Osage Kid."

"My God. I didn't know *he* was in Texas!"

"Oh, Lord, have mercy. Not . . . him!"

Now, this just about tickled Ellis Starr half to death. The one thing I learned about Cherokees during my stay with the Starrs is that Cherokees have a perverse sense of humor. A Cherokee will take a joke and drive it forty miles down into the ground before he's finished with it, and Ellis Starr was one of the worst. In the seconds before Sam called for Ellis to come out, Ellis pushed the joke about the Osage Kid to its limits.

"The Osage Kid is one mean chigger," he said to his already fear-riddled hostages. "I know he scares me. There just ain't no tellin' what he'll do. If I was ya'll, I'd stay just as quiet as I could. You don't want him comin' in here mad clear out of his head."

We were all on our horses, and the horses pushing into a gallop, when Ellis came charging out of the bank, mounting his horse in a run and laughing like a fool. By this time most of the town had rallied; men were running out of buildings and firing rifles at us. Ellis was still laughing even when the instantly deputized townsmen mounted up in pursuit.

I didn't realize just how well I could ride until we were running from that posse. As brutal as Sam's horsebreaking lessons had been, he sure taught me how to ride a horse good. And because of all the gun practice when the Starrs shot at the sheriff and the league of sheriff's men chasing us, hoping to catch us before we reached the Red River, hell! I shot too. I was just a kid! I didn't want to get hung. Even if being strung up and being forever known as a member of the notorious Starr gang guaranteed getting my picture in the newspapers. In the throes of running for my life, I didn't find the prospect of legendary fame to be all that appealing. Then, too, I had no idea at the time that Ellis Starr's warped brand of humor had given rise to an enduring western legend.

Me.

Once we crossed the Red River and made it into the Territory, and then finally into the Starr compound, I figured our troubles were over. But they weren't. A whole new batch was waiting for us. When we rode into the yard we found Belle pacing the barren ground and so mad, she looked fit to be tied. While we'd been away, Belle had gotten into a squabble with their Choctaw neighbors. A member of the offended neighboring family had stopped her buggy as she was headed home from church prayer meeting. Yes, Everett, Belle Starr went to church. Every Sunday and every Wednesday, weather and outlawry escapades permitting. (I told you the woman had no sense of shame.) Anyway, this Choctaw fella rides after her buggy and stopped her in the road. Then I guess he says just as politely as he knew how, "Miss Belle, you tell Sam we're still waiting for our money an' he better get it quick like he promised."

Of course Belle says, "What money?" and the fella fills her in on the news that Sam has agreed to pay for his family's lost horses, and as his family needed the money, they'd appreciate Sam paying up promptly. Now, Belle's biggest downfall was that she never really understood Indians. She might legally be Cherokee, but she didn't have a drop of Cherokee blood, therefore it was beyond her to understand just how fragile a male Indian's pride can be. It is especially tender when a woman he is not married to picks up a horse whip and proceeds to flog him about the head and shoulders with it.

While she was giving this fellow a good thrashing, Belle informed him that he and his kin were not going to get any money out of her Sam. In her mind she and Sam had found those horses, and finders being keepers, they had been well within their rights to sell off the herd in Catoosa. Of course Belle did not admit to having done this while she inflicted damage on the Choctaw family spokesman. Nope, she denied any and all knowledge of the horses and accused the injured party of malicious slander and attempted coercion of innocent folk.

Things hotted up after that. The threats that had been made without Belle's knowing, the same threats Sam had managed to smooth over with promises of repayment (which is why he had to rob the bank), erupted once again. Not only that, but the next day, when Belle was in the buggy, driving herself to the store, shots were fired and she'd had to take refuge with a friendly neighbor until it seemed safe enough for her to make it back to the compound. During the next two days, while she waited for Sam to come home, she fumed herself up into a wrathful state. No one shot at Belle Starr and lived to tell about it. Oddly enough, Belle had a majority of the outlying community on her side. Folks for and against Belle Starr had begun to take shots at one another from behind trees and from inside bushes. This bushwacking spree either killed or badly wounded friends and opponents while the helpless damsel in question was completely safe inside the well-guarded compound. But she heard all about it. Oh, yes, she did. Every time a good friend of hers got plugged, she was almost immediately told and the news made her even madder.

This was just the trouble Sam had hoped to avoid. The kind of trouble he knew would get started if Belle got in the middle of the brewing fight. He had been right on all counts. Folks were going after each other, and it was down to him to stop it. The trouble was, now that blood had been spilled, paying off the debt of the missing horses with a sack full of dollars wasn't going to work. In the Cherokee mind, blood could be met only with blood. Especially the blood that had been spilled on his wife's behalf.

We weren't home barely five minutes when Belle started in on Sam about how their neighbors were getting "real uppity" and about how they had threatened her. She couldn't get over the fact that they'd had the audacity to shoot at her. Belle simply could not believe anyone would have that kind of nerve. As we unsaddled our exhausted horses, led them into the corral, a hyped-up Belle, waving her arms and yelling her head off, followed Sam around like a horny hen intent on a disinterested rooster.

"Dammit, Sam! I'm tellin' ya, them people need a good killin'!"

Sam picked out a fresh horse, put the bit in its mouth. Taking a cue from their younger brother,

William and Ellis chose out a couple of fresh horses for themselves. Sam led the new horse out of the corral gate with Belle still behind him, still carrying on about their no-good neighbors. Ignoring her, he stopped before me, lifting my chin with his hand as he looked me hard in the eye.

"Charlie, there's one more thing I want you never to forget. Never foul your own nest."

Everything inside me went cold. I knew he was going out to fight to the death. I was fully prepared to fight by his side. At that moment I wasn't afraid of being killed. I was more afraid of the blackness that would be my life without Sam Starr to shine as my sun and my moon. He was everything to me—father, brother, hero. He was a man's man. The genuine article. He was everything I ever hoped I would be. When he took his hand away, I felt the first pains of losing him. When he lightly tusseled my hair, I knew he was saying good-bye. In desperation, I tagged after him as he went for his saddle, begging him not to go just as loudly as Belle was yelling for him to go and teach their offensive neighbors a much-needed lesson in manners.

As Sam and his brothers mounted up, Sam said to Belle, "Charlie goes. See to it, woman."

As soon as she heard that, Belle shut right up. I guess the finality of the moment hit her just as hard as it had me. Then she started in on Sam about not going, that they could find another way out of the mess. Sam just looked down at her and kind of smiled a lopsided smile. Then his hand caressed the side of her face.

"You know I have to go, Belle. *S-gi-dv nu-s-di.*"

Then he righted himself in the saddle and turned his horse's head. "See that Charlie gets enough food to take him home. An' some money too. Fifty dollars ought to do it."

Belle's son, Eddie, and daughter, Pearl, lived in the East somewhere. Exactly where, I never knew. In their absence, Belle had mothered me about as well as Belle Starr knew how to mother anyone. Having a boy around had given her maternal instincts a lift. She was unhappy that Sam wanted me to leave, but because he'd ordered it, she didn't say a word. She simply turned and went inside the house. Contrary to popular fiction depicting Belle wearing the pants in the family, being the boss over her Indian husband, I know from firsthand knowledge that when Sam Starr told Belle to do a thing, the woman obeyed. I would have given anything if she had argued with him, told him he wasn't going anywhere and that she was going to keep me. But she didn't. And in her silence I felt my banishment and Sam's death.

I think the thing that hurt and confused me the most that day was that Sam didn't bother looking back as he, his brothers, and four cousins, rode out. I was all alone in the yard, watching them go. Sam's brother Ellis did look back, and because he was Ellis, he had a grin on his face that was five miles wide as he hollered, "Be seein' ya, Kid!"

I heard the others laugh. The Osage Kid. It was a damn fine joke. And I looked like a joke, standing there, my long, thin legs with knobby knees poking tents in my baggy britches. My hair, grown out from the severe bowl cut the sisters had given me, looked like a blackbird's nest perched on top of my head. I was wearing a faded red shirt four times too big for me and tucked into my baggy pants. My feet were bare. My only mark of an outlaw was the six-gun holstered at my side. Sam Starr left me that day, easy in his mind that I could and would use that gun. That I was good enough. In our too-brief time together he'd managed to set my feet on the Man Road. Or, as he called it in Cherokee, *Asgaya Nunohi.*

I've always known that he wasn't laughing at me, that he was laughing because of my seemingly harmless appearance. But I wasn't harmless and Sam Starr knew it. More important, on the day he left my life forever, I knew it.

I've enjoyed a lot of freedom in my life, Everett. That freedom did not come cheap, nor did it come by accident. I have been free because Sam Starr taught me how to be just as ruthless as times decreed I had to be in order to be free. But because deep down Sam was a caring person, inadvertently he taught me to care for and protect those who were weaker than myself. And like Sam, I've never made a big fanfare of my singular virtue. Protecting the weak is simply a thing a man does, what he is expected to do. It's the quality that makes him a man. Without that quality, he's just a thing on two legs. I have done my best never to let Sam Starr down. Just as I didn't let him down when I safely took myself home, riding through a thoroughly lawless Territory. Sam expected me to do it, and I did.

Belle didn't come out of the house again until long after Sam was gone. It was a superstition she had. She said if she watched him go, she'd never watch him ride home again. I knew in my heart that this was the one time her superstitious practice didn't matter. Sam already knew he wasn't coming back. In her heart, I believe Belle knew it too. After being widowed twice, I believe Belle could feel it when death was coming for her man. But Belle wouldn't give into it. No, sir. Belle Starr wouldn't give the death angel credit where credit was due. What she did instead was busy herself with my leaving. She showed me everything she'd packed in my travel bag, all the foods, explaining which I should eat right away before it went to spoil, which ones would last the longest, and the extra change of clothing she'd stuffed in there against the weather turning cold and wet. She also gave me fifty dollars in five-dollar notes and then she helped me hide some in my clothing and then hide the rest in places in my saddle. Belle didn't hold with putting money in a bag. Bags were too easy for some no-good person to grab. When I was all set to leave, she kissed me good-bye.

Emotion was strong in her tone as she instructed the boy she'd come to care for. "Charlie, once you get clear of the canyon, go wide around the nearest towns. Stay to the woods till you get more up-country, where the name Starr is more fable than fact."

"Yes, Miss Belle."

Belle Starr drew the child to her for the final time. His arms wrapped her waist tightly as he lightly sobbed against her skirts. Stroking the back of his head, she said softly, "You've been a joy, Charlie. I'm gonna miss you somethin' hard."

"I don't wanna go!" he wailed.

Belle firmly pushed the boy away from her. "We gotta do what Sam says." Briskly, with the back of her hand she brushed a tear from her cheek. "Get yourself gone, Charlie. An' don't you be afraid of nothin'. God's angels will be a-ridin' with you."

I left. And I cried steadily for the first hundred miles. I missed Belle, I even missed her singing. When I closed my eyes to go to sleep in the cold camps I made each night, I saw her in my mind just as clearly as I had seen her that final day. She was standing in the yard, her right arm straight up in the air, waving to me as she watched me go. Belle's watching me leave reconfirmed what I already knew. We would never see each other again.

Just like poor old Blue Duck, as I made my way homeward, a completely undeserved celebrity went before me. The Territory back then had the telegraph and newspapers, and a few of the bigger towns were even on the telephone. The Territory had something else as well. Balladeers. Today they're called bullshitters, but back then they were balladeers. Don't get it in your head that these fellows wandered around strumming guitars and singing inspiring ditties. They didn't. What they did do was tell great big fat lies for food and drink. The bigger the lies, the more food and whiskey they received courtesy of their attentive listeners.

It was in the first town I felt safe enough to enter to treat myself with the purchase of a few apples and a wedge of cheese, that I heard about Sam Starr. That little town was all abuzz about its visiting balladeer. In the mercantile I was all but ignored as I made my purchase and the customers gabbed with the merchant.

Charlie was pushed by a lounging man's rear end as the man blocked the center of the counter. Charlie dropped an apple and stooped to retrieve it before it rolled away. Grabbing it just in time, he righted himself, placing all of his apples safely on the end of the counter. It was then that the store owner noticed him, looking down at him over half glasses. Russell Spinner was an awkward-looking man. Tall and rake-thin, he had an unusual amount of dark, curly hair. He also had an Adam's apple in the middle of his neck that rivaled the apples Charlie chose for purchase. But his hair was his primary feature, growing all over his head and face and sticking out of his ears and nose. His body hair grew so thickly on his arms that when his sleeves were rolled up, he looked like he was wearing a tight-fitting hairy sweater beneath his shirt. But Russell Spinner was a kindly man and he loved children. Having been a homely child and now a homely adult, Russell Spinner especially loved homely children. The Indian child at the end of the counter more than qualified. Not only was the child homely, he was raggedy to boot.

"Hey, little tadpole," Russell laughed. "Didn't see you down there. Whatcha buyin' today, son?"

"Apples, sir. And some cheese, please."

Russell rubbed his chin thoughtfully. "Your mama send you inta' town, son?"

"Yes, sir."

"Think maybe she gave you enough money for all them apples an' a wedge of cheese?"

Charlie took out a five-dollar note, unfolded it, and held it straight between his two hands. Russell laughed. The child had just enough, but what he said was "Looks like she give you enough for apples, cheese, an' a big ol' piece a' stick candy for a treat."

"Yes, sir." Charlie nodded. "She surely did."

Charlie's presence was promptly forgotten as Russell cut into the cheese wheel and talked again with the adult customer. Charlie's mouth was watering for the apple. He bit into it, enjoying its flavor, ignoring the adults until he heard the name Sam Starr. His mind turning so rapidly he was no longer able to think or behave like a normal child, Charlie pushed his way past the leaning man and slapped his hand on the counter, demanding to know, and in a tone that set Russell Spinner back on his heels, everything he had to say on the subject of Sam Starr.

Russell Spinner no longer viewed his smallest customer as a tadpole. The manner of the kid combined with the lethal light that had begun to shine from those black eyes reminded him more of a baby diamondback. Russell felt a prickle of apprehension, and he wasn't alone. The other man had stepped away from the counter, fully relinquishing his space to the boy, who had to stand on tiptoe to glare at Russell Spinner.

"Who told you Sam Starr was dead!" Charlie demanded again.

"Now, son," Russell stammered, "don't get yourself all worked up—"

"Tell me!"

Russell Spinner told him. "There's a fella just over at Miss Emilia's. But it's been in the newspapers too, son. The fella that come to town's just got more details than the newspapers had, an' all I'm just sayin' is what he said."

Russell Spinner offered not one more word. Hastily he bagged up the boy's purchase, plus a very big piece of stick candy. Russell remembered to breathe again after the child left his store. Then he laughed because he felt foolish. Foolish for having been almost mortally afraid of a ragged little boy. But there had been something about that boy. Something dangerous. Russell Spinner retrieved a bottle of tonic from the shelf behind him, uncorked it, and took a big drink.

"I'm feelin' a mite dipsy too," his customer said. "Mind if I have a swalla?"

Russell handed the bottle over. Then he started a new conversation. One that had nothing to do with Sam Starr.

Charlie headed first to his horse, which he'd left tied out behind the mercantile. With effort he prised out two five-dollar bills from the snug hiding places in the battered saddle. Then he took himself over to the café/saloon, owned and operated solely by Miss Emilia and her husband, Zebulon Murphy. As Miss Emilia's was something of a family place, no one looked twice at the child entering the establishment. The man he was looking for was holding forth and enjoying a fine supper for his balladeering efforts. Charlie cut every bit of that short.

There was no sitting room at the table, but Charlie wasn't interested in sitting. He tapped the man repeatedly on the shoulder until, annoyed, the man turned his head. With a start he looked into a pair of the coldest and blackest young eyes he'd ever encountered.

"There's a couple of fellas that want to talk to you outside."

"An' just who would they be, son?"

Charlie unfolded one of the bills just enough to reveal the pen-and-inked likeness of a president.

The man looked from the bill to the boy. "There's two of 'em?"

"Yep. Said they need to talk to you for five minutes. No more than that."

The man stood and followed Charlie out.

I never did ask that man his name. Who he was wasn't important to me. What was important was what he had to say about Sam. Away from the crowd and behind the saloon where it was just that man and me, he ended his roll of roaming entertainer and gave me the barest facts. Sam had been ambushed. In my mind's eye I saw the gun smoke, I saw Sam's horse rear in fright and twist, making Sam a more viable target for the bullets that struck him. I even saw the bullet that skimmed Ellis's head, almost taking his ear off. I saw, and I heard. And I wished to God that I had been with them.

I gave the man the two bills and neither of us spoke as he took the money and left. I wanted to cry, Everett. I was desperate to cry. My whole body hurt, I needed to cry so bad. But I couldn't. I went to my horse, climbed into the saddle. I headed home to the Osage Hills. But I traveled slowly, purposely taking my time. Time I needed to quietly grieve for Sam.

A week or two later it was in Tulsy Town that I heard the biggest lie a balladeer could tell. The True Story of the Osage Kid. The Territory's newest and most bloodthirsty desperado. In those early days of Tulsa, a kid with a loaded gun on his hip and a bit of money in his pocket didn't cause that much of a stir. I had thirty dollars left from the fifty, and in Tulsy I used every penny to buy myself a hot bath, some clothes that fit me right, and a hot meal. Clean and feeling dapper, I was alone at a corner table, enjoying my meal and listening with one ear to the balladeer spouting off his mouth for the paying crowd. Imagine my surprise when I heard that I was the by-product of Sam Starr's defilement of an Osage maiden. Naturally the maiden in question was a princess, never mind that there has never been such a thing as an Indian princess. Anyway, Sam was supposed to have kidnapped her and kept her out at his daddy Tom's place, where he forcibly impregnated her. Then a few years later Belle came along and said Sam would either free his love slave or stand by and watch while Belle gunned her rival down.

Sam had enough heart to send the Osage woman away, but the woman was by now in love with Sam. As an act of revenge for his spurning her in favor of Belle, she took Sam's only child with her, raising the boy to be a wild Indian. It wasn't until the child was nearly full grown that Sam was reunited with his son. By then the boy was so wild that Sam and Belle had to chain him up in the barn until he was tame enough to go out robbing and killing with Sam.

Every head in the place turned when I started braying laughter. What made it worse was, I couldn't quit laughing. I hadn't been able to cry for Sam, but boy I could sure laugh like a fool in his honor. Somewhere in my mind I heard him laughing right along with me. It was a very healing moment, and it left me feeling alive again.

There were more idiot tales about the Osage Kid, but I won't bother to repeat them. The one I've told you is my favorite. Anyway, as you might imagine, no one equated the scrawny boy briefly in their midst as the Territory's newest villain, so I was never afraid I would be recognized. But back home it was a different story.

Days after the Starrs, with me in tow, set out for their home country, my mother went to the authorities to report my father and me as missing. The Osage police were good trackers. Within no time at all they found my father's body. They picked up my tracks pretty fast too. To the sharp eyes of experienced trackers, the truth of what happened was more than evident. They found the camp where I'd stayed with the Starrs. They found my bandaged foot marks where I'd stood over the cowboys, shooting them to death, and then they followed the blood trail made by the cowboys being dragged. That trail led the trackers to the two bodies buried in shallow-dug graves. Now, the rest of the Territory might be baffled about the identity of the Osage Kid, but my own people felt in the know.

And they were waiting for me.

Once I made it home, I barely had time to kiss my distraught mother, when the authorities came for me. Ripped from my mother's arms for the last time, my young butt was slung into the reservation jail. While I was in there, I heard the news that Belle was in great difficulty. I was scarcely in the position to ride to her aid. I was looking at a trial for murdering two white cowboys and scheduled either to hang or spend the rest of my life in prison. The degree of the sentence depended on just how guilty the jury found me. You'll notice that there was never the slightest flap over the question that I might be innocent, or that the defunct cowboys might have needed, as Belle would have said, a good killin'.

My deliverance from a very uncertain fate came from a totally unexpected source.

Père Blanc.

Not the Major, whom I had been counting heavily on, but the old priest I would have sworn had no idea who I was. But, dusty black robes flying, that desiccated old Jesuit marched himself straight into that jailhouse and demanded his son be returned to him.

Père Blanc's one and only conceit sprang from the fact that he was a Jesuit, a member of the only priesthood in Catholicism claiming a direct link with Jesus Christ. Because of this, Jesuits are considered to be the real princes of the Church. Jesuits are trademark bullies, arrogant, and possessive beyond belief. If a Jesuit converts you, he owns you. Père Blanc had converted and baptized me, ergo, I was his property and no jumped-up worldly lawman was going to say different. But what made the hair on my neck stand up was that when push came to shove, Père Blanc could outlie a balladeer.

Without blinking an eye he swore that I had been at the school during the time of the killings, on punishment because I was a rotten son he had to beat regularly. (At least that part was true.) My punishment during this particular time was to miss the summer break to visit my parents. Because of my unrepentant sins, under his constant supervision, I stayed at the school doing menial labor, learning the error of my ways. He stated that he personally had been given the task of telling me that my father had been horribly killed. And because I was so rotten, instead of praying for my father's soul like a dutiful son, I had, instead, run away. According to Père Blanc, I had been gone less than two weeks.

Tops.

He further declared that hanging me for a crime I could not possibly have committed was tantamount to child murder. He also shouted that the state of Texas could take its petition for extradition and go twist in the wind. His little boy had not robbed any bank with any damn gang. That the only evidence that I was the Osage Kid rested heavily on the fact that I was Osage and I was just a kid!

With a Catholic priest ready to testify to this story under oath, the Major ordered my prompt release. But on the condition that I be returned forthwith to the Catholic school and remain there without any type of a holiday from the place until I was sixteen years of age.

As they opened the cell door and I faced Père Blanc, hanging by the neck until I was dead, dead, dead didn't seem all that injurious. As I looked up into those bright, penetrating pale blue eyes set into a sun-darkened and heavily lined, craggy face, I knew Père Blanc knew that

I had killed those cowboys, knew that I had robbed a bank with the Starr gang. I also knew that old man was going to beat the pure-o-tee hell out of me until I made a satisfactory confession and was granted absolution.

He did.

But as I took my punishment without so much as a whimper, that old man never whipped me again. Instead, whenever I felt my juices rising and acted accordingly, he stuck me in the kitchen, working with the girls. The first few times, it was as humiliating as it was meant to be. An Osage male was not supposed to wash dishes like a woman. But after I met Cassie DuPree and felt myself sinking inside her light green-blue eyes, which were so innocent and lovely, I went out of my way to get into trouble. I was careful to always kick up rough about the kitchen punishment. If Père Blanc ever got it into his egg-shaped skull that the kitchen was where I actually craved to be, he would have gleefully put me to a more manly enterprise.

Shoveling out the manure in the stables.

Now, Everett, before you get all hot about me talking about your mother, remember this. I knew her first. I loved her first. You never did know her. You could not possibly miss her the way I have, so that gives me the right to talk about her.

As you already know, Cassie was more French than she was Osage. And as I told you earlier, a French/Osage girl was promised practically from birth in marriage to a suitable French/Osage man. I certainly knew Cassie's fate, and I knew I should have had better sense, but I couldn't stay away from her. She was the most beautiful girl God ever put on this troubled planet. And I think I fell in love with her the second she lifted her face and warmed me from head to toe with her smile.

I think, as it was torn down long ago, that I should

tell you a bit more about the school. It was a big two-story structure made of brick and wood. The perimeter was a wall. Another brick wall sectioned off the play yard, one side for the girls, the other for the boys. It was meant to keep the sexes separate, but the wooden door at the back end allowed access. That door was called the Chore Gate, because when boys were given the hard chores of chopping wood for the kitchen, which was located on the girls' half of the school, or unloading the supply wagons, which came twice monthly, the older boys had to go through via the Chore Gate. As a consequence, the gate was never locked and the boys sneaked into the girls' play yard just about any time they wanted to. I liked to go into the girls' yard, but not for the same reason as the other boys. The girls' yard had big oak trees and grass. The boys' yard was denuded. The grasses were mown down not only by the few grazing horses but by the rough-and-tumble games the boys played in all weather. The few trees that had once stood had either fallen under the ax or had fallen victim to high winds that had occurred during thunderstorms. As a result, the boys' field was open and dusty. Not a good place for a solitary person such as myself to sit alone and mourn his fate. So I started sneaking into the girls' yard and then I would creep into the small wooded area. In this hiding place I could watch, if I wanted to, the girls having their play time. I wasn't really interested, I was trying to piece back together my broken heart.

Then one day a particular little girl caught my eye. She and her friends were playing a game of, of all things, horses. Prancing around and whinnying and shaking their heads in an imitation of spirited horses. Watching her cavort around was just about the cutest thing I had ever seen. She was so tiny that when she tried to dance like a horse, she looked more like a little fairy dancing on a leaf. I pulled my legs up to my chest, rested my chin on my knees, and forgot everything else as my eyes followed her every movement.

I think I fell in love with her right then, but maybe I fell in love with her the next day. Wanting a closer look at her, I volunteered to help chop wood for the kitchen. I held a steady rhythm as I split kindling and watched that fairylike little creature at play. That day she and her friends weren't playing horses, they were playing hopscotch, and the way she hopped on one leg inside the marked-off squares held me mesmerized. She was so light on her feet that she wasn't really hopping at all. She was lifting herself off the ground and setting herself down again with a grace that defied the laws of gravity. And with each movement her waist-length brown hair just seemed to float and settle. I chopped and watched her until the lesson bell rang and she became lost inside the pack of girls hurrying to answer the summons. Then, as she stood in the line, our eyes met. She didn't smile or giggle or wave, she just looked at me. And that's when I realized her eyes were too light. So light that at first I thought she didn't have normal eyeballs. Afraid that maybe she might be blind, and wanting a better look, I scooped up an armload of kindling and hauled it toward the kitchen. She was still looking at me as I passed her. Up close, I realized she wasn't blind and that her eyes weren't solid white. Her eyes were soft green. It was when I stopped and gawked that she smiled a tiny, shy smile. I was still standing and staring like a dolt when the line began to march into the classroom door, Sister Rosalyn nodding to each girl passing her. When my little girl—that was the way I was beginning to think of her—passed the nun, Sister Rosalyn placed a firm hand on my little girl's head, forcibly turning her face to the front. I heard the sister say something like "Cassie, what have I told you about staring?"

Cassie, that was her name. I must have mentally said her name at least a thousand times throughout the rest of that day and into the night, and then, when I dreamed, I dreamed of her, dancing in the sunlight, the brightness sparkling the crystal wings growing out of her shoulder blades.

Now, after spending so much time as a member of the Starr gang, chopping wood was something I could really do well. Sister Angelica, the nun who ran the kitchens, quickly saw my potential and placed me permanently on the wood chore. So after that I no longer had to sneak into the girls' yard, I could just walk right in, go about my chores, and watch my little girl. I did this for weeks, each day hoping that would be the day I would finally speak to her. At last, when the opportunity finally came, if felt like a gift from God.

Watching him out of the corners of her eyes, Cassie giggled. The dish she handed him to dry was slippery, and his hands were big and clumsy. He struggled not to drop it as he applied the sodden drying cloth. He was standing closer to her than he needed to. She could feel the heat of his large body. Plunging her arms deep into the sink of sudsy water, she felt him bump against her. He was careful to make the brief physical contact seem like an accident. She knew it wasn't.

Before he left school for that fateful summer holiday, she knew of him only as the boy everyone loved to pick on. When he came back he had a fearful reputation. It was said that he had ridden with outlaws. That he had killed people. The boys who used to bully him mercilessly left him alone. Even the nuns seemed to be afraid of him. Charlie lived his days in silence, doing his lessons at a separate worktable, eating alone at a place in the back of the large dining hall. In the afternoons he chopped wood. His evenings were spent in Père Blanc's office, being taught the Catholic religion on a one-to-one basis. Some nights Père Blanc's roaring voice could be heard all the way into the dorms.

"Damn your eyes, boy! Pay attention. I'm trying to save your immortal soul!"

The boy named Charlie Jones was considered by the majority to be beyond Père Blanc's attempts at salvation. Young Charlie had crossed the line of God's forgiveness when he'd used his summer holiday to kill two unarmed men and then ride as a member of the Starr gang. No one expected such a boy to come to the aid of a little girl who had fallen from a swing. But he had, abandoning his wood-cutting chore, running to her and picking her up, carrying her all the way to the dispensary. And he stayed with her, holding her hand as the stinging iodine the nurse applied to her badly abraded knees caused her to whimper and her chin to bobble as she tried not to cry. When her knees were bandaged, he was still holding her hand as he walked her down the long, dimly lit corridor that led to the girls' dormitory. There was a large window at the end of the hallway. From a distance, the window looked like stained glass. It wasn't. The window had been cunningly painted by Sister Rosalyn, and the scene she chose was of a guardian angel following behind two children as they crossed a bridge.

Walking the hallway, the two living children came into the light streaming through the translucent colors. The girl stopped, lifting her face. The painted face of the angel seemed to melt against hers. Transfixed, Charlie stared at the double image. He looked up at the window, then again at the faylike girl.

"You look like her."

Cassie slowly opened her eyes and peered at him questioningly. "I look like who?"

Charlie pointed to the window. "Like the woman painted on the glass."

The girl shook her head. "Oh, no. No one is allowed to look like her. She's a blessed angel."

Charlie squeezed her hand. "I—I think maybe you are too. An angel, I mean."

She lowered her head, her hair folding forward, hiding her face and her blush. "My name is Cassie."

"I'm Charlie."

She looked at him again, her odd-colored eyes searching his. "Did you really kill people?"

Charlie felt his heart clinch. He so badly wanted to be her friend. He knew his telling her the truth would most probably lose him that friendship. But denying something that was true would not keep truth away.

"Yes," he mumbled. "I—I killed two bad men."

She leaned in close, her voice a husky whisper. "Were they very bad men?"

"Yes. They killed my father."

She squeezed his hand. "I think you are a brave person. I wish I was brave."

Charlie looked at her incredulously. "But you are brave. When the nurse poured the stinging stuff on your knees you didn't cry once. I know I would have cried."

Her smile was as radiant as the tinted sunshine lighting her face. "Honestly?"

"Yeah. That stuff must have hurt a lot."

"It did. But I was brave only because you were with me."

Charlie's young chest puffed with pride.

She stood closer to him, their shoulders touching. "I'm glad you're with me now too. This school is a big place and I am a small person. I get lost a lot."

Immediately protective, Charlie tightened his hold on her petite hand. "Don't worry about getting lost anymore. I'll always find you, Cassie."

"Swear."

"I swear."

"Double swear."

"I double-double swear."

Cassie giggled mischievously. "Don't ya know you're not supposed to swear in school?"

It confused him the way she could laugh so hard at such a weak joke, but to be polite, he laughed with her.

As the years passed, their friendship grew. Cassie was right in the description of herself. She was a small person. Each time she slipped her hand into his, the bones of her fingers reminded him of delicate little bird bones. Her face was heart-shaped, her eyes pale green, her long, fine hair a rich brown. Her one physical flaw was that she was too thin. The years hadn't padded her out the way they should have. Charlie worried about delicate little Cassie primarily because he enjoyed worrying about Cassie. It made him forget the high walls around the school that kept him in. He remembered the walls only during the times Cassie was gone and he was virtually alone in the school. Every holiday, especially during the three whole months of summer when the other students were gone, Charlie remained behind with the nuns and Père Blanc. If it weren't for his daydreams and fretting about Cassie, he would have felt every inch the prisoner he was. In effect, his mania for Cassie helped him remain sane. But even he knew that he worried about her too much, especially when she played dodge ball with the other girls, a game he constantly pleaded with her not to play. He didn't like the game because the ball was big and it moved too fast. He was certain that if it hit her, it would break one of her little bird bones. But Cassie was quick, just in time she would twist away as the ball sailed past her. Only when it hit someone else, not his Cassie, did Charlie release the held breath. When the game was over, she came to him. He tried to ignore her as he pouted and wielded the ax, splintering the wood. But he couldn't pout forever, and she knew it. She was smiling from ear to ear when he eventually looked at her.

"How many times," he scowled, "have I asked you—"

She quickly placed her hand against his frowning mouth. "I'm never afraid when you're watching me, Charlie. And when I'm not afraid, I'm too fast for the ball."

He took her hand away, held on to it the way he tried to hold on to his anger. "Just promise you'll never play when I'm not here to watch."

Her smile became dreamy. "I promise."

Satisfied, he grunted and set the ax aside. "Good. Now let's practice your math lesson. Did you remember to bring your slate?"

Cassie lost her smile, her expression instantly changing to startled. "Oh, no!" she cried, and scampered away, running quickly for the classroom hall, the place she'd last seen her slate board. Although he loved to watch her run, like Belle, he never watched when she was running away from him. Instead, he closed his eyes and counted off the minutes they were apart. His eyes opened when he heard her running back to him. Then he would enjoy the sight of her, enjoy the way the strong white sunlight seemed to caress her, cause her dark hair to shine.

Forgetting her slate and needing help with her math were both signs of Cassie's second flaw. She was not a good student, the nuns forever lamenting that although Cassie was the sweetest girl in the school, mentally she was not the brightest flower in God's garden. Charlie didn't mind this flaw one bit. That she was a bit slow meant too that she was totally without guile. Nor was she strong-headed. Sam had warned him about strong-headed women. Loving his Cassie meant he would never have to worry about a strong-headed woman getting her hooks into him. But the best thing about Cassie being a trifle dim was the way she always looked up to him. And not simply because he was almost six feet tall. She looked up to him and depended on him because Cassie was firmly convinced that her Charlie was the smartest person in the whole world. When they were together, she somehow managed to make him believe it too.

This time when he closed his eyes against her leaving, he didn't count the minutes. What he did was dream about the day they would be old enough to leave school and he would build a little house among the blackjacks and oaks. Next he dreamed of the day the house would be filled with babies. Babies he and Cassie would make together. In a bed. He was concentrating hard on the latter, when she returned and tugged on the sleeve of his shirt. When his eyes snapped open, she beamed her happy smile, proudly showing him her slate.

"I found it!"

"And did you remember your piece of chalk?"

Cassie gasped again, shoved the slate into his hands, ran away. When she returned a second time, Charlie's eyes were shut and he was grinning.

"Are you dreaming?"

"Yes," he answered, his eyes remaining closed.

"Is it a good dream?"

"The best."

"Am I in the dream?"

"Oh, yes."

That was the day, in their secret place under the oaks and while Cassie labored over the math problems on her slate, the tip of her pink little tongue protruding between her lips as she concentrated, that Charlie gave her her first real, grown-up kiss. He had kissed her before, little kisses that didn't count. This one did. And Cassie responded, letting go of her slate as she wrapped her thin arms around his strong neck and kissing him with all the love she had to give. From that point on, they considered themselves to be lovers. Lovers with secret signals.

Like the accidental bump he gave her as they washed the dishes. That bump actually meant the coast is clear. Pantry. Now. The kitchen was very large and the nuns and older girls moved silently while doing their tasks, washing down cooking counters, mopping the floor. Cassie and Charlie were at the sinks, soaping and rinsing plates and bowls, drying and stacking them to one side. When the kitchen tasks came down to these few, the sharper-eyed nuns retired from the kitchen. All but Sister Angelica, who was almost legally blind and wore spectacles so thick that her eyes were magnified to a startling effect. From where she stood on the far side of the kitchen, the pair at the sinks were nothing more than moving blurs. Cassie turned away from the sinks, drying her hands on her apron as she walked for the pantry. Seconds later, Charlie followed, quietly opening the pantry door and slipping inside. Almost before he closed the door, Cassie jumped into his arms and they kissed and kissed until they heard Sister Angelica's voice telling the others that it was time for Vespers. Charlie and Cassie then slipped out of the pantry, joining the organized march taking place past Sister Angelica, and she counted off heads, making certain all her charges were accounted for. Charlie's and Cassie's hands remained joined until they were in the hallway and the line of girls went one way and he another.

Just before he let go of her hand he whispered, "Meet me tonight, our place."

Cassie felt the trembling beginning in the pit of her stomach. Everything inside her told her that meeting him outside the dorms late at night was dangerous, foolhardy. If they were caught . . . she forced the thought away. Being with him was necessary. She needed his nearness the way she needed air to breathe. From the day they met, Charlie had filled up every part of her. But they had been children. In those days, every part of her had simply meant her heart, mind, and soul. Now they were young adults, and the remaining part of her that he longed to fill was by the Church, and by her family obligation, forbidden. Meeting him in the darkness meant he would beg again and she would be forced to refuse him—again. And to be honest, she didn't know if she could. Her body was crying out for his, and before their fingers slipped apart and Charlie went his way to the boys' dorm, she quickly nodded that she would meet him.

Marching in the line to the girls' open dorm, where she would change from her day dress into her church dress for evening prayers, Cassie's heart was already racing with anticipation of the late-night meeting. Charlie was wildly exciting. He was so tall and feral-looking. Everyone was afraid of him, not only because of his size and looks but because of his prevailing reputation. It had not faded with time as Père Blanc told Charlie it would. If anything, Charlie's violent reputation had grown right along with him. Grew because he intentionally made it grow. He used it as a shield, a shield to protect Cassie. Especially since she'd come into her woman's time.

At the onset of her monthly flow she began having trouble with the chore boys who were permitted to be inside the girls' yard. When they weren't occupied with their given chores, those boys came after her like dogs sniffing after a bitch in heat. All of them were aware that Charlie was her special friend, but none of them realized just how special until Pete Bernard tried to force himself on her. Pete had used his weight and his superior strength to pin her against a tree. He laughed as he ground his hips against hers.

"I got something for ya, Cassie."

She had been so afraid, her voice had frozen. She hadn't been able to scream or cry. Suddenly, there was Charlie taking hold of Pete by the neck and throwing him down to the ground. Charlie kicked Pete hard in the middle. Pete doubled up as air exploded from his mouth. Charlie kicked him again.

"You ever touch Cassie," Charlie growled, "and I'll kill you. Pass the word."

Pete did. From that moment on, no one messed with Cassie, not even the older girls, who thought they ran the girls' dorm and had the right to boss everyone except the nuns. No one argued that Cassie was protected by Charlie Jones even though it was common knowledge that as soon as Delbert Jakomin decided it was time, he would come for Cassie and marry her.

But, please God, not for another year, Cassie prayed. Please, please. Just let me have one more year with my Charlie and I won't ever ask for another thing. I swear.

By this time in my life, Everett, I was getting close to sixteen. My mother had long-ago remarried and had another child. During this time I believed that it was because of her new child that she forgot about me. I had no way of knowing that before I had been released from jail my mother had been bullied into signing me into Père Blanc's custody, that, in effect, he had accused her of being an unfit mother. Shame kept her away and made prisoners of us both. I couldn't leave the school and she never came to see me. Not even once. So outside of Père Blanc making me his prime occupation, continuing to privately teach me the Gospel, I believed I had no one to really care about me. Except my Cassie. For years she filled the ache in my heart and she was the only reason I opened my eyes each and every morning. Because of my clinging reputation as the Osage Kid, it wasn't hard for me to bully everyone in school. (Except Père Blanc.) So I had no problem getting the other boys and girls in the school to help me sneak Cassie out of the girls' dorm at night. They even acted as lookouts while we were together. In those stolen moments I courted Cassie like a storm.

In the soft glow of the crescent moon, Charlie eagerly waited for her. He caught the image of white, seemingly floating above the ground like a ghost. He pushed away from the trunk of the tree he leaned against and raced toward the form. Cassie leapt into his arms, and he kissed her, crushing her against him.

"I was afraid," he said huskily, "that you couldn't get out tonight."

"Sister André took a long time going to sleep," she whispered. "I thought she would be awake all night."

Charlie set her down, took her hand, and held it tightly. Together they ran to their private spot, where a blanket already lay waiting. There, they lay down, holding each other tightly, kissing, whispering, snuggling, and vowing their eternal love.

Cassie's hair flowed to her small waist. She was so indescribably beautiful, it beggared his imagination. In the year they had been seriously courting, they had progressed to the point where Charlie was allowed to remove her nightdress. In the moonlight he was allowed to look at all of her. Touch her.

Kiss her budding breasts. And although she would not allow him to remove all of his clothing, he was permitted to take off his shirt and shoes. Lying on his back, he closed his eyes as Cassie explored his heaving chest with her hands and her soft lips. He gritted his teeth, the pain of this chaste courtship, exquisite. When he could stand no more, he cried out and rolled away from her, huddling on his side until he was able to bring himself under control. Each time it was taking longer and longer. He had no idea how much more he could endure, but the notion of being without her touch, her sweet love, was wholly unacceptable.

When he was able, he turned and lay on his back, his hands beneath his head as he gazed up at the glistening stars. Cassie snuggled in close, resting her head in the hollow of his arm. It never ceased to amaze him that Cassie was only vaguely aware of her power over him, that she never took advantage of the fact that her less than one-hundred-pound body was able to completely crumble his one-hundred-and-fifty-plus body. Instead, she worried about him when he trembled violently, her cool hands there to wipe away the sweat pouring from his face.

"We shouldn't do this, Charlie. It makes you ill."

"It's a good sickness, Cass. It's the best."

"You're sure?"

"Oh, yeah. Please don't stop."

But she would stop, leaving him frustrated but more madly in love than ever.

He turned his head and their foreheads touched. "I'm leaving school this summer. And when I do, I'm gonna clear-cut a place on a hill that I've already picked out in my head. I remember it from when I was a kid. It's a real high hill, Cass, and I'm gonna build a us house on it. A good house. Then I'm gonna come get you. Père Blanc will marry us and we'll be happy forever, Cassie."

"How many rooms are in the house?"

She already knew, because this was a plan they discussed many, many times.

"Three. One for the kitchen, one for just sitting, and one for us and the children to sleep in."

"How many children?"

"Five. Three boys for me, two girls for you."

"It will have to be a big sleeping room."

"It will be, Cass."

"Swear?"

"Double swear."

"You're not suppose to—"

"Swear in school."

Laughing, he rolled on top of her, careful not to crush her with his weight. As he kissed her and she kissed him, she tried to forget that their shared dream would never come true. She was destined to marry Delbert Jakomin, a man ten years older than herself. For all of her life she had known Delbert Jakomin by sight, but until last summer he had never approached her, had never spoken to her. She had been promised to him as a bride when she'd been no more than a baby in her mother's arms. Delbert Jakomin was a big man, and it was said that he was wild. Last summer, when she voiced her concerns, hoping the discussion would lead to the subject of Charlie, her father had quickly cut her off. Marriage, he said, would settle Delbert Jakomin down. That all any man needed was a good woman to put him right.

"Del knows you're ready, that you're a prime woman now. He'll be comin' for ya soon, girl. You just be patient an' you won't be needin' that school no more."

Cassie's dainty little brain remained in a panic. She'd promised Charlie that she would talk to her father about him, let him know how they felt. She tried again, and her father, misunderstanding, left the house. When he came back, he had Delbert Jakomin with him.

"Girl, your man's come to call," her father said proudly.

Cassie moved as if she were lost in a thick fog as she helped her giggling mother make supper and her father visited with Delbert. After the meal, the courting couple were given permission to sit together outside in the darkness. One hour spent in his company was all the time she needed to know that she was not the right woman for Delbert Jakomin. Like Charlie, Delbert was a quick thinker. But unlike Charlie, Delbert had no patience with a slower-witted person. Sitting side by side on the bench on the back porch, Delbert talked and talked about things she didn't understand. When she tried, asking what she thought were pertinent questions, she felt his hot temper rise.

"Are you really stupid, or are you just puttin'-on stupid?"

Charlie would never have said that. He would have laughed and then he would have done his best to explain so that she would understand. The way he did his best to explain multiplication.

"Don't worry about the X, Cass, it's not important. Just remember that when you see a three and a one, the problem is asking you what number would you have if you had three ones."

"Six."

"No, sweetheart. You would have six if the problem asked what number you would have if you had three twos."

The corner of her mouth twitched. "I don't like trying to do this in my head, Charlie. I do better when I can draw the sticks on my slate and then count the answer."

"But you can't have your slate when Sister makes the class do multiplying drills."

"I know," she said, beginning to weep. "Sister always makes me sit down first. And then everyone laughs."

She would cry and Charlie would hold her, making her feel better. Delbert Jakomin did not try to hold her. What he did was leave, taking his formidable temper with him. He did not try to see her again for the rest of the summer. It became plain, even to Cassie, that Delbert Jakomin felt as trapped as she. She longed for Charlie, who was still shut up in the school, and she prayed every night that Delbert would do what was beyond her power to do.

Break off their betrothal.

He didn't. Now the time for Charlie to leave school was getting closer and closer. She knew she wouldn't be in school anymore when Charlie finished building the house and came back for her. But she couldn't bring herself to say it. If she didn't say it, there was still hope.

Wasn't there?

"I will always love you, Charlie," Cassie said with tears in her voice. "Forever and ever. Even after I'm dead."

Charlie sat up smartly. The mere mention of death sent a cold chill through him. He had seen death. He had even meted it out. Death was not romantic. It was terrible.

"Don't say that!" he snapped. He looked back at her, his expression churning fury. "Don't ever say that again."

Cassie pulled herself up beside him. "But don't you want me to love you forever?"

"You know I do. I just don't want to hear any talk about you being dead."

She kissed his cheek. "People don't really die, Charlie."

"Yes, they do, Cass. They die deader than a dog."

Everett, I can almost feel you getting hot, so I will briefly pause here to answer your question. No. I never did anything more than innocently love your mother. But that wasn't because I didn't try. I was a virile young man and she was a beautiful young woman. So of course I begged her. On my knees and half crazy from wanting her. But she was promised to your father and never mind that she loved me, Cassie took the promise seriously. No matter how we felt about each other, she saw it as her duty to honor the promise her father had made to your father, Delbert Jakomin. At the tender age of fourteen, on the day she went to the church to marry him, in spite of all of my begging and crying, she went to him so pure, she was whiter than a lily.

And I was hog-tied and gagged in the cellar.

• • •

The news Cassie dreaded, pretended would never come, came on a bright and sultry May morning, when Sister André informed her that she was permanently dismissed from kitchen duty.

Clutching the front of her nightdress, Cassie asked a typical Cassie question, "Why?"

Sister André fought back the smile, straightened her slight frame that was all but lost inside the novice's blue and white habit. "Because, my dear, you have a more important task to fill your day. You must prepare for your wedding."

Cassie's hand clutched the material between her breasts more tight. "I—I'm getting married?"

"Of course you are. Tomorrow afternoon. The bridal dress will be brought to you after breakfast for the fitting, and then for the remainder of the day you will be receiving final instruction."

None of this was a mystery to Cassie. She had seen other girls being prepared. The bridal dress belonged to the school, each bride fitted into it by laborious basting up or letting out, each measure dependent on the bride's shape. When the sisters finished with the dress, the bride was then bathed and dressed like a novice nun. In this holy garb she was taken under the escort of older nuns to the chapel. Well into the night she received lengthy instruction on the subject of being a wife, made confession, and then endured the bridal mass. Cassie had been told that the bridal mass was beautiful, that all the sisters sang and that the chapel was filled with flowers and candles to honor the purity of the bride. Cassie knew she would like that part, that being the focus of such a lovely mass while dressed in the blue and white habit, she would feel almost like the Holy Virgin. What she would not like was the part of the preparation intended to keep the purified bride immaculate in mind and heart before her marriage. Under close watch she would be shut up in the chapel for the entire night. And that meant she wouldn't have the opportunity to meet Charlie in the darkness. She would never again kiss his mouth, his huge body, or feel herself become lost in his strong arms. And without Charlie she would never feel safe again. Cassie whimpered as she felt herself shattering, dropping shard by shard into a blackened void.

Charlie looked for Cassie all of that day. It wasn't until the supper meal, and while he was in the cafeteria, that he finally heard about the wedding. The boys were excited, anything to do with sex, even a holy event, sent their young blood jumping. The older girls serving the food were subdued, shuffling through their duties as they thought of the bride, who was now shut up in the chapel. Any girl over the age of twelve knew that her own wedding day was rapidly approaching, and because marriage was the great unknown factor in their young lives, the marriage of a classmate was seen as a sobering event.

Yet most of the girls could not fully understand why Cassie DuPree, now the oldest girl in the whole school, had managed to remain unwed for three years past her first menses. No one, not even Charlie knew the reason why Cassie had made it to almost fifteen before the marital ax fell.

Cassie had made it through into a more mature age simply because the chosen groom had to be shamed into marrying her. Coerced, the better term. Delbert Jakomin did not want to be married. He wanted even less to be married to a girl he knew to be hopelessly dense. True, she was pretty and mild-natured, but he couldn't talk to her. He hated the way she looked at him with those blank grass-green eyes, letting him know that there was precious little going on between those delicate, shell-like ears. How could any man plan a life with a woman who couldn't even follow the flow of easy conversation? What kind of helpmate was that? Worse, what would their children be like? Delbert could not picture himself as a breeder of idiots. A supremely proud young man, the mere thought of being saddled with a dim-witted wife and equally dim children, gave him the shudders.

Had Charlie known the mind of the groom, he most probably would have gone over the school wall and run to Del-

bert. It is even conceivable that the two of them might have found a way out of their mutual dilemma. But Charlie didn't know, nor could he ever imagine any man not wanting his Cassie. A mental impression quickly formed of the man Charlie had never seen. An image so clear and corrupting that it became fixed. Permanent. He saw Delbert Jakomin as a great slathering beast eager and primed to force himself into Cassie's tender flesh. The vision was so horrific that Charlie could even hear Cassie screaming, calling for Charlie to save her. Horrified by this last vision, he jumped up from the long dining table and ran to the one man he believed could and would help him.

Père Blanc.

Charlie went straight to Père Blanc's small office. He did not pause to knock, he barged straight in, finding the old priest kneeling before his private altar. Livid that he would be interrupted during his evening prayers, Père Blanc stood to his feet.

"Charlie Jones," he fumed. "You are a thoroughgoing rascal. You know better than to rush in—"

"This is an emergency."

Père Blanc blinked his watery blue eyes. "There's a fire?"

"No, Father. A sacrilege is being performed."

Père Blanc stepped back, his expression alarmed. "We have a heretic in the school? A son or daughter of the devil practising the dark craft?"

"No, Father. It's not that kind of sacrilege."

Père Blanc's face reddened with anger once again, his voice rising to its notable shout. "Then what are you babbling about, Charlie Jones? You'd better be quick with the telling, or I'll fetch the strap!"

"You're about to marry off an impure girl."

Père Blanc's eyebrows shot all the way up his balding head, the effort smoothing many of the lines from his weathered face. Then his features settled, became a pruny scowl. "That's impossible," he railed. "I've just heard the child's confession. I am at peace in my mind that she has never lain with a man."

"But she has." Charlie slapped his hand to his chest. "By

all that's holy, I swear to you, Father, Cassie DuPree laid down with me."

Shaken by what he'd just heard, Père Blanc pulled out a chair and ordered Charlie to sit. While the young man made his confession, Père Blanc prowled the room. This was a terrible situation. Père Blanc knew that there was more at risk here than simply a young man's infatuation. There was the threat of the continuing existence of his school. Père Blanc paced more rapidly as he thought of all of those young souls who would be wrenched from his care. Even more awful, he thought of those young souls being doomed to become Quakers. And that was exactly what would happen if the Jesuit school was forced to close because of scandal. There would be only one school left on the Osage Reserve. That damnable Quaker school.

Père Blanc placed a hand on his brow and stopped pacing. Recovering his wits, he moved to stand in front of the young villain he should have allowed the law to hang.

"Did you penetrate that girl?"

Charlie thought at length. He knew he should say yes. He knew he should lie, say anything that might help to save Cassie. On the other hand, if he said yes, only God knew what would happen to her, what she might suffer until he was able to marry her and protect her. Cassie was so delicate. She would never understand or survive public scorn and ridicule. To save her from that, and hoping that the dried-up old man before him was still enough of a man to understand how a young man felt, Charlie forced himself to tell the truth.

"No, Father."

Confused, Père Blanc was even more angry, and in his anger he shouted at full volume, "Then kindly tell me exactly what you did with her!"

Père Blanc listened, and after a few minutes he calmed down. The situation was not as terrible as he had first believed. But it was still bad. By Church law, the girl was virgin. He certainly did not approve of the way she had been behaving, but her carelessness with propriety was more to do with Charlie. The girl had simply been too easily led. Besides, this minor indiscretion had been forgiven when the child asked to be absolved of any sins of omission. As during her confession she hadn't mentioned Charlie's name, Père Blanc could now safely assume Charlie to be her greatest omission. Now that she was safely locked up in the chapel for the night, technically, a perfectly pure bride would be delivered for the wedding.

However, if the girl talked, confessed to her parents that she could not go through with the marriage and why, they would not view their daughter's moonlight escapades with Charlie Jones as being technically innocent. In their minds the girl would be tainted and they would hold the school responsible for her corruption. He would deal with her, but first he must deal with Charlie.

Twenty minutes later, his black robes flying, Père Blanc made his way back to the chapel. His entrance startled the sleeping sisters and frightened Cassie. With a wave of his hand he dismissed the sisters, all of them hurrying to cover their sleeping-capped heads as they scurried off to the sacristy. Sitting up in the cot, Cassie held the thin blankets up against her nose, her large eyes peering fearfully at the angry priest. Père Blanc sat down on the opposite cot.

"Young lady, I've just heard of your misdeeds." When Cassie uttered a gasp, Père Blanc raised a hand. "Please do not add to your sins by attempting to deny the truth. Charlie Jones has told me all of the sordid details. I have had him locked up."

Cassie dropped the blankets, her hands covering her mouth as she began to cry. "Please, please, Father, don't do anything to my Charlie."

"What happens to him, my dear, depends largely on you. If you tell anyone, anyone at all of the disgraceful way you have behaved, I will see to it that Charlie goes to jail for a very long time."

"NO!"

"Yes. Charlie has committed a very serious offense."

"But, Father? Didn't I commit it with him?"

Her ingenuous question momentarily stymied the old priest. Slapping his knees, Père Blanc bellowed, "My child, you are losing sight of the issue. I am offering you a chance to save him from prison. Do you or don't you want to save him?"

"Y-yes, Father."

"Then this is what you must do. You must make a holy oath to me here and now that you will never again speak to, or be alone with, Charlie Jones. You must also vow that what passed between you will go no further than your confessor. You will not tell your parents, you most certainly will not tell the groom or any member of his family. Do you understand!"

"Even if they ask me?"

"They will not ask you!" Père Blanc boomed. "They will have no reason to ask you."

"But what if I should see Charlie and he says hello and—"

"You will not respond."

"Ever?"

"Not ever."

Cassie puckered her little face and began to weep.

Père Blanc lost the last of his patience. "If that is your answer, then I have no choice but to send for the law."

"No, Father!" Cassie screamed. "I promise. I promise. Please don't lock my Charlie in a jail."

Père Blanc stood, lightly touched the back of the sobbing girl's head. "Your sins are forgiven, my child."

Père Blanc left the chapel.

I was over six feet tall and Père Blanc had shriveled even more with age. There was no way he could overpower me fairly. So, he had done the next best thing. Circling the chair he had me sitting in, me unsuspecting and crying like a baby, he used something heavy and hit me on my head. That was the last thing I remembered.

The next morning I woke to the sound of the church bell ringing. I found that I was trussed up good and tight, lying on my stomach, my arms and legs tied together behind me. A gag was halfway down my throat. It was pitch-black in that cellar. Which was a good thing. In the privacy of darkness, I was able to weep and rage, as my darling Cassie promised to love, honor, and obey Delbert Jakomin.

My beautiful Cassie was gone. The girl who promised to love me for the rest of our lives was lost. And the small spark inside me making me capable of loving anyone fully and completely flickered out.

The whole time I was down there, I suffered every pang known in hell. I just knew I could hear my Cassie crying as my sordid and bitter imagination ran riot. The images I saw behind my eyes do not bear repeating. You'll never understand what all of that did to me, Everett. No one will. Cassie was my beautiful little angel. She was never intended for mortal man's use. Not even mine, although given the chance, I would have taken it. But I would have been tender with her, because I knew what she was; perfect, God's greatest work of art. I didn't trust Delbert to know or appreciate that, and time proved me right. He didn't.

Père Blanc left me in that cellar for two days. The nuns came in during the first night, untied me, gave me food and water. The canny old priest knew I would never kill a nun, but he was smart enough to know that I wouldn't hesitate to kill him. That's why he didn't come to the cellar himself. On the third morning he plucked up the courage to face me.

I have no idea what stopped me from snapping him apart like a wishbone. I hated the man. Hated him for saving me from hanging, only to cast me into a living hell. The fact that he was a priest didn't cut any cheese with me either. I was finished being Catholic. I was finished being his prime occupation. And when he held the lamp close to my face, I could tell that he read all of that in my eyes.

He became unspeakably sad and he seemed to shrink even more as he said softly, "Go with God, Charlie." He turned and slowly went back up the cellar stairs. I never saw him again. Finally freed from the cellar, I ran to my dorm room, packed my bag, and walked out of that school that very morning.

Like Sam Starr, I did not look back. And I finally understood why Sam hadn't. There was no point. The life and the love I had known in that place was finished. Looking back on all that was lost to me served no purpose.

S-gi-dv nu-s-di.

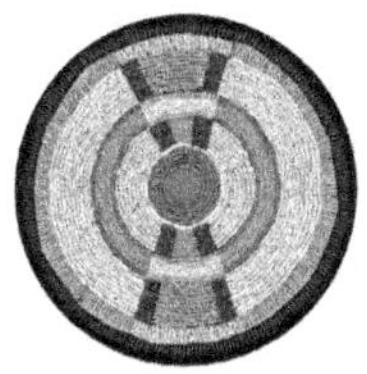

CHAPTER SIXTEEN

Everett closed the cover of the notebook and his red-rimmed eyes. Exhausted, he went to sleep. Two hours later, 8am, Katie woke up. Slipping on one of Everett's white T-shirts, she came out into the living room and found him sound asleep in the recliner. His face was wet from the tears seeping from beneath his lids. She had half a mind to read the journal resting in his lap, find out just what C.R. could possibly have said that would have a strong man like Everett Jakomin crying in his sleep. But she didn't. Instead, she turned and went to the bathroom and began filling the tub.

The next thing Everett knew, he was being wakened. "Come on," Katie ordered as she tugged on his arm. "I've got just what you need."

Seeing the way she was dressed, or not, depending on a person's point of view, Everett immediately brightened, coming fully awake. "Really?"

"Not that," she chuckled. "It's something you need a whole lot more."

Everett was soaking in the tub when Katie came into the bathroom holding a steaming mug.

"I hope that's coffee."

"It isn't. It's cocoa and brandy, guaranteed to send you off to sleep as soon as your fat head hits the pillow." She sat down on the edge of the tub, handing over the mug.

"I can't drink this," he said in a grumbling tone. "I can't afford a good sleep. I don't have the time."

"You didn't finish the memoirs?"

"No. I still have two more journals to read."

"Is it strong stuff?"

"Very."

Katie turned her angry face in profile. "I hope to God he isn't telling you you're his long-lost son."

Everett chuckled heartily. "Hey, don't I wish. That would make me his oldest son, heir to everything." He raised a dripping hand from the water and rested it on her bare leg. "I hate to disappoint you, but he was not my father."

Katie heaved a dramatic sigh. "Well, buster, I think I am disappointed. All of that lovely money. And it could have been ours. All ours." She sighed again. "At least Nath will be relieved. Can you imagine how he'd react to the news that his wife is also his first cousin?"

Everett laughed loudly. "You know, I'd completely forgotten about those two."

Katie stood to her bare feet and stretched and yawned. Then her arms slowly dropped. Everett sipped at the spiked cocoa as he watched her breasts move beneath the cotton fabric. Katie had great breasts.

"I have to go," she said abruptly. "I have to make sure my temper-tantrum girls didn't burn the house down. Then I have to head over to the café to make certain the staff didn't do the same thing to my only means of livelihood."

Sitting up, Everett caught her arm. "I don't want you to go."

Katie looked at him for a moment. "I'll make a deal with you. You take a nap and I'll come back. I'll even fix supper again. What do you want?"

"Spaghetti."

Katie leaned toward him and kissed his mouth. "Spaghetti it is. But only if you promise to get some sleep."

"Okay, okay, okay," he lied. "And could you bring something else?"

"What?"

"Some of your clothes? You know, to kind of throw around in the bedroom."

At first she looked startled, then she grinned, kissing him again.

After he dressed he made a fresh pot of coffee. It was almost nine. The store didn't open to the public until ten, but by this hour employees would be coming in. Everett dialed the number and after five rings Tommy Knife picked up. "Hey," Ev said casually. "Just thought I'd check in and see how everything's going over there."

"We've been really busy," Tommy replied. "But not with selling and raking in the dough. Folks are coming in here like swarms of bees hoping to find you and get the latest news about the Joneses."

Everett sighed wearily. "Then if you can handle being manager a bit longer, I'm staying put."

"What about tomorrow? You gotta be at the funeral!"

"Yeah."

"So I just open up an—"

"No. The store will be closed tomorrow."

"Outta respect?"

"Yeah. Outta respect."

Everett hung up, poured himself a cup of coffee and

went into the living room, picking up another journal. C.R.'s wake was scheduled for that night, and he didn't have time to spare on such a petty thing as sleep. He thought seriously about asking Katie to go to the wake with him. He could certainly use the support, but the idea of taking her to a wake made for a grim second-date theme.

"Oh, to hell with it," he said out loud. "Last night got off to a grim start, too, and turned out great."

What he did not say, what he couldn't bring himself to admit as he opened the cover of the next journal, was that even the thought of Katie not being with him made him afraid. Afraid because even though she was only partway into his life, he knew he couldn't face being alone again.

Ruthless.

That's what people said of me, and it was the truth. Only they don't know the half of it, Everett. When I finally left school, the Territory days were just about over. The surviving outlaws were old men, but a new breed of crooks were eagerly taking their place.

Oilmen.

I was determined to join their ranks. All the collateral I had in the world was my father's tract of land and my own young body. One I hung on to. The other I sold to the highest bidder.

And the highest bidder was Jacob Black. Emma's father. Old Jacob was a full-blood, just like me. And the man liked the way I didn't take any crap from anybody. There was oil on my father's land, and I knew it. But I wasn't about to do what the others were readily doing. Leasing out their land. But neither did I have the money to get at the oil on my own. So I promised to become Emma's husband in trade for the full rights to Jacob

Black's land and a commitment on any family land if and when it became available.

Before Emma and I were even married, I had leased out a small section of Jacob Black's land, and with the money from that hired my own drilling crew to work my father's land. I was eighteen, hard in body and in mind. The tag Osage Kid and the reputation of being a killer and outlaw persisted. Newly formed oil companies gave small, independent wildcatters hell. But me they were leery of. To make certain-sure, as Sam would say, that they remained leery, I walked around wearing the six-gun Sam had given me, slung low on my hip. And I freely used that gun. Every time a white face appeared on my property, the man either wanting to know how I was doing, or thinking to strike a deal with the crazy Indian kid, I opened her up.

I was a pretty good draw. Fast. Accurate. They got the message. Not too long after they stopped coming around, my first well came in. Big, bold, black, and rich.

Charlie and his crew of six felt the ground tremble. The entire wooden derrick was shaking. The wooden beams sounded wails of screeching protest against the restricting nails struggling to hold the construction together. As the ground shook harder, loud rumbling deafened the wide-eyed and fearful men. The entire derrick was threatening to tear itself apart into a giant, splintering deathtrap.

"Run!" Charlie screamed.

In their haste to escape, Charlie and his crew completely forgot that the derrick platform was over four feet off the ground. Charlie remembered just as he stepped off into air, arms and legs flailing. And behind him a solid six-foot-wide plume of thick oil erupted, shooting skyward.

"SHITTTTTT!" he shouted as the force of the eruption threw him farther into space.

He landed yards from the platform just as the gusher reached the top of the massive derrick and sprayed down on the earth, turning the ground and the men lying prone on it physically black.

For a few moments, all anyone could do was lie there, watching the erupting force they had created. The sheer power of it was numbing. Finally, Charlie threw his oil-soaked head back, laughing, unable to stop. Luckily for him, his foreman, Roger Jackson, was more experienced.

Roger scrambled to his feet, slipping and sliding under the assault of oil raining down and covering ground.

"Let's get a cap on this mother!"

Four hours later, and still covered with the residue of the strike, his shoulder-length hair hanging in matted clumps, Charlie drove the wildcat company truck as fast as it would go. He was going for Cassie. He no longer cared who knew that he loved a married woman. He didn't care about anything. He was rich now. Rich enough to buy Delbert off. Rich enough to buy Cassie a divorce. Rich enough to pay off Jacob Black and get out of his promise to marry Jacob's daughter, a little girl named Emma.

Charlie was too rich now to worry about hurting some little girl's feelings, and because he was rich, he was free. That was all the hard-earned money meant to him. Freedom. His and Cassie's. After nearly two long years apart, they would be together. No one would ever again tell them what to do. They would be married, and if it made Cassie's Catholic heart feel better, hell, he'd buy the annulment of her marriage from the Pope himself.

Shamelessly he drove right up to Delbert's house. To the side there was a sagging clothesline, laundry flapping in the breeze. Laundry his Cassie had hand-washed and hung out to dry. Four mangy dogs barked as his truck pulled in. He kicked one squarely in the head, sending it off howling as he bolted from the truck cab. The remaining three dogs groveled, giving way to the Alpha male.

Before he reached the front porch, Cassie opened the door, stepping out into the bright sunshine. Charlie's heart stopped on a dime. He hadn't had so much as a sight of her since their last night together at school. And in that time he couldn't believe it possible, but she had grown even more lovely. Her hair fell behind her like a dark veil, almost touching the backs of her knees. She was slender, her face beaming with youth. It pained him to admit it, but Delbert seemed to be taking good care of her.

As she stood there, staring, seemingly unable to believe it was really him after all this time, her beautiful mouth fell open. As Charlie raced toward her, she was so happy to see him that she forgot everything else. Just as he reached the porch, she sailed readily into his arms.

It felt so wonderful to kiss him. To be held by him. To hear his voice, his laughter. She didn't care that he was filthy. So filthy that his eyes looked like white holes in his face. She'd missed him so much that every day had seemed an eternity. And the nights spent in Delbert's bed a torturous hell. Delbert wasn't brutal, but neither was he loving. He did what he did and then he rolled over without speaking. He didn't speak much during the day either. He never bothered to explain where it was he went or when he would be back. It made it hard for her to have his supper hot, just the way he liked it. Delbert was a good eater. He liked the food she cooked, giving her a backhanded compliment, "Cooking is the one thing you can do."

Too soon Charlie pushed her away, holding on to her shoulders as he laughed and spoke in a rush. He spoke so fast, she couldn't follow what it was he was saying.

"I hit, Cassie. I hit it big. Do you know what that means?"

"No."

"It means that I've got money now, sweetheart. A lot of money. I can take you out of here. You'll be my wife. Mine, Cassie." He began to pull her off the porch. "Come on. Let's get out of here. Now. Right now!"

Cassie began trembling as tears began to flow. She pulled away from him, her arm easily sliding out of his oily grasp. She felt her heart breaking all over again as her wonderful Charlie stood there looking so hurt and confused. Cassie sank to her knees. Sitting on the backs of her legs, her long hair curtaining her face, she rocked back and forth, weeping inconsolably.

Charlie knelt down, took her chin in one hand, raising her chin, forcing her to look at him.

"I can't," she wailed. "I can't go anywhere with you. Not now. Not ever."

"I don't give a damn about your marriage, Cassie!" Charlie yelled. "I don't care about anything except you."

Her trembling increased as in a voice so soft he had to strain to hear, she said, "I'm gonna have a baby."

Charlie felt everything leave him, turn him hollow. As the reality of what she said penetrated, he became an empty shell. He had no heart. No blood. No mind. He was an empty chrysalis and hope, the butterfly, swiftly fluttered away.

His legs gave out from under him, his begrimed body landing dully on the dusty ground. All he could do was sit and stare at her. Delbert might have let Cassie go, but he would never let go of his child. And Cassie would never leave her baby. Not for anyone or for any reason.

It took a long time of just staring at her as she sat there, silently weeping, to realize that no amount of money on earth could buy her freedom now. Charlie's enemy had won. Somehow he managed to pull himself to his feet and walk away, knowing full well that he was walking toward a life empty of every emotion except one.

A consuming hatred of Delbert Jakomin.

I got two more wells going, paused long enough to marry Emma, and went back to work, staying with those wells until they came in. During this time I heard that Cassie had lost that baby. That she had lost it in her sixth month and that expelling that thing from her body had almost killed her. But it was too late for me to go back and get her. I was married now too.

Poor little Emma. I really do feel bad about her. When we first married she was a sweet little thing. But

I didn't love her. I couldn't. I promised her father I would honor her, and take care of her. That's exactly what I've always done. Old Jacob got his money's worth.

Your mother, my Cassie, had two more miscarriages before she became pregnant with you. I knew that because I'd made it my business to know everything that was going on with Cassie. So I also knew that your father was told, right to his face by the doctor, that Cassie shouldn't be pregnant again until her body was a bit more mature. She wasn't even eighteen yet, and another miscarriage could mean her life.

Well, your father wanted a son and Cassie was his wife. In less than a year after Delbert was warned, Cassie was pregnant again. I don't know if you're ever going to thank me for this, Everett, but the sole reason you're alive is because I went to that doctor and paid the man a thousand dollars cash money. In those days, a thousand dollars was worth about a million. To earn this under-the-table money, he had to put Cassie, who was only two months pregnant, in the hospital and keep her there until she delivered.

Please don't go all misty on me. I didn't give a fig about you. I just didn't want her to die. And if saving her life meant paying a doctor to hover over her twenty-four hours a day until her baby was born, I was willing to pay the man. Plus, being in the hospital, where she could simply rest, pulled her out from underneath Delbert's thumb.

I don't have to tell you Delbert's always been a drunk. He could have been rich if he hadn't poured the profits he received from leasing his land right down his stupid throat. I won't soft-pedal it, Everett. The man was an idiot. What made it worse was that he thought he was so damn smart. He built Cassie a fine house and he bought himself even finer cars. Then he got it into his idiot head that he was an investor, sinking his money into the stock market. I know you know where that eventually led. But before he lost his money, he was living fine. To me, he had it all. And the thing that baked my biscuits was the fact that if he hadn't had French blood in his veins, he would never have gotten his hands on my Cassie. So for that I hated him. As a matter of fact, I began to hate the whole French race. I still do! I won't eat French food or drink their damn wine, I hate them so much. I know it's popular history to believe that the Germans started both world wars. Son, go back and read the history books again. I think you'll be surprised to find that it was France who pushed Germany into war—twice! And then when the Germans pushed back, the French immediately surrendered and waited for the Americans and the British to rescue them. My suggestion is, if that kind of bonehead thing ever happens again, the loser of the war, as a penalty, should be made to keep France.

But never mind all that. Let's get back on target. So, there I am, married to Emma, and by this time Emma knew exactly how I felt about Cassie. She knew because I did the stupidest thing a husband can ever do. I told her. But not until we were six months into our marriage and I realized that my wife was in love with me. For some reason, I just couldn't go along with that. I felt it was unfair. Oh, it was okay for us to be married and get along all right in the bed together, but this love business outside of the bedroom gave me the whim-whams. So I sat Emma down and told her the whole story about me and Cassie, and while I was telling her, Emma just seemed to change right before my eyes. I had married a sweet girl who wouldn't have said boo to a goose, and what my confession accomplished was to turn her into a screaming damn harpy. After that, if I couldn't account for every minute I was away from her, Emma would commence yelling and crying. I was still young, dumb, and thick-headed enough to believe that I didn't have to explain my whereabouts to anybody, especially my own wife. As a consequence, Emma pitched a lot of fits, and I was getting to the point where I couldn't stand the sight or sound of her. Our marriage was all but over by the time Cassie was in the hospital pregnant with you.

In the meantime, my personal life might be in shambles but my oil wells were sure doing great. So great that Emma's brother was looking to go partners with me on his piece of land. I knew there was oil under that ground. By that time I could smell oil better than anyone in the state. So I was really wanting Emma's brother to partner with me instead of leasing out his allotment.

As a persuader, I bought him a car, because he wanted one so bad. Well, the fool killed himself in it. Her whole family started throwing ashes in the air because the blockhead had been doing about twenty miles an hour in reverse when he went over a cliff, but I seized the opportunity to remind old Jacob about our deal. The upshot is, the day they were burying Emma's brother, I wasn't at the funeral because I was drilling a well on his land. A simple twist of fate, or a case of remarkably bad driving, got me that land. And five more oil wells. Because of that car crash, I'd been spared the headache of having that fool as a partner. But old Jacob watched me real closely after that. He was too afraid of me to ever accuse me directly, but I know he believed that I had somehow killed his son.

I didn't.

However, that did make three dead men the general public laid at my feet. The two shot-up cowboys and Emma's brother. But nobody could prove anything, and I was busy sinking wells. Imagine the glee when there finally was a case against me that could be proven.

Attempted murder.

The victim—Delbert Jakomin.

For a long time, Everett, I thought I had a lock on my

feelings. I had gotten to the point that whenever I saw Cassie with Delbert, I didn't foam at the mouth like a rabid dog. Believe me, that was progress. Seeing her with him when all of us just happened to be in town at the same time and Cassie would pass me by and look through me like a piece of glass would completely tear me up. Then Emma would have to hang on to me to prevent me from pulling my gun out of the holster and shooting Delbert. If you counted the times Emma saved your daddy's life, you'd run out of fingers and toes. Anyway, sometime before Cassie fell pregnant with you, whenever I saw Delbert, I wasn't going for my gun anymore and Emma wasn't having to hang on to my arm. It wasn't a giant leap in emotional progress, but it was enough of a jump to fool me into feeling safe, like nothing would ever get at me or hurt me again.

What a young loony I was.

It was raining the night you were born. In fact, it was pouring. It was one of the worst summer storms we'd had in a long, long time. Which was why I was home and not on a drill site. Emma was mad at me again. I hadn't called her that whole day, and she was just sure it was because I hadn't been working at all, that I had spent the day hanging out at the hospital. I wasn't interested in trying to convince her otherwise, so I was ignoring her while I worked out tally sheets figuring my profits and losses and figured out how to avoid the latter. Then the telephone rang.

Frankly, until that phone call I'd forgotten about Cassie. I mean, she was in a hospital with doctors and nurses all around her. All she had to do was eat, sleep, and swell up. Then she'd have the baby, and if it was a boy, hopefully Delbert would leave her alone and she wouldn't be in any more danger.

The call was from the hospital. Cassie had delivered a healthy son. Unfortunately, and this is what reached me, Everett, turning me cold with rage, Cassie hemorrhaged and they were unable to stop the bleeding.

Cassie was dead.

My Cassie. My sweet, lovely Cassie.

I hung on to that old ringer telephone earpiece, pressing it so hard against my ear that it almost went straight through my skull. I saw her in murky sunlight, running for me. Then I saw her in moonlight as she knelt in front of me, her face and young body so beautiful, she took my breath away. And then I heard her, just as clearly as if she had been on the other end of the telephone line.

"I love you, Charlie. I promise I will love you forever and ever. Death isn't the end. It isn't."

I screamed and started running out of the house. Emma, not knowing what the hell was going on, tried to stop me from running half-dressed out into the pouring rain. I threw her so hard, she bounced off a wall. I heard her squawk like a chicken as she hit, but I just kept on going. Then she stood on the porch, screaming her lungs loose as I cranked the automobile engine over in sheeting rain.

Everett, if you've never hand-cranked a car in slamming rain, you have missed a treat. Somehow I got the engine to kick over and then I drove like a madman to the hospital. When I got there, I scared the nurses half to death when I banged through doors like I owned the place. Who could blame them? I was soaked, half-naked, wearing only a pair of oily jeans. I was also completely crazy, running through the halls and screaming Cassie's name.

I'd let her down, you see. That was the thing making me the most nuts. I hadn't saved her from a loveless marriage. Then I'd paid strangers to take care of her when it was me she needed the most. And the whole time I had been worrying about how much money I was making, my Cassie lay dying, surrounded by strangers. Now she was dead. My Cassie was dead. But I had it in my crazy head that if I kissed her, she'd come back to life, that the second she did, I would pick her up just like I had done when she'd fallen out of the playground swing and run. Delbert would have his son. Emma would have enough money to see her beyond her years. They could have everything. All of it. Every last damn bit of it. The one thing, the only thing I wanted, was my Cassie. So I tore up that hospital, looking for her.

And I found her.

In a room all by herself, lying on a bed looking tiny and pale. By this time doctors and nurses were yelling and clawing at me, trying to drag me back, but I had strength known only to the thoroughly insane. I was flinging doctors and nurses everywhere, throwing them off me. And when I got to Cassie, I kissed her and I kissed her, but . . . she wouldn't come back.

Because she couldn't.

She couldn't.

"Cassie!" Charlie screamed into her cold face. "Cassie! Don't leave me. You promised you wouldn't! You promised. Cassie, come back. Please come back."

Tears blinding his eyes, Charlie lay his head on Cassie's stilled chest and wept. He said her name over and over. Again he put his mouth on hers, trying to blow breath into her. When a nurse touched his bare shoulder, Charlie growled like a feeding lion, warning the woman off. The doctor Charlie had paid handsomely to care for Cassie sent the nurse an understanding nod.

"We'll just give him some time. Just a little time. There's no hurry. None at all."

At 3pm Katie had been in the house for about an hour. Spying Everett in the living room, she tiptoed back into the kitchen, closing the door. He seemed so engrossed in what he was reading, she would have sworn he didn't even know she was in the house. And then he shouted, "Katie!"

Startled, she dropped the bowl she was going to use for the spinach salad and ran. She found him holding the writing pad tightly in his hands. His entire body was shaking and he was weeping uncontrollably. Terrified for him, Katie started yelling.

"Stop reading it, Ev!"

"No!"

"What's he telling you?"

"My birth day," Everett wept. "He's telling me about my birth day." Sitting up in the recliner, he literally begged, "Katie, please hold me. And for God's sake, don't let go."

I heard laughter. In a stricken daze I looked up from Cassie to all the worried faces crowding the room. None of them were laughing, but someone was. Someone not in the room. There could be only one person able to laugh at a time like this.

Delbert.

Once again the doctors and nurses made a futile effort to stop me, but nothing could stop me. Like a furious bull, I was charging for the man doing the laughing. The man responsible for killing my Cassie.

Delbert and two of his brothers were standing outside the nursery. One of your uncles was holding you. To be fair, it was one of your uncles doing the laughing. I guess it was because he was so pleased that you were such a strong, healthy baby. But any expression of happiness at that point only drove me more over the edge. I had grown almost another three inches since leaving school, and because of a hearty appetite, which Emma catered to, and the rough physical labor filling almost every hour of my days, I had bulked up considerably. As a result, the thing that was going after your daddy was a moving wall on two legs. I remember the look of absolute fear in his eyes just before I plowed right into him. Then, right there in the hospital corridor, with his brothers and a large number of the hospital staff trying to stop me, I beat the living hell out of him.

While I was beating him unconscious, someone called the police. By the time the police got there and put a gun to my head, I had beaten Delbert so badly, he was more dead than alive and had to be admitted to the hospital.

I, of course, they carted off to the jail. I was so covered with Delbert's blood that they had to hose me down before putting me in a cell. While they were blasting me with the fire hose, beating me against the wall with the force of water, washing that accursed French blood off my full-blood Osage body, I heard the guards laugh.

"We gotcha, Charlie! Took some years, but we gotcha!"

Emma's father went with her to the jail. He waited in the police office as Emma was escorted back to the cell where her husband was confined. Jacob Black sat wearily down. He deeply regretted marrying his daughter to Charlie Jones. Why Emma still loved him after what he had done to her brother, and now this . . . disgrace, was more than Jacob Black could understand.

But Emma did love him. With an intensity that bordered on unnatural. Jacob had to sit by and say nothing as Emma's so-called husband walked all over her broken heart. When Jacob fully understood how little Charlie Jones regarded his Emma, Jacob begged Emma to either allow him to kill Charlie Jones or to show some pride and come home. Emma would do neither.

It was only tonight, when Charlie had laid his hands on

her, throwing her against a wall, that it seemed Emma had finally had enough. After Charlie roughed her up and drove off into the night, Emma had called her father and asked him to come get her. The second he heard her say over the telephone that she was going to divorce Charlie, Jacob didn't spare the horses going to fetch her. But moments after she was safe in her parents' home, a knock sounded at their door, and a policeman stood on the front stoop.

Emma stood there, hearing the whole ugly tale, and not one tear did she shed. Jacob and his wife, Margie, were thoroughly aghast. Charlie was in jail. He had all but killed another man with his bare hands. And not just any man, but a man who had just lost his wife to childbirth. Jacob had to hold Margie up because as she heard the deplorable tale, she went into a faint.

But Emma didn't budge. She just stood there, listening, not one trace of emotion showing on her young face. Then she said to the policeman, "You're quite sure Mrs. Jakomin is dead?"

That was it. Emma's one and only question. And said in a tone of seeking assurance rather than fixing a fact in her mind.

"Yes, ma'am, she's dead."

Emma released a slow breath, then hurriedly turned, retrieving her coat from the wall hook. "Take me to my husband."

She didn't want her father to come with her, but Jacob insisted. Charlie was so crazy that if he further shamed Emma by refusing to see her, Jacob wanted to be there for her. Then he would tell the jailers to throw away the key to Charlie's cell. Now, watching his daughter leave with the guard, all Jacob Black could do was wait. And pray Emma would find the grit to tell Charlie Jones to his no-good face that he could just go ahead and rot.

Charlie was soaked. Trickles of water twisted around the curve of muscles, each droplet taking its time traveling the expanse of his bare chest. Sodden jeans were molded against his legs like blue-black skin. He sat on the cot, his spine resting against the wall, one leg dangling over the edge of the narrow bed, the other bent at the knee, his bare foot planted squarely on the thin mattress. His arm was balanced on the top of the knee as he sat staring vacantly at the far wall. He was conscious only of his pain. He breathed and exhaled pain every time he thought of Cassie lying so small and alone in the hospital morgue.

"Please forgive me," he whispered. "Please, Cas, please." His throat tightened. He could only make a low, moaning sound. He went quiet when he heard the jailer. Hearing the footsteps approaching his cell, Charlie forced himself to go blank. He appeared completely indifferent to his circumstance by the time the jailer appeared on the other side of the bars. Only his eyes moved when Charlie glanced in the direction of the cell door. There stood Emma, and standing just behind her, the guard.

"Open the door," Emma commanded.

"He could get violent again."

Emma turned her head and sent the guard a withering look. "Either you open the door or you give me the key."

Frowning, the guard unlocked the cell door. After Emma entered, the guard closed the door, locking it again. "Miz Jones, you just give a yell whenever you're ready." The guard then sauntered importantly away.

Emma slowly approached Charlie. He wasn't looking at her now. He was staring again at a spot on the opposite wall. Emma was livid, but she was also happy. Cassie Jakomin, the woman who had plagued their marriage from the very beginning, was dead. That meant that whether he liked it or not, Charlie was Emma's now. Never again would she have to spend the hours he was away from her worrying that he was with Cassie. Nor would she spend any more sleepless nights alone in their bed terrified that he and Cassie had run away together. Now that Cassie Jakomin was dead, Emma no longer saw the need to divorce the man she loved.

And she did love him. She loved him passionately and completely. She'd fallen in love with him on their wedding day, when he'd folded the blanket away from her face and softly promised, "I will not harm you."

He looked big and rough, but when he took her to his bed, he was so gentle, so kind. He went slowly, bringing her out of her fear and then into a passion that burst into millions of stars. Throughout their marriage, Charlie never failed to make love to her just that way. And if he could make love like that with a woman he merely respected, what must he be like with the woman he loved with every ounce of his being? That question nagging her, Emma became insanely jealous of Cassie Jakomin. Her jealousy changed her into an embittered shrew, refusing to believe him when he vowed to the heavens that he and Cassie had never made love.

What did she look like? A fool? Did he really expect her to believe that for a man like him Cassie Jakomin had never fallen down on her back and spread her legs? Of course she had. And that newborn baby of hers was Charlie's too. Emma just knew it. Charlie steadfastly refused to give his own wife his children, but he was giving them to his whore. It was just a pity that this baby hadn't died like the others. But this time Charlie had made certain that the child lived. He didn't think she knew about his paying the doctors, but she knew all right. It was just his bad luck that this time the baby survived and his precious Cassie died.

Emma pushed all of that from her mind, concentrating instead on the fact that Charlie was finally free of Cassie. And because he was free, there would now be no reason for him to withhold himself. Now he would give his wife his children. Emma had won. It was time now for her to be gracious, prove to him that he still had something to live for.

She sat down next to him. In a voice Charlie had never heard her use before, a voice that did not wheedle or whine, Emma spoke to him.

"Charles, I want you to stop feeling sorry for yourself and put your mind to getting out of here."

His vault-dark eyes drifted to the corners. Both were silent as Charlie coldly regarded her.

"You're a mess," she said tightly. "And you'll catch your death in those wet britches. I'll bring you some clothing from

home. But before I go, I want to put a few things straight. You are my husband, Charles Jones. Mine. And the minute this jail cracks open and you walk out a free man, you'll find me waiting and with our bags packed. We're going on a honeymoon. We will stay gone until this whole business blows over. When we come home, I'll be telling my parents that I'm going to have a baby. And that won't be a lie. Do you hear me?"

He stared at her, his eyes flat, unresponsive.

"I know you loved her, Charles, that all you ever needed or wanted from me was my land. That hurt me, but it doesn't hurt so much anymore. From this day forward, we can both change, have a real marriage."

He turned away from her, leaning his upper body solidly against the cold brick wall. She placed a warming hand on his bare shoulder.

"I promise I won't ever get in your way," she said. "I won't yell at you ever again. I'll do everything I can to be the kind of wife you need. In return, all I'm asking you is that you pick yourself up, be a man, and get yourself out of here."

He jerked his shoulder and Emma took her hand away.

"I'm not your enemy, Charles. I never have been. Your enemies are all outside this jailhouse. If you give up now, then they've beaten you. And if you give up on a life with me, then you've lost the one person completely on your side."

Charlie turned, his head still leaning against the wall as he studied her through narrowed eyes. This woman was a stranger. She looked exactly like Emma, but the hardness she projected was totally alien to the Emma he knew. He found that surprising and vaguely fascinating. As if to probe the hardness and depth of this new person, he said, "I love Cassie. I can't love anyone else. I don't mean to hurt you, Emma, it's just . . . it's just the way it is. The way it will always be."

He was listening. She didn't care for what he said all that much, but at least he was listening. Which meant she had his full attention. A thing she rarely enjoyed. Generally she would yell, or cry, and he would remain as responsive as a dirt clod.

"I know," she said softly. "And I know how much you're hurting."

Charlie waited for Emma's threats and condemnations. None of those materialized. Even more amazing, she remained as dry-eyed as a well-digger's ass in Idaho. He waited again, and while he waited he remembered all the times when, no matter what he said, Emma was firmly convinced that he and Cassie had been together. She refused to believe him when he swore that he never even saw Cassie. Which was the truth. Seeing Cassie always tore him apart. No matter how much he wanted her, he would never debase their love by seducing her into a sordid affair. Cassie was too pure for that. Some women were ordinary and some were meant to be on a pedestal. Cassie was the latter. But he couldn't stop wanting her. When he made love to Emma, he kept the room dark and his eyes closed.

And made love to Cassie.

Cassie!

Just the thought of her name made everything inside him seize into a tight fist. It hurt so much that he doubled up and bowed forward. Emma steadied him with her hands, bringing her face close to his, speaking to him gently but firmly.

"Charles, I understand what you're going through. I know what it is to love someone you can't have. But I'm asking you now to pull yourself together. I'm asking you not to let them put you in prison."

"I deserve to go to prison, Emma," he sobbed. "I left her all alone. Don't you understand? She was always afraid when she couldn't see me. And her fear killed her. I, killed her!"

Emma snorted down her nose. "Charles Jones, the only person you almost killed was Delbert Jakomin. Do you really want to go to prison for a man like that? A man who wouldn't even listen to the doctors when they told him not to make his wife pregnant again?"

Charlie raised his eyes. The hatred that radiated from those eyes caused Emma to flinch. But then she recovered.

"It was him that put that baby in her, wasn't it?"

"Yes," Charlie rasped. "It's Delbert's baby. I've told you a thousand times, and I'm telling you for the last time, I have never touched Cassie."

Emma took a deep breath, released it. Now, finally, she believed him, and because she believed him, his going off to prison was the last thing she wanted. She lowered her voice to a whisper, speaking in a rushed staccato.

"Delbert deserved the beating you gave him, but I'm telling you something, if you go to prison, he'll be a happy man. Is that what you want? Cassie's killer singin' and dancin' in the street while you're a jailbird?"

Unbeknownst to her, Emma said exactly the right thing. It had been said before, in a different time, a different place, but for the same reason. Revenge. Charlie remained silent for a moment. Her hands still against his shoulders, her face so close to his that they shared the same air, Emma could feel the heat of his anger as it quickened, began to smolder. Emma fanned the flames.

"You're gonna have to beat him again, Charles, but this time not with your fists. This time you'll have to use your head."

Emma stood up. "They told me they'd let you make a phone call. I'm gonna go now. I'm gonna get you some hot food and some dry clothes. While I'm gone, I expect you to think long and hard about just who you should call. You don't have many friends out there, so don't waste your time on someone you just hope might help. Think instead of someone who needs to help you, and then you call him."

He looked up at her shyly. "You promise you'll come back?"

Her heart ached to hold him, to comfort him, but she knew better now. Charlie seemed to respond more favorably to strength. If a strong-headed woman was the kind of woman he wanted, then that was the kind of woman he was going to have.

"Yes, I'm coming back."

She reminded him of someone, but in his present state of

emotional turmoil, he couldn't remember who. Years later, he would.

Belle Starr.

And Charlie would fall into playing to Emma exactly the way Sam had played to Belle.

His tormented expression had almost left his face as he watched Emma walk to the cell door. Her spine was ramrod-straight when she called for the guard. She said good-bye and a few other things he didn't hear as he flogged his brain, trying to think of who this tear-free, hard-headed person masquerading as Emma Black Jones might be. He gave up trying as the cell door banged behind her and she left. But outside the cell room, just after the last door was closed and Emma knew he couldn't see or hear her, she collapsed against the wall and waited for the dizziness to pass. Playing at being a strong-minded woman had taken just about all the starch out of her. Her only hope was that she would progressively get better at it because for a beginner, it was emotionally exhausting.

Twenty minutes passed. During that time Charlie dwelled on everything Emma had said. But he thought about other things too. He thought about Delbert. He thought about Cassie. He thought about revenge. As he completely concentrated on that, a voice from the dim past came to him.

"Never go after an enemy when your heart is full of hate. You wait until your mind goes clear. . . . Then you get him on your own ground. And you let him see the bullet coming."

Charlie sat straight up. His mind was going clear, and as it cleared, the name of the one person he should call came to him. Hurriedly, he left the cot and yelled for the guard.

Emma returned with food, clothing, and a flask of hot coffee. A now-more-animated Charlie appreciated all of it. He was clothed and wolfing down sandwiches, when a young man wearing an eastern suit and tie and very thick glasses appeared outside the cell. The guard unlocked the door, and as the young man entered, Charlie and Emma simply stared at him. The young man was nervous, pulling on the high-starched collar and slightly loosening the tie.

"My name," he said shakily, "is Peter Waterman. I'm the—uh—lawyer you asked for."

A slow smile tugged at the corners of Charlie's mouth. So, this was the infamous snapping-bobcat lawyer for Rockefeller Oil. The one everybody laughed about because he had made the mistake of letting it be known that he would have liked to be a cowboy. Now Charlie understood why everyone laughed. Peter Waterman stood no more than five feet five and couldn't possibly weigh over one hundred and twenty pounds. And he was Jewish. New York Jewish.

Charlie suppressed his own laughter. Rising from the cot, he felt like a massive oak shading Peter Waterman as the two men faced each other for the first time in their lives.

Charlie extended his hand. "I'm Charles Jones." With a slight turn of his head as he shook hands with Peter Waterman, he acknowledged Emma. "And this is my wife."

Emma's spine straightened with pride. Then Charlie again took her by surprise when he used an additional endearment. "Sweetheart, would you excuse us, please? Mr. Waterman and I have a lot to discuss."

As she moved past him, Charlie stopped her, lightly kissed her lips. "Thank you. With all my heart, I thank you."

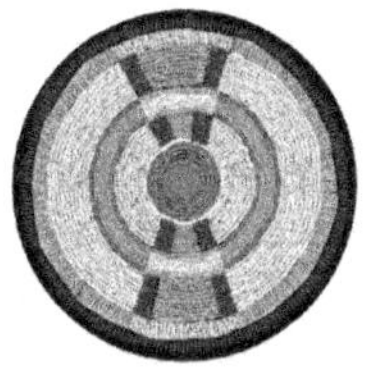

CHAPTER SEVENTEEN

Katie held on to him for a long time, and during that time Everett confused her. When she had run to his aid, he'd been practically hysterical. Then he just became still, concentrating on each page he read. Gradually she let go of him, then stood by the chair, at the ready should he need her again. Minutes ticked by. Absently his left hand groped the end table beside the chair. When it found the near-empty pack of cigarettes, Everett, still reading, fished one out and lit it. She suspected he was smoking without even realizing what he was doing. She didn't want to leave him, but at the same time, she could smell the spaghetti sauce beginning to burn. She tossed a mental coin and the sauce won. Everett's brows were furrowed and he blew smoke against the page he was reading as Katie turned for the kitchen.

Peter Waterman got me out of jail the next morning. On his advice, I paid Delbert off. I paid handsomely,

Everett. It cost me ten thousand dollars, but Delbert dropped the charges. Four days later, I left with Emma for England. We had a nice honeymoon. Emma might never be the woman I loved, but while we were in England, she became my dearest friend.

When we came home, we started building the house. That project ate up practically every minute of my day. As the house was being built, Emma was always changing her mind about the rooms and so on, which made the architect crazy and, in turn, me. It took over a year to build that house. We had been living in it only a few months when Emma discovered that she was pregnant. At first she was so happy she was practically singing. That quickly changed. Harry was a hard baby for her to carry. In the first months she was constantly sick, and when that eventually passed, her arms and legs became so swollen that her skin felt tight and feverish. Her doctor was so worried about her that he all but lived with us during her final months of pregnancy. Now, I could cope fairly well with all of that, but then there came the day that I came home to find brick masons building walls around the house. That just about burned me to the marrow of my bones.

From the time I was eleven until I was sixteen I had lived behind brick walls. If it hadn't been for Cassie, being locked behind a high wall would have made me stark, staring nuts. Now Cassie was gone and what was my wife doing?

Building brick walls!

I went after her. I didn't care if she was laid up in the bed with her arms and legs the size of giant sausages, I wasn't going to allow her to wall me up inside my own damn house. We had some kind of fight, both of us yelling so loudly that the doctor came running. I'll never forget the way that man came into the room with such speed that the instant he stepped onto one of the Persian rugs, the thing folded like an accordion and he slid the rest of the way in.

Well, that got me and Emma to laughing, and then she stopped, a peculiar expression coming over her face. Then she took off in a hurried waddle and locked herself in the bathroom. The doctor and I could plainly hear what was going on. He even timed it with his pocket watch. I'm not kidding, Everett. Emma peed for five straight minutes. When she finally came out, damned if her arms and legs didn't look normal. Then she pranced right up to me, tiptoed, and looked me dead in the eye.

"Those walls are going up, Charles Jones."

It was the same tone she'd used the night I had been in jail, I knew she meant it. In the meantime, here's what was going on with Delbert. And everything I'm about to tell you is solid fact. I know because I was having the man watched. My reason? Well, it had gone beyond revenge. My reason had become a tiny bit side-tracked. The reason was you. Like it or not, you were all I had left of my Cassie, and I started worrying about you the same way I had once worried about her. At first it was only because I knew she would want me to look out for you, then it became more than that. It was because you looked like her. You have your father's coloring and build, but you've got your mama's face. And I know you probably don't remember this, but until you were seven, you were towheaded. You were the prettiest little blond Indian baby in the whole world.

I couldn't help it. I loved you.

It was because of you that I laid off Delbert, that is until he started cutting loose with a woman named Sherry Philbin. She was a white woman your dad met somewhere and brought home to live with him. Sherry Philbin was just about the sorriest piece of trash I ever hope to meet. Your dad has always been a good drinker, but after he hooked up with Sherry, he really got going after it. They had parties in my Cassie's house that could sometimes go on for a week. And there was two-year-old you in the middle of all that rowdiness.

I sent Peter over to talk to your aunt, pay her to take you out of that house and home to live with her. She did, and a few weeks later, when Delbert finally sobered up enough to notice that his son was gone, he sent Sherry out to fetch you back. Sherry was falling-down drunk when she drove your daddy's brand new Cadillac car over to your aunt's. Your aunt wasn't going to let you go with Sherry, but Sherry had a gun and threatened her with it. Your aunt was calling the police as Sherry drove off with you in the car. She had plowed headlong into another car by the time the police came on the scene. Sherry was laughing as she climbed out of the demolished car. The people in the second car weren't laughing. Sherry was sitting on the side of the road, smoking a cigarette, when the police asked about the baby they were told she had with her. To that Sherry yelled, "I ain't got no damn baby!"

The police just left her sitting and smoking while the police were finding you in the backseat of Delbert's car, your little head split open like a ripe melon. While the ambulance was racing for the hospital, the police telephoned me. I was already at the same hospital my Cassie had died in when the ambulance arrived and they came running out of that thing carrying you into emergency. I was also there during all the critical hours the doctors battled to save your little life. Legally, I had no right to be there, but I wasn't about to leave you the way I had left Cassie. To further secure my place by your bedside, I had Delbert forcibly barred from the hospital grounds. Here's something else you should know, something that made me respect and treasure

Emma. Please bear in mind that during this time period, Emma was very pregnant and uncomfortable ninety percent of the time. She came to the hospital anyway, and when I was so exhausted I couldn't sit up straight, she spelled me, sitting by your side while I slept on a pallet on the floor. While she sat by your bed, she sang to you softly and held your little hand. It was during those hours that I forgave Emma for the walls she was building around our house. Considering what she was doing on your behalf, that woman could have told me she wanted to build walls around the moon and I wouldn't have griped.

A few days later you woke up. I know you don't remember the two people who were both laughing and crying when you finally opened your eyes, but those two people were me and Emma. Then we had to leave, walk out of the hospital in order for Delbert to come in. And as we were leaving, Emma said to me, "If you let him kill that baby the way he killed Cassie, I will never forgive you, Charles."

I just about admired the fire out of Emma, and never mind that we were on the hospital's front lawn and it was broad daylight, I kissed her right on the mouth.

Emma went on home, but I went to my office, yelling for Peter. I wanted to sue Delbert for custody of you. In fact, the whole idea excited the pants off me. Peter calmly sat in a chair while I paced and raved. Finally, when I ran out of steam, Peter pointed out the dark side of my idea. Even though both of us knew that Emma would have stood by me in such a venture, my stepping forward to claim another man's child would do me irreparable harm.

You have to bear in mind that in that long-forgotten era, a businessman lived by his word and a handshake. An adulterer was viewed as the lowest life-form, his word untrustworthy even on an airtight contract. Then, too, there weren't such things as fostering out or legal guardianships when a child had one or both parents, or even close relatives, to take it in. In those days families looked out for their own. Only a total orphan could be adopted. You did not fit the criteria. You had a parent and you had relatives. Therefore, the only way I could get you would be to fraudulently claim you as my blood son. Which would make me an adulterer and completely ruin me.

As I said, Emma more than likely would have gone along with it, but I couldn't bring myself to shame her. She had already had enough to live down with folks stopping just shy of calling me a murderer and a crook. My going to court to fight for you would have given rise to a whole new load of rumors, and I knew Emma did not have the strength to live through the shame and heartbreak of something like that. Besides, as Peter pointed out, good intentions quickly fade when cold reality sets in. Later on down the line, when we had lost everything and Emma was lumbered with another woman's black-sheep son, he said Emma would crack, most likely even take her bitterness out on a helpless child. She would do that, Peter said, because Emma was only human and that's what humans do. His being a Jew in those days, a slow-moving target for ridicule and hate, Peter knew all there was to know on the subject of negative human behavior.

I sat down and I thought the whole thing through. Then I said that there was no way I could allow you to go back to Delbert. Then Peter said, "You don't have to. There's a better way. I've got a maneuver Solomon himself would have envied."

"And what do I do?"

"You keep your mouth shut and your checkbook open while I do my job."

This time when Peter went to court, he went with your auntie. He petitioned the court to have you removed from Delbert's custody and placed into hers.

For my part, I shuffled twenty thousand dollars into her bank account to prove to the judge that she was financially able to care for you into adulthood. On the basis that she was hale and hardy and a closely related adult of sound financial means, and taking into account your father's scandalous lifestyle, your aunt's petition was duly granted.

The day you were out of the hospital and safe with your aunt, I went after Delbert. My purpose in financially ruining him was to prevent his ever regaining custody of you. During all of that back-room plotting with some good old boys deeply connected with Wall Street, I'd forgotten about Sherry. But why would I even think about her? Other folks were doing a good job where she was concerned. To me, Sherry Philbin was old news. Your father stands guilty for Sherry. If Delbert had been any kind of man, he would have supported her in her hour of need. Remember, he was the one who ordered a drunk woman to drive over and pick up his son. If he had owned up to the blame for what happened, because the woman had only been doing what she'd been told, believe it or not, I would have respected him for it. But nothing was ever Delbert Jakomin's fault, and you know for yourself that that's true.

So, being that kind of man, he blamed Sherry for the accident and then for losing him his son. He left her at the mercy of everyone within a hundred-mile radius who was having their say about her to her face, and more often than not, cheerfully spitting in her face. Trapped in a hopeless situation and with a worthless man, Sherry started drinking more heavily. When he wasn't going around town moaning on about how depressed he was that his son had been taken away from him because of a witless drunk woman, Delbert was home drinking right along with her.

I know if Sherry'd had the money she would have left the state and that would have been that. But she didn't have any money and because I and several of my well-placed friends were undercutting the stocks high-roller Delbert had heavily invested in, he was quickly losing his money. His finances were becoming so critical that he was selling the furniture out of his house to keep him in booze. Their hope of finding jobs was out of the question because I had made it out of the question. Before you think I was a hardhearted bastard, let me remind you of how precious you were to me. Let me also inform you that at this point the doctors were concerned that the head trauma you had suffered would manifest in epileptic seizures. One doctor was even giving your aunt lessons on what to do if you had a seizure. She was scared to death and so was I. In fact, I was calling her every day, listening to her go on about how afraid she was that you might have a seizure and she wouldn't remember what the doctor said for her to do. I was afraid of that too, but mostly I was afraid of what your life would be like if you started having seizures.

There wasn't any medication in those days to control or ward off the fits, and because the fits couldn't be controlled, epileptics were treated little better than lepers. If you had started having seizures, your young life would have been over. You would still be breathing, but any prospects of being a whole person would have been taken away. Epileptics weren't allowed to go to school, learn to drive, or vote, and in some states they were not allowed to marry. So when the doctors told me of their concerns, did I hate Delbert all over again?

You bet your shorts I did.

Not only that, but I felt that I had once again miserably failed my Cassie. I wanted to kill something, but the best I could do was step on Delbert like a rodent. But on good advice from my old hero Sam Starr, I went after him with a cold heart and I let him see the bullet coming. I got him off alone, on my ground and with no witnesses. It wasn't a hard thing to do. He was getting desperate, and the loon thought I was going to help him. As difficult as it was for even me to believe, he still had no idea just how bad an enemy I was. Oh, sure, I'd once beaten him half to death, but he'd come out of that pretty good. I'd given him a lot of money to drop the charges, remember? Because Cassie had never told him about us, he'd been fairly confused as to why I'd beaten him. Peter Waterman shrugged him off with the excuse of my being an old school friend of Cassie's who had been a bit too emotionally distraught following her death. Blinded to everything except the money Peter waved under his nose, Delbert accepted the story. After that, because we traveled in such different circles, I didn't have any more public dealings with Delbert Jakomin. He hadn't even known that I was the cause of his being barred from the hospital. The police kept him pretty busy about the accident, and then, when they'd done all they could, the hospital staff intervened, claiming you were too critical to be seen. He most certainly had no idea I was the cause of his losing his son. So as gullible as a newborn babe, he met me out on an old drill site, where it would only be the two of us.

The gray December sky was low to the ground and a brisk prairie wind whistled and creaked through the timbers of the abandoned derrick. Bundled up in a long wool coat and wearing a homburg and fur-lined leather gloves, Charlie felt reasonably warm. He paced a small path beside his parked car and smoked a cigarette, impatiently waiting for Delbert Jakomin to arrive on the site. In spite of all his cries for modernization, Delbert Jakomin lived on Indian time. Meaning he rarely glanced at clocks, the idea of being late foreign to him. How could anyone be late if he showed up on the day he was supposed to? However, Charlie existed in the world of schedules. Waiting for Delbert to show up whenever he wanted to irritated Charlie.

The designated meeting place was known on the geological map as Number 17. Despite the latest scientific assurances that this site held a rich deposit, Number 17 had been a powder-dry hole. Charlie mentally renamed the site College Boys' Folly. And he never again listened to geologists when his own nose for oil disagreed with their so-called findings. He maintained the derrick on Number 17 as a reminder of the type of misfortune waiting for him should he ever again allow himself to be swayed by yammering outside voices. The still inner voice that had once guided him through a territory of outlaws when he was only ten, and then guided him through the dangers facing a young Osage male who dared to play for high stakes in a white man's game, had tried to warn him about this site. The silent derrick was a costly monument to his turning a deaf ear to that voice.

Charlie leaned against the car, squinting at the somber sky as he smoked. He hated this time of year. Gray, drizzly days and the month of December brought back too many memories of Cassie. They were separated for longer periods of time during the summer, but he could cover her absence during those two months by working in the nuns' kitchen garden until he was physically exhausted. When she went home for Christmas, because of the inclement weather there was very little for him to do other than mope.

They didn't have proper gifts for each other, only little things that they made. Charlie drew pictures. They weren't very good, but Cassie liked them. She always gave him the same type of gift. A Christmas star. She spent hours folding the piece of paper just right, using a pair of scissors to make tiny cuts along the folds. When the piece of paper was folded out, like magic the piece of paper had been transformed into a lacy star. Charlie saved each and every one. He had six. One for each previous year of their shared special love. Cassie's stars were all he had left of her, and he kept them in a hidden drawer in his desk. When he took them out and carefully touched them, he could see her as she worked on her gift while he told her exciting stories about outlaws. He couldn't remember any of the stories, primarily because he made them up as he went along, but he could see her in fine detail as she artfully handled the scissors and listened.

Once upon that time he had enjoyed cold weather. Especially at night, when they would meet at the bottom of the stairs in the girls' wing. After his nightly lesson in Père Blanc's office, Charlie made a great noise walking down the hallway to the boys' wing. Then he would take off his boots and slip down the corridor to the girls' wing. He was already waiting in the shadows when Cassie came easing down the stairs. Cassie knew how to tell only one lie to the nun whose cot was near the door of the girls' dormitory. She always said she had to go to the bathroom. That nun was convinced Cassie had the smallest bladder in the world. Then the nun would drift back to sleep, unaware of the length of time Cassie was supposedly in the toilet.

Because she was wearing only a cotton nightgown and a pair of socks on her feet, Cassie was always cold by the time she came down the stairs. Charlie had the luxury of an old robe, and he opened it up, welcoming her into his warmth. During those wonderful stolen moments, Cassie's arms were wrapped around his chest as he held her and covered her with the robe. And he blessed the cold nights. The colder the night, the longer she stayed, because she dreaded the chilly climb up the stairs and the cold bed waiting for her in the frigid dorm room.

"I want to sleep with you," she mewled.

"Someday sweetheart," he promised. "Someday when we have our own house. On rainy days we'll stay in bed together all day if we want to. We'll hold each other just like this and snuggle down in the blankets."

"And no one will tell us we can't."

"That's right. No one will be able to tell us anything, not ever again."

"Because you'll shoot them."

"Right between the eyes, Cas, right between the eyes."

• • •

Charlie heard a car. He threw down the cigarette, his shoe grinding it out, smearing it into an unrecognizable mash. Then he stepped away from his car and stood with his feet wide apart, a shootist's stance. In long strides Delbert Jakomin approached, thoroughly unaware that he had been the destroyer of a priceless dream the day he'd married Cassie.

I let him talk for a good long time. I heard every word the man said. He wasn't thanking me for being there to help him out of a financial hole. No, not Delbert. His attitude was arrogant. It was his opinion that because we both had Osage blood, I was obliged to help him. That's when I told your father in no uncertain terms exactly who I was, the man who loved Cassie, the man who would avenge her death by any means possible.

Every speck of blood left his face. His eyes went wider than a pair of coffee cups, and for a good five minutes he couldn't say a word. But when he eventually found his voice he said the unforgivable. "You're mad at me because of that little dummy?"

I flattened him, Everett. I'd sworn to myself I wouldn't touch him, but my hatred took charge. Before I could blink, Delbert was sprawled on the ground. Then I walked away. As I headed for my car, he was yelling about how he'd tell everybody about me. He did. I must admit that more than a few listened. After a while, folks began to stop and think. There were a few in the area who knew that while we had all been in school together Cassie had been my girl. But then they had to consider the kind of priest Père Blanc had been. If anything untoward had happened between me and Cassie, they knew Père Blanc would not have married Cassie to Delbert.

And then there had been all those years in between. Except for the one time I had charged to her house, begging Cassie to run away with me, she had not so much as looked in my direction. All the time she had been married to Delbert, Cassie had conducted herself in a blameless fashion. Any speculation occurring later occurred after I had beaten Delbert. What had boggled more than a few minds at the time was the way Emma had condoned the beating. Emma, bless her, had said, "When they were children, Charles and Cassie were friends. Because of the way she died, I don't blame him a bit for losing his temper. My Charles cannot abide any man who isn't protective of his own wife."

Not long after our meeting on the prairie, Delbert's tales of my threatening to destroy him because of my love for his dead wife reached Emma. She smiled, even laughed, inviting the other ladies to laugh with her. When they did, the tide of public opinion turned against Delbert. As there had been no witnesses to this dramatic meeting, his accusations were quickly viewed as the delusions of an alcohol-soaked mind. As far as the public was concerned, especially in the face of Emma having one baby after another, any further speculations regarding our marriage were cast aside.

That's when your father finally saw the bullet coming. Finally realized just how dangerous his enemy was. But he had one weapon in his arsenal. You. But for a long time I didn't worry about his ever regaining custody of you because his most crippling blow happened on the night he lay in bed asleep with Sherry. She put a gun in her mouth and pulled the trigger.

Delbert had used Sherry like a lightning rod. Through the many years that she lived with him, she had been good for deflecting blame away from himself. He lost his son because of Sherry. He was going broke because Sherry was spending all his money. Nothing was his fault; it was hers. I have to be honest, the whole thing made me physically ill. It made me wonder if he hadn't treated my Cassie in the same way, making her feel worthless, always to blame for anything that didn't please him down to his toes. At any rate,

Sherry's death shook the community. It also obliterated any hope Delbert ever had of getting you back. Delbert Jakomin became a nonperson, and I was finally satisfied. I had paid him back for Cassie, you were healthy and safe, and now I could forget him.

For years your aunt didn't say anything to me about his coming around to her house. You were his son, and blood is thicker than bank accounts. It was only when Delbert's visits became too much for her that she called me and told me everything. That's when I knew what he was up to. He was trying to regain possession of the one weapon he had in our private war. As quickly as I could, I made arrangements to take you out of the line of fire. I had you sent off to boarding school.

I'm only sorry that when you were grown enough to come home for good that Delbert managed to have the last word, build an animosity between you and me that stretched into decades. Or at least when he died he thought he'd had the last word. Neither he nor I ever believed that I would approach you with the whole truth. Then again, neither he nor I ever suspected that I wouldn't have one son to my name I felt I could trust with my final secret. Especially not Matt. So here it comes, Everett, the real reason I'm writing to you. The real reason I've chosen to place myself entirely in your hands.

I hope you're sitting down.

CHAPTER EIGHTEEN

The spaghetti sauce smelled good. Hungry now, Everett climbed the steps to the back porch, drawn to the garlic-heavy odor wafting from the kitchen. The moment he had completed the final journal, he'd left Katie and the house without a word. He went for several walks around the block. He had to keep moving, had to be by himself. He felt somewhat liberated now that he knew the full truth. For the first time in his life he felt whole, all of the pieces to an old puzzle finally in place. But the price C.R. asked for sharing these truths was outrageous. Hell! It was a felony! But as Everett turned for home and Katie, he knew that despite the illegality of the venture, he thoroughly intended to honor C.R.'s request. But not because doing so would see an end to the brouhaha between himself and the Jones boys and pave the way for Matt's grudging approval of the marriage between Nath and Hayley, but because after everything he had learned, after the private time he had spent with C.R. rehashing the trials and pitfalls of C.R.'s life, Everett knew that what C.R.

asked for was right. Everett would do it because he wanted to. He honestly did.

As he entered the kitchen, Katie was talking on the wall telephone, standing with her back to him.

"Kara, I can hear Gemma yelling in the background. You tell her I said that I am a grown-up person and I'll come home when I'm good and ready." Lengthy pause. "No, I have no idea when that will be. Everett needs me to be with him right now, and I have no intention of leaving him while he does." Another pause. "Kara? Does the word *tough* mean anything to you at all?" Katie glanced in Everett's direction, rolled her eyes, looked quickly away, and spoke again into the telephone.

"What? Oh. I'm making spaghetti. Why? Do you want some?" Impatient sigh. "No, Kara-Marie, I did not make coleslaw. Because you're the only person in the whole wide world who eats spaghetti and cole-slaw mixed together like vomit. Now, do you want some spaghetti or not? All right, fine. Yes. You can call the café and have Maybelle pack you up a tub of coleslaw. Well, use Gemma's car and go get it. Then you can run by here and get the spaghetti. Yes, I put black olives in the sauce. Happy? Good. I'll see you when you get here."

Katie hung up.

Turning, she looked at Everett standing in the doorway. "Are you absolutely sure you want to take on me and my two lunatic daughters?"

Everett grinned. "Yeah. I'm sure."

Shaking her head as she left the wall phone, she muttered, "You've got a lot of guts, Jakomin. Sit down. Your supper's getting cold."

Katie pushed her plate away, leaned forward, resting her arms on the table, waiting as Everett lit a cigarette.

Exhaling smoke, Everett spoke softly. He looked

past her, as if intently watching something distant. "You know, I can still remember the first time I ever saw C. R. Jones. It's kind of amazing when you consider that at the time I couldn't have been more than five years old. I guess at that age it's only the dramatic or traumatic that sticks. Nath remembers falling out of a tree. My son Bobby remembers his first day at kindergarten, and my daughter Martha remembers Anna giving her a crayon box. A big crayon box with a gold and a silver crayon in it.

"But it seems to me that the day I met C.R., my whole brain came awake. I remember that day and *everything* that happened in the years after that day just as clear as a bell. It was a hot day and I was sitting on the bottom step of the front porch of my auntie's house. Because it was a hot, I was wearing just a pair of white cotton underpants. I was peeling an orange my aunt had given me. I lived with her, you see. My dad's sister. My aunt Gladene. My dad was a drunk, Katie. The courts gave my aunt full custody of me when I was about two or three. My dad wasn't supposed to come around me, but he did. I remember that he stank. His breath, I mean. It was always sour, and I hated it when he picked me up and kissed my face. I asked my aunt Gladene why his breath was so bad, and she said it was because he was pickling himself with alcohol.

"Anyway, there I was, peeling my orange, when I felt someone staring at me. I looked up, and across the tattered lawn was this tall man. He was the best-dressed Osage man I had ever seen. A lot of men wore suits, but nothing like his suit. I was too young then to know anything about England or Savile Row, so I had no idea why his suit seemed so special. I only know that it did and that he looked like a king.

"I don't remember if I'd ever heard of C. R. Jones before that day or if I had just passed it off the way kids do, so it's only natural that I would have an idea that was who the stranger was. What I do remember is feeling afraid of the man. Afraid because of the way he looked at me. He wasn't hateful or mean-looking, he was intense. When his eyes met mine, I felt I had been nailed. Literally. He stared at me for a long, long time and I couldn't move one muscle.

"He called me over to him, and for some reason I went. But being afraid of him, I made sure to keep a good distance back. I stood there, a little shaky-legged boy in underpants, holding my orange, while this man silently inspected me from head to toe. Then he squatted down so that we could be on eye level, and he said to me, 'You look just like your mama.'

"Well, that floored me. Nobody in my family ever talked about my mama. Except to say that she was dead. So I piped right up and asked this perfect stranger if he really knew my mama.

"C.R. just kinda smiled and said, 'Yes. I knew her very well. So far, you're a credit to her. Stay that way.'

"Then"—Everett lifted his shoulders in a slight shrug—"he just stood up and walked off. He never came back, even though I hoped he would. I wanted him to tell me about my mother. You've got to understand that I was kind of desperate. I didn't even have a picture of my mother. All I knew was that her name was Cassie and that it was bad to speak about the dead. My auntie firmly believed that speaking of the dead would call a ghost. She was terrified of ghosts. I had a feeling the man in the suit wasn't afraid of ghosts, that he wasn't afraid of anything, most especially the ghost of my mother. I looked for him every day, hanging around out in the yard all the day long, waiting.

"The next time my father came around, I made the mistake of telling him about the man in the suit. Well, that started a whole new world of hell. It was the first time my father ever hit me. I mean, he hit me so hard, I bounced off a wall. I didn't feel any pain, just a fuzzy feeling in my head as I lay on the floor. I could hear my auntie screaming, 'You hurt his head! You hurt his head!' Then my dad got scared, leaned over, and spoke into my face. 'Try to move, son. Try to move.' But I couldn't move. I couldn't even move my fingers. The next thing I knew, he was gone and a doctor was there, shining a light in my eyes and saying, 'Everett? Can you hear me?'

"I was in bed for two weeks after that, the doctor coming every day to shine lights in my eyes. My dad stayed away the whole time. Once I was completely well, he began to come around again. He never apologized for hitting me, what he did do was start in on how I shouldn't be stupid. That I was a big boy and I should know who I should be talking to and who I shouldn't. He told me that if I ever saw the man in the suit again that I should run away. That the man in the suit was an evil person only a stupid little boy would ever talk to.

"From that day on, the word *stupid* peppered his vocabulary. Just like the day I told him I was getting married. He didn't say congratulations, what he said was, getting married is stupid. He stopped short of calling Anna stupid, because by then I could whip his butt, so he just stayed with my being stupid."

Everett shrugged. "Anyway, on the first day of him telling me I was stupid, he never let up on that or C.R. He made me feel ashamed of myself and terrified of C.R., making him seem like the devil in the flesh. But the man who scared me the most was my dad. He had a lot of hate in him, plus, he was drinking more and enjoying it less. The booze wasn't agreeing with him, but he drank it anyway. Sometimes he was so falling-down drunk that my auntie ran him off with a gun.

"I was in the second grade and walking home from school on a very cold and wet day when I heard my dad and my auntie going at it inside the house. When I heard the shouting and the tussling going on in the house, I hid in the bushes. I hid even more when their physical fight moved outside onto the front porch. My auntie was hitting my father over the head with the butt end of the rifle, and it was during that momentous occasion that I heard my auntie yell C.R.'s name as a threat. This was a woman who'd never even mentioned C. R. Jones, and now she was throwing around his name with every swing she took at my father.

" 'I'm callin' C.R.!' she yelled. 'I'm callin' him an' this time I really mean it!'

" 'You damn woman,' my dad yelled back as he tried to protect his head, 'I'm takin' my son an' ain't no one's gonna stop me.'

"She smacked him a few more times and he left, wiping blood off his face as he passed right by where I was hiding. I stayed in my hiding place for a long time. Finally, when I couldn't stand being cold and wet anymore and I hoped the coast was clear, I crept out and ran to the house. The front door was locked, so I had to bang on it and yell for my auntie. She quickly let me in and then she locked the door behind me. Then she gave me the bum's rush to my bedroom and told me not to come out until she was off the telephone.

"While I changed my clothes, I could hear her talking, but I couldn't hear what she was saying. A few minutes later she came to my room and took me into the kitchen to warm me up with some heated sugar-milk. I didn't see my dad after that. To be honest, as the months passed, I didn't ask where he had gotten to because I didn't want to know. I just enjoyed the peace of his being gone.

"Then, just before Christmas, he started coming around again, but not around my auntie's house. He started waylaying me as I walked home from school or when I was walking around town. He wasn't drunk during those times, but he was acting crazy. I think that scared me more than his being drunk. He was talking about C.R., about things that made no sense and making me swear I wouldn't tell my auntie he was seeing me. I didn't tell her. What I did do was start wetting the bed every night. I know she guessed the reason for it, because shortly after that I was sent off to boarding school.

"My dad somehow gained permission by then to see me when I came home to my auntie's for Christmas. Each and every Christmas Day he'd come over clean and sober and remained on his best behavior so she would have no complaints. What saddened me over the years was the way he deteriorated. Each year he was worse than the year before, and not just physically. I was big enough by then to know I could take him if he got rough, but having to listen to him as he babbled, never being able to follow the line of his conversations, was worse than his taking a swing at me. And he ended each sentence with 'You know what I'm sayin'?' Mostly I nodded as if I did, but once when I was sixteen and rude, as sixteen-year-olds tend to be, I popped up with some remark I meant purely as sarcasm.

"He was sitting in a wing chair and smoking a cigarette at the time. He stared at me until that cigarette in his hand burned down to his fingers. Then he stabbed it out and said, 'You're your mama's boy all right.'

"I know it hurt my auntie's feelings when I stopped coming home for the holidays. My Christmases became pretty lonesome, but being lonely was a lot better than being anywhere near my dad. I couldn't stand looking at him, but mostly I couldn't stand having to listen to him. Staying at school was my means of escape. I was so grateful for that escape that I got down on my knees every night and thanked God that I had an auntie who loved me enough to pay the bills to keep me in school.

"During all of that time and since, I've been thanking God for the wrong person. She would have paid if she could, but she couldn't. It was C.R. who paid for everything—bed, board, education, even the clothes on my back and the shoes on my feet. And I never knew." He pressed his lips firmly together. In a voice nearing a husky whisper, he said, "I swear to God, Katie, I never knew."

Everett looked off, cleared his throat. Looking at her again and in a more steady tone, he continued. "When I was a kid, I hated my father. When I was grown, especially after I married Anna, I did make an effort to love him. Anna believed devoutly that no one is ever born bad, that something caused a person to go bad. She said if I found out what that something was, then I would be able to understand and forgive my father. With her pushing me, I did some digging into my father's past. By this time I didn't have my auntie to fill me in on details because she had passed away. As a matter of fact, she had passed away just a few months after Anna and I were married.

"Now, my auntie had never been sick a day in her life. The last day I went to her house to pay her a visit, she seemed as right as rain. We sat out on the front porch, snapping beans and laughing and joking. We were in the middle of a good laugh, when she turned in her rocking chair and took a good, long look at me. Then she said, 'Ev, I am so pleased you've settled with a good wife. Now I guess I can leave.' I said something like 'Where you gonna go? Hawaii?' She threw a bean at me, told me I was still just a silly boy, that Anna sure had her hands full being married to me. The next day she was dead. Just like that." Everett snapped his fingers. "Dead. A neighbor found her in her kitchen garden. She was wearing her gardening dress and her old sunbonnet. I guess she wanted to make sure her vegetable rows were clear of weeds before she went. I think she must have had a bad heart for a long time and just didn't tell me. It had to have been something like that, Katie, else how would she know her time was so near? Her house was just as clean as a whistle and—"

"Everett."

"Huh?"

"You're wandering."

"Oh." He shook his head, then continued. "Okay, so there I was, married to Anna, and outside of her, her family, and my own sprinkling of first cousins, I didn't have much of a family left. That's when Anna really started pushing me to make peace with my father. I think it was just to make her happy that I got into the task of investigating my father's past.

"All I really found out about my mother was her age when she passed away. Except for the year, a fixed date for her passing wasn't listed. I'd always known that she had died shortly after I was born, but I had no idea that her death and my birth practically coincided. Anyway, I showed the things I'd found to Anna, and together we wrongly surmised that her passing at such a tender age, leaving my grief-torn father with a newly born infant, had set him off on a wrong road. Well, Anna was incapable of critical thought, but I certainly should have known better. Especially after I found out about his second, and I use the term loosely, wife. Trust me, Katie, the newspaper clippings about *her* were real eye-openers.

"Her name was Sherry Philbin, her age was twenty-eight, and the cause of her death was listed as a suicide. But it was the way she committed suicide that kept the presses rolling for a while, and in the clippings, bingo, C.R.'s name finally came to light. But only once.

"What happened was, Sherry had committed suicide in the bed while my dad was sound asleep right beside her. At first the newspapers seemed to be on my father's side, concentrating on Sherry's peculiar method of checking out. Then the press releases became scornful, insinuating that perhaps my father had watched her put the gun in her mouth and pull the trigger. After that, they were wondering, in print, if perhaps he hadn't pulled the trigger himself. Then my dad was hauled into court and after a long trial, he was acquitted. But it wasn't over. Not by a long shot. On the day my father walked free, C.R. was stopped by a reporter as he left the courthouse. As a well-to-do concerned citizen, C.R. was asked his opinion on the matter. C.R.'s quote burned a hole in my brain. He said: 'His technical innocence notwithstanding, Delbert Jakomin would appear to be the singular catastrophic phenomenon in the lives of two defenseless women.'

"So, what he said in words that would not get him sued to hell and back was, my dad killed Sherry. Not only that, but that my father had killed my mother. Suddenly everything my father had been babbling during my growing-up years made complete sense. Now I knew just what he'd been saying when he'd gone on and on about C. R. Jones blaming him for everything. It seemed more than clear to me that what my father had been saying all along was all true, and I finally had the proof there in my hands. What I did not do was ask the crucial question, why. Why would C.R. blame my father for my mother's death? Why would he even care about the death of a young woman he barely knew? But primarily, why would he then purposely set out to destroy my father? Turn him into a gibbering drunk?

"I didn't ask the questions because I was young and hotheaded. I was also deeply ashamed for all the terrible things I had felt for my father throughout my life. If you want to point to the very thing triggering the feud between me and C.R., there it is. Our feud escalated when I fished my father out of that old house he was in and brought him home to my house. He was very sick by then. So sick that his own doctor no longer cared if he drank or not. His doctor said it wouldn't make any difference one way or the other. But Anna was pregnant with Martha. The smell of cigarettes and alcohol made her violently ill. I quit smoking and I wouldn't bring my dad any booze. Well, not smoking only made me jittery, but not being allowed to drink made my dad a raving lunatic. I'll never understand how Anna handled him during his tirades, but she did. I took care of him as much as I could, and all the while I was cleaning up the messes he would make in his underwear, I blamed C.R. Just like my father had been incapable of blaming himself for anything, I fell right in line. I pushed it right out of my head that in every dispute, there are two sides."

"And now you have both sides."

"Yes," he said wearily. "I certainly do. A side I never expected. C.R.'s side is simple. He hated my father because he loved my mother. He would have married her in a heartbeat if people hadn't conspired against him. Then he had to stand by and watch my mother endure a loveless marriage. It twisted his mind, Katie, but I can understand it. Any man who has ever totally loved a woman is completely able to understand what that must have done to him. And because I understand, I—"

He turned away, made a show of rubbing his eyes for a few seconds. Then he sat up quickly. "Where was I?"

"Never mind," she said quickly. "The subject's a bit too much for me to handle too. Tell me what happened after you were born."

"Okay. Like I said, the real feuding began on the night I was born, but as the years passed, things went from bad to worse and Baby Everett was pig-in-the-middle. I would have stayed in the middle if C.R. hadn't taken me away from my father and placed me with my aunt. When my aunt couldn't keep my father away from me, she called C.R. and he had me placed in an expensive school in the East. You remember me saying that my dad threw the word *stupid* at me a lot?"

Katie nodded.

"Well, while I was in school, C.R. didn't think I was such great shakes either. Both C.R. and my dad believed I had inherited a lot more from my mother than my looks. The way C.R. tells it, my mom was a little slow, but at the same time he made it sound her most endearing trait. From what I gather, her being dependent on C.R. to explain things to her was total. Now, C.R. might have loved that to bits, but remembering the months my father was in my house gives me a terrible insight into the kind of marriage my mother had with a man like my dad.

"Anna was far from simple. The truth is, the woman could have outthought me with half her brain tied up. Needless to say, you and Anna have a lot in common. Anna was also something else, she was patient to a fault, but even she knew a thin-skinned moment or two when my dad was peevish and sullen with her. He didn't like having to tell her what he needed while she was battling morning sickness and having to clean up after him. He expected her to know what he needed and jump to do it.

"I lit into him many times on Anna's behalf, but mostly I kept my mouth shut because she said dealing with my sick father was her ministry, that it was God called. I told her to let me know the minute God stopped calling. When she was in her eighth month and my dad's haranguing became too much even for her, I happily checked him into the hospital. Up until the moment he died he spent his time griping about how stupid the nurses were, how the one thing he couldn't abide was an idiot woman. Now, can you imagine how a timid, slow-witted girl fared with someone like that? Especially when you consider during the time they were married he was young and healthy, really able to bully her into the ground."

Katie shuddered. "That Sherry person must have

been some kind of woman if she could take that kind of garbage."

"Don't give Sherry too much credit," Everett chuckled. "She shot herself, remember?"

"Oh, yeah."

"Anyway, C.R. probably thought I was a dim bulb too. He would have thought so, because he was getting my school reports and frankly, my grades sucked eggs. In school I liked sports. It didn't matter what kind; if a ball was involved, I was on the team. We had study hours each night from seven to nine, and those study hours are the only reason I didn't flunk out. It was only during the mandatory study hours that I actually cracked open my books. So I passed my classes, but believe me, there wasn't any skin left on any of my teeth.

"C.R. said that the kindest remark a teacher ever made about me was 'Everett Jakomin is not a happy student.' That's pretty much what the nuns used to say about my mom. Which is why I now understand the look."

"What look?"

"The look C.R. gave me the first time I stood up in the council and asked a relevant question. I've never forgotten the way he looked at me as he sat at the council table. He stared a hole right through me the whole time I stood at the back row, challenging what he'd said. His expression was a mixture of amazement and approval. What I didn't know was that look also meant he was finished coddling me. That I had just proven to him that I had a brain and I wasn't afraid to use it. Another thing I didn't know was that my getting the loan to start up my business had all been down to C.R. That he'd smoothed the way while I'd just blundered in. I guess he was also ready with the safety net should I make a hash of my business. After that council meeting, whenever we confronted each other, he treated me like an equal. In other words, he didn't spare the punches, and neither did I. The most important thing I did not know was that I was fighting someone who was handicapped. That my one advantage during our many confrontations was that I was Cassie's son. The last piece of her left on this earth. And he still loved her too much to destroy me the way he could have if he had so chosen."

Katie sat up smartly. "Excuse me, but you keep going on about C.R. loving your mother beyond the grave. While that's extremely romantic, it leaves me to wonder about his wife."

"What about her?"

"Well, she was alive and your mother wasn't. Doesn't it stand to reason that her love would gradually ease him out of his love for your mother?"

"Ordinarily you'd be right, but there was nothing ordinary about C. R. Jones. He married Emma to get his hands on her land. After they were married, he started liking her, and lastly he cared for and respected her a great deal. In his writings he talked about her at length. He said he was proud of her, he said she was the best wife he could hope for, and that she had been his best friend. She was all that and something else."

"What?"

"She was part of a package of things he'd never wanted. As amazing as it sounds, C.R. never wanted to be a rich man. Money and power were only tools. Tools he planned to use to free my mother. After she died, they were tools he used to beat down my father and protect me.

"Emma was a tool too. Not only did Emma provide him with the necessary means to begin his fortune, later on she protected him from any hint of scandal and then went on to become one of the state's great ladies.

"But all the man ever wanted was a little house on a hill among the blackjack trees and my mother. Because of the times they lived in, this sweet, little ordinary dream was beyond his grasp, and after she was gone, all he felt he had left was the absolute love he had for my mother. It was the one thing no one could take away from him. From the very beginning, their innocent love was an unbreakable bond between them, and after she died, C.R. never wavered. He cared for his wife and he appreciated her, but in his heart he belonged to Cassie. And Emma knew it."

Katie sat back, utterly astonished. After a moment she thought about what she hadn't heard, the unspoken issue that had been running through Everett's discourse like a strong undercurrent.

"C.R's asked you for a favor that's a real whopper, hasn't he?"

"Yes."

"Is it against the law?

"Oh, yeah."

"State or federal."

Everett laughed, "Does it matter?"

"Yes, it does. I want to know just how much trouble we're going to be in if we get caught."

"We?"

"We," she replied adamantly. "Because I know you're gearing up to tell me you're going to do whatever *it* is. And, Everett Jakomin, if you're going to prison, I plan on being in that cell right along with you."

"What about your kids?"

"Well, here's the glorious part. In their brazen attempt to win me away from you, they did something that just about made my socks roll up and down with glee."

"What?"

"They cleaned the house. Everett, if those two girls can do a thing like that without my yelling, then as far as I'm concerned, they're weaned enough to take care of themselves while their mama's in the slammer."

He hid his laughter behind a hand, but his smile was

evident in his eyes. "Katie, I love you for wanting to help, but it's too dangerous. Besides, I'm the one who owes C.R. my life."

"Oh, pull the other one. I owe him quite a bit myself, and if he needs help, I'm there. Your choices come down to this, either you let me help you, or I do everything I can to stop you."

"And just how would you stop me?"

"I'd call Matt."

Everett gasped sharply. "You wouldn't do that."

"Wanna bet?"

The hand holding the cigarette toyed with a bread crumb on the table as Everett thought quietly. Finally he said, "This isn't a joking matter, Katie. I have it within my power to give C.R. the one thing life denied him. The only thing he ever wanted. If you tell Matt, he'll get in my way and refuse his father's last request. C.R. knew he would, that's the real reason he turned to me, gave me the power to make or break Matt if I had to. Now do you understand just how important this is?"

"Oh, of course I understand. And it doesn't change a thing. I'm helping you, and that's final." Katie glanced at her wristwatch. "What time is the wake?"

"It starts at nine." His eyes met and held hers. "I kind of hoped you'd come with me."

"Why were you hoping? I brought a dress because I'd already assumed I'd be going."

"You did?"

"Everett! You told me to bring clothes. What else was I supposed to think?"

Embarrassed, he wormed around in the chair. "Katie, when I said that, I was, in a roundabout way, hinting that I'd kind of like you to consider marrying me."

Her eyes flared. "What about my kids and their fleabag cat?"

Everett sat back. "Yeah, I'll take those too."

Her elbows on the table, Katie placed her head in her hands and stared blindly at the tabletop. "My Lord, the man's serious. The cat I can understand, but the kids—"

Everett's large hand encircled her wrist. When she looked up, he could see tears forming. Katie's natural impulse was to make a joke of everything, but the unshed tears sparkling in her eyes gave her away. She loved him, and that love made her afraid. He could feel that fear rapidly pulsing through the veins in her wrist.

"Katie Little Hill?" he said tenderly. "Would you please do me the supreme honor of marrying me?"

Her voice a squeak, and her chin trembling, Katie said, "Yes. Yes, I will."

Everett brought her hand to his lips, softly kissing her curled fingers. "Now that you've promised to be my wife, I guess I can trust you with the rest of it." He squeezed her fingers. "I want you to listen hard, Katie. It's important you understand everything I'm about to tell you. I can't take your wanting to help me seriously until you completely understand what I'm going to be doing."

She took her hand away and stood. "Hold that thought. I've just gotta have another cup of coffee."

Her eyes were dazed and her arms flat on the tabletop when they heard the knocking on the back porch door. Everett rose and walked out of the kitchen. From the porch Katie heard her daughter Kara speaking to Everett. Still too discombobulated to budge, Katie was still seated at the table when Everett came back into the kitchen, Kara timidly following behind. Katie raised her eyes, but she wasn't looking at her daughter, she saw only Everett. The love she'd felt for him took on a new force. In those seconds, she fully realized just how much she and C. R. Jones had held in common. Both had loved devotedly and from afar. But now the love she had borne alone for so long was returned and there was a promise of a happy, shared future. This was the single treasure C.R.'s money could not buy.

She stood and raised her chin in determination. "Ev, I am going with you."

He rolled his eyes anxiously in Kara's direction. With Kara present he couldn't argue the point. There was very little he could say beyond, "Uh, you real sure about this, Katie?"

"Yep."

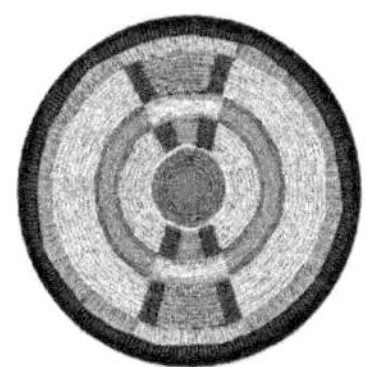

CHAPTER NINETEEN

Kara felt the tension in the room. There was some kind of secret signaling going on, and it upset her. Lately, her life had enough secrets to fill the Rose Bowl. Now, here she was, in the middle of yet another secret. Her mother and Mr. Jakomin were having a staring match, and it didn't appear likely it would be ending anytime soon. Kara did what Kara did best. She stepped into the middle.

"Hey, Mom," she said timidly. "I got the coleslaw. I—I just came for some spaghetti. You said I could."

Katie's attention switched to her daughter. Then she said quickly, "Ev? Where do we keep the Tupperware?"

"In the cupboard above the sink."

"Well, that's too high for me to reach. You'll have to get it down."

Being a very observant girl, Kara did not miss the "we." Katie inspected the plastic containers Everett offered down to her. After saying "This one will do," she moved briskly to the stove, loading the container with spaghetti.

Everett looked back at the ashen-faced teenage girl. He had casually known Kara all her life, but now he was seeing her with the eyes of a soon-to-be-stepfather. Kara was a pretty girl. Both of Katie's girls were pretty. Gemma he knew to be highly strung, reed-thin, intensely living her life as if it were a race. Kara was taller than her older sister and leaning toward plump. Her plumpness was the hallmark of a kid who didn't get out much, who instead led the life of a sedentary student. Kara was the kid who strove to please, making all of those straight A's Katie was so proud of, while her sister Gemma actively rebelled and argued constantly with Katie. Mother and first daughter going at it hammer and tongs made Kara the invisible child, her presence noted as the kid who didn't give anybody any trouble.

As a result, Everett guessed Kara was using food to compensate for being ignored, while volatile Gemma gobbled up Katie's concern. Everett knew he could handle a kid like Gemma without too much difficulty because her feelings would always be right out there in the open with no surprises. But Kara was a deep-water kid. Unless it was prized out of her, no one would ever know just what she was thinking or feeling. He knew, too, that if he wanted to win over Katie's girls, his best bet was to win over this one. If he followed Katie's example, bypassing Kara and concentrating on Gemma, he just might find himself swimming against Kara's silent disapproval for the remainder of his life.

"Kara?" he said. "Would you come with me into the living room for a minute?"

Woodenly, Kara nodded. In the living room she sat stiffly on the edge of the couch. Everett sat close to her and turned in her direction.

"Kara," he said gently. "I've asked your mother to marry me."

Kara's eyes clicked to the corners. Everett hastened to continue.

"Now, I know you and your sister will be thinking this is all happening too fast, but really it isn't. Your mama and I have known each other for a very long time, and in the last year or two we've known that we have special feelings for each other. It's just now that we've admitted our feelings and decided it was time to do something about them."

Kara's jawline tightened.

"If it makes you feel better, my youngest son doesn't like the situation very much either, but what I told him and what I'm telling you is this. Your mama and I are grown-up people. We both love our kids half to death, but neither of us is prepared to let our kids run our lives. No matter how any of you feel about it, she and I will be getting married. However, it would be nice if one or two of you found it in your heart to approve, maybe even come to the wedding."

"I have a father," Kara said dully.

"Yes, you do. Just like my three kids have a mama. She passed away a few years ago, but that doesn't make her any less their mother, just like your daddy being away doesn't make him any less your daddy. Katie and I aren't asking to take anyone's place. All we're asking is to be allowed to fill their space. It's a fair request, Kara.

"I will promise you that I won't try to daddy you or your sister any more than either one of you wants me to. And I won't try to change or interfere with the relationship between you girls and your mother."

Kara moved on the couch, turning a sullen face toward him. "After you marry my mother, where are we going to live? Our house or yours?"

"I hadn't exactly thought all of that through."

"Why not?"

This kid's petulant attitude was beginning to get on

his nerves. Trying to keep his tone patient, he said, "Look, to be honest, I haven't thought beyond the most important thing, which was to ask Katie to marry me. Now that she's said yes, the next thing we'll do is plan the basics of where we're going to live and what kind of furniture we're going to have. But that's all right. That's what engagements are for."

"Then you won't be getting married tomorrow?"

"Uh, no. That I can definitely promise."

"And maybe you and Mama could be engaged . . . for years?"

"Don't push your luck, Kara. I'm not a young man. At my age, I can't afford to hang fire for more than six months."

She bowed her head. Feeling he'd been saying all of the wrong things, he moved closer to her, their shoulders touching as he placed his hand on hers.

"Kara, I'm not the kind of person who'll just march right in and start telling you what you can do and when you can do it. But I'll tell you what I will be. I'll be one of the best friends you could ever ask for. And I'll be the guy ready to go to bat for you when things feel kinda out of your control. I'm pretty good that way, and any one of my kids can tell you I'm a very dependable person."

She took her hand away, wiped at a tear streaking her face. Then she stood. Everett remained seated as she surveyed the spartan living room. He had no idea what was going on in that mind of hers, so he hazarded a guess.

"Kara, you may not have to worry about living here. My kids still think of this house as their home. Can you imagine what they'd say if I brought in a new wife and her kids took over their old bedrooms?"

"Yeah," she muttered. "They wouldn't like it."

"No, they wouldn't. They want this house and me, come to that, to stay just the same." Everett's hands slapped his knees. "So, I don't know what to do. This house is big enough for all of us, but I wouldn't want you and Gemma fighting with my kids just because you two want to redecorate their old bedrooms. On the other hand, I wouldn't feel comfortable selling this house and going over to live in your mama's house." He looked up at her. "I'm kinda hoping for a suggestion here. Feel free to jump in anytime."

The corner of her mouth twitched. "Well," she offered in a subdued tone, "maybe you should think about building . . . a new house?"

Everett canted his head to the side as he considered the suggestion. When he'd thought of getting the kids, one at a time, involved with the prewedding decision-making, he hadn't believed the scheme would work. Actually, he'd fallen back on an Anna trick. She used to involve the kids in every decision, from what to have for the night's supper to where they should go on family vacations. She used to say that if the kids helped do the choosing, they wouldn't gripe if things didn't work out exactly as planned. Everett remembered the horrendous vacations they'd known as a family. Then there was the memory of one or two meals that had been so awful, the dog ran away when the scraps landed in his bowl. Their own choices or not, the kids griped anyway, but admittedly not as badly as they might have had the ideas for the Grand Canyon and the spinach casserole been forced on them.

Still testing Anna's system, he said, "You really think a brand-new house might do it, huh?"

Kara sat down on the couch, surprising Everett with her sudden and lively animation. "Yes! Don't you see? It would solve everything!"

Everett bird-eyed her. "Why do I get the feeling we're no longer talking about your mama and I getting married?"

She blushed and became still.

"Kara?" he coaxed. "If there's something really important, something your mom should know, I think—"

"If I tell you a secret, will you promise not to tell Mama until I say it's okay?"

Everett's eyebrows rose. After raising three children, he knew that a child turned to an adult for help only when that kid was in trouble. Trouble too big to trust their know-it-all peers for advice.

"How big a secret are we talking about?"

"The biggest."

Everett's eyes narrowed, and he pursed his lips. Her eyes fluttered with relief when he said, "I'm pretty good with big secrets."

She smiled. She had a pretty smile. He felt she needed to smile a lot more. Kara took a deep cleansing breath, let it go. Then she moved in closer, her voice dropping to a near whisper.

"Okay, here goes. Gemma isn't going to college. She didn't send back the college application forms the way she told Mama she did."

"Why not?"

"Because she and Ed are going to get married. They, uh, kinda have to."

"Oh, God."

"Yeah!" Kara said, her tone urgent. "But think about this. If you build a new house for Mama, Gemma and Ed could live in our old house. I know Mama doesn't believe it, but Gemma is even more afraid than Mama that she's going to end up with a baby on each hip and no husband. Maybe if Gemma and Ed had a house, didn't have to start out living in a rented trailer the way my mom and dad did, their marriage would work out all right and they'll be happy."

It was a dim hope, but it was all Kara had. Sensing how much she cared for her older sister, he couldn't bring himself to take that one hope away, tell her that even if the young people were handed life on a platter, there were still no guarantees they would be happy. Any couple believing that they *had* to get married were starting off badly. Marriage was something people had to want desperately. Everett was living proof that any guarantees of happiness resulting from a forced marriage just weren't that thick on the ground. But Kara was young, and young people lived in an enviable world of hope.

Again he placed his hand over hers. "When exactly does Gemma plan on telling Katie about Ed and the baby?"

"She was going to tell her last night, but then she and Mom got into a big fight about Mom going out with you. Gemma wanted Mama to stay home so they could talk, but Mama took it wrong. She started in about Daddy, about how he didn't care two hoots about us and that the reason he didn't care was because they'd made the mistake of getting married too young. I guess you can figure out how that part upset Gemma. And Mama wouldn't stop. She can be like that. Once she gets going, a bulldozer couldn't stop her. Mama went on and on about how she deserved a good time, too, and that nothing we could say was going to stop her from going out. Then Gemma got really mad. Gemma always gets mad when she's scared. Anyway, she said some pretty wild things about Mama driving Daddy away and how she was the reason he never came back. The fight really got worse after that."

"Where were you during all of this?"

"In my room. I was kinda crying, hoping they would stop yelling and just start listening to each other. Then I was trying to think up ways to make everything better."

"Cleaning the house was your idea, wasn't it?"

"Yeah. I thought if we showed Mom we could be responsible, be real grown-up and dependable that she—"

Everett picked up her limp hand and held it tightly between his. He didn't have to hear any more. Now he completely understood why Katie's girls had been so hostile to the idea of him. It wasn't as he or Katie believed, that the girls were being loyal to a father they barely knew. The truth was, his first date with Katie had come at the worst possible moment of their young lives. Then while Katie had been with him, he could almost picture the two frightened girls putting their heads together, trying to come up with a way to soften Katie up before Gemma hit her with the news that her worst fear for Gemma's life had been realized. But the housecleaning scheme hadn't worked because Katie had only turned around and left again. And why? Because she thought he needed her more than her girls needed her.

Everett felt supremely selfish. While he wallowed in that, not saying anything, Kara became suddenly afraid that she was losing the one friendly adult in the camp.

"Please, Mr. Jakomin," she begged. "Don't tell Mama. Not yet. Maybe if we wait until she's really happy about being engaged, she won't go crazy when Gemma and I tell her about Ed and the baby."

"Ooooooh, I wouldn't count on that," he said with a hollow laugh. "And from now on I think you should call me Everett."

She nodded as her face crumpled. Watching her, he saw Kara for what she was, what she had always been. The family peacemaker. But the trouble with being a peacemaker is that no one ever considers the possibility that the peacemaker could do with a bit of peace herself. Most especially, any peacemaker dedicated to the thankless challenge of standing between Katie and Gemma. This kid needed a friend. Everett decided to be that friend. He wrapped an arm around his step-daughter-to-be and held her close, laying the side of his face against her crown.

"Now that you've told me, I don't want you worrying about it anymore. As a matter of fact, I want you to stay completely out of it. In the next few weeks there's going to be a fair amount of screaming and quite possibly not just over Gemma and Ed. But none of it will be your responsibility, Kara. You didn't start any of the trouble, and you can't fix it. So what I want you to do while all the sand is being thrown in the air is take my car."

Kara shot up right in his arms. "You mean your *'Vette?!*"

"That's the one." He looked down into her aghast face. "You can drive a stick shift, can't you?"

She swallowed hard. "I—I drove a stick shift over here. It's Gemma's car, but I can drive it because I've got my licence! Wanna see?"

Chuckling, he settled her down. "I'll take your word for it. Anyway, what I want you to do is take my car and use it to have a good time. And I mean a real good time, Kara. I want you to cut loose. You are hereby ordered to spend every minute of your free time profiling through Olla. Think you can handle that?"

"Are you serious? The minute I drive that car, I'll be the most popular girl in the whole high school."

She looked up at him, her young face streaked with tears. In a tiny voice she said, "So . . . you're gonna tell Mom?"

"Yes. That's why I'm letting you drive my car. Call it a payback for not being able to keep your secret. But I won't tell her right away. First I'm gonna want to talk to Gemma and Ed. Together. Got that?"

"Yes."

"Good. And the minute you give Gemma the message, you tell her you are no longer her go-between, that if she wants to worry someone with her problem, she's to worry me."

"Please—please don't be mean to my sister," Kara said inside a sob. "She's so scared and I love her an awful lot."

He hugged her tightly. "I know you do."

Kara rested for a moment in his strength, becoming very glad that Everett Jakomin had come into her life. And not just because of the Corvette. Her tone shy again, she said, "Do you think my idea of a new house is pretty good¿"

"Kara, I think your idea is just the ticket."

"Does that mean I'll be getting a big bedroom just for me¿"

Everett laughed. "Definitely. And maybe even your own television."

"What do you think of the idea of our new house having a swimming pool¿"

"I think you're pushing your luck. But, hey, nice try."

As they dressed, Katie tried to finagle the reason behind Everett and Kara having their heads so closely together, why they had been speaking in whispers. Everett bent at the knees as he looked over her head into the dresser mirror and brushed back his hair. Seated at the dressing table, she watched him in the mirror.

"I couldn't believe it when I saw Kara hugging you. Kara isn't a hugger. What on earth did you say to make her act that way¿"

Everett patted down the hair near the part. "I just told her how much I loved you. That I knew a little something about kids and that your having two kids didn't scare me a bit."

"And that was it¿"

"Yep." He placed the brush on the table and concentrated on straightening his tie.

"Why don't I believe you?"

He gently pushed her hair away from her shoulder and kissed the back of her neck. "Do you have any idea how much fun this is?"

"How much fun what is?"

"Dressing together. Don't you think that's fun, Katie?"

"I think you're avoiding giving me a straight answer."

"And I think you're being a party pooper."

"Everett," she said, trying to keep her voice stern. It required a great effort. He was now nibbling the length of her neck, setting off a flurry of butterflies in her stomach. "We happen to be going to a wake, not a party."

He turned away from her. "Hey! When life's this much fun, even a wake's a party."

Katie had a few more things to say, but the telephone rang and Everett went to the night table to answer it.

"Dad," Nath said, his tone firm but his voice a trifle shaky, "I'm going to the wake with Hayley, and you can't stop me."

"Fine."

"What?"

"I said that's fine. I think you should be there to support your wife. This is a very stressful time for her."

Nath was silent for a few seconds. "Dad? Have you been drinking?"

"Not yet." Everett hung up. Clapping his hands together, he said, "Well, the whole gang's gonna be there. C.R.'s last hurrah aughtta be a corker."

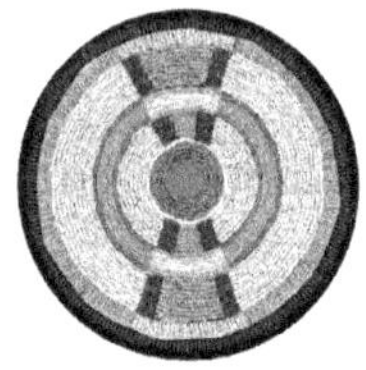

CHAPTER TWENTY

"What a dump!" Katie exclaimed sarcastically. She and Everett walked the graveled drive choked with cars. The impressive house and front gardens were fully lit. If she hadn't known this to be a private home, she would have sworn it was a fine old hotel. "You'd have thought with all of his money, C.R. could have afforded a nicer house."

"Oh, he did live in nicer house," Everett joked. "This is just the gate cottage. His house is behind this one."

Shaking her head, Katie grimaced as they bisected the gleaming walls of parked Cadillacs and Mercedes. "I see the poor arrived early. Must have heard about the free food."

"And the free booze, Katie. You can't expect people to get maudlin stone sober."

A hearse was parked close to the house. The driver stood just outside the vehicle's door, smoking a cigarette. Spotting Everett and Katie, the driver quickly lost the cigarette. He nodded to them as they walked by, his expression respectably mournful.

Standing just outside the massive front door, Katie and Everett adjusted their clothing, Everett his tie, Katie smoothing any wrinkles from her dress. Then they looked at each other.

"Here we go," she whispered. "I'd advise us both to enjoy the booze and food as much as we can. Tomorrow night we'll probably be feasting on bread and water."

"There's one other thing I forgot to tell you."

Katie looked up at him, her expression stricken. "What now!"

"I don't have time to go into it. It's a little too detailed. But just try not to look surprised by anything you hear me say."

The butler answering the door was highly surprised when he opened it to Katie and Everett. He was in time to hear Katie yelling, "*Damn* you, Jakomin!" Then they turned to the startled butler, their faces creasing with false smiles as they said in unison, "Good evening."

Just inside the massive foyer, the two Johnstons stood solemnly, acting as dignified greeters. The elder Johnston spoke to Everett in a papery voice.

"Mr. Jones is on view in the main room. The family are in the small parlor, being comforted by Archbishop Hearly. They will be joining their guests directly."

The unspoken question hung between Everett and both Johnstons. Katie's heart was beating furiously in her chest as Everett nodded. She caught the conspiratorial gleam in the old men's eyes. The gleam brightened when Everett began to speak with authority.

"I will need to meet with Matt, David, and their wives just as soon as the family prayer time has finished."

"Of course," the elder Johnston said. "But before I replay the message, would it be possible for you and I to have a private word?"

"Certainly."

Johnston caught Everett's elbow. "Perhaps we should speak nearer the library."

Everett allowed himself to be led to the other side of the foyer. Katie remained by the side of the younger Johnston. She couldn't hear a word passing between Everett and the elder Johnston, and with their heads turned, it was impossible to read their lips. Then the old man led Everett fully into the library and closed the doors.

Twenty long minutes passed. During that time, more guests arrived, the women subdued with grief, the men looking stricken to the core. She heard one man mutter something disparaging about Harry, but he was silenced by a warning look from a woman, apparently his wife. The younger Johnston spoke softly to the guests and they filtered on by, passing Katie without a second look. Finally the library doors opened, and as Everett and the elder Johnston approached, she heard the mortician say, "Leave it with me. In the meantime, please avail yourselves of Mrs. Jones's hospitality."

The main room was in Katie's view, on the scale of an elegant stadium. It was filled with finely dressed people wandering about, speaking in hushed tones, and walking on tiptoe around the opened casket. From where she stood she could see C.R.'s sleeping profile, his slightly raised head resting on a silky pillow. Looking at him, Katie's stomach became a hard knot and her body began to shake like a leaf being battered by a cold winter wind. A waiter bearing a silver tray containing filled wineglasses passed. Without waiting to be offered a glass, she hooked one, knocking back the contents in a single go.

"I didn't realize you were such a little drinker," Everett teased.

"Nerves," Katie rasped.

"Nerves?"

"Yeah. I'm losing mine. Rapidly."

Looking back over his shoulder, Everett saw the doors to the small parlor open, family members beginning to file out. The Jones boys looked ashen. Their wives were snuffling into handkerchiefs. The elder Johnston quickly corralled Matt and David.

"Try to get a grip, Katie," Everett whispered against her ear.

Matt looked away from the mortician, his gaze finding and angrily settling on Everett. Then Matt turned, Kelly, Irene, and David following him back into the parlor.

Everett took Katie's cold hand. "Okay, honey, it's showtime."

Her mouth was suddenly dust-dry with only a hint of the wine she'd tasted. Her heartbeat was rampant. In a weakened cry she squeaked, "Where'd that waiter go!"

Matt prowled, while on the couch placed in the center of the room Kelly sat next to Irene. David stood in front of the fireplace, his back turned on everyone in the room. Katie, perched on the edge of a chair, sat directly behind Everett as he stood solemnly, his hands behind his back, his feet well apart. The atmosphere in the room was so charged that she wished she had a bottle of wine and a carton of cigarettes. She badly needed both to bank the riot going on inside, but for Everett's sake she sat perfectly still, her spine ramrod-straight, hoping to God she looked as if she didn't need anything.

"Matt? David?"

Matt stopped prowling, David turned and looked back at Everett over his shoulder.

"Would you both be seated, please. What I have to say is very important. I will try to be as brief as possible."

Matt sent Everett a look of pure hatred. As he sat down beside Kelly, David dispiritedly crossed the room and flopped down beside Irene.

Matt darkly eyed Katie for a moment, then dismissed her presence as he barked, "Shouldn't we be waiting for Harry?"

"This discussion does not include Harry."

Matt and David glanced meaningfully at each other. "I think you should know," Matt said, "that we haven't been idle. We've had conferences with our best lawyers, and they've assured us—"

"If you want to listen to lawyers," Everett said firmly, "go right ahead. But as of now, you are no longer entitled to take any advice from any lawyer connected with Red Bird Oil."

"And why not?" David scoffed.

"Because they work for me."

Kelly and Irene turned pale. Matt and David jumped to their feet and in loud voices called Everett every vile name that came into their heads.

Through it all, Everett, the man with the power, said nothing. He waited until the furor settled, Matt and David were more in control of their tempers.

"If you will be seated," Everett said calmly, "I will continue."

Their eyes throwing daggers, Matt and David complied.

Everett began again. "Your father, by the full authority under the terms of his will, has left everything in my hands. And by that he meant Red Bird Oil, the banks, the refinery, the Rocking J—everything."

Again Matt and David jumped to their feet. "You sonofabitch!" David shouted. "The Rocking J is mine! Mine and Irene's. There is no way Dad could give the Rocking J to you!"

"Yes, he could. And if you refuse to be quiet, you will never understand why he could."

Irene grabbed David's arm. "For God's sake, sit down, Dee."

"But, Irene! The Rocking J had nothing to do with Daddy!"

"How we gonna find out it didn't if you don't stop hollerin'?"

Reluctantly, David sat down beside his wife.

Matt was still standing, his eyes radiating his near-uncontrollable rage. "You've already read our father's will?"

"I've read a copy of it, yes."

"When?" Matt demanded.

"Just a few moments ago. It was a copy given by C.R.'s attorney to the Johnstons."

"Why would undertakers need a copy of my dad's will?"

"It was necessary in order to legally carry out the terms of his . . . disposal."

"Disposal!" David cried. "What the hell are you talking about now?"

"Forgive me. *Disposal* was C.R.'s expression. He meant, of course, his funeral. Those final preparations are directly linked to the distribution of his estate."

"I fail to see any link," Matt seethed. His face twisted with loathing, his voice ragged and feral, he said, "If you think for one second that my father's trusting you to bury him has any tie with Red Bird, that you can just waltz in and take it all, then you're in for the fight of your life."

"I'm not trying to take anything," Everett said somberly. "What I'm trying to do is talk. But a talker needs a listener. Are you going to go on making noise and choking on your pride? Or are you going to shut up and listen?"

Matt stood defiantly a moment longer. The fire in his eyes continued to burn brightly, but he finally yielded to Kelly's urging and sat down. Everyone remained quiet for an interminable amount of time. When Everett knew he had their full attention, that there would be no further outbursts, he began to speak.

"The Johnston brothers have the funeral firmly in hand. It will take place tomorrow morning at nine. The headstone has been prepared, the grave is ready. The will is to be read tomorrow evening, but only on the condition that certain essentials are unanimously agreed to by everyone now present."

Everett looked into each face. No one moved. No one blinked.

Everett quickly continued.

"Matt, barring any further threats against my life, you are to remain president of Red Bird Oil. David, you are still first vice president. Harry is to retain his position at the bank. Everything is to remain the same except for one minor change. For the next five years I am to be chairman of the board of directors over Red Bird and the banks. The reason I have been placed in this position is to prevent a family bloodbath. C.R. chose me for a number of reasons. Those are unimportant. His primary reason was that he knew he could trust me."

David's eyes rounded in sheer amazement. Matt ground his back teeth. "Well, I don't trust you. And my father didn't have to protect—"

"Yes, he did. Each of you is exactly where you belong, in the jobs you do best. Any scrambling to change places would only spell disaster for everything C.R. built. But because none of you would see it that way, he had to devise a strong-arm method to keep the three of you in place before it began a catastrophic family brawl.

"Too many people depend on you three for their livelihoods. C.R. knew their interests would become lost in the scuffle if his sons started warring one against the other. My job is to see that this does not happen. For the next five years"—Everett tapped his chest with his index finger—"I cast the deciding vote on any disagreement among the three of you. I also have the power to fire anyone who steps out of company line. After five years, if I am guaranteed a continuing peaceful coexistence, I will be free to sign over my controlling shares."

Matt sounded a scoffing laugh. "And how do we know you'll leave everything in place, that after five years you'll step down and out of our lives?"

"All I can give you is my word."

"I'm afraid that's not good enough."

"Then you are in for a very long five years."

Like a timid student, David raised a hand. Everett nodded and David spoke. "When you sign over the shares, will they be divided equally between us?"

"No. Those shares will be held in trust."

"For our children?"

"Yes. But the primary recipients will be the grandchildren produced by my son and Matt's daughter, Hayley."

Kelly gasped sharply. David and Irene, knowing full well the meaning behind Everett's statement and both fearing the worst was still to come, locked hands.

"What grandchildren?!" Matt shouted.

"As I said, the grandchildren that will be born from my son, Nathaniel, and your daughter, Hayley."

Kelly's eyes went wider. Irene mouthed *Oh, my God.* David looked, with a high level of anxiety, toward his astonished brother.

Everett stood calmly with his hands clasped behind his back. Katie did a quick check that he hadn't crossed his fingers while telling a big fat lie. She didn't put it past Everett to use the momentum of the situation to save Nath's young behind while the saving was good.

But Everett's fingers were uncrossed, his manner composed. As difficult as it was for even Katie to believe, Everett was telling the truth. Then she did a quick read of the others. Irene and Kelly looked frightened half out of their minds. David was gnawing a hole in his thumbnail. Matt Jones was going purple in the face.

Oh, what she wouldn't give for a bucket of wine right now. Then the time bomb that Kelly, Irene, and David had been afraid of exploded.

"You mean to stand there and tell me," Matt thundered, "my own father expected me to sell my daughter off in marriage to your son¿"

"No! What I'm telling you is that two months prior to your father's death, your daughter secretly married my son. Not only did your father know about the marriage, he went to great lengths to make certain you couldn't touch it. All he's asked me to do is stand in his place, protect what he built, and protect his granddaughter's marriage.

"My son's a good man," Everett continued hotly. "He's better than this family deserves. And C.R. knew it. You, Matt, are the reason your father left everything to me. He knew everyone was worried about Harry taking over, but Harry has always been your smoke screen. Mutual dread of Harry would put everyone in your corner, and that's exactly what you were counting on. You may have had an entire state fooled, but you didn't fool your father. He's always known just how strong you are, just as he's always known just how weak Harry is. The other thing he knew was that David will always follow wherever you lead. Against the two of you, Harry would be out in the cold before he ever knew what hit him. C.R. was afraid for Harry. He needed an outsider to protect his weakest son. And that's exactly what I intend to do. So, Matt, I'm putting you on notice. If one word of this conversation leaves this room, finds its way to Harry, completely destroying what's left of his pride, you and David are out. Harry will get everything."

The blood in Matt's face drained. His jaw dropped,

his eyes glazed over. Everett waited for Matt's eyes to rekindle with anger. They didn't. Matt simply sat there with the vacant look of a man who had just witnessed his champion Labrador mowed down in the street by a speeding ten-ton truck. Completely deflated, Matt sagged against the couch.

Everett regarded Matt from beneath his brows. In a low but steady voice he continued. "Matt, let's move away from threats and talk to each other in a reasonable fashion about our kids. I want to assure you that until yesterday, I didn't know anything about their marriage. But, C.R. being C.R. seemed to know about it from the first day. That's when he made arrangements in his will to prevent their marriage being contested."

Matt didn't respond in any form or fashion. Giving up on him, Everett turned to David. "Now, would you like to talk about the ranch?"

David snorted down his nose. "I'm almost afraid to."

"Don't be. Actually, it's fairly cut and dried. On Peter Waterman's death, you and Irene inherited the house and all the outbuildings. The land was never Mr. Waterman's to give. The dollar-a-year fee you've been paying without knowing why was to cover the terms of a long-standing lease between C.R. and Peter Waterman. Because of a promise C.R. had made to his father, C.R. was not free to sell any part of his land, but he could lease it. Which is what he did, and that lease was good only for the length of Peter Waterman's lifetime."

Irene yelped, "Then my daddy never owned the Rocking J?"

"No, he did not. But you could own it, Miss Irene, if you were married to one of C.R.'s sons."

The dawn of realization slowly began to spread over her face. Her voice was full of laughter as she exclaimed, "Well, those old foxes! No wonder they were so tickled when Dee an' me got together."

"They were more than tickled." Everett smiled broadly. "They were delirious." Becoming more serious, he paced a few steps. "None of you may realize this, but C.R. was a die-hard romantic. In fact, it was his one weakness." He looked at the four faces regarding him intently. "To him the most important thing in this life was love. The type of love shared between a man and a woman. Which was why, when any of his sons came to him and professed this kind of love, C.R. was prepared to do anything to make certain his son got the girl of his choice."

Suddenly, his senses flying down a long, dark tunnel like a speeding express train, Matt was transported back in time. In that brief second he was again that young man standing nervously in his father's office, confessing his love for Kelly, and her condition. Instead of his father demanding he get rid of the girl, his father had stunned him by neatly arranging a wedding that very same day.

Matt next became indescribably sad. Saddened that his own daughter knew she could not come to him about the young man she loved, that his father had been forced to extreme measures to protect her. Protect her because he didn't trust his son. He hadn't realized his father felt that way, and knowing it now, Matt was crushed. He ran a hand over his eyes, wiping away welling tears.

Noticing her husband's distress, Kelly leaned in and whispered in his ear. "Everything is going to be all right, Matt. Your father hasn't taken anything away from you. Not really. He loved you very much. But he had to do what he thought would be best for the whole family."

"I know," he said. He turned his head, his eyes locking with hers. "And he sure did a good job, didn't he?"

Kelly smiled warmly. "He was C.R. What else would you expect?"

Feeling calmer, Matt looked squarely at Everett, listened without anger as Everett Jakomin continued speaking to David and Irene.

"There is a condition I'm about to present to you that will not be addressed in C.R.'s will. If you agree, my name as owner of the Rocking J will be stricken from the will's list of assets."

Irene leaned forward. "What are Dee an' me supposed to do? Give one of your sons our unmarried daughter?"

Everett chuckled. "No, fortunately for all of us, I've run out of eligible sons, and the one condition I'm supposed to put to you is very easy. If all goes well by tomorrow evening, I will happily sign the deed to the Rocking J, making you and David the rightful owners. Which also means you will no longer be required to pay the annual one-dollar fee."

"Well, that sounds like a deal," Irene chortled. "An' it'll sure take the strain off our budget."

Frowning, David lightly admonished his wife, "Honey, you pick the damnedest times to crack jokes!"

"Yeah, but, Dee, if ya can't laugh in the face of adversity, then what the hell good is it?"

Everett was biting down on his lower lip, fighting a laugh as David threw his hands in the air and yelled at Everett. "You'll have to forgive her, Mr. Jakomin. My wife is what Will Rogers and Gracie Allen would have had if they'd made a baby."

Everett pealed laughter.

Katie watched the four people sitting across from her. Now that all of the harsh truth was out of the way, they seemed to be perking up, laughing along with Everett at Irene's good-natured expense. When the laughter subsides, all the previous tension was gone. Eyes that were no longer hostile followed Everett as he paced back and forth, outlining C.R.'s last but most important requirement.

"David, Irene, both of you must promise absolutely that following the funeral services, you will not go home. You must promise that you will stay away from the Rocking J for the remainder of the day."

"Well, that's not a hard promise!" Irene bayed. "We're all going to be here for the reception. Lord only knows how long that thing's gonna last. Then there's the reading of the will in the evening, and then—"

Everett raised a silencing hand. "What I meant to say is the ranch must be completely deserted. If there is one human being anywhere on the ranch, you and David forfeit the Rocking J."

In stark confusion, the four Joneses muttered among themselves. Then Irene leaned forward, again trapping Everett with her piercing gaze. "By human beings, are you meaning the ranch hands?"

"Oh, for God's sake, Irene!" David cried.

She looked at him levelly. "Dee, you an' I both know that Phil Brant, while he is one of the best hands we've ever had, is not something anybody would call a human being."

Everett jumped into the conversation. "Miss Irene, when I said human beings, I meant Phil Brant too."

Irene turned back to Everett. "Well, what are you gonna be doin'? Rustling our stock?"

"No." Everett laughed softly. "I won't be taking a thing."

The four Joneses muttered again, David the more vocal, saying, "This just doesn't make any sense!"

Irene broke from the pack and over the buzz of voices yelled, "Are you sure this Looney Tune thing is something C.R. wanted?"

Everett did not fight the smile. "Yes."

Irene was still amazed, so much so that her eyes were wide and her mouth was rounded, giving her the appearance of an awestruck goldfish. "Mr. Jakomin? Are you a medicine man?"

Behind his back, Everett crossed the fingers of both hands. Katie watched as his fingers folded over and locked tightly. *Here comes the big fatty!*

"Yes, ma'am. I guess you could say I am."

When Matt opened the parlor door, Harry's voice could be heard from the main reception room. It wasn't hard for the six to visualize Harry standing beside, perhaps even in front of, his father's coffin as he eulogized the immortal C. R. Jones.

"As I am now the head of the family," Harry said loudly and proudly, "I ask you all to lift your glasses in a farewell toast."

Matt's eyebrows were knit together as he turned his head level with his shoulder and frowned at Everett.

Everett smiled faintly, shrugged, and mentally quoted Sam Starr. *S-gi-dv nu-s-di.* That's the way it is.

Matt blew steam from flared nostrils.

David offered Irene his arm. "It's going to be an interesting five years."

"Yeah," Irene agreed. "Five years of peace. How the hell are any of us ever going to get used to that?"

Her fears and worries for her daughter's secret marriage behind her, Kelly felt almost giddy. She slipped her arm through Matt's. As the two of them began to walk forward, Kelly glanced back to Everett. Her smile for him was warm, grateful. With the turning of her head, her bright coppery hair swirled, surged like a frothy tide, obscuring her features. The fleeting touch of her blue eyes, the warmth of her private smile, were gone.

Katie did not much care for the exchange between Everett and Kelly Jones. Never mind that she understood the gratitude expressed in Kelly's glance, having another woman look at Everett that way set her teeth on edge. Katie tightened her hold on Everett's arm. When he looked at her, she said, "You know, you're good in a crisis."

Everett brought his face closer to hers. "Honey, we're still not out of the woods. Don't get cocky on me now."

"Humor me, Ev. I love you and I'm proud of you."

Thinking of Ed and Gemma, Everett whispered feverishly, "Honey, just promise you'll always hold on to that. Especially, oooh, let's say, in a few days from now."

"Why?" she squawked. "What's happening in a few days from now?"

"Let's just take one thing at a time, okay, Katie? We're still in the middle of this mess."

"Whatever you say, big boy."

Matt's two children and their guests waited just outside the parlor in the foyer, trying to look interested in what Uncle Harry was saying. Matt, leading the procession out of the parlor, walked straight for his daughter.

Seeing her father and the intent look on his face, she realized that he knew, he absolutely knew. Hayley's eyes dilated in fear. Before she could speak, Matt seized her by the shoulders, pulled her off her feet, and kissed her solidly on the mouth. Setting her down, he looked past her to a suddenly very nervous Nath Jakomin.

Matt extended his hand. Harry's oration drowned out Matt's words to everyone except those in the foyer. "I understand you're my son-in-law."

Nath glanced quickly to his father standing stolidly behind Matt Jones. Everett sent Nath a meaningful look. Gulping the lump in his throat, Nath's fear-riddled dark eyes slew back toward Matt. In a raspy voice Nath responded, "Yes, sir, I am".

"You love my daughter?"

"With all my heart, sir."

Matt nodded his grudging acceptance. "Then . . . that's fine, son. With your permission, we'll save the formal announcement for another two months. I'm certain my wife will want to throw a huge party and invite everyone she believes will be good for an expensive gift. Two months should be just enough time for her to plan the event."

"Yes, sir." Nath gulped again.

Matt's words were appropriate, but his handshake was brutal. Especially for an artist. Nath could almost hear his knuckles breaking. And while his hand was being mangled, Hayley threw her arms around her father's neck.

"Oh, Daddy. I love you so much. I just know you're going to love Nath too."

"Of course I will," Matt said, squeezing Nath's hand just that little bit harder.

When Nath got his hand back, he couldn't stifle his cry of relief. As he tried to work the pain out of his knuckles, Matt lifted a brow and spoke to Everett. "I hope my being a bit firm with your boy isn't considered a firing offense."

"No, it isn't. I have a married daughter too. I did a bit more than squeeze my son-in-law's hand when they came home from their honeymoon."

Harry, still pontificating his father's lengthy list of virtues, stopped short as hearty laughter erupted in the foyer. He frowned, furious that his two brothers, and at a time like this, could stoop so low as to yuck it up with Everett Jakomin. Harry managed to recover before his audience was equally distracted. Terri sat in a chair close to him, looking up at her husband adoringly. Harry went on with what he had been saying as if the group in the foyer were of no interest to him. And once his father was buried, he would begin his plan of action. Harry called it slash and burn. Slash down the dead wood of the Jones empire and burn it up quickly before it sprouted enough new growth to make a challenging comeback.

That's what Daddy would have done. Harry was sure of it.

• • •

Now that the worst part of his job was over, Everett wanted to leave, but he couldn't. Not without speaking to Emma Jones. Leaving Katie to trap one of the wine waiters in a corner, Everett made his way through the crowded room to where Emma Jones sat in a high-backed chair near her husband's coffin. When she saw him approaching, Emma regally dismissed the people surrounding her. She even dismissed the bishop standing behind her queenly chair. Everett sat down on the arm of a sofa and leaned toward her.

"You look lovely, Mrs. Jones."

She canted her head, looking at him with clear eyes and offering an enigmatic smile. "Shouldn't you be calling me Emma?"

"If I may."

"You may. There was a time, when you were a small child, I believed you would end up calling me Mother."

"I know."

She arched a brow. "You do?"

Everett blushed deeply. "C.R. left a—a letter for me. In it he told me about the car accident, how you stayed by my bed."

"Did he now?" Her expression became apprehensive. "A-and what else did he tell you?"

"That you are the loveliest wife any man could ever hope for. That you are a genuine great lady, that he has always been so very proud of you. He's also asked me to watch over you in his place."

Large tears came into her eyes, spilled down her cheeks. "He-he said all that?"

"Yes."

Her head bobbled on her neck as she struggled to preserve her shaken dignity. A trembling hand took his, holding on firmly as she looked back to the coffin, staring quietly at her husband's sleeping profile. "He's gone now," she barely said. "He's not mine. Not anymore. I have to give him up. Don't I."

As it was not a question, merely an affirmation of what they both knew, Everett remained silent. Emma Jones was not a woman to welcome anyone's pity. Her spine straightened, her tears ceased, her features becoming fully composed. Everett placed a hand over the hands already joined as Emma Jones said softly, "Good-bye. Charlie."

In the same way Emma Jones had once stationed herself by a tiny boy's hospital bed, Everett never left her side throughout the remainder of the evening. When it was time to leave, Everett kissed her hand. "I am always near. Mother."

"I will depend on that," she answered.

It was a beautiful day for a funeral. The sun was bright, the cornflower-blue sky cloudless. Only a whisper of a breeze stirred. Birds sang in trees bordering the cemetery. The coffin was slowly lowered into the ground. The seated Jones family, which now included Nath, wept copious tears.

Guests swarming the burial site like the multitude awaiting their share of the five loaves and seven fishes followed suit. The only ones not moved to tears were Everett, Katie, and the two Johnston brothers.

Standing well back of the funeral party, these four carefully avoided eye contact. As family members stood and in turn approached the grave, tossing down a red rose of remembrance on the sealed casket, Everett, Katie, and the two Johnstons turned, walking out of the cemetery.

The afternoon was like the morning. Except that it was boiling hot. Everett stood on the side of the hill, watching the dirt road that cut straight through the Rocking J. David and Irene held to the bargain. The Rocking J was completely deserted. Katie sat on a blanket, a bottle of wine between her blue-jeaned legs.

Now that everything was ready and waiting, Katie was drinking straight from the bottle. She was trying to get drunk, but it wasn't working. If they were about to go to prison, regretfully, she'd be stone cold sober for the occasion.

Leaving the cemetery, Everett had known a few last-minute qualms himself. Back at his house, both he and Katie changed hurriedly into the necessary clothing. In a dead run out of the house, they grabbed the needed shovels and pickaxes out of the garage and stowed them in the trunk of Katie's car. It was then that Katie noticed that the Corvette was missing.

"Ev! Where's the 'Vette?"

"Kara's got it."

"She's what?"

Everett closed the trunk lid. "I told her she could take it out for a spin. I left her the keys on the kitchen table."

"Don't you think the 'Vette's kind of a powerful car for my baby daughter to be driving?"

Everett kissed Katie's nose. "Kara's not a baby. Besides, I promised her that as long as I was her daddy, she'd have a good time."

"Kara has a good time," Katie said defensively.

"I know." He shrugged. "But from now on her good times just got better."

She snorted. "If we get through this, you mean."

Everett's hand against the small of her back propelled her toward the car's passenger side. "Yeah, this and a few other things," he muttered.

"What?"

"Nothing, honey. Get in the car, please."

Speeding away from his house, Everett had been close to changing his mind. Even closer to changing it as they followed the map C.R. had drawn for him, leading them to this very spot. A knoll, surrounded by protective blackjacks.

A knoll that Peter Waterman had years before told

David and Irene to leave strictly alone, that it was not for any reason to be cleared for grazing. He'd said it was a sacred Osage site, that he had assured the Nation he would leave this place undefiled. David and Irene continued to believe just that.

As C.R. would have said, What a load of mule muffins!

Everett turned at the waist and looked back, past Katie, to the grave and the simple stone that read *Cassie.*

All this time, Everett thought, *she's been here.*

He remembered the one and only time his father had ever taken him to his mother's grave. There wasn't a headstone, only a plaque set in the ground that read *C. Jakomin.* He could see himself again as that little boy placing flowers across the plaque. Now that he had a full understanding of the situation, he knew that his father had not taken him to the cemetery out of love for his long-dead wife, but to prove to a stubborn son that his mother was indeed dead. Delbert's mission was accomplished. Everett stopped asking questions about her. But not because of the grave. As young as he was, he knew that his father, Delbert Jakomin, simply wasn't interested in talking about his dead wife. He wanted to talk only about C. R. Jones, pound it into the boy's head that anyone named Jones was their bitter enemy.

Everett also remembered, as he stood by what he was told was his mother's grave, that he'd felt nothing. And then he remembered feeling ashamed and guilty because he'd felt nothing. Now he understood why and the age-old guilt melted away.

His mother wasn't there. She'd never been there. Which was why a sensitive boy hadn't felt her presence. Delbert Jakomin never suspected that what he had consigned into the ground had been nothing more than a weighted coffin. If he had loved her, he would have known, exactly the way Everett had known when he buried his much-loved Anna. A cherished wife missing from her own funeral would have sent any normal husband on a tear through the countryside in search for her. But not Delbert. He buried that box and walked away just as quickly as he could. But while he was planting rocks, C.R. was busily spiriting his lovely Cassie away.

C.R. and Peter Waterman—and the Johnstons—brought Cassie home. To the site where once C.R. had planned to build her a snug little house.

Tell me about our house again, Charlie.

Well, it's going to be two rooms. Three, if you count the kitchen. One room will be just for sitting. The other room is where we will snuggle together in our own bed.

And pull the quilt over our heads when it storms?

Yes. And hold each other tight.

Forever?

Forever, Cas.

Looking now at his mother's simple grave, Everett finally felt her presence. Felt her so strongly that his hands trembled as he removed the dried roses C.R. must have placed in the vase at the head of the grave most probably a day or two before his own death. Her gentle presence was so strong that it damn near broke Everett's heart. Even after placing a good distance between himself and her grave, he could still feel her.

Everett put the heels of his hands to his eyes, pressing back tears. Then he took a deep breath, expelled it, and concentrated on watching the narrow road below. Moments passed, and then he saw a brown tail of dust rising up behind a pickup truck speeding along the dirt road. His shoulders shook slightly, laughing in much-needed relief, as Katie, who had also spotted the pickup, wailed, "Oh, God, Ev! We're body-nappers!"

Suddenly he loved Katie so much, he wanted to shout it to the sky. But considering the situation and Katie's mounting hysteria, now did not seem the opportune moment. However, when he looked at her, the love he felt shone from his eyes and was apparent in his tone as he laughingly said, "Cork the bottle, baby. C.R.'s here."

Those two frail little old men proved to be a lot stronger than they looked. With Katie pitching in, the four of them grappled the simple pine coffin off the flatbed of the truck. Carrying it by the rough handles, the four hefted it up the incline to the grave site, a grave Everett and Katie had spent hours digging with the shovels and pickaxes.

The four people were sweating profusely and breathless by the time the coffin was finally set down beside the open grave. Katie and Everett sat down and rested while both Johnstons inspected the grave-digging efforts.

"Could have been a foot or two deeper," the youngest ancient had the nerve to say.

"It's fine just like it is," the elder said. "In the old days, nobody went in for that six-feet-under crap. It was just dig as best you could and be done with it."

The elder Johnston looked hastily at Everett. "We have papers you'll need to sign before we can allow you put him in. Then we could help with the burying if you'd like."

Everett glanced at Katie as she leaned wearily against him. She looked sweaty, dirty, and whipped. Even so, Katie shook her head and communicated with her eyes. Everett silently agreed. The burial would be private and personal. Exactly the way C.R. wanted.

Everett looked up to the two morticians. "I appreciate your offer, but Katie and I will see to it ourselves."

The elder Johnston smiled.

The younger Johnston moaned. "Oh, no. We forgot all about the headstone. It's still on the blasted truck."

Everett hauled Katie to her feet and they followed behind the Johnston brothers as the four glumly slumped back down the hill.

As heavy as it was, the stone marker proved easier to manage than the coffin. Using ropes, they dragged the stone, and with just the barest amount of maneuvering, the stone went into place as if it had leapt there all on its own.

Katie fell in an exhausted heap. She didn't move as Everett went back down to the truck to sign the necessary forms in which he assumed full responsibility for the earthly remains of one Charlie Bear Chief. Everett couldn't suppress the chuckle as he read the deceased's listed occupation.

Vagrant.

But on second thought, it fit. *Vagrant* meant more than simply penniless. It meant wanderer. Vagabond. That description fit Charlie Bear Chief, alias the Osage Kid, alias C. R. Jones, right down to the soles of his restless feet. For without his beloved Cassie, that was exactly how he had seen himself. A lonely wanderer in the world of the living. He loved and was loved, but never again in the same sweet and innocent way he and Cassie had loved each other. One of the wealthiest men in the state of Oklahoma had been an emotional pauper.

Everett signed the forms.

Katie stood next to him, holding his hand as she and Everett stood quietly at the foot of the two graves. One grave was grown over with hand-clipped grass. The aged stone was carved with just one name: *Cassie*. The other grave was brand-spanking new. On the plain white stone marker had been carved one name: *Charlie*.

Everett knew that he would come here often to clip the grass and leave flowers. The hidden graves would always be tended. The two souls sleeping peacefully side by side would not be forgotten.

The sun was going down. Everything was unnaturally quiet. So quiet that it raised the hackles on the back of Katie's neck.

Looking at the graves, Everett forgot Katie's presence as visions unfolded inside his mind. First, there was a scrawny boy with a gun on his hip. Then he could see two desperately-in-love young people vowing their eternal devotion in the moonlight. Next, a young, virile man lay belly-down on the ground alongside his crew of men. His head was tipped back and he was laughing as black oil gushed from the depths of the earth, rushed up the tall frame of the wooden derrick, shot toward the sky. Then the plume of black gold sprayed the surrounding area, completely soaking the men lying sprawled on the shaking, thunder-rumbling ground.

They were great visions. Wonderful memories. And these secret memories would always be safe. Everett had burned all the writing tablets in the backyard barbecue pit just after he and Katie came home from the wake.

Katie looked up at him as Everett squeezed her hand. To her inexpressible relief, Everett nodded that he was finally ready to leave.

Their hands entwined, they set off together down the hill. As they walked, another memory jogged, and Everett paused, looking back over his shoulder. Katie watched him worriedly as an odd expression passed over his face.

"You know something, honey," Everett said with a slight laugh. "In my head I know C.R. was an eighty-five-year-old man, but in my heart I can't see him that way. Not anymore. In my mind he's younger than me! Does that sound crazy¿"

"No. It doesn't sound crazy at all. It sounds nice."

As Everett stared at the graves, he imagined he saw an apparition rising from the freshly turned soil. The image of a little boy stood inside the mist. As the child stepped forward, he changed, was transformed into the image of a strong young man. This final image prevailed. And through this whorling specter the name carved on the headstone became bold.

CHARLIE

Everett swayed and Katie quickly moved to help him maintain his balance. Wrapping his arm around her, he pulled her close, kissing the top of her grimy, sweaty head. He hugged her again, almost squeezing the breath out of her as he realized that he would not, as he'd worried, live under a cloud of guilt. With a clear conscience he would look the Joneses squarely in the eye. Most especially Emma, whom he knew without a shred of doubt had finally and forever released C.R.

During the funeral, and in full view of hundred of witnesses, and while the members of her family crumbled in grief, Emma Jones had remained steadfast, knowing quite well that she was putting on a show, burying a man who was happily missing his own funeral. In all probability she knew exactly where he was, where he had directed Everett Jakomin, Cassie's son, to bury him. Emma Jones was no one's fool. Especially not C.R.'s. She knew C. R. Jones inside and out. She would, because C. R. Jones had been nothing more than an alter ego and Emma the co-conspirator in the great fraud. For decades, this concoction blocked the truth from the world, that the real man it represented had been married heart, soul, and mind to someone else. But through it all she remained by his side, an active participant in the hoax. Now, in her own way, Emma was free too, and

Everett could keep her free as long as he never admitted something they both clearly understood. That the huge gravestone in the cemetery was just a rock shadowing more rocks.

The very real man, the man Emma loved but never actually had, Charlie, was here. In a simple grave on a hilltop overlooking the land he had loved, lying forever beside the only woman he had loved. The only witnesses to his passing had been Everett and Katie. Everyone was free now, Everett most especially. The past was no longer troublesome for him, not since Charlie had come into his life and shone a great light on their shared history. The image that was the youngest member of the Sam Starr gang, knowing Everett finally understood, that there was nothing left to teach, wistfully smiled, faded.

Caught up in the exhilaration of having briefly made that young man's acquaintance, Everett's arm shot up toward the sky, and he gave a shout that filled the silent prairie.

"Be seeing ya . . . Kid!"

Coming Soon!

RAINWATER ON THE WHITE ROAD
a.k.a. The Misty Hills of Home

MARDI OAKLEY MEDAWAR
author of *The Glory Days of Buffalo Egbert*

A spellbinding saga of a Native American family through three generations of triumph, tragedy, and love.

Defying her family to be with the man she loves, a beautiful Native American makes the fateful decision to marry into the brawling, hell-raising Osage clan. Over three decades, the two will themselves fight to make a place of their own amid an Oklahoma land-scape of dust and oil rigs. Through the good and bad times, and through the strength of their five sons, this re-markable family will gain courage from their age-old traditions...and hold passionately onto the rugged land they call home.

Now Available

Howard Moon Deer Mysteries

Books 1 - 5

She is the Turquoise Lady, dressed in Indian jewelry and a cowboy hat, who came looking for a new life and instead found murder and betrayal. A year later, Wilder & Associate have been hired by the family to see if they can solve the mystery of her disappearance after the police have failed…

Turquoise Lady is the newest of the Howard Moon Deer mysteries.

For more information

visit: www.SpeakingVolumes.us

www.ingramcontent.com/pod-product-compliance
Lightning Source LLC
LaVergne TN
LVHW020525100826
845148LV00010B/1335

* 9 7 8 1 6 1 2 3 2 7 7 2 3 *